Jessie Wells lives with her husb[and in] Merseyside. She has always written i[n and] worked as a journalist on the *Liverpoo[l*] as a freelancer for various nationa[l] newspapers before moving into finance. She loves nothing more than getting lost in her imaginary worlds, which are largely filled with romance, communities bursting with character and a large dose of positivity.

 instagram.com/jessiewellsauthor

Also by Jessie Wells

The Good News Gazette

SAVING THE GOOD NEWS GAZETTE

The Good News Gazette

Book 2

JESSIE WELLS

One More Chapter
a division of HarperCollins*Publishers* Ltd
1 London Bridge Street
London SE1 9GF
www.harpercollins.co.uk
HarperCollins*Publishers*
Macken House, 39/40 Mayor Street Upper,
Dublin 1, D01 C9W8, Ireland

This paperback edition 2023
1
First published in Great Britain in ebook format
by HarperCollins*Publishers* 2023

ISBN: 978-0-00-847586-4

Printed and bound in the UK using 100% Renewable Electricity
by CPI Group (UK) Ltd

For Olive

Chapter One

'I'm closing down the business.'

My stomach starts rolling, over and over, like a snowball gathering speed down a hill frosted with soft white powdery flakes.

In the twelve or so months since I took a deep breath and pressed 'send' on the first edition of *The Good News Gazette*, Alan Parry, of Parry's Carpets, has become the newspaper's biggest and most consistent advertiser. In fact, the double-page advert he religiously takes out in every issue provides almost half of the meagre advertising income that makes up the wages for my co-worker Ollie Marsh and me. So the fact that he's selling his business is very, very bad news.

I look across my desk at Ollie, engrossed in designing the next edition's front page, and press the speaker button so that he can learn of our fate in real time.

'As you know, Zoe,' Alan blusters as I picture him on the other end of the phone, nervously picking at the sample squares of carpet as he tries to get through this break-up call, 'we've been thinking about retiring to the Costa del Sol for some time. Now that the kids are married and we've got cash in the bank, it seems like a good time to go. Plus, the wife's ready for a boob job and they're cheaper over there. All of which means...'

'You won't be advertising with us anymore,' I say forlornly, sticking my thumb into my mouth and biting down hard on the nail.

'No.' His voice seems smaller and less frantic now. 'Sorry about that, love.'

'We'll miss you, Alan,' I tell him, even though we'll miss his money even more. 'When are you closing? Will you be wanting to take out a "thanks to all our customers" advert? Or a "closing down sale" ad?' My attempt at trying to milk him out of every last penny is so transparent it's almost indecent.

I stick my thumb back in my mouth, biting harder now with small, repetitive movements. A new heat is prickling my face and damp seeps into the space under my arms. Thank goodness that, in Westholme at least, people prefer good old-fashioned phone calls to Teams meetings or video calls. While my voice is just about maintaining the illusion that this latest turn of events is no big deal, all the signs are there that, visually at least, I'm a mess.

'I don't think so, love,' Alan replies gently. 'We've been winding things down for a while so we're on limited stock as it is. We'll close the doors for good four weeks Friday, once the bargain-hunting vultures have had their pound of flesh.'

Across the desk, Ollie's blue eyes flash with alarm and there's a sheen across his unusually furrowed brow. Even his blond quiff has flopped. I pull my thumb out of my mouth and shrug my shoulders back.

'Quite understand, Alan,' I chirp. 'And, on behalf of *The Good News Gazette*, I'd like to thank you for your custom over the past few months. Ollie and I have very much appreciated it and we wish you all the very best for the future.'

'Er, OK, thanks,' he replies uncertainly.

'Goodbye then, Alan.' I plaster on a smile because I remember someone telling me that smiling makes your telephone voice sound better, then say again, more firmly this time,

'Goodbye.'

There's a deathly silence once the line goes dead. Ollie's forehead is now on the desk, and the new angle at which I'm looking at the top of his head only strengthens my belief that he secretly has highlights.

I think back to the business manager's handbook I've been reading recently in my quest for overwhelming success. This is the sort of scenario in which it is imperative I take control, show true leadership, reassure my colleagues – or in my place, colleague – that there are many bumps in the long and winding road to success.

'Come on,' I say instead. 'Let's go to the pub.'

———————

One pinot grigio and a bag of Scampi Fries later, I've rallied.

'Don't worry, Ollie,' I soothe. 'This is to be expected. Every new business goes through ups and downs.'

'I know, I know.' He traces his finger around the ring of water left on the table by his glass. 'But we're hardly fresh and exciting anymore. We've been going for over a year now. Do you know that the percentage of new businesses that fail in their first two years is staggeringly high?

'It's all right for you, you can just move in with Sam and live happily ever after in his nice house...'

He pauses, then tilts his head towards me. 'In fact, why haven't you and Charlie moved in with Sam yet? It doesn't make any sense, paying for two homes when you could all just live in one.'

'Can we stick to the problem in hand?' I fix him with my most

3

authoritative stare. 'Stop being so defeatist. It'll all turn around soon. We just need to work out a way to let potential advertisers know that we're the best possible medium through which to reach their target audience, that's all. A way that allows us time to work on the stories and do our freelance stuff while also touting for new business.'

'Yes, obviously that's what we need,' he tuts, rolling his eyes. 'But we haven't got that right now, have we?'

I sink further into my chair and scoop the crumbs out of the bottom of the greasy packet with my fingertips. Ollie grimaces, but I continue undeterred.

'Who do we know?' I muse through crunches. 'Who is it that could point us in the right direction?'

I delve deeper into the smelly remnants of the Scampi Fries bag. Ollie shakes his head at me and looks away, disgusted. His gaze settles momentarily on the wall above my head, where an old photograph showcases Westholme in its heyday, when it was a pretty farming hamlet rather than a suburban jungle.

'Why don't you call Daniel Lewis? He's got a list of contacts as long as your arm and, given his multi-millionaire status, appears to know a thing or two about how to make a business work.'

I shake my head vigorously. 'No way. It's one thing working with him on the Parade, but quite another going to him with *this*.'

'You're wrong. He's exactly the person we should be asking for help.'

'Move on,' I say firmly.

Ollie lifts a hand to his hair-do and fiddles with a few strands at the front, trying to put the oomph back into his quiff.

'What about Sam then?' He pulls his phone out of his man bag to check his image in the camera function. 'He runs his own business. He'd help for sure.'

'We don't need rescuing!' My tone is sharper than I intend and I stop myself. 'Sorry.'

Ollie gives his rearranged quiff a final glance of approval then lays his phone down carefully on the table, the beginning of what looks like irritability tugging at his smooth features.

'Are you genuinely not getting how close we are to having to shut down this entire operation right now or are you just pretending for my sake?'

My shoulders sink into my body and I ask myself what Michelle Obama would do. I read a profile piece on her last year and she's unwittingly had a hand in most of my decision-making processes ever since.

Michelle wouldn't let something as minor as a lost advertiser get her down. She would charm the advertiser back into the fold and find another two in the process. She would turn this situation around and make it ten times better than it was before. In short, she would rise to – rather than wimp out of – the challenge.

I straighten my spine and take a gulp of my drink. 'Look,' I say, in the manner of the former First Lady addressing the nation. 'This is a blip, an obstacle, like that time I only realised it was "own clothes day" at school when I dropped Charlie off in his uniform, or when he announced on Christmas Eve that he had written a new Christmas list but that it was fine because Santa would just *know*. It's one of those moments where the situation seems impossible, but somehow you conjure up enough magic to pull a rabbit out of the hat. That's all we have to do here: find the rabbit and pull it out of the hat.'

Ollie sips at his vodka and cranberry and pulls a face.

'Fine words, oh wise one. Except, right now, we haven't got a hat, let alone a rabbit.'

I turn to Michelle for an uplifting retort, but she seems to have nipped off for a coffee break.

'And,' he continues, 'unless we find both pretty quickly, we can say goodbye to *The Good News Gazette* and hello to a pretty uninspiring future on the dole queue.'

5

I'm heading back into the office, trying to picture what someone would wear to join the dole queue and wondering whether the dole queue is even actually a thing anymore, when I get the call.

Mercifully, I'm alone, having left Ollie lingering around the doorway of Cath's Caff, hoping to see his now girlfriend, Adina Eliade, before Cath catches him and orders him to either buy something or be on his way.

Cath recently decided to haul the café into the twenty-first century by dropping the 'Caff' part that used to form the second half of her business name, but I'm still finding it hard to refer to it simply as 'Cath's'. It's like referencing Ant without Dec, or Kate without William – entirely possible, but not quite right.

'Zoeeeeee!' the voice on the other end of the line trills. 'How the hell are you?'

My heart sinks. It's Amanda, my old boss whom I followed down to London all those years ago. It was she who landed me the reporting job on a national tabloid, long before I got pregnant with Charlie. She's still down there, and while I like her in theory, in practice she always leaves me feeling like I'm floundering around in some sort of Northern back alley while she's sipping cocktails in The Shard.

'How's life in the suburbs?' She giggles as though she's said something incredibly witty.

I force out a laugh, even though I'm not sure what the joke is. 'Oh, you know, same old, same old.'

'What about that paper you set up?'

'You mean *The Good News Gazette*?'

'Yeah. Great idea by the way. Advertising taken off yet?'

I unlock the office door and push my way inside. 'It's getting there.'

'Good to hear,' she says, as though she couldn't care either way. 'Quick call. I have a proposition for you.'

I pause. 'Go on.'

'I've been tasked with launching a new national magazine and I'm assembling my team. Naturally, you're the first person I phoned.'

My spine, fingers and toes start to tingle simultaneously. I clear my throat. 'What do you mean?'

Amanda laughs. 'You know exactly what I mean. It's time, Zoe. It's time to come back to London.'

Westholme Community Facebook page:

Kim Hughes: Believe Parry's Carpets is closing down – gutted!

Stevie Scott: Anyone know when the sale starts?

Chapter Two

'What do you think? Fancy it?'

A shiver erupts down the back of my neck. 'Er—' I manage before Amanda continues.

'It'd be a deputy editor role so you'd be working with me, which would be bloody brilliant, and they're throwing cash at this thing for some reason, so the money's good for a change. Plus, there's an apartment coming up in my building too. On your new wage you'd totally be able to afford it.

'Lovely area, great schools… Just think, no more reporting on community fetes or writing about wheelie bins – no offence. I'm talking big stories, celebrity interviews, a half-decent salary. We'd have a bloody ball!'

My mouth opens and closes, like a goldfish swimming around and around in a bowl, flapping about but never gaining ground.

'It's great what you've done with that newspaper – all that community stuff.' She's still talking. 'But you know you'll never be happy just plodding along with local news. Not with your ambition. Now your son's getting a bit older, don't you want something more?'

Amanda stops then and attempts to backtrack.

'But there's nothing wrong with staying where you are if that's what you want. London's not for everyone.'

I still haven't spoken, so she jumps in again. 'I've got to run into a meeting now, but I'll email all the details over. We're still in the early stages so there's plenty of time for you to think about it – but don't take too long.'

'That sounds like a brilliant offer, and I really appreciate it,' I reply, throwing in a few other regretful clichés for good measure. 'But it's really not something I can take on at the moment.'

My life's here in Westholme now. My family's here, my friends are here. *The Good News Gazette* is here. No, my London days are well and truly over.

But I'm still chuffed to have been asked.

There's a buzz around the Parade tonight as my boyfriend Sam Milner and I head to Westholme's own Spanish restaurant, El Corazón. (That word still makes me cringe by the way – boyfriend. Can you even have a boyfriend when you're thirty-four or do they instantly become your partner?) It's a warm August evening and the residents of Westholme are out in full force, chatting, laughing and even reading the latest edition of *The Good News Gazette*. A wave of doom washes over me, taking the feel-good factor with it. The *Gazette's* my paper, my baby. And, right now, it's a dead man walking.

I clip-clop along, my hand enclosed firmly in Sam's, as uncomfortable in heels as I ever was, but prepared to make an effort on this occasion, and vow to put all thoughts of the *Gazette's* slow demise out of my mind. My chestnut waves have not yet dropped, my floral tea dress feels cool around my legs and, determined to find something positive to focus on, I congratulate myself on the unfamiliar feeling of having chosen the right thing to wear.

The Parade has been transformed since Daniel Lewis's company started ploughing money into it. What was once a plain concrete square is now populated with tables, chairs and huge planters filled with flowers that spill over the edges, cascading pretty colours down each side. The shopfronts have had a refurb and, these days, the hanging name signs share the same black font rather than the mishmash of varying quality designs they displayed before.

My favourite part, though, is the pretty area in the centre of the flagged square that's been created around the magnolia tree. Despite its very existence being under threat this time last year, the memorial to Stan Kemp, Westholme's late barber and the husband of local powerhouse and volunteer extraordinaire Margaret, is now framed by a small garden that's still in full bloom.

Fairy lights adorn the pillars supporting the shelter that overhangs the shops, providing a magical glow to the outdoor space, while locals enjoy an end-of-week drink in front of Cath's (Caff).

The alcohol licence that her Italian nephew Antonio managed to secure for the former greasy spoon café before he returned home a few weeks ago has given the place a whole new clientele. Now, generations X, Y and Z sit alongside each other as they enjoy the relaxing effect that the combination of sun and alcohol can bring.

A few doors down, even more locals are sitting outside Vino, the wine bar that opened up last month, watching the water fountains that periodically erupt from the ground and passing comment on how cosmopolitan it all feels.

We stroll past Vintage Vibes, the new clothes boutique that contains a level of periodic glitz and glamour that I suspect could only be rivalled by the wardrobe of Starr – the artist formerly known as Edna Jones. Despite being well into her eighties, she can still be found manning the till at her dance shop, Pink Performers, a few doors down – that is, when she's not uploading videos of herself trying out the new dance crazes on social media.

Further on is The Lower Story, the beautiful book shop that I still love to retreat to when real life feels like too much. The Bakehouse is another such haven. Paula Carr, my old salsa partner and relatively new friend, opened it a few weeks ago and it supplies one set of diet-dooming cakes and pastries to passing trade and another to the diners at Cath's.

In the centre of the Parade, the mini-supermarket that takes up two units has managed to hold on to its position of King of the Walk. This is despite the fact that it continues to sell week-old fruit and confectionery so cheap you're convinced you've missed the bargain of the century if you don't buy it.

Most of its customers aren't too bothered about the questionably fresh produce it offers up as a token gesture. Locals tend to stay loyal to Bob's Greengrocer's, where Bob sells loose fruit and veg downstairs while Ollie and I work from the floor above, trying to bring good cheer to the people of Westholme.

Out of the corner of my eye, I see someone trying to catch my attention.

Adina, Ollie's girlfriend, is grinning at me, her dark hair tied back in a loose ponytail that stands out against the crisp white of her shirt, waving with one hand while juggling a tray with the other.

'You look beautiful,' she shouts, her Romanian accent ringing out against the background of Northern voices and I wince as heads turn and look out for a stunner, then turn back when they realise she's talking to me.

'Date night,' I reply as we slow down to chat, glancing up at Sam. He has an irritating ability to look good when he's not even trying, so at times like tonight, when he does make an effort, the effect is impressive.

'It's our one-year anniversary,' he adds, squeezing my hand, 'so we're off to El Corazón.'

Adina's eyes soften. 'Very romantic. Have a lovely evening.'

Sam grins back at her and moves his tanned arm to my shoulders. 'Oh, we will,' he says confidently. 'I'm certain of it.'

When *The Good News Gazette* revealed that a Spanish tapas restaurant was opening up at the Parade, the level of excitement reached such dizzying heights you'd have thought Soho House was launching an outpost in Westholme.

Even now, eight months on, you still have to book early for weekend reservations, which means the place is always lively, bustling, with an ambiance that could best be described as 'sophisticated good cheer'.

Visitors tend to be sold on El Corazón before they've even walked through the door, thanks to the hunger-inducing aroma of garlic, onions and spices that scents the Parade every evening, enticing diners in through the senses alone.

But that's just the starter. The main course is everything that lies behind its glass frontage.

Square tan leather bar stools sit beneath a long bar that runs down one side of the restaurant, with backlit shelves bursting with bottles of wine providing the 'wow' factor. Across the floorboards, slightly scuffed wooden chairs are set around small rectangular tables. The bottom part of the walls is covered in panelling, a marked contrast to the exposed red brick above, while a chandelier and side lights cast a soft glow upon the room.

In the background, the gentle strains of Spanish guitar music mingle with the clinking of glasses, the tinkling of cutlery and the delicious accent of owner Rafael Alvarez Lopez, as if to emphasise the authenticity of the whole thing.

El Corazón is so completely different from anything we've ever had in Westholme before that it always prompts a shiver of excitement whenever I step inside. It's a tangible reminder of how far our little town has come since the day a few of us got together to try and save the once tatty Parade.

I look across the table at Sam and smile. He has the sort of tan you'd expect from someone who spends his days outside teaching kids' football, therefore being present for the odd five minutes of summer to which the UK is treated every now and again in strange months like October or March.

His light-blue shirt flatters his colour and the golden flecks in his green eyes are dancing in the candlelight. He stretches his hand across his mouth, smoothing over either side of his freshly shaved jawline with his thumb and forefinger, then drops it when he realises I'm watching him.

'Happy?' he asks.

I squeeze his fingers across the table. 'Very.'

I'm not going to put a downer on the evening by telling him about the lost advertiser, and there's no need whatsoever to mention the London offer, seeing as I'm not going to take it. It might make Sam feel unsettled and he's right – it *is* going to be a good night.

Rafael sets down a tray and starts unloading steaming plates of tapas. I inhale deeply as the delicious scent of tomatoes, garlic and paprika wafts through the air and up over his head of thick black hair.

'Thanks, Rafa.' I gently separate my hand from Sam's. 'This looks delicious.'

'Only the very best for Westholme's lovebirds.' He winks at us both and I jokingly roll my eyes at Sam, before realising he's fully on board with this level of cheesiness.

'Twelve whole months since we became an official couple,' he replies, beaming. 'Best year of my life.' He laces his fingers back through mine and engages me in an intimate smile.

'I leave you now.' Rafa bends into a mock bow as he backs away. 'Enjoy your meal.'

As he returns to the front of the dining room, I do a quick check of my phone to make sure I'm not missing any messages from Mum telling me that Charlie's been abducted or ended up in A&E again.

Thankfully, with the exception of a few news alerts and texts from my best friends Emma and Beth telling me to have a great night, the screen is clear.

When I look up, Sam's watching me, a little line forming between his thick brown eyebrows.

'Everything OK? You're quiet tonight.'

I smile. 'I'm always quiet.'

'More quiet than usual.'

Seconds tick by as I weigh up the benefits versus the cons of telling him the truth, then finally I groan.

'Sorry, Sam, I wasn't going to say anything tonight, but Parry's Carpets pulled a huge regular advert today and I'm worried. It's a massive chunk of advertising revenue to lose.'

Sam sighs and his expression folds into creases, his eyes filled with concern.

'No wonder you're quiet.'

Then the lines melt away as his face brightens and his mouth curls into a smile.

'Did I mention that I wanted to upgrade my ad for the football academy to a bigger one? That should cover the loss in advertising.'

He leans back in his chair, satisfied that the problem has been rectified, but my heart sinks, in spite of – or maybe because of – his generosity. He's kind of missing the point.

'Thanks, Sam, but it's really important that we build up the business through real, genuine advertisers; people who believe in what *The Good News Gazette* is trying to achieve and think we're an attractive advertising proposition.'

He flinches. '*I* believe in what you're trying to achieve.'

I reach for his hand again and squeeze it. 'I'm sorry. I know you do.'

Rafa's return to the table prevents any further awkwardness, and he presents two champagne flutes and a bottle of cava with a flourish. 'On the house,' he declares, as he skilfully removes the cork and fills my glass with a whirl of bubbles. 'Happy anniversary to the perfect couple. *Salud.*'

Sam beams, clearly overjoyed at our 'perfect couple' status.

'Thank you, mate. And if we have half as happy a life together as you and your wife seem to have, then I'll consider it a success. Any words of advice you can give us?'

'That is very kind, my friend,' Rafa replies as he moves on to Sam's glass, 'but we have to find our own way when it comes to love.' He pauses. 'There is one piece of advice I've always lived by though.'

We lean in closer, eagerly anticipating his words of wisdom.

'Always let your heart rule your head – because your heart will have the final say anyway. It's not enough to just feel it here…' He touches his head. 'You also have to feel it here.' He presses his palm against his chest and I assume he's referring to his heart rather than his lungs.

'I'll drink to that,' says Sam, clinking his glass against my own. 'Cheers!'

'Cheers,' I echo, wondering why I suddenly feel so uncomfortably exposed.

Westholme Community Facebook page:

Paul Gregory: Tried that Spanish place for the first time last night. Some great scran. Can thoroughly recommend.

Johnny H: Yeah it's all right, but have you seen the size of the dishes? I had to order 4 of them just to fill me up.

Paul Gregory: They're called tapas, mate. Snack-size dishes. Very popular in Spain.

Johnny H: Not in my hotel in Benidorm, they're not.

Chapter Three

B y the time I pick Charlie up the next morning, he's clearly already had way more sugar than government guidelines would advise.

He's dancing around Mum and Dad's kitchen chanting football songs and doing daft little routines to accompany them, a great boy-shaped bundle of energy whooshing around the house like a mini whirlwind.

'Good grief, Mum, what have you given him?' I ask, wondering how long it'll take for this 'high' to wear off and vowing to stay here until it does.

'Oh, nothing much; we had a few cans of Coke hanging around that your dad wanted me to get rid of, so we gave Charlie one last night.'

I watch him, running around the kitchen now like a hamster on a wheel.

'He's like that after one can of Coke last night?' I check, doubtful.

'I've had a couple this morning, too,' Charlie confirms.

Mum, who I suspect can tell by now that he's overdosed on the white stuff, sticks her head into the fridge on the pretence of retrieving some apples.

'It's only a little bit,' she says, her voice muffled by the presence of an unusual abundance of broccoli. 'Won't do him any harm.'

It is one of life's great mysteries that my beautiful mum manages to remain the petite size eight she was when she married my dad while simultaneously filling every inch of cupboard space with the sort of nutritional crap Channel 4 regularly makes documentaries about.

A wave of guilt hits me then, as I remember that Charlie only stayed here in the first place so I could celebrate my anniversary night with Sam.

'Don't worry, Mum, I'm sure he'd have had much worse at home by now.' I clock her look of alarm. 'Only kidding. Anyway, what's with all the broccoli? You're not trying to put Bob out of business by selling broccoli from your fridge, are you?'

Mum smiles, attention successfully diverted, and pushes her dark-brown bob away from her face. 'I don't think anyone could ever put Bob out of business. Nowhere else sells strawberries half as nice as his. No, it's your dad. He's finally decided to shed a few pounds and seems to think that a bowl of broccoli soup a day will do the trick. But he's been eating the stuff for two weeks now and I don't think he's lost anything.'

'Tell me about it,' I sigh. 'It was all right when I was in the weight-loss zone. But now every day feels like a battle trying to keep it off.' I pause, then voice my thoughts out loud. 'Although working so close to The Bakehouse probably doesn't help.'

Mum stops her busyness for a moment and pulls up a chair at the kitchen table, focusing on me for the first time since I arrived.

'How are things at work?' she asks, pushing a pile of leaflets aside to make space for the coffee she sets down before me. 'Still finding lots of good stories?'

'Well, yes, but it's not really the stories that are the problem; it's the advertisers.'

She frowns and I spot a lone grey hair peeking out of her right eyebrow. 'What's wrong?'

'Oh, I've just had a key one pull out. Not a problem, I'm sure I'll be able to replace it.'

I love the way that, no matter how old I get, just the very mention of someone giving me grief is enough to send Mum into full-on warrior pose.

She's sitting up like that now – shoulders straight, hackles definitely raised, ready to do battle with whoever has been brave enough to take me on.

'Honest, Mum, it's fine – all part of business. I need to find a way of getting more advertising in, that's all.'

The click of the front door diverts our attention and my dad walks in, a copy of the *Daily Star* under the arm of his battered grey hooded jacket that hangs just far enough over the belly of his blue factory-issue trousers to cover the pudgy flesh of his tummy. He sees me and grins.

'Hello, love.' He drops the newspaper onto the table and uses his arm to give me a quick squeeze around the shoulders instead. 'How did your night go? I hope he pulled all the stops out for you. Very lucky guy, that Sam.'

I squeeze him back. There was a time not too long ago when any comment on my date night would have felt more like a put-down than a harmless joke. But since I decided enough was enough and told him so, Dad's made such an effort that I no longer live in nervous anticipation of his jibes.

'What's this about a diet, Dad?' I look him up and down. 'Surely a man with your physique doesn't need to think about losing weight.'

'That's what I told the doctor when I went to get my knees checked out,' he replies, unzipping his top. 'But he said it'd be a good idea to shed a few pounds and it's done you the world of good losing a bit of beef, so I thought I might have a go.'

I smile, grateful for the back-handed compliment. 'So where does broccoli soup come in?'

He pulls back his chair and slumps into it like a sack of potatoes. 'I saw this bloke on Facebook saying that a bowl of broccoli soup a day could help you lose weight so I thought, well, it's an easy way of doing it isn't it? The stuff tastes foul, but if it knocks the pounds off, I can take it.'

'How much have you lost so far then, Dad?'

He scratches his head. 'That's the strange thing. I've been eating it like it's going out of fashion but the scales haven't moved.'

I consider this for a moment. 'Have you changed anything else about your diet? Cut out the beer or the cakes?'

'Well, no, of course not. That's why I'm eating the soup – so I don't *have* to change anything else.'

'Dad!' I start to chuckle. 'Broccoli soup alone won't help you lose weight. You've got to cut out some of the other stuff or you're not going to lose any weight.'

He looks across at my mum. 'So, I've eaten a gallon of that green gunk for nothing?'

I sigh. 'Yes!'

'Oi!' Mum shouts.

'Sorry, love, but it's bloody awful.'

Dad looks so dejected that I say the next part before I've had a chance to think it through.

'Why don't you come to Slim City with me? The leader there, Barb, will show you how to lose weight and you won't have to eat any more broccoli soup to do it.'

He pulls a face. 'I don't know about that. I'm not really up for listening to a group of old fatties talking about why they can't stop shovelling junk into their gobs.'

'It's not like that, Dad,' I say. 'Look at me, I go and I'm not an old fattie, am I?'

'Not any more,' he concedes.

'And you won't be the only guy – there's a few men in my group and people of different ages. You might even enjoy it.'

He pulls a face and glances over at my mum for reassurance. 'What do you think, Sue? I don't want to look stupid.'

'Oh, Dad.' I move out of the chair to wrap my arms around his shoulders and rest my head on the back of his neck. 'You've been eating green soup for the past fortnight as though it's some magical calorie-busting medicine. I think that ship's sailed, don't you?'

Last year, Charlie's teacher staged one of those awful 'let's talk about what jobs your parents do' sessions. The type that are held under the guise of helping nine-year-olds map out their career options but really just allow the teachers to suss out parental hierarchy.

Apparently, it was during this employment exposé that Charlie proudly revealed his mum was the woman behind *The Good News Gazette*, and I have received almost weekly calls from the school office about the latest 'good news story' heading my way ever since.

I'm convinced Mrs Pople, the headteacher, now views me as the editor of her own unofficial school newsletter. And while it's an assumption that I push back against at every available opportunity, my lack of success so far means that not only have I agreed to write about the school litter-picking session taking place at the river today, I've also been roped in to take part.

So, after collecting Charlie from football practice, we headed here. To the river that runs around the perimeter of our little town, where a rainbow of rubbish is currently littering its banks.

Sam has managed to swerve the enticing proposition of cleaning up other people's trash on the basis that he has upwards of twenty kids waiting for him on the football field, so it's just me here. And loads of other equally unenthusiastic parents. And our hyperactive children.

Charlie has been so excited about this event that you'd truly think it was a primary school version of Glastonbury, when the only similarities it shares are the fact that a) we're all wearing wellies, and b) we're stood knee-deep in household waste. I'm not sure that kids should even be around this stuff, but Charlie's having such a good time using his litter picker to pinch his friends' backsides that I've decided to forgo health and safety for one day and let him enjoy himself instead.

At least *he's* enjoying himself. The wind whips around my face, catching at yesterday's blow dry and tossing it around my shoulders with little regard for the fifteen quid I paid to have it done, and I wonder for the tenth time today whether we really *had* to spend our Saturday afternoon doing this.

Mrs Pople is looking similarly dishevelled and as she reprimands Rafa for using the litter picker as a makeshift cricket bat, I suspect she's feeling the same.

'Mr Alvarez,' she shouts, brushing aside a grey, frizzy piece of hair that's escaped from her low bun as she stumbles over an ant hill. 'Will you please remember that the litter pickers are on loan and are absolutely not to be played with. Any breakages will have to be paid for by the person...' she glares at the children '... or *people* responsible.'

Rafa looks over at me and rolls his eyes and I give him a return eye roll in sympathy. I feel like, these days, I'm rolling my eyes on an almost continuous basis.

'Charlie,' Mrs Pople continues. 'You're a sensible boy. Most of the time. Can I trust you to hand out the bags?' Charlie nods enthusiastically and my heart sinks at this further confirmation that my boy is going to be a people pleaser like me.

'Everybody, you'll each receive three bags; one for general rubbish, one for aluminium cans and one for plastic bottles. It is absolutely *imperative* that you don't get them mixed up.'

Flushed at the faint praise, Charlie takes the roll of bags from her and starts diligently passing them to his classmates, including a girl with intricate plaits who has been singing 'Somewhere Over the Rainbow' in a loud American accent since we arrived.

'You should all have gloves,' Mrs Pople instructs, 'so please use them. The last thing we want is any injuries. And can I also remind you of the absolute need to avoid potentially hazardous waste, sharp objects and clinical items such as needles and syringes. Parents should keep a watchful eye over their children at all times and if you have any concerns, you must see the project manager, who is...' She consults her clipboard. 'Me. Immediately. Charlie's mum, Mrs Taylor, will be taking photographs for *The Good News Gazette*, so if there's any reason why you don't want your child to be pictured, please can you let her know.'

I smile and nod, despite it being news to me that I was taking photographs, and mutter, 'It's *Ms* Taylor,' before accepting that no one can hear me anyway and whipping out my phone. I remember my business book and look for the positives in the situation. *Any social gathering is an opportunity to make new contacts,* it says, so I look around to try and sniff out any decision-makers whom I might be able to tap up for advertising.

'Are you the girl with the newspaper?' a gruff voice interrupts my train of thought and I turn to its source. A woman with a long, pointy face and excessively long, mousey-brown hair plastered flat to her head stands in front of me, hands on her hips.

'Yes I am,' I reply, attempting a smile in case she's quietly overseeing thousands of pounds' worth of advertising spend.

'Right, well, I suppose you'll want to do a story on our Chelsea.' She looks past me towards the little singer who's now moved on to 'Follow the Yellow Brick Road'. 'You've probably heard of her already. She's a *performer*.' She says this last bit with a meaningful look in her eye, as though the word alone is enough to indicate the high level of regard in which she should be held.

'Oh, right.'

'Yeah, she's performing in the Liverpool Empire's Christmas panto this year. *The Wizard of Oz*.'

'How fascinating.' I try to look more fascinated than I feel. 'Dorothy, I presume?'

The woman looks over at her. 'No. The director felt the role of Dorothy was a little...' she leans towards me, then whispers '... *limiting* for her.' Straightening up, she adds, 'So she's going to be a munchkin instead.'

I press my lips together to imprison the giggle that's trying to escape, then, spotting an empty can of lager, make a great show of seizing it with my litter picker so that Mrs Pople is aware that I'm putting in the required amount of effort.

'You can do a piece on her if you like.'

'Er, OK.' The can keeps slipping out of the plastic picker's grasp.

'Would she get a lot for it, like?'

I reluctantly pause my activity. 'A lot of what?'

'Cash? You know, for selling her story?'

'We don't buy stories.'

'Oh right.' Two vertical lines deepen between her eyebrows, then she shrugs back her shoulders. 'Never mind. We'll go to the *Mirror* instead.'

I relax into a warm smile. 'Do you know, Ms... Or is it Mrs?'

'Mrs Turner.'

'Mrs Turner, I think that's an excellent idea. I'm sure the journalists there will be delighted to hear from you.'

And with that I pop the lager in the 'aluminium cans' bag, whip out my phone and take great delight in texting Ollie the tale about the one that got away.

I've introduced a new treat into our Saturday night proceedings: a treat from Paula's Bakehouse. Now that I'm virtuous and rarely eat sweet stuff, I really look forward to indulging myself with my two favourite treats: cake and Charlie . And Sam, obviously. Which makes it three, I guess.

Even the exterior of Paula's Bakehouse is a feast for the eyes. A huge arrangement of pastel-coloured flowers has been positioned around both the door frame and the huge window, with more potted flowers flanking either side of the door.

Through the glass frontage, cakes, pastries and breads of all shapes and sizes provide an enticing showstopper of a display.

It is, by far, the most attractive shopfront in the Parade. And, these days, the bar is set high.

An old-fashioned bell dings our arrival as we enter, and I hold the door open to let two teenage girls chatting excitedly about tonight's *Strictly Come Dancing* launch show pass us before we step inside.

It's a different Paula who greets us today from the one I was introduced to at salsa class last year. Her pasty skin looks healthier, possibly because her cheeks are permanently flushed from being constantly on the go. She's also swopped the harsh knot hairstyle in which she used to arrange her hair for a sleek, side-parted low bun and now wears a crisp white catering jacket which makes her look every inch the professional baker.

She grins a welcome as we walk in, but the semi-circles of shadow under her eyes suggest she hasn't had much sleep and I'm sure I see her stifle a yawn.

'My favourite customers,' she exclaims as we reach the glass counter that runs along the side of the long, narrow shop, smiling as Charlie presses his nose against the glass to better examine his cake options.

'I wasn't sure you'd have anything left this late in the day,' I say, relieved to see there's still plenty of choice.

'I wouldn't usually, but I overestimated how much I'd sell today, so take home as many as you like.'

We chat as she goes backwards and forwards, serving up the cakes we select and a few more besides, as she explains why she's so tired.

'It's the lads on the estate. You know that boarded-up house across the road from mine?'

I nod. I've been to Paula's house on the Orchard Estate a few times now, usually to pick up Charlie after a playdate with her son, Sean.

'They've been getting into there and hanging out, playing loud music, drinking and whatever else all through the night.' She sighs. 'They're so loud, they're keeping the whole road awake.'

'Hasn't anyone called the police?'

'What do you think?' She pulls a face.

'I've got to get off the estate,' Paula continues, then, eyeing Charlie, who, having pickpocketed my phone, is now fully engrossed in a game on it, drops her voice to a whisper. 'I need to move Sean away from that gang.'

My spirits plummet. 'Are they really that bad?'

Paula sighs. 'They're getting worse. Stealing everything they can get their hands on. I caught one of them trying to nick Sean's bike from the path when he came in for a snack the other day. I yelled at him and he ran off, but if I'd spotted him five seconds later, both he and the bike would have been gone. I'm too scared to let Sean ride out on his own now in case they try and pinch the bike off him while he's on it.'

I gasp. 'Oh no, Paula. That's horrible.'

She pauses, then says, 'Aren't you worried about Charlie? After all, you only live around the corner from the estate.'

I check that Charlie's still distracted by my phone.

'I'd be lying if I said that moving hadn't crossed my mind,' I say quietly. 'It won't be long before he'll be asking to go out on his bike too, but right now just the thought of it brings me out in a cold sweat. But I love our home. I'm not sure that I could go through with a move.'

Paula ties the box of cakes with some coloured ribbon and passes them across the counter.

'Wrong though, isn't it? That just a few lads can spoil what could be a lovely place for everyone. The estate would be all right if it wasn't for them.'

And we spend the next ten minutes debating nature versus nurture, the failed social policies of various successive governments and whether there could ever be a better pairing on *Strictly* than Rose and Giovanni.

Westholme Community Facebook page:

Sheila Pople: Thanks to all the pupils and parents of Westholme Primary School who helped with the river clean-up today. The hard work and positive spirit perfectly displayed the values of good citizenship we uphold here at Westholme Primary.

Elise Harvey: Was down there walking my dog today. Didn't see much good citizenship on show from the kids peeing into the river using a beer bottle for target practice.

Chapter Four

There are twenty thousand newspapers lying in bundles at my feet.

Twenty thousand issues of *The Good News Gazette* that came with no moving instructions save for the delivery driver who unloaded them at the back door of Bob's Greengrocer's, shouted merrily, 'Good luck in shifting those' and drove off with a cheery wave.

I stare at them and ask myself once again why I continue to use a printing firm which clearly exists only to produce endless challenges for me to resolve.

A tuneless whistle meanders into hearing range, confirming that Ollie's finally arrived somewhere in the vicinity of the office. I open my mouth and holler his name. On the fifth call I hear his footsteps approaching, then he appears behind me, wearing a pair of skin-tight tracksuit bottoms and an equally tight blue T-shirt.

He stares at the scene before him, then pulls a face. 'That'll keep you busy for a while.'

I look him up and down, distracted from the immediate

problem by a seemingly more pressing one. 'What are you wearing?'

His chest puffs up a little. 'Oh, this?' he says, referencing his outfit with a flourish of his hands. 'Sorry, I know it's not strictly office attire, but Margaret's away so I stayed at Adina's last night.' He shrugs his rounded shoulders. 'No time to get changed before work this morning, I'm afraid.'

Despite my irritation, I can't help but stare at the contours of his chest through his ultra-thin T-shirt. Ollie never has been and never will be my type, but I'll give him this: those hours in the gym have certainly paid off.

I point at the newspapers. 'The printers have just dumped them here again. What happened to the papers going to the distribution centre?'

Ollie shrugs. 'No idea. Why don't you call them back to move them?'

Storm clouds are gathering in the already grey sky, and I weigh up my chances of the delivery driver making a return trip.

Nil, at a rough estimate.

'I think it's going to rain,' I reply instead. 'They could be pulp by the time they get back. We need a Plan B.'

Ollie scratches his head. 'I think you need a Plan A before you can have a Plan B.'

I sigh. 'Whatever. The only plan on the table right now is that we need to move them – and fast. Let's see if Bob will let us use the back room.'

When I started up *The Good News Gazette* last year, Bob Dunning and his son Lawrence offered us the use of the office above his grocers shop for free. Now, over twelve months later, Bob still refuses to take any rent from us, arguing that what we're delivering in positivity to the community is worth far more to him than any cash we could offer. Yet he's come to my rescue so many times that it's very clear who's getting the better end of this deal.

He might be seventy-odd, but he's still shifting bundles at twice the speed of Ollie, who's more concerned about getting ink on his T-shirt than he is with getting the newspapers somewhere dry before the heavens open.

'Thank you so much, Bob,' I puff as I work up a sweat, half-dragging, half-lifting the papers into the large store room that for a few months last year became my weekly salsa retreat.

It's the first time I've been in here since the lessons wound up and I inhale deeply, letting the stench of rotting cabbage leaves transport me back to those much-missed sessions.

'How's Lawrence doing?' I ask, recalling Bob's ballroom dancing son who temporarily brought Cuba to Westholme and, quite frankly, got my previously large backside back into gear again.

Bob beams, pausing to scratch his scruffy grey hair with his permanently grubby fingernails. 'He's great, thanks, love. Back on the cruise ships with Ivanka again. They're in Hawaii right now.'

'Probably sipping cocktails and thanking his lucky stars his days of selling spuds are over,' Ollie snorts, oblivious to Bob's wounded expression.

The bundle-moving process seems to be taking forever and I'm wondering whether we'll still be here, doing this, by the time the next issue is due to hit the stands when Bob pauses to look at the front page.

It's one of my favourite – but least hard-hitting – splashes since we launched: a story about the bunches of flowers that have been spotted around Westholme lately with nothing but a note attached to them saying that it's hoped they'll bring happiness to the recipient's day.

I first heard about it on the Westholme Community Facebook

page, where people had posted photographs of the beautiful bunches they'd found. But despite asking everyone I can think of, including Margaret Kemp, leader of the Westholme Gardeners and general font of all knowledge when it comes to community kindness, I'm still no nearer to being able to identify where they had come from.

So, until I can write a story about the person behind the bouquets, I'm simply reporting on the flowers as and when they turn up instead.

'I'll have to show the wife this,' Bob says, glancing at the front page. 'Might cheer her up a bit. She went out this morning to find all her car windows smashed. There was nothing inside to take, but they wrecked the car.'

'Oh no.' I pull a face. 'Any idea who did it?'

Bob shakes his head. 'One of the neighbours saw a bunch of lads running away and thought it was the Orchard Estate boys, but we've got no proof so they'll probably get away with it again.'

I frown. 'Again?'

'There's been a few cars down our road targeted lately.' He hauls another bundle of newspapers in through the door then wipes his forehead with the back of his hand. 'I don't know if they're actually trying to nick the cars or just make a mess of them. Either way, someone's got to put a stop to them. They're running rampage through Westholme at the moment.'

'Those lads are little scumbags,' adds Ollie, his eyebrows knitting together in an expression of anger I rarely see from him. 'They still shout stuff at Adina when they see her and I know it frightens her. Obviously they never do it when I'm there.' I see his pecs tighten through his top. 'They wouldn't dare.'

I stifle a smile.

'Course they wouldn't, Ol. Those pants would scare anyone off.'

He glares at me. 'Speaking of stylistic expertise, I've been meaning to ask whether you've disposed of the last of those paisley dresses yet. You know, the ones you used to wear before you got all trendy? Although admittedly, they must have been a fabulous form of contraception.'

'Ollie!' I hiss.

'Especially the green and brown one,' he adds.

Bob chuckles. 'Even *I* remember that one.'

And I spend the next half an hour acting as the punchline to a series of fashion jokes told by a millennial in skin-tight bottoms and a baby boomer in a Fair Isle jumper.

'I've come up with a plan,' I tell Ollie once we're back at the office.

'Fabulous,' he says dryly. 'I do love your plans. Which particular problem is today's plan going to tackle? World poverty? Our poverty? Bob's fingernails?'

Despite my determination that everything will work out fine, I was awake for hours last night trying to work out how to conjure up a shed-load of previously uninterested advertisers.

It wasn't until daybreak, when the light started creeping around the edges of the curtains and making its way inside my bedroom, that the answer finally came to me.

Gloria Bridges. The woman who specialises in guiding female entrepreneurs to greatness. The one who saw enough greatness in me to ask me to save the Parade. She'll know how I can generate more advertising. She'll know what to do.

'I'm going to go back to basics and speak to Gloria,' I tell Ollie.

He smirks. 'It took you long enough.'

'What took me long enough?'

'To come up with what is a fairly obvious solution.'

'Erm. I think you'll find I'm the only one who's so far come up with *any* solution.'

I'm about to launch into a diatribe when a knock on the door stops me mid-flow.

We exchange a split-second glance. Visitors tend to come under one of three categories. The first is a very valued breed: Those Who Bring Us Stories – and they fall into subcategories of their own – blindingly brilliant (rare), decent story (less rare), mediocre (more common) and not worth getting out of bed for (very common).

The second category is little short of a pain in the backside: Salespeople.

The third and final category is that elusive jewel that I lie awake at night praying will pay us a call: The Potential Advertiser.

Waiting to see who's behind the door is like an all-or-nothing game of *Blind Date*, which is why Ollie and I are watching it with the intensity of two people aware that their entire financial existence depends on the identity of the hidden figure.

Very slowly, the door creaks open and the face of a man I vaguely recognise emerges. It takes me a moment to place him. He has large, ruddy cheeks and a sweaty forehead and as he trundles into the office, a body that suggests he's as big a fan of saturated fat as I used to be comes into view.

His eyes flit around the room and then, spotting me, they shrink into the extended creases of a warm smile. 'Hello, Zoe,' he greets me in a big, booming voice and, just in the nick of time, I remember who he is.

'Norman Woods,' I boom back, standing up and heading over to the door to greet him. 'What a lovely surprise. How are you?'

'Great, thanks.' He grasps my hand in both of his and pumps it up and down so energetically that I fear for the safety of the Home Bargains bag swinging violently from his wrist. A sharp smell of body odour and past-its-best aftershave pierces my nostrils and I turn away quickly so he doesn't see me grimace.

'Come on in. Would you like a drink?'

He shakes his head and pulls a bottle of Lucozade out of the bag. 'Got my own, thanks, Zoe. Like to have refreshments for the bus journey.'

I stare at him for a second, then nod my head in lieu of being able to add anything to that particular line of conversation and introduce him to Ollie instead.

'Ollie, I don't know if you remember Norman from our *Northern News* days?'

'Ah, yes.' He clearly doesn't have a clue. 'Good to see you again, Norman.'

'I don't remember you,' replies Norman, frowning.

'Ollie used to work in Design.' I guide him over to the couch and away from any of the comments Ollie could be gearing himself up to make.

'So, Norman…' I gesture for him to sit down and observe with fascination the way he glugs his Lucozade, with his entire mouth around the bottle neck. How does he even manage to swallow it like that? I force myself to focus. 'To what do I owe the pleasure?'

The bobbing of his Adam's apple indicates that he's managed to take a bona fide gulp and he pulls the drink away from his mouth, eases himself into the couch and very slowly screws the top back on.

'Remember you used to do stories about the old cinema when you worked for that other place?'

'Of course. It was supposed to be turned into retirement apartments, wasn't it? What happened in the end?'

Norman presses a hand down on his navy cord trousers. 'The deal fell through. It'll be down to the owner. Hard as nails, that one, although clearly no common sense, letting that lovely building go to rack and ruin. That's why I'm here. She's selling it again.'

I raise my eyebrows. 'Really? What a shame. I suppose that's put paid to any hopes you had of bringing the cinema back to life then.'

'Good grief, no,' he splutters, his rough cheeks a shade of purple. 'Quite the opposite, in fact. I thought we could buy it.'

'Who?' I'm confused.

'The good people of Westholme, of course.'

I've clearly missed something.

'Where's the money coming from, Norman?' Ollie shouts over from his desk.

'That's where you come in.' Norman lowers his voice and looks around as if to make sure no one else is listening, although given that there's still only Ollie and I here, it's pretty obvious he's safe.

'OK,' I say slowly. 'I'm going to need a few more clues.'

'You sorted the Parade out, didn't you? You saved that.'

'Well not exact—' I start, before Ollie, who is usually the first to remind me that we only succeeded on a technicality, interrupts.

'She did,' he confirms. 'Tell us your plan, Norm.'

Norman looks momentarily stunned by the sudden shortening of his name, then rallies and launches into his speech.

'I don't have a plan as such, but since the Parade business, everyone says you're the woman to come to in order to get stuff done. Westholme folk threw money in to hold that carnival last year, right? I was thinking they could do the same thing here – you know, raise enough money to buy the cinema then get it up and running again.'

I blow air through my lips. 'That sounds like quite a task, Norman. And not really something I can help you with, I'm afraid.'

'But if we don't buy it, he will. He'll knock it down and let them build a supermarket there instead. He's already got his people working on it – I've seen vans with his company name on there for weeks now. We might be too late. It may be a done deal.'

'*Who'll* knock it down, Norman?'

Norman leans forward, his face earnest. 'That rich bloke. Daniel Lewis.'

I freeze.

'What do you mean?'

Norman drops his voice to a whisper. 'I have…not spies, exactly…but people in Westholme who provide me with information.'

Ollie squeaks with the laughter he's trying to hold in and I throw him a look.

'Carry on, Norman,' I press him.

'It's probably something to do with all that Parade business last year. He couldn't get his hands on that, so he's going after the cinema now, I suppose.'

My head's spinning.

Daniel, who has done so much to turn the Parade into a beautiful space we can all enjoy.

Daniel, who believed building a supermarket in Westholme would create jobs for the community.

Daniel, whom people still don't completely trust.

'Are you absolutely sure you're right, Norman?' I'm breathing more quickly than usual.

'I'm one hundred per cent sure I'm right,' he confirms. 'He's *definitely* going to buy it. Which is why I think *we* should instead.'

I allow myself to glance at Ollie, whose confused expression mirrors my own.

'Can you believe the nerve of that man?' I mutter, vaguely aware of my lips pressed tightly together, of a head that's shaking from left to right, a small but defiant *no*.

Sensing weakness on my part, Norman continues with renewed gusto.

'I'm sure we'd be able to raise the money. I'd help out. People would love to see the cinema re-opened. And I have lots of photos of the original interior of the building that we could use when it comes to redecorating. With that big Hollywood movie being filmed here soon, I thought the actors could come to the grand opening.'

'Woah, woah,' I say, still reeling from this new information and alarmed at the speed at which this project is taking off, despite the fact that I've already said no to it. 'Aren't we getting a bit ahead of ourselves here? It's one thing raising a few thousand to stage a carnival, but quite another to raise...how much?'

'I'm guessing two hundred grand.'

I gasp. 'Two hundred grand to buy the cinema? Plus, even more to decorate it and get it up and running again I assume?'

'Another fifty grand,' Norman replies cheerfully, as though I regularly raised this sort of money and would simply need to make a few calls for it to be done.

Norman unscrews the cap of his Lucozade bottle and wraps his lips back around the top of it. The whole action makes me feel a little bit sick.

I stand up, a gentle hint that he should do the same, and fetch my jacket and keys from the other side of the room.

Norman presses his big hand down on one side of the couch to lever himself up out of it, splashing the luminous orange liquid on one of the teal cushions on his way up.

'Oops, sorry about that,' he apologises, looking down at the bright stain making its way across the fabric.

'Don't worry about it,' I snap, punching my arms into the sleeves of my jacket.

'Er, where are we going?' Norman asks, bewildered.

'I suggest you go home and write a strongly worded letter to the local council reminding them of the strong opposition Daniel Lewis faced the last time he applied for planning permission to build a supermarket.'

'Great!' He nods his head enthusiastically. 'And where are you going?'

'I,' I reply defiantly, 'am going to Liverpool.'

'Uh-oh,' Ollie says, his wide grin at odds with his doom-laden verbal warning.

'Why are you going there?' Norman's head is spinning from my face to Ollie's.

Ollie fixes me with his eyes, bright with excitement, and I nod to confirm exactly why I'm going there.

'Because,' he declares with glee, 'she's going to find Daniel Lewis.'

Westholme Community Facebook page:

Jimmy Hunter: Heard the cinema's up for sale. More retirement apartments on the way then.

Rita Hollingworth: How disappointing. I always hoped that someone would come along and rescue it.

Jimmy Hunter: Nah, less opportunities for dodgy dealings with community businesses. Council probably wouldn't allow it.

Pete Owen: You still here then, Jimmy?

Chapter Five

My insides feel like the contents of a washing machine as the lift swoops me skywards towards Daniel Lewis.

It's been a few months since I last met him for coffee, when, come to think of it, he did mention something about the cinema.. He must have been sussing out how likely I was to stage a revolt against whatever dastardly plan was forming in his head.

I've been trying to extract the conversation from the recesses of my mind all the way here so that I can re-examine every word and discover whether there were hidden clues in what he was telling me. But even on closer examination, I can't spot any tell-tale signs that he was about to try and destroy Westholme all over again. He's clearly become even more sophisticated in the execution of his plans.

An injection of bitterness surges through my veins, coiling the spring of my anger just that little bit tighter. I can't believe I actually thought he'd changed his ways.

I glare at the illuminated light of the lift panel, which is moving at a snail's pace through the numbers. By the time it reaches the top floor, I've wound myself up to such an extent I'm like a shaken bottle of prosecco ready to explode.

The doors ping open, launching me into a bright shiny world of glass and chrome. I look around as I power up to the reception desk. Still as perfect as I remember it.

A blonde receptionist with super-glossy waves and a flawless complexion smiles at me and I'm suddenly aware of the contrast between our appearances. Her dark-purple shift dress, flawless make-up and buffed nails scream 'perfectly polished'. I make a mental note to add 'paint nails' to the increasingly long list of tasks I have to complete in order to look half decent.

I glance down at my trousers – the ones with the pulls at the bottom where the heels of my boots keep catching them – and my swirly patterned shirt. I hastily refasten an open button and wish I'd gone home to change first. Then I see Daniel through the double doors and anger hijacks any remnants of shame.

He's talking to someone, his height putting him at a distinct advantage when it comes to establishing who's in charge. His dark-blue suit fits snug across the width of his shoulders and the brightness of his white shirt highlights the olive tones of his skin.

A light coating of gel holds his neat, dark hair in place and his dark-brown pupils look huge, despite the distance between us.

He sees me then and for a split second his expression lightens, his eyes flashing a welcome that feels warm and genuine. I almost smile in response. Then I remember why I'm here and shoot daggers in his direction as I stomp past the receptionist, fling open the double doors and march towards him.

The man he's talking to pauses to check what's captured his attention. Then Daniel utters a few words to him and walks slowly and deliberately towards me, eventually meeting me in the middle of the corridor.

'I can't believe you've done it again,' I fling at him once I'm a few feet away.

His shoulders jerk back. He's startled by my verbal assault, his eyes filled with surprise behind the dark frames of his glasses.

'Hello, Zoe,' he says briskly, and I see he's lost absolutely none of the pompous streak that used to grate on me even on those rare occasions I found him almost bearable. 'I'm glad that Candice managed to contact you. Unfortunately, she's double-booked me. I'm due to head out to another appointment shortly.'

'What? No, I—'

'Sorry, Daniel.' An attractive redhead whom I recognise from my last visit to Daniel's office hurries up the hallway waving a notepad. 'You only asked me to call Ms Taylor ten minutes ago. It's at the top of my "to do" list,' she adds hastily, looking from Daniel to me and pulling the sides of her mouth taut by way of an apology.

Daniel's eyebrows knit together into a frown and I wonder how genetically blessed a person would have to be to frown so much yet still have a resting face that's so wrinkle-free.

'I'm confused. Then I assume I owe the honour of your visit to another purpose?'

All this cross-purpose talking has thrown me off my stride. I scramble to pull together the various threads floating around in my brain in order to hit him with the same dynamic, kick-ass persona I'd rapidly created on my way over here.

'You didn't manage to turn the parade into a supermarket, so now you're knocking down the old cinema instead, aren't you?'

For the first time since I arrived, Daniel moves his gaze from me to Candice. They exchange a look, then she says quietly, 'I'll move your one-thirty appointment,' and scuttles off.

Suddenly self-conscious in my surroundings, I look through the glass walls surrounding me and into meeting rooms where blokes in suits and women in heels are watching the scene with obvious interest.

When I turn back, Daniel's staring at me again. 'Let's go

somewhere more private,' he says, turning on his heel and leading me briskly down the corridor like a schoolgirl being marched to the headteacher's room.

Daniel's office is still the same. Still huge. Still shiny. Still streak-free. I hover cautiously inside the door, unsure of where to put myself in this minimalist haven that wreaks of his power.

The last time I visited Daniel at his office over the Parade business, I inadvertently allowed myself to be psychologically manipulated by the seating arrangements. So, this time, when he invites me to sit down on the low red couch, I remain resolutely standing.

He shrugs, a careless move that causes me to launch into The Reason I Am Here with renewed vigour.

'I cannot believe you're so hellbent on this supermarket deal that you're now knocking down one of this town's oldest buildings to do it.'

A smile tugs at the sides of his mouth before, realising, he quickly recovers his usual stern expression.

'What's wrong with knocking it down to build a supermarket?' he snaps back, his eyes boring holes into my own. 'No, wait, I remember from the last battle I had with you, you're vehemently opposed to anything resembling progress.'

'Yet you're brave enough to do battle with me all over again when I oppose *this* development too?'

Daniel's eyes glint with something which, if he had the personality, might indicate mischief. He pauses for a minute, as though he's considering what I've just said.

When he speaks again, his voice is softer.

'So determined to cast me as the bad guy, aren't you?' he says quietly, shaking his head, and for one unexpected moment, my stomach is back in the elevator, dropping all the way back down to the ground floor.

When he looks back at me, his dark stare is so intense, so penetrating, that, like the glare of the sun, it is just too uncomfortable to look at. I look at the power trip red couches I'm determined will never again see the imprint of my bum instead.

He clears his throat and gestures towards a big rectangular table near the floor-to-ceiling windows.

'Zoe, will you *please* sit down? I have a business proposition I want to discuss with you. And you're too intimidating when you're standing up.'

A business proposition? Despite my determination that I'll be the one in charge here, I'm thrown, so I stalk over to the top end of the table, where I slide my bottom onto the corresponding seat.

I suspect I've taken his usual place, but he doesn't try and claim it back. He buzzes through to Candice to bring us some coffee, then moves deliberately towards the other end of the table, where he sits facing me as if we're opponents in a high-stakes game of chess. One in which both players have extra-long arms.

'I mentioned to you a few months ago that another firm of property developers had submitted an application to turn the old cinema into retirement apartments,' he says. 'You may be aware that that application was turned down due to the plans not being deemed in keeping with the area.

'The owner of the cinema decided at that point that she would keep the cinema and try to revive its fortunes. Lewis & Co. were engaged and we undertook a great deal of work in order to ensure it was structurally sound and that the remainder of the renovations were aesthetic only.

'After some work had been completed, the owner changed her mind about investing further in the cinema and prepared it for sale. However, the board of Lewis & Co. reminded me of the need for this company to increase its corporate and social responsibility commitments to the areas which we serve. We have set ourselves ambitious targets which we fully intend to hit through the careful implementation of a CSR strategy.'

I can feel my concentration waning. He sounds like a politician.

'As we are in the business of property, we have decided that one of our primary offerings should be to renovate where we can, while empowering local people to take control over key elements of their communities.'

Daniel pauses and takes a deep breath. 'In that spirit, we have worked out an agreement with the owner of the cinema that will allow a community business to rent the building, on the understanding that that business will have the right to have a purchase offer considered once they're in a sound financial position.'

I let his words sink in. 'What do you mean, a community business?'

'A business that's committed to positively benefiting society, driven by and accountable to the local community. A business whose primary aim would be to turn the cinema into a fully functioning picture house again.'

A wave of excitement flutters in my chest and I do my best to bat it away. But *Oh my goodness! A fully functioning picture house! The picture house I used to go to as a child, brought back to life for Charlie and me to enjoy together! That's amazing!*

That's what my brain says. What I actually say is, 'And how does that involve me?'

Daniel looks briefly at the table, his gaze faltering momentarily, and then continues.

'I would like to offer you a paid position as project co-ordinator. The role would be part-time, so you could combine it with your other responsibilities. You'd be free to choose your own hours and it would end once the cinema is up and running.'

My brain is whirling as it tries to keep up with the speed at which this information is coming through.

'You would, however, be working alongside me. This project is important to me and I'd want to be involved in its progress and kept up to speed with developments at all times.'

Just as quickly as they'd started to soar, my spirits plummet.

'But we'd kill each other,' I blurt out.

He allows himself a reluctant smile. 'On the contrary. I think we'd work well together. You have the contacts and the goodwill of the town on your side, I have the labour and the business acumen on mine. It is my belief that our combined qualities could produce something very special.'

I gulp. It sounds as though he's envisaging our offspring, not a revived local cinema.

'I mean,' he continues quickly, 'if you were to come on board with this, it could result in a fantastic new venue for our community, don't you agree?'

A gentle knock on the door heralds the arrival of coffee and Candice nudges it open with her foot before setting the drinks down on the table and withdrawing silently from the room.

Daniel rests his chin on his thumb and taps his lips with his finger, waiting for me to speak. I stare down at the glass table as I try and work out what to say, and feel victorious when I spot the marks my fingers have left on its surface.

Eventually he can stand it no more. Pushing his chair back, he gets up and walks around the table then perches against the middle of it.

'You haven't said much. Any initial thoughts?'

I curse each and every blood vessel in my face as I feel them working overtime to pump the tell-tale colour of shame to my face.

'Embarrassment, obviously,' I mutter. 'I thought you wanted to knock it down.'

He stifles another smile.

'Anything else? An overwhelming desire to apologise bubbling away alongside the sense of shame maybe?'

Oh, this is mortifying.

I reach for my mug.

'Sorry,' I mumble, swallowing the word in a sip of coffee.

He smiles. 'What was that? I didn't quite catch what you said.'

Good grief, is Daniel Lewis actually teasing me?

'I seem to have misjudged you,' I force out.

His expression turns serious now.

'You do that a lot.'

I take another sip of coffee in response.

A moment or two pass, then Daniel raps his fingers on the side of the table,

'Can I take it you're happy to be on board then?'

I place my mug down on its coaster. 'Er yes…no…I'm not sure. No,' I answer, the last 'no' being more decisive than the first. 'Thank you for thinking of me, but I don't have the time. Plus, I'm not sure how well you and I would work together. We have different…attitudes towards our community.'

He flinches at that one, and I feel as though I've struck a low blow, given that the main reason for our differing views towards our community is that I wasn't beaten up and left for dead at the Parade when I was a teenager in the way that Daniel was.

'Sorry,' I say again. 'I didn't mean to…' He waves his hand and shakes his head, and I fall silent.

'I know there's a lot to think about,' he picks up the conversation, 'so I'll have Candice email you a formal offer with the salary details and you can mull it over.'

He pauses and pushes his glasses up the bridge of his nose.

'But please do me one favour—'

I look up at him and see an unexpected flash of vulnerability in his eyes.

'Don't say no just because it's me.'

———

Westholme Community Facebook page:

Paul Gregory: Can the binmen please stop sticking the wheelie bins back in front of the doors of the terraced houses on Parsons Way please. I know there's hardly any pavement there to leave them on, but my elderly mum was trapped in her house all day yesterday because she couldn't move her wheelie bin out of the way.

Jimmy Hunter: It's not the binmen, it's the Orchard Estate gang. I spotted them the other day. They're doing it on purpose.

Chapter Six

I 'm back in the queue at Slim City, along with my best and oldest friends, Emma Ronson and Beth Hurst. Having finally reached my goal weight three months ago, these days my intermittent attendance is more about catching up with the girls and making sure I haven't gained half a stone while I wasn't looking than trying to win Slimmer of the Week.

But Barbara Theasby, the Slim City leader, likes to wheel me out as an example of what can be achieved when you put your mind to it. Therefore, I smile gracefully in the manner of a celebrity at a hospital opening and offer my tips for weight loss – most of which are definitely not Slim City approved – then head home before I'm tempted to join the rest of the class at Greggs.

Today though, it's absolutely vital that I attend. Because today, I'm expecting a plus-one – Dad – and I don't know who's more nervous about his much-mooted attendance, him or me.

I'm standing in the queue for weigh-in, checking my phone over and over, waiting for the text that will confirm he's either arrived and is in the car park or (and this is the one I'm expecting) he's bottled out.

Emma's chatting to the woman behind us, who, unlike everyone else, is decked out in jeans and a heavy jumper, and I turn to her as Beth tries to placate her crying baby.

'It's Donna's first week,' says Emma by way of introduction.

'Again.' Donna grins sheepishly.

I give her a warm smile. Heavy clothes at the first weigh-in, light fabrics from there on in. Any self-respecting returning Slim City member knows that trick. As does Barbara, which is why the only reaction Donna's outfit garners is a quick up-down, followed by a wink of approval before she moves on down the line.

I watch Barb for a moment as she tuts at the same heavy outfit on one of her regular attendees, her short light-blonde bob covered in so much hairspray that her whole look reminds me of one of those little Lego figures with the plastic hairstyles you just stick on top.

Further along the queue is Cath Waters from the café. She became a fully-fledged member of Slim City last month after a particularly glutinous afternoon which saw her, Ollie, Adina and me try out Paula's new range of cakes in the name of product testing. And while I'm sure her intentions were good when she first joined, a few weeks in she's become one of the more rebellious attendees who pays her money but makes no effort whatsoever to stick to the diet.

Beth's dressed in an odd combination of blue-patterned maternity leggings and a red, sheer leopard-print shirt, thereby conforming to the Slim City rule of light fabrics but not perhaps the general rule of outfits that make sense. However, the fact that she's a new mum means she has a free pass to wear whatever takes the least amount of effort, so her unusual look doesn't raise so much as an eyebrow among the other women in the queue.

In addition to her unconventional outfits, Beth tends to come attached to her own semi-permanent weight-gain these days:

twelve-week-old Darcy, who clings to her long bob, entwining her fingers in it until it's more knot than hair.

I study Beth now, noticing the dark shadows shading deep hollows around her brown eyes and the roots that are threatening to turn her caramel waves grey.

'How's the week been?' I ask, keeping my tone light, as though nothing about her appearance gives me the slightest cause for concern.

'Hard work, isn't it?' she says wearily. 'It's a good thing we're so in love with her because it's only the endorphins that are keeping us going right now – there's very little else in the engine.'

Darcy is one of those rare breeds of babies who appear to need no more than four disjointed hours of shut-eye a night. If she were a CEO, she'd be killing it. Unfortunately, the only thing she's killing right now is Beth, who hasn't had two consecutive hours of sleep since Darcy was born.

Beth glances wistfully at a lady further down the queue. With her smooth blonde curls, perfectly applied make-up and baby sleeping blissfully in an expensive-looking pram, she looks like something out of a Pampers advert.

'That's Louise,' I whisper. 'I was talking to her last time I came. Her baby's a sleeper. Darcy's not. The two experiences are like chalk and cheese.'

Beth bites her lip and swallows hard.

'It does get easier, you know,' I add.

She looks at me with such despair that it's all I can do not to throw my arms around her and tell her everything will be all right, then she flashes me an uncertain smile.

'I hope so, Zoe. I really hope so.'

My phone vibrates in my pocket and I pull it out quickly.

'Dad's here,' I say, giving her a quick hug. 'I'll go and get him. Wish me luck.'

My dad, the same one who scaled the roof of the Parade dressed as a bat only last year, who has a catalogue of jibes and a tongue that could cut you in two if you caught the wrong end of it, is absolutely bricking it.

He's standing outside the town hall, a sheen of sweat covering his face despite the cool air, all but trembling as I try and convince him to step inside.

'I don't know about this, love. What do I need to come here for anyway? I can lose weight myself at home. I'll just cut down on the beer. And eat more soup.' He points at his protruding stomach. 'I'll have this off in no time.'

'Come on, Dad, it'll be all right once you're inside.'

He starts backing away. 'I think I'll leave it today. Maybe next week.'

I probably would have lost him at that point, if it wasn't for Emma popping out to answer a work call.

As soon as she's ended the conversation, she heads straight over to join us.

'Terry!' She greets him with an embrace and a kiss on the cheek. 'Zoe told us you were coming. How lovely to see you.'

'Dad's having cold feet,' I say with a wink.

'What?' She takes her cue. 'A big man like you? Aw, you don't need to worry about us. We make look scary but we're a bunch of softies really.' She links her arm in his and chats incessantly as she guides him inside. 'Come on, I've saved a seat for you. Let's go and have a chat with Barb – you'll love her.'

And as Dad looks at me helplessly over his shoulder, I follow them into the building, wondering what delights the next hour will bring.

'Right, Terry,' Barbara says, looking my dad up and down. 'What brings you to Slim City today?'

Dad glances at me and I give him an encouraging nod.

'My doctor told me I needed to lose a bit of weight and seeing as how Zoe managed it, I thought, well…it must be pretty easy so I'll just come here and I'll lose some too.'

'Hmmm.' Barbara presses her lips together in a way that makes her mouth look very small. 'As Zoe will also tell you, it's not always that easy. But I applaud you for giving it a go, nonetheless. Would you like to step on the scales and we'll see how much you weigh?'

Dad moves to take his jacket off.

'No—' Barbara jumps in. 'Leave that on this week. You can take it off for the next weigh-in.'

Her eyebrows arch as she registers the number on the scales. 'Right,' she mutters. 'We certainly have our work cut out for us with you, don't we?' Then she turns back to the new member's book she's filling in and jots down a figure that I can't quite make out.

'OK, Terry,' she says, moving on to the next section of the page. 'What's your target weight?'

Dad looks at her, then at me, then shrugs.

'I dunno. Twelve stone?'

Barbara looks him up and down. 'Have you ever *been* twelve stone?' she asks, clearly dubious that such a figure might be possible for my dad.

'Maybe, forty years ago. We didn't go in for all that weight-loss malarky back in our twenties.'

Barbara gives him a death stare. 'Maybe you should have done. That way, you wouldn't have ended up overweight and joining us in your sixties.'

She writes 'twelve stone' into the target weight box. 'Why don't we start off small. At least that way you might feel as though you're achieving something.' She slams the cover of the book shut and hands it over to Dad. 'Plus, it would be nice to set a goal someone might actually hit for a change.' She looks at me and her tense expression relaxes into a semi-smile. 'Present company excluded, of course.'

The members of Slim City have been indulging themselves rather too much for Barbara's liking and she is – to excuse a pun – on a roll.

When she gives us all a very warm welcome at the start of the class, I'm optimistic that we might be in for an easy week. But the moment she reaches Cath – who, admittedly, often acts as a trigger to Barb's emotions – it becomes clear that none of us are about to be let off lightly after all.

'Cath, you've put on three pounds in the last week alone,' she barks. 'How did that happen?'

My dad turns to me, eyes wide. I pat his knee in what I hope is a reassuring fashion. Cath rolls her eyes and conducts a cursory chew of some non-existent food while she thinks about her answer.

'It started with a caramel cupcake back at the café after class,' she replies eventually. 'A bit of a reward after weigh-in.'

'But, Cath,' Barb says, checking her spreadsheet, 'you put on two pounds last week. What made you think you deserved a reward?'

Cath smiles, confident of this one small win. 'For coming to class.'

'Cath! You don't get a reward for simply turning up to class. Especially not when you've *gained* weight. And it might have started with a caramel cupcake, which in itself is bad enough, but

I suspect it didn't end with one, did it? What happened after you ate the cake?'

'I had a millionaire's shortbread.'

'And then what?' I spot a vein pulsating in Barb's neck.

We're all shifting uncomfortably now, aware that once one of us has riled Barb, the rest of us are likely to get it in the neck too. Not for the first time, I wonder why any of us actually come here.

Even Cath looks as though she's lost her footing.

'I don't really want to say, Barb.'

'Catherine, where did it lead?'

Cath mumbles something under her breath.

'What did you say, Cath? When you got home you moved on to Cheesey Wotsits?' A second vein is visibly throbbing now.

'Two of them.'

'Two Wotsits?'

'Two bags.

'Two bags of Wotsits?'

'Oh, Barb.' Cath sighs, leaning back in her chair. 'By that point I knew I'd gone well over my calorie allowance, so I thought I might as well carry on.'

Barbara's face is purple. I'm seriously worried that those veins in her neck might explode with the pressure of our collective failures.

'I hate to point out the obvious, but when you're partaking in the Slim City life plan, you shouldn't even have Wotsits in the house, let alone be eating them as a snack.'

'I forgot to mention the Cadbury's Dairy Milk the day after.'

'*Cath*,' a woman hisses further down the row, 'it's Slim City, not a confessional.'

Barbara sinks down into the nearest seat and rests her head on the palms of her bony hands.

'I think at this point it's irrelevant to even ask whether it was a single or family-size bar.'

'It was a fam—'

'Stop.' she shouts abruptly. 'What made you buy all this rubbish in the first place? It's meant to be apples and rice cakes all the way.'

'It's for my new fella, Ralph, you see. He likes his weekend treats.'

'But Ralph's not getting any weekend treats, is he, Cath?' Barbara trills. 'There's none left by the weekend. Because you've eaten them all in the week.'

Poor Cath. There was a time when I was the subject of this ritual humiliation, but since my heart-to-heart with Barb and the weight loss that subsequently followed, Barbara regularly calls on me to offer the other members hints and tips, which is confidence-boosting and mortifying all at the same time. And I sense this is where she's heading now.

'As we all know,' she starts. 'Zoe managed to achieve her goal weight a few months ago. Not only that, she's also managed to maintain it, which, as our lifetime members will tell you, is often the most difficult part.

'Zoe, can you offer Cath some words of advice?'

Either side of me, Emma and Beth chuckle. They still haven't got used to my rise from the ashes to become the poster girl of Westholme's Slim City chapter.

'Er,' I start, sparks of heat prickling my face, 'write down everything you eat?'

'Exactly,' confirms Barb. 'Write down EVERYTHING that you eat on a sheet of paper. Although in your case, Cath, you may need an entire exercise book rather than one lone sheet.'

'I do still cheat now and again,' I intervene, keen to show some moral support.

Cath looks hopeful. 'Really?'

'Oh absolutely.' My reply is emphatic. 'I've had a four chocolate bars and a bottle of wine over the last week alone.'

Barb shoots me a warning look. 'But we wouldn't want to encourage *that*, would we, Zoe. After all, it's that kind of behaviour that led most of our members here in the first place.'

'Of course not.' I fall into line. 'All I'm saying is, you don't have to stick exactly to the diet. You can cheat a little bit – you just need to rein it in for a few days before weigh-in. Then you'll probably get away with it.'

'Although clearly we would not recommend that as a sensible course of action,' Barbara interjects. 'Now, does anyone at all have a weight loss they'd like to share with us?'

The room falls silent.

'Right then,' she says, her voice resigned. 'Can I suggest that due to there being no contenders at all, we might bypass this week's City Slimmer award and move on to the weekly raffle instead? After all, it's the only loss most of you will have had this week.'

I give in to the weekly post-class Greggs trip this week. Something in me crumbles and I find myself filing into the little shop and picking out cakes along with the rest of the Slim City crew.

Part of it, at least, could be deemed altruistic. I want to stick close to Beth for as long as possible today. I remember how hard it is having a newborn baby and how isolating it can be. I don't want Beth to feel that way.

'Has your mum been around much?' I ask her as I tap my card on the machine.

'Oh, you know,' she says, her hand buried in the pram, stroking Darcy's face. 'She's popped by with Adam a few times, but it always seems to be when they're on their way to some party or other. She only stays long enough to have a cuppa and pose for photographs with the baby that she can post on social media along with the hashtag "blessed".'

I give Beth's arm a sympathetic squeeze as we file outside the shop. When we were growing up, her mum was, like my own, a homely, kitchen-based type who was more concerned with getting their hands on the best cut of beef at the butchers than on a toy boy.

But after Beth's dad announced five years ago that he was moving to Blackpool to live with a woman he'd been having a twelve-year affair with, her mum drew up a new list of life goals. She joined an online dating agency, got together with Adam, a plumber twenty years her junior with a big group of friends apparently determined to party to their graves, and has never been quite the same since.

'I'd feel blessed if I spent most of my life on the ale,' Emma quips.

'Emma!' I glare at her. She spots Beth's expression then checks herself and nudges her shoulder with her own.

'Sorry, chick.'

Beth shakes her shoulders, as if shaking off her sadness, and smiles widely.

'Enough about me. Tell me how *you're* both doing.' She turns to me. 'How's work going?'

We're hanging around outside Greggs now, eating our cakes out of their paper bags. I point at a nearby bench and the three of us assist Beth as she does a forty-seven-point turn with the pram in order to park it just so, then we squeeze up together on the wooden seat.

'Honestly? It's not great.' I debate whether or not to tell them about Daniel's offer and hover for a minute on the side of 'not', but I'm desperate to bat the idea around.

'But I have been offered a part-time job,' I say slowly.

'Oh yeah?' Emma mumbles through a mouthful of pastry. 'What's it doing?'

I inhale deeply. 'This is just between us, OK?'

'Course,' Beth confirms.

'Go on.' Emma waits expectantly.

'Daniel wants to bring the old cinema back to life. And he wants me to be in charge of the regeneration project.'

They both gasp in unison.

'What?' I look at each of them in turn.

'Daniel Lewis?' checks Beth. 'The rich bloke?'

'How much is he paying you?' asks Emma.

'Yes,' I confirm to Beth, then to Emma I add, 'A lot.' It's true, it is a lot. So much, in fact, that I had to read and re-read the offer letter several times to make sure there weren't any hidden job responsibilities in there.

'Enough to keep the wolf from the door for a while?' asks Beth, frowning as she runs the idea through various checks in her head.

'Well, enough to pay for Christmas if I'm careful with it.'

Emma's watching me, eyes narrowed slightly. I can even see a proper, bona fide frown, which, on someone as overly reliant on Botox as Emma appears to be, is an unusual occurrence.

'What does Sam think you should do?'

I look down at my cake, a triple chocolate donut, and wonder why I bought it.

'I haven't told him yet.'

'Why not?' Naturally, that's from Emma. but even Beth looks a bit worried.

I shrug. 'I haven't seen him much lately. He's been so busy with the academy and I'm so busy with everything...you know what it's like. I'll tell him when I next speak to him.'

'You should definitely take the job,' Emma says.

'You think?' My heart lifts a little at her words.

'Absolutely,' she replies, nodding. 'I loved seeing how fired up you got about the Parade. It's good for you, having a cause. You seem, I don't know, more alive or something when you're doing this sort of thing.'

'Really?' I know I'm grinning.

'Definitely.'

'I don't know if this is a good idea,' Beth manages as Darcy starts wailing. We all fall silent as Beth stands up and hooks her out of the pram.

'Why not?' I feel like a balloon that's been popped by a Nerf gun.

'Sam's not going to—' Darcy's ear-piercing scream takes priority over whatever else she was about to say, and her various demands over the next fifteen minutes make it impossible for me to steer the conversation back to me again.

It's probably no bad thing. I'm not sure I would have liked the answer anyway.

Westholme Community Facebook page:

Barbara's Slim City Westholme: May I remind all of our Slim City members that a lot can be gained in seven days – and a lot can be lost too. Please remember that it's the losers that are the winners at Slim City. Just something to think about when you're about to start on those Wotsits, **Cath Waters**.

Chapter Seven

The next bouquet of flowers turns up at on the doorstep of Paula's bakehouse. No one knows how they got there, or even when they got there, but Paula couldn't be more excited at her discovery.

She pushes open the door into *The Good News Gazette* office, her face flushed and her eyes bright, despite the ever-present bags that have taken up residence beneath them.

'Look at this,' she exclaims, spreading out her hands to reveal a stunning combination of pink and white carnations, their buds starting to open to reveal the pastel hues inside, along with vibrant pink roses whose bright shades provide a pop of colour, violet irises, and gypsy grass poking out through the stems and petals of each flower.

'Paula, they're beautiful.'

I move out from behind my desk in order to see the bouquet in all its glory. As I approach, I notice a note attached. 'What does it say?'

She opens it and reads, 'Your cakes make the world an easier place to be.'

My heart melts a little bit at the words. 'What a lovely sentiment.'

'Isn't it?' Paula strokes a petal gently. 'Have you had any luck finding out who's behind them?'

'Nope. I really thought that featuring the story in *The Good News Gazette* might do the trick but there's been nothing. No feedback, no suggestions of who it could be, nothing.'

Paula grins. 'Whoever it is, they can keep 'em coming. It's certainly made my day.'

I sling my arm around her and squeeze her shoulders. 'It couldn't have happened to a nicer person. If only we could find out who it is that's behind it all.'

She sighs. 'I'd love to imagine it's a gorgeous hunk of a man with millions in the bank who's looking for a ready-made family. But, knowing our luck, it's more likely to be a stalker with a flower fetish.'

I'm writing an advertising feature about drainpipes and it's led me to this sad conclusion: there is not one single interesting thing about them.

Across the desk, Ollie's working on a freelance design project for an agency in Liverpool about a luxury spa, which is infinitely more interesting than writing about plastic tubes. But then last week he had to take orders from a client who made him redesign a brochure five times, so I suppose we all have our crosses to bear.

This is how we're both managing the lack of advertising at the moment: by combining freelance work with the *Gazette*.

The problem with a place like Westholme is that it's so small, no one really needs to advertise. We all know every pub, shop and restaurant (it helps that there's only three of those and one is actually a takeaway with eight plastic seats and a Formica table) so advertising is pointless. If you're a regular at one pub then you're not going to – embarrassing incidents aside – suddenly shift allegiance to another. Beauty salons and hairdressers are doing a roaring trade anyway and builders are usually found through the Westholme Community Facebook page rather than newspapers. It's a really hard sell at the moment.

But I've arranged to meet Gloria's latest mentoring group tomorrow after she suggested I pop along so that we could chat about some of the tactics that might help attract more advertisers. Plus, a woman who has already assured me she has a *huge* budget is coming into the office later to talk about advertising her new business, so I'm keeping everything crossed that she'll provide an answer to our woes. Or at the very least divert our attention from them and save me from having to work for Daniel Lewis in order to make ends meet.

'What's up?' says Ollie, distracted by whatever's on his screen.

I sigh. 'Nothing.'

He looks up and tuts. 'Stop fretting, you're worrying too much. It'll all be fine.' He clocks my expression then says, 'Well, at least worry about something else. The advertising issue's getting old. Have you done anything about saving the cinema yet?'

I ignore him and start tapping harder at the keyboard.

'Speaking of which…' he raises his voice to be heard over my clacking '…what happened when you went to see Danny boy the other day? You said on your text you'd update me when you saw me. Yet here I am. Seen but not updated.'

I glance at the random letters of the alphabet I've been furiously typing into my screen and hold down the delete button to erase them all.

'Oi!'

I lift my finger off the button and look at him haughtily.

'So. What. Happened?' he repeats slowly.

'Daniel isn't buying the cinema.'

'Oh.' Ollie's face falls and I strongly suspect he's disappointed by the lack of drama that that sentence brings with it.

'But he wants to restore it. And he wants me to do it with him. In a part-time, paid position.'

His expression falters for a moment, then his face lights up in delightful anticipation of the words that are to follow.

He leans back in his chair, clasping his hands together, the sun zinging flashing stars off the teeth he spent hours in the dentist's chair yesterday having whitened before putting it all on his credit card. 'Naturally you said yes?'

I suck my bottom lip in and start chewing on the side of it.

'Please, please tell me you said yes.'

I shrug. 'I don't think I'm going to do it.'

'Why the hell not?'

'Because it would be the worst idea in the world,' I huff, turning my attention back to removing the disorganised letters of the alphabet off my screen one by one.

Ollie props his elbows on the desk and rests his chin in his palms. 'And why would that be? Are you frightened by the raw, animal magnetism that clearly draws the two of you together?'

I stop deleting and glare at him. 'Very funny. I just think... I don't know. It doesn't seem right, that's all.'

'Because of Sam?' Ollie's dropped his playful expression, but the look he's giving me now is even worse. Now he appears almost sympathetic.

I stand up and remove my dirty coffee cup from the table. 'Nothing to do with Sam. I'm busy trying to make us our millions. I haven't got time to be renovating cinemas too. Coffee?'

'You know I can't,' he moans, distracted from his line of questioning.

'Ah, that's right. Forty-eight hours, the dentist said, didn't he? Which means you've got another...' I look over at the clock '... twenty or so hours to go. Never mind, Ol, you just keep sipping that tap water, safe in the knowledge that if the energy prices get too high, we can farm you out and use your teeth as solar panels.'

I wink at him, then turn the tap on and squirt washing up liquid into the sink. 'Just kidding.'

'You, meanwhile,' Ollie shouts over, 'can keep knocking back the coffee. And carry on pretending that the decision you're about to make will have absolutely no consequence whatsoever on the *Gazette*, your relationship with Sam or indeed your nervous system.'

I spin round, startled by his words.

'What did you just say?'

'About your nervous system?' He's in his element.

'No, the other stuff.'

He smiles widely to make sure I can see his megawatt grin in all its glory, then winks.

'Just kidding.'

Westholme Community Facebook page:

Paula's Bakehouse: Thanks so much to whoever left me that beautiful bouquet today. Such a lovely surprise. I'd love to know who you are though?

Peter Mason: It was me. Just send a few boxes of those chocolate cupcakes my way and we'll call it evens.

Chapter Eight

The group of women being mentored by Gloria – the woman who sat on the boards of some of the biggest businesses in the UK before retiring back to Westholme – might have changed, but the vibe in the library's meeting room is still exactly the same.

Just like the last group of disadvantaged women that included Paula and former model turned vintage shop owner Eva, this group is chatty, sassy, cautious, battered and bruised. Having spent a couple of months working on their own business plans, the women are delighted to pitch in to someone else's. And between them they have numerous suggestions as to how I might be able to make the *Gazette* more profitable.

'Leaflet drops worked well for me,' says Alice, a woman with straight brown hair and a black hairband who started her own estate agents a few months ago.

'I do well at community events.' This is from Penny, owner of a cheese hamper business that's been an overnight success.

'Do you do much on Facebook?' Julia, a sweet young thing who makes wax melts, asks and my heart sinks as I realise that her very question means my social media efforts have clearly not been effective enough.

Gloria, as awe-inspiring as ever in her fuchsia lipstick and matching, towering heels, flashes me a sympathetic smile and straightens the lapels of her grey jacket. 'Let's go direct to what Zoe wants the end result to be. What is that, Zoe?'

I think for a moment.

'I suppose it's a bigger profit.'

'And how do you think that can be achieved?'

'Through advertisers. That's the only way it *can* be achieved, other than charging for the paper, which is something we'll never do.'

Gloria places a hand on her hip. 'In that case, you need a way to reach more of them. And I assume it's business owners you're looking to target, isn't it?'

I nod. 'That's right. And the more money they have to spend, the better.'

'OK,' she says thoughtfully. 'You'll need to go to some networking events then. They're a good way to meet other business owners and to also let people know what *The Good News Gazette* is all about.'

'I've looked into those. But they tend to take place at breakfast, when the only deal I'm concerned about is the one that will convince Charlie to get dressed and brush his teeth so I can get him to school on time.'

'Can you escape in the evenings at all?' Alice asks, tapping her Biro on the table. 'I go to an after-hours networking do once a month that's specifically for the property sector. Estate agents, conveyancing and commercial property solicitors, that sort of thing. They do something different each month. There's a cocktail party next week at The Titanic hotel in Liverpool. A nautical theme apparently, probably something to do with the venue.'

Now *that* sparks my interest. There's tons of money in

property, isn't there? Everyone says so. And I love cocktails. It's tailor-made for me.

'Alice, that sounds perfect, if you're sure you wouldn't mind me coming with you?'

'No problem.' She grins. 'Friend me on Facebook and I'll send you the details. In all honesty, I'd be glad of someone to go with. I'll chat to anyone, but even I find these events daunting at times. Just remember to embrace the dressing-up part. There's usually more men than women so you need to show you're up for being as daft as the blokes are.'

'Don't worry,' I say confidently. 'Daft I can do. And it just so turns out I have the *perfect* outfit in my wardrobe at home.'

———

The road to hell is paved with good intentions.

So, it appears, is the road to Vintage Vibes, the clothes store that former model Eva opened up last year.

Through her little shop at the Parade, she's introduced me to a world of clothes that appear to have been crafted with me in mind, a still-slightly-curvy-despite-my-weight-loss figure. Stepping inside Eva's charming, shabby-chic boutique is like disappearing into a magical world with beautiful clothes that are unlike anything I've ever seen before.

I adore it. But its very existence makes my bank account weep. So, the last thing I need when I'm trying to be good with my money is for her to stick her head out of the door and beckon me inside.

'Zoe,' she shouts across the Parade, her willowy frame clad in a multicoloured maxi skirt, biker boots and a red chunky jumper that sets off her flawless brown skin. 'You've *got* to see this dress I've put aside for you. It has your name written all over it.'

My heart sinks and soars at the same time. If Eva thinks it's got my name written all over it then it will have. Which means, despite my best efforts, the dress will be reserving a place in my wardrobe.

I approach the shop like a woman condemned, with sweaty palms and a pounding heart, but the moment I step onto the plush grey carpet that adds even more luxury to the pretty store, I can't help but beam.

From Peter Pan tops to the most stunning evening dresses, dozens and dozens of items hang tantalisingly from the silver railings set up against the flocked silver paper that adorns the walls. Black satin, pillar-box red wool, pure silk...there are so many fabrics from across the eras just desperate to be touched, tried on and ultimately bought. I sigh. My newly discovered love for vintage means a constant battle between my head and my heart.

'Come on then,' I say, my voice heavy with resignation. 'Let's see what I'm about to spend my money on.'

Eva grins, a gesture that makes her chiselled face look even more striking and flicks her black curls, highlighted with threads of honey, behind her shoulders. 'Wait one minute and I'll get it. But brace yourself – this one's a beauty.'

Moments later she emerges from the back room of the shop with the most beautiful dress I've ever seen in my life. A strapless red crêpe creation, it has a sweetheart neckline and a wrap skirt that gathers at the top of the thigh and looks like it literally just sashayed out of a Christmas movie.

'Told you you'd love it,' chirps Eva, the curves of her mouth forming a smug grin.

'I have nowhere to wear it.' I sound like Eliza Doolittle.

'You *find* somewhere to go to wear this dress,' she argues. 'Why don't you try it on?'

Try it on. Yes, that's what I'll do. I don't usually buy anything after I've tried it on.

'Great idea,' I reply. 'Hopefully it will look awful on me and I'll leave here without it.'

———————

I feel like a movie star. Granted, an X-rated movie star, with the tight bodice creating the sort of cleavage even *I* would stare at and the wrap skirt revealing a piece of leg that definitely needs a good dose of self-tan, but a movie star all the same.

'I'll take it,' I holler from behind the curtain, trying to keep my hair piled on top of my head as I stand on my tiptoes and check my reflection in the mirror, imagining how I'd look if I was six inches taller and another stone lighter.

'Knew you would,' Eva shouts back. 'That's why I didn't share it on social media. It would have been gone in a flash and I didn't want you to miss out. Do you want to pay now or in instalments?'

I look at the price tag again and ignore the voice of The Money Man, the star of a previous *Good News Gazette* story who so successfully helped me get my finances back on track earlier this year, ringing in my ears.

'In instalments please.' I poke my head out from behind the curtain. 'It's not like I'm going anywhere posh anyway.'

Eva laughs. 'No one is. Maybe that's why business is so slow at the moment.'

'Oh no, really, Eva?' I pop my head back in and carefully undo the zip. 'I can't believe people aren't snapping these clothes up – they're beautiful.'

'I'm not sure that the locals get it,' says Eva. 'I've seen a lot of comments on the community Facebook page about this just being a glorified second-hand shop.' She pauses, then adds. 'I don't suppose you know any celebrities, do you? A few social media posts from someone famous would make all the difference.'

I'm wracking my brains, but I haven't met anyone famous in a long time. In fact, round here, Daniel is probably the most famous person I know. Not that I can imagine him in a dress.

'Not really.' I reply. 'But we'll have Lily Lonsdale here for a while when they start filming that movie next month. Maybe she'll pop by and pick up a few of your clothes.'

'As if,' scoffs Eva. 'They're filming on the Orchard Estate, aren't they? Why on earth would they go there?'

'No idea. But it's a psychological thriller or something, so I suppose they're trying to make it look gritty.'

'Gritty or grotty?'

I consider this. 'Maybe both?'

'Little chance they're going to need vintage costumes then,' Eva muses, her voice glum.

'You never know. Lily Lonsdale might have already found you online. Maybe she's counting the days until she can make it into Vintage Vibes.'

Eva snorts, and, unable to add anything constructive, I pull my jumper over my head and step out from behind the curtain.

'Take care of her,' I caution, giving the dress one long last look before I hand it back to Eva.

'I'll guard her with my life.' She clutches the crêpe to her chest.

And I take out my card and put down the deposit on the dress that I'm not even sure I'll ever get to wear.

Westholme Community Facebook page

Billy Twistle: I see *The Good News Gazette*'s looking pretty thin this month. Not many adverts in it.

Steve Owen: It's not the adverts that are the problem, it's the news stories. Must have run out of good news. Always said it wouldn't last.

Stephanie Porter: That's what we're missing on here – more little rays of sunshine like you. Cheers Steve!

Chapter Nine

I t's a strange feeling, dressing up as an octopus to go on a night out, but the theme of the evening is 'nautical' and I'm nothing if not conformist.

Fortunately, I'm also a multi-tasker – which is how I ended up with an octopus outfit sitting in the bottom of my wardrobe in the first place.

I'd mistakenly ordered an adult costume rather than a children's one for Charlie's 'under-the-sea' day at school last year while watching a boxset with a glass or three of wine. Long story short, the get-up arrived, I reclaimed my 'Worst Mother of the Year' crown, and, to add insult to injury, I forgot to send it back within twenty-eight days so had to pay £27.34 for the privilege.

But every cloud and all that, and the silver lining to that particular scenario was that, when Alice's invitation came, I had the perfect 'nautical' outfit ready to go.

I'm feeling a wave of self-satisfaction at, for once, being unwittingly organised for such an event and even if I do say so myself, I'm looking pretty good. Well, you know, for an octopus.

The taxi makes its way along the industrial setting of what is known locally as the Dock Road, a long thoroughfare unpunctuated by traffic lights that runs along the mouth of the Mersey towards the north of the city.

Those visitors to the city who know nothing of this area's past or future are unlikely to be impressed by this part of town. First iron railings then a huge, thick wall separate the road from the series of docks that lie behind it, areas filled with history that once provided access to another world. A world of tobacco and rum importation, emigrants excited to embark on new adventures and, much to our eternal shame, slaves being carried across the Atlantic to their fate.

In parts, it is distinctly run-down. Another area of the city that could be written off as past its best. But as the taxi nears the entrance to The Titanic hotel, the juxtaposition of present and future becomes clear. Because The Titanic heralds the start of a new beginning; one which includes the planned transformation of the River Mersey waterfront and much of the city's docklands.

The Titanic was the first sign of real change in this part of town – the part where Everton's new football stadium is currently taking shape – and it still fills my heart with joy every time I see the difference that the combination of good taste and money can make. I feel a rush of pride as the taxi turns into the cobbled car park of the hotel and I anticipate how different this area will look in years to come. It's going to be amazing.

For now, however, there's the small matter of paying the taxi driver, and I thrust a thick pink arm through the two front seats to hand over the cash, leaving him chuckling as I try and climb out of the car.

This operation is a feat in itself, and I work up a sweat manoeuvring the padded costume that envelops every part of me from the knees up out of the car in a way that doesn't result in me leaving half of its tentacles behind.

I've arranged to meet Alice at the bar, so I head inside the industrial luxe surroundings, clamber on to one of the bar stools and order a mojito while I wait. A few funny looks are being cast my way, but I console myself with the thought that plenty of people will soon be here dressed as dolphins, sharks, sailors and pirates. Admittedly, I'll still look weird, but at least I won't look weird alone.

There must be another do at the hotel tonight, as there's a steady stream of people heading through the doors now, dressed in a variety of raunchy outfits that suggest a pimps-and-vicars or other such themed event might be taking place alongside ours.

I take another sip of my cocktail as I watch the partygoers filter through, then pull my phone out of my bag to browse through it while I'm waiting. I scan the notifications. Three unread messages and four missed calls – all off Alice. I open up the texts and start to read.

Zoe, I got the theme wrong, it's naughty, not nautical! Hope I've caught you in time.

Just tried to call you, the theme is naughty, I repeat, naughty. I read the email wrong. Just popped back to change so I'll be a few minutes late.

Just tried to call you again. Text me back so I know you got this message.

I look up to see even more people dressed up in costumes that are definitely not nautical filing into the bar. Around me, sexy secretaries and men in shirtless collars and cuffs are staring and pointing. My face is the only part of me that peeks through the costume and even that's now pink too.

A wave of horror jabs at the back of my neck and then continues its journey all the way down my back and round into my chest and tummy. *Please let this not be happening, please God please let this not be happening.* But I'm still here. This is actually happening. This is the *worst* moment of my life. Ever.

I'm about to call a cab and flee when Alice appears, looking perfectly dressed for the occasion in a naughty nurse's uniform.

Perhaps unsurprisingly, she spots me immediately.

'You didn't get my message,' she says, her expression of horror mirroring my own.

I shake my head, which probably looks to her like I'm just shaking my face. 'I did not.'

We stare at each other for a moment, not quite sure what the solution should be to this particular problem, before I voice what appears to be the only plausible one.

'I'm going home.'

I'm not sure whether I've been rescued by or thrown into the clutches of Graham, a five foot two damp specialist who has told me more about the subject over the course of the last sixty minutes than I'm sure I'd need to know in an entire lifetime.

Alice, who used to work with him many moons ago, spotted him as I was about to leave. Despite the fact that the only nod he's made to the night's theme is a T-shirt that reads *I'll show you mine if you'll show me yours*, he and Alice somehow managed to convince me that the do would be made all the better by the presence of a huge octopus and he hasn't let me go since.

'It's a fascinating topic, you know, dry rot,' he says, visually excited that he's being given the opportunity to talk about his specialist subject, even if it is to a puffy pink sea creature.

'I don't know if you've ever actually seen dry rot in all its glory, but it's a magnificent thing. Big, fleshy, red bit in the

75

middle…it's like a big, rotting fish. Not unlike your outfit actually!'

He howls with laughter at his joke while I gulp the remains of my mojito and look around for Alice, who conveniently needed the toilet five minutes into proceedings.

I've been here an hour now and haven't had so much as a sniff of potential advertisers. In fact, the only time I've spoken to anyone other than Graham was when he headed off to the toilet after his first two cocktails and passed me on to a group of blokes he knew, Jasper being the only one whose name I can remember.

After they'd finished with the octopus jokes, they were very keen to tell me about themselves, their opinions and the overwhelming success of their own businesses. And while it led me to wonder why they felt the need to be here in the first place, I bit my tongue and just kept nodding anyway. No one showed even the slightest bit of interest in the *Gazette*.

'There was one house I was called out to,' continues Graham, stroking his comb-over across the top of his head, 'where the dry rot ran underneath the floorboards of the entire ground floor. The whole family had to move out for a month while my team did a complete floorboard replacement. Made a beautiful job of it they did, you never would have known there'd been a problem.'

This. Is. So. Boring.

Not just standing in a supermarket queue or finding yourself on a train with a dead phone battery kind of boring. I mean the sort of boring that makes you feel as though the life is being sucked out of you, bit by bit, by the person talking at you with such complete self-absorption that they're hoovering up any energy you might have had in order to power their own mouth.

Which. Won't. Stop. Moving.

It's at the point that I honestly believe this is how I might die, verbally pinned up against the wall by Graham the damp specialist, that a hand clamps down on his shoulder, spinning him around so he's facing the other direction, before a voice I recognise all too well filters through the jumble of other noises in the room.

'Graham, how are you? The damp business still going well?'

I dare myself to look over Graham's shoulder. And there, defying the dress code to instead wear one of his many suits, is the person I least want to see when I'm decked out as an octopus with a face as pink as my tentacles.

Daniel Lewis.

My next move is probably neither sensible or achievable, as I try and turn away before he notices me and in doing so manage to bump into a waiter who's so far done a successful job of handing bright-pink cocktails out from a tray. The resulting crash is loud and messy, with pink liquid splashed all over the walls, other people's costumes and the bottom of Graham's jeans, which at least now have *something* naughty about them.

'I'm so sorry,' I whisper to the waiter who's scurrying around picking up pieces of glass off the floor. 'Wait – you'll cut your hands. Let me help.'

The very act of attempting to bend over to help him sends even more glasses crashing to the ground as my huge costume takes on a life of its own, seemingly determined to take down every drink in the room.

I try and shuffle round on my haunches to collect the debris, but then the waiter steps back into me and I lose my balance and topple over like a Weeble, until I'm lying on my back on the floor.

I look around for back-up, ideally in the form of the two people who dragged me inside in the first place. But Graham has completely disappeared while I can just make out Alice's face in the distance, her laughter ringing out at the back of a crowd gathered around me that now stands five-deep.

In fact, the only person that I vaguely recognise is Daniel Lewis. And he's making his way towards me, smiling as though the whole toe-curling incident has made his entire night.

'Zoe Taylor,' he says, reaching out his hand to help me up. 'I thought that was you.'

Despite my better judgement – and mainly because it's the only way I have of standing upright without potentially smashing a window or two, I use him to lever myself up, trying to channel Amal Clooney accepting George's hand in those many pictures I've seen of her stepping on and off boats. Even allowing for the fact that I've never seen her do it in an octopus costume, I'm still aware that I'm failing dismally.

'Daniel,' I manage with extreme politeness. 'How are you?'

He studies me. 'Good. But confused as to what a nice girl like you is doing in a place like this.' He looks me up and down. 'Dressed in an outfit like that.'

I have my grey Converse, rather than my boots on, so feel shorter and less 'boss lady' than I do when I'm wearing heels. And that's before we even take into account the fact that I'm the only person in the room, if not the entire world, who's chosen to dress as an octopus tonight.

Daniel, on the other hand, has never seemed so tall. He looks good, again, with his deep-brown eyes, thick eyelashes and a smattering of dark stubble grazing his jaw. And stylish. Always stylish.

I'm formulating a witty retort when someone stands on one of my tentacles and I have to grab Daniel's arm in order to avoid being dragged across the room.

Steadying myself, I am hit by the humiliating realisation that there is nothing Amal Clooney-esque about me at all. Even dignity is a concept to which I relinquished all claim the moment I walked through the door.

'Honestly?' I start to reply. My expression, I know, acknowledges my defeat. 'I have no idea.'

Daniel uses his other hand to grip the underside of my forearm until I'm in a more upright position, then looks down at me with an acceptable degree of sympathy.

'Would you like me to take you home?'

I hesitate as I weigh up my options. And I curse myself for giving him the satisfaction of knowing I need his help to get me out of this, the most embarrassing of situations.

That said, even I know when I'm beat.

I sigh. 'Would you mind?'

'It would be my pleasure.' He sets down his water on the tray of a passing waitress. 'I only came to show my face because I'm one of the people who set this group up, many moons ago...' He looks around. 'And this was certainly not the type of networking association I originally had planned.'

My tale of how I came to be dressed as an octopus amuses Daniel no end, and I'm forced to re-tell it at least twice during the drive home.

'So, you thought that by coming along to the group you might pick up some advertisers?' he repeats, trying to get his head around the whole thing.

'Yes.' I nod. 'I thought it was a professional organisation.'

'Where they asked people to dress up as sea creatures?'

'Point taken. Although I'm not sure that the naughty theme was any more professional.'

'Touché.'

We fall quiet for a moment, and the silence feels awkward. Despite the many miles we covered in his car last year when I dragged him around the local area in a bid to convince him not to demolish Westholme Shopping Parade, it feels strange now that we're not on either side of a battle. Different.

I shiver, which is strange considering the amount of synthetic material I'm swaddled in, and he does something with the controls to make the car warmer.

'So,' he says then, 'did you think any more about my proposition?'

'Not really,' I lie. I feel the weight of his eyes on my face as he glances at me sideways.

'I assume Candice emailed you the job offer?'

'She did,' I confirm. 'It's a very generous wage.'

'You get what you pay for.'

His fingers squeeze the steering wheel so tightly that it makes his knuckles look white in the reflection of the moon, then he clears his throat.

'The very fact that you've dressed up as an octopus to go to a networking event is a clear indication that you would benefit from a little assistance.'

I raise an eyebrow in response.

'In return for helping me to get the cinema back on its feet, I would be more than happy to introduce you to potential advertisers and any other connections that might help *The Good News Gazette* to succeed.'

A flicker of excitement kicks in as images of a beautifully restored art deco cinema float into my mind – quickly followed by the delightful thought of our newspaper packed with adverts.

'I must admit, it's not the *least* tempting offer I've had this year,' I say, winding a tentacle around my fingers.

He slows down to let a boy racer in an old Astra zoom past, then checks his rear-view mirror. 'But?'

'Not enough time, too much of a juggle, concerns that not enough people would get involved…'

'Didn't you feel that way when you agreed to go up against me over the Parade?'

'Well, yes,' I admit, the winding of the tentacle getting a little quicker as I blush at his unintentional double entendre.

'So why did you agree to take that on?'

Good grief, he's relentless.

'Because I thought it was important. I thought the Parade was a big part of our town.'

'But you don't think that about the cinema?'

'Yes…I mean, no…I mean…' I stare out of the window into the darkness. I have no idea what I mean.

He turns on the music system and a slow, sexy Mick Jagger track powers into action. Lowering the volume he says, 'Look, there's no pressure. But I think with your know-how, your…' he hesitates '…spirit, you'd be the perfect fit for this. And I suspect this arrangement might be good for you, too.'

I'm about to ask him what he means when he says, 'I'm sorry, I don't actually know where you live. Which way is it from here?'

My heart lurches in my chest as I realise I didn't completely think this through. Fortunately, the fact that my mum's at mine babysitting for Charlie means there's no way I'd invite him in for coffee anyway, even without all the associated subtexts that come with it. But in my panic to escape the non-nautical party, I hadn't processed this one small fact: Daniel's going to see where I live. And it's a world away, in every sense, from where he resides.

I quickly do a mental recce of the outside of my home. Red ex-council house brick, surrounded by dozens of other identical semis and a few terraces, white PVC windows and front door, a red roof, pots of dead geraniums either side of the front step. The flowers looked beautiful in the height of summer, and I felt every inch the domestic goddess. Now that we're hurtling towards winter, they look like someone buried a pile of weeds in a plant pot and tried to call it art.

Even as we approach my road, I feel a sense of discomfort wash over me. I love my house once I'm inside it and the door's shut. It's a haven of cosiness for Charlie and me. But I feel like I'm seeing my surroundings with new eyes. With Daniel's eyes. And they're falling short.

I can tell by the subtle movement of his head as various urban landmarks catch his eye that he's taking it all in. But, he doesn't make any comment. There's no false compliments or musings on how gentrification may one day reach this particular part of Westholme.

I sit there, babbling about anything that comes into my mind to try and distract him. I want to tell him that it was only ever meant to be temporary, that I wanted the dream house, just like him. That once upon a time I really believed I'd get it.

Instead, I simply say, 'It's here on the right,' thank him for the lift and promise I'll give the job some more thought.

Then I step out of his world and back into mine.

Westholme Community Facebook page:

Eyelash Lucy: Word of warning to anyone going to the multiplex – take your own snacks. Just paid the best part of £20 for two drinks and a couple of popcorns.

Tracey Cook: You bought snacks at the multiplex? Schoolgirl error. Should stop off at Home Bargains before going to the flicks.

Phil Ryder: Knew I should have asked you out at school. Always thought you'd be a cheap date

Tracey Cook: You should have – I bought my sweets from the penny sweet shop back then!

Chapter Ten

It's Friday night and Cath's Caff is packed with children hungrily guzzling slushes, milkshakes and freakshakes piled high with squirty cream, mini-donuts, Haribos and chocolate that look like the best and the worst things on the planet all in one go.

I'd love to be one of those mums who gently reminds her children of the dangers of consuming so many artificial substances in one sitting and successfully nudges them in the direction of the carrot sticks and hummus, but I'm not that strong. So not only is Charlie tucking into the concoction of chemicals; I am too.

Sam shakes his head and smiles as he sips his smoothie and watches the two of us drowning ourselves in a sea of sugar and fat. It wasn't too long ago that I would barely eat a chip in front of him, let alone one of these monsters, but as time's gone on it's become more and more difficult to hide my inner pig. Plus, these days I mostly stick to the Slim City plan, so given that the moments when I go off the rails are few and far between, I justify it by telling myself that everyone deserves a treat sometimes.

'How was school today, Charlie?' he asks, resting back against the padded surroundings of our booth.

Charlie looks up from his freakshake, cream and chocolate sauce dribbling down his chin, and gives Sam a thumbs-up. I had suggested we share one but Charlie's refusal had been emphatic.

'I think that's all you're going to get for the time being,' I say, laughing at his determination to devour the entire creation. Like mother, like son.

Sam grins. 'OK then, I'll ask you instead. How was *your* day? In fact, I'll rewind a little. How was your night last night? Did you win best fancy dress?' He chuckles. 'That picture you sent me… Well, it was something else. I bet you stood out in the crowd.'

'You have no idea.' I sigh, recounting the story of how I came to be the only octopus in a room of risqué outfits.

After laughing for way longer than politeness allows, Sam pulls himself together and says, 'Please tell me it was worth it and that you picked up some advertising along the way.'

I dig my spoon into my shake and polish off a mouthful, buying myself some time before I reply.

'No advertising leads as such…but I did receive an interesting proposition.'

'Oh?'

'Yeah,' I speak slowly, dragging out each syllable in order to allow me the space to choose my words carefully. 'Daniel Lewis was there and he asked me to help him out with something.'

Sam frowns. Despite fifteen years having passed since he was a bystander in the attack that put Daniel in hospital, their shared history reminds them both of a time they'd rather forget. I've done my best to smooth the waters, but just the mention of the other's name is enough to change the atmosphere. Like it's doing now.

Sensing the shift in dynamics, Charlie breaks off from his gorge fest. 'Daniel Lewis, is he the one with the really cool house?'

A storm cloud settles on Sam's face.

'We dropped him off last year. Before we were together,' I hastily explain.

'Right.' He's searching my face as though trying to solve a puzzle. 'What was his proposition?'

I dig into the shake again and pull out a spoonful of chocolate, pretzels and ice cream.

'He asked me to spearhead a campaign to bring the cinema back into use,' I speed-talk, popping the spoon into my mouth.

Sam exhales loudly.

'And what's in it for you?'

I swallow. 'He'd help me pull in more advertising.'

'But I've already said, *I'll* help you with advertising. *I* can have a word with people.'

Charlie drops his spoon onto the table with a clatter. 'I feel sick,' he groans. He starts rubbing his tummy. 'And my stomach hurts.'

I turn to him, glad of the distraction.

'Oh, Charlie, I knew we should have shared one. Don't eat any more.'

He groans again. 'Can we go now?'

Sam's face is full of concern. 'Are you OK?' He looks at me. 'Is he OK?'

'I think so. Just overindulged, haven't you, little man? We've all been there.'

Sam smiles at my joke and I relax a little.

'I'd better take him home. You're welcome to come if you like, though?'

Sam pauses for a minute. 'You know what, I think Charlie needs you to himself tonight. Plus, I've got work to do anyway. Why don't we leave it this evening? I'll see you both at football tomorrow.'

'Oh, OK.'

I try not to act too surprised, even though Sam usually always jumps at the chance to hang out at our house. On the other hand, it's been a busy week and I haven't seen much of

Charlie. It would be nice to have some quality mum and son time with him.

So that's what we do, spending a blissful evening curled up on the sofa, guessing at the questions on *Who Wants to be a Millionaire* and getting the answers wrong, just like we always used to.

I'm playing a cat and mouse game with sleep that I seem to be losing. It's three twenty-five a.m. and, aside from the odd moments when I drifted off only to wake with a jolt minutes later, I haven't slept at all.

I know exactly what it is that's keeping me awake. I'm wrestling with the position Daniel's put me in. Even without the advertising opportunities he's promised, there's a teeny part of me that's attracted to the idea of taking on the cinema. The whole reason I started *The Good News Gazette* in the first place – apart from to generate an income – was to make people feel better about Westholme. We went one step further with the Parade and now there's a chance to make even more headway with the grand old dame of Westholme that for too long has stood derelict, just waiting for someone to come along and make her beautiful again.

Yes, it would mean additional work and possibly less time with Charlie, who seems to be growing up and away from me right before my eyes. But it would also mean another jewel in Westholme's crown; a place Charlie and I could make even more memories. Add Daniel's offer of help into the mix and it's looking like a seriously sweet deal.

There's one big, massive, fat 'but' in all of this though.

Sam.

He and I have been plodding along quite happily. The last thing I want to do is rock the boat.

The entire night is a blur of tossing and turning, trying to make the right decision, the one that will mean as little as possible in my life has to change.

But by the time Emma texts the next morning to ask me what I've decided to do about Daniel's job offer, I finally know what the answer should be – and it's not the one I was expecting.

Westholme Community Facebook page:

Steven Arnold: Fire in the road next to ours on the Orchard Estate this morning. Local lads set an unoccupied property alight, giving people who already want to see the place burnt down even more ammunition.

Alan Boyd: Hmmm, noticed setting things alight seems to be their new thing.

Elaine Short: That's not new. I live on the estate. Learnt a long time ago not to let my pets out after hours.

Chapter Eleven

Despite Norman informing me otherwise, I suppose I'd laboured under the misapprehension that, thanks to the structural work Daniel's company had already carried out on the building, Westholme's cinema was now a slightly dusty jewel, a rough diamond that needed little more than a spring clean to have it up and running again.

The reality is entirely different.

For a start, the auditorium is filled with rubbish. Literally, rubbish. Lolly ice wrappers, empty salt 'n' vinegar Chipsticks bags, Woolworths carriers. It's like a dumping ground for the nineties. I've already spotted mould on the seats and I can almost hear my lungs protesting at the amount of damp I'm inhaling. But, since making the decision to turn its fortunes around, I've thought of little else but how beautiful it will look when we're done with it.

'Granted, it doesn't look great right now,' Daniel admits, batting a giant cobweb out of the way in order to continue his descent down the aisle. 'But you can see it has the potential to be amazing.'

With a penchant for old properties that I witnessed when he showed me around his renovated home last year, Daniel Lewis is transfixed. I watch him taking in the little quirks of the building, clearly entranced by the character, the balcony that hangs over our heads, the idea that so many people have sat right here, in these seats, watching so many different films before us. To the unimaginative mind, it is indeed an eyesore. But I'm already carried away by the romance of it all. Despite the mess, the place is magical.

'Look, Daniel,' I gush, butterflies fluttering around my stomach as I take in the original coving. 'Look at all this history. It could be transformed into something truly stunning.'

He smiles. 'Which is exactly what I thought when I saw it a few months ago. I knew it would be right up your street – I'm just surprised it took *you* so long to realise it.'

'Well…' I look at the floor, kicking one foot against the other. 'I just, you know, with *The Good News Gazette* and everything… There's been a lot going on.'

'I know,' he says, looking at me thoughtfully as though he really does. 'Anyway, I've spoken to Joanne—'

I scrunch up my nose as I try to work out who Joanne is.

'The owner,' he reminds me. 'And, as I said, she's happy to rent it to our group and then offer the option to buy at a later date. That will take the pressure off in terms of trying to find the money to buy it outright.'

'It's very kind of her to agree to that,' I reply airily. 'Do you know this Joanne well then?'

He turns away slightly and rubs his fingers over one of the seats. 'Let's just say I've had dealings with her. Anyway.' He turns back to face me. 'You came to the right conclusion in the end, I'm glad to see.'

'Hmmm.' I look around. 'Now all I have to do is come up with a way to raise the thousands of pounds needed in order to get this off the ground.'

'If I remember rightly, you didn't have any money this time last year when you decided to stage a ten thousand pound carnival,' he shoots back. 'That small fact didn't seem to stop you then.'

I sigh and wander along one of the rows of seats, trying to take in the building from every angle. 'You're right. I did it before, I can do it again.'

Daniel walks slowly around the auditorium, examining the ornate cornicing and red velvet curtains still hanging in front of the screen.

'Do you know how long it's been closed for?' he asks.

'I remember writing about the cinema well over a decade ago for *The Northern News*, and it had been empty for over a decade then. It was all down to dwindling attendance figures and the cost of keeping the place going.'

'Yes, I can see that would be a challenge.' He rubs his chin. 'But not an insurmountable one. Have you had any ideas about who we should recruit to help us with this? Board members as such?'

I gather my thoughts, eager to show him how 'on it' I am. 'There would be me, Gloria would be an obvious choice, Lynne would be great with her fundraising background, and maybe Sam would help out too—' I stop as I see his expression change. 'Well, maybe not Sam, he's really busy with the football academy...but there would be plenty of people who would want to be involved, I'm sure of it. And we'd need them. Let's face it, there's plenty of work to do.'

He looks around the auditorium and for a split second, he looks daunted.

'Come on, don't tell me you're afraid of hard work, Daniel Lewis.' I laugh nervously. Now that I've committed to this, the last thing I need is for him to back out.

Saving the Good News Gazette

He looks at me in a way that makes me feel unsettled, although I have no idea why. 'You know I'm not.'

We fall silent and I drop my eyes to the floor. It's strange, these little acknowledgements of information that we each have about one another.

'And you – are you sure *you're* up for this?' he asks. 'Even if things get rough?'

I smile now. '*You* know I can't resist a challenge.'

He gives me that look again. 'I certainly do. It's decided then?' he continues. 'We're going to revive the Westholme cinema?'

I smile. 'I guess we are.'

He extends his hand towards me. 'Ms Taylor, it appears we're in business.'

'I may live to regret this,' I reply, placing my hand in his warm large one and trying to ignore the feeling of inappropriate intimacy it brings.

He treats me to a rare grin and something flips deep in my stomach.

'You probably will.'

Ollie falls about laughing when I tell him what I've gone and done.

'Never let anyone tell you you're not predictable,' he says through chuckles. 'If there's something that needs saving, *you*, Zoe, can be relied upon to save it. And that applies whether it's a shopping centre, a cinema or even the town's least popular man.'

I frown. 'What's that supposed to mean?'

He's still laughing. 'Nothing! I just think it's nice, that's all.'

'What's nice?'

'That you've found enough common ground with Daniel to be able to work together on such a lovely project. I'm sure Sam must be over the moon at the idea of sharing his girlfriend with a rich, good-looking, high-flying bachelor. It's certainly making me feel all fuzzy inside.'

I shake my hair out of my face and continue typing. Ollie doesn't know *why* Daniel and Sam can't stand to be in the same room as each other, but he's picked up on enough of the signals to know that they don't get along.

'You *have* told Sam, haven't you, Zoe?'

'Not yet, but there won't be a problem. Sam is an adult. Daniel is an adult. I am an adult. We're all perfectly capable of making this work.'

'Ooh, how mature and grown-up you all are,' Ollie says, a mischievous glint in his eye. He claps his hands together in delight and says with mock excitement, 'I can't tell you how much I'm looking forward to seeing this unfold.'

I glare at him. 'Ollie, you are wicked. I promise you, it will be fine. I'm going to tell Sam about it tonight and there'll be no problem at all. You'll see.'

I'm right – I know I am. So why am I feeling more than a little apprehensive at the thought?

Every now and then, Mum invites Charlie for a midnight feast sleepover. I haven't worked out exactly how that's different from the other sleepovers that take place there, all of which appear to involve a massive consumption of everything that's bad for a nine-year-old boy, but I decided long ago not to dwell on the specifics. Not when Charlie's absence gives Sam and me a valuable opportunity to order something that isn't pizza or McDonald's through the delivery app.

Tonight, it's Chinese, and it's as I'm serving up the mains at his black-glass kitchen table that I decide to broach the subject I've been dreading.

I take a deep breath. 'I met with Daniel today,' I start. 'At the old cinema.'

His jaw shifts slightly to give his face a harder edge that I almost never see.

'Right,' he says, picking up his wine glass and clinking it against mine. 'Cheers,' he mutters, taking a gulp. 'What was that about?'

'Well,' I respond carefully, 'you know that the cinema's been on my mind since that guy Norman came to see me about it, and that Daniel Lewis has asked me to lead a project to renovate it?'

I pass Sam the egg-fried rice and start spooning sweet and sour king prawn on my plate.

'Hmm,' he replies, by way of acknowledgement.

'Daniel's actually offered me a job. He's going to pay me to help bring the cinema back to life. And it will be part-time, so I'll be able to juggle it with the *Gazette* too. So that's good, isn't it?'

Sam says nothing, just watches me and waits.

My cheeks feel hot. I carry on spooning the sweet and sour, careful to avoid looking him straight in the eye. 'Anyway, I wanted to know exactly what it would entail, so I asked him to meet me at the cinema to chat more about it.'

Even just the mention of the cinema has caused my heart to beat just a little faster as that familiar feeling of being all fired up by something starts to make its presence known.

'Sam, it's beautiful,' I enthuse, unable to contain my excitement. 'You should see all the old art deco features that are still there, just as they were one hundred years ago; it's incredible.'

I pause and try to weigh up his reaction, but his expression is blank. This is a different Sam to the easy-going, laid-back one that I know. I want *that* one back, so I carry on talking, hopeful that if I plough on with my chatter then he'll make a return.

'In fact, it was so incredible,' I continue, 'I told him I'd do it.'

Sam stares at me, rice in one hand, glass still in the other. 'Why would you do that?'

'I need the money,' I say in a very small voice. 'And the advertisers. And I think it would be a lovely project to be involved in.'

He tilts his head to one side, a silent question as to what I'm playing at.

'And it didn't occur to you to talk to me about it first? That I might have some thoughts about the idea of my girlfriend spending who knows how many hours a day with another bloke? Especially when it's *that* other bloke?'

I'm stung.

'I spend hours every day with Ollie and it's never bothered you.'

'I thought he was gay until he started going out with Adina.'

'What are you talking about?' I glare at him and he drops his eyes.

'You know…' he shifts uncomfortably '…with the way he is.'

'He's not gay,' I say firmly. 'A bit camp, maybe, but he's very, very straight. Not that it even matters.'

'Of course not; you know what I meant.'

We both fall silent and I turn my attention to my food, stirring the rice until it's coated with sauce.

'I hardly even see you anymore,' he says, and I can tell he's sulking. 'If you're not working on the *Gazette* you're doing your freelance stuff, and if you're not doing that, then you're with Charlie. Not that I'm complaining, of course, I know you should spend time with Charlie but…'

I almost spell out to him exactly how much it sounds like he's complaining, but then consider whether I'm really in the mood for a row.

Probably not.

'Forget about the cinema,' I soothe instead, reaching across the table and lacing my fingers through his, even though it's actually the last thing I feel like doing. 'Let's talk about you. Are things still as busy at the academy?'

For a moment I think he's going to pull his hand away, then he thinks better of it, stabs his fork into a prawn and decides to let it go.

Westholme Community Facebook page:

Alan Boyd: Anyone heard these rumours about the cinema being brought back to life?

Tori Hindle: Ah, how cute

Eyelash Lucy: That'd be great. I've watched all the boxsets now so need something new to see

Linda Browning: Not watched that Marie Kondo one on decluttering yet though, have you love?

Eyelash Lucy: Cheers Mum!

Chapter Twelve

If there's one thing I can say for Daniel Lewis, it's this: he certainly knows how to hold a meeting.

We're in one of the Parade's units that's been turned into a site office and there's a sense of anticipation in the air that suggests our volunteers are expecting a gathering far more exciting than the one I suspect is actually about to take place.

A flip chart stands in the far corner, posh coffees and sandwiches have been ordered in from Cath's and a stack of cakes easily identifiable as Paula's are laid out on a trolley, which is currently parked next to the white partition wall by the door. It's a different offering entirely from the supermarket biscuits and instant coffee I used to serve up at the Friends of Westholme Parade meetings and, admittedly, a much more attractive one.

I clock at least three of our members eyeing up the Viennese whirl, and steel myself against the sticky red conserve and buttercream combo oozing out of the golden pastry base. I'm in the zone diet-wise again and am determined not to be lured out of it by Paula's creations. Also, one of those ogling the cakes is

Norman, and he's a lot bigger than me. I wouldn't fancy my chances if we had to battle it out.

Norman was the first person I approached when drawing up my fantasy list for our newly formed cinema revival group, although deciding who else to add to it was tricky. After all, the Friends of Westholme Parade were magnificent in helping me save the Parade (albeit by default) last year, but this would be a different project altogether so needed additional people on board.

Norman needed no persuasion. He accepted the invitation with all the emotion of an actor receiving an Honorary Achievement Award at the Oscars. Given that my decision to bring the cinema back from the dead had been strengthened by the respect I had for Norman's lifelong dedication to the cause, his reaction was probably justified.

Margaret was next on my list. She's been involved in fixing Westholme for so long that I wouldn't even have tried to attempt this without her.

I asked Eva from Vintage Vibes to join because, as someone in her twenties, she could add a viewpoint that everyone else was lacking. She's a whizz with social media and knows more about trends than anyone else on the group could ever hope to grasp, so it was pretty clear we needed her.

Then there were Colin and Lynne. They were a must – Colin on account of his surveying knowledge and Lynne because she did such a great job of crowdfunding for last year's Westholme carnival.

This time I wanted Emma on board too, because although in theory I could take care of the PR and marketing for this venture, in practice there just aren't enough hours in the day.

I hadn't so much invited Starr to be involved as been told by her that she was going to be, as, with her background in the arts, she was probably the most qualified person in Westholme to be on the taskforce – her words, not mine.

Gloria had ducked out of this particular project, saying old age was slowing her down, which I suspect was a kind way of saying she'd had enough of Westholme politics to last a lifetime.

I haven't asked Sam and he hasn't offered. Bit awkward, that one.

And then, of course, there's Daniel. Or there soon will be, according to Candice, his PA. She's been dispatched to greet us this morning, and has come equipped with explanations about him being held up at a previous appointment and a promise that he'll be here shortly.

The noise of chatter slowly fills the room as those who were on the Friends of Westholme Parade committee greet each other like long-lost friends while Emma manages to introduce herself to everyone within the space of three minutes. Norman stands awkwardly on the sidelines, nodding at Colin and Margaret's conversation until Margaret kindly invites him to join in, and Eva's busy on her phone.

It's interesting watching how they all interact and I move from group to group, making polite small talk and telling them all to help themselves to tea and coffee but keeping the clingfilm firmly on the sandwiches until Daniel arrives.

I've dressed as a woman on a mission today, which, in theory, I am. That means my favourite navy midi dress and coordinating ankle boots. I've developed a thing for navy lately. It seems to have all the slimming effects of black, without the draining ones.

I've learnt about stuff like this since losing weight – fashion and colours and what looks good. I always thought that sort of information was frivolous, self-indulgent mumbo jumbo, but it makes a difference, to me anyway. It makes me feel as though I can hold my head up high, rather than wishing I was invisible so no one could see how awful I look. I like it.

Eventually, Daniel powers in, muttering apologies. He closes the door firmly behind him and I notice that everyone in the room sits up a little bit straighter as it becomes clear that they're in the presence of Someone Very Important.

Emma remembers him immediately and winks at me. 'What?' I mouth back, eyes wide, then turn away before she can mime a reply.

Daniel pulls up the seat at the top of the table that everyone has, naturally, left free for him, which prompts me to finally declare the meeting officially open.

'Right, everyone, shall we make a start?' I begin, keen to portray myself as the very image of leadership.

'For those who haven't officially met him before, which is…' I glance around the table '…well, just Norman actually…this is Daniel.'

Completely at ease in his natural habitat – i.e. sitting around a board table – Daniel opens a black leather notepad, writes the date and 'Westholme Cinema Meeting' in neat cursive writing, then looks up expectantly, dark eyelashes magnified through his glasses.

'Good morning, everyone.' He nods in a formal fashion. 'Can you all introduce yourselves, please?' He's greeted with absolute silence and I sense the heavy weight of all eyes turning to me.

My palms feel a little sweaty, but I remember I'm wearing navy and brazen it out. 'Great idea,' I enthuse. 'I'll go first.'

I look around at the warm, smiley faces. 'You all know me but I'll introduce myself anyway. I'm Zoe Taylor and I'm the editor of *The Good News Gazette*. I'm also a mum and I live here in Westholme.'

I nod encouragingly at Starr, who's sitting next to me in a mustard woollen minidress, a pair of red tights covered in stars and black ankle boots with little block heels.

'I'm Starr,' she says as she grandly picks up the baton. 'I'm an octogenarian. Those of you who are old enough may remember me from my performing days.' She's met with a room-full of blank stares so I jump in to save her blushes.

'Starr used to be a dancer in the West End,' I explain.

'I did,' she nods proudly. 'And in Liverpool. I knew The Beatles, obviously.'

It's not the first time I've heard this claim and as no one can verify its veracity, I call quickly on the far saner voice of Margaret, who, as ever, is ready to support me.

'Margaret Kemp.' She dips her crown of coarse brown hair. 'I help out where I can.' Given that we all know modest Margaret's just made the understatement of the year in an attempt to sidetrack the praise I was about to bestow on her, I move on to Colin, whose surveying knowledge was instrumental when we were plotting to save the Parade.

He clears his throat. 'Colin Thornton,' he says, unzipping his red fleece with one hand and scratching the middle, bald part of his head with the other. 'I worked as a surveyor for years before I retired. Now I spend most of my time doing jobs in the house for Lynne.'

'Hey!' Lynne digs him in the arm and we all laugh as they share a warm look. 'Lynne Thornton,' she says, flipping her shoulder-length blonde hair behind her slim shoulder. 'Used to work in the arts and did a bit of crowdfunding in my time. Retired last year and now project-managing Colin's work. The only beetles I know are the ones I dig up in the garden.'

Norman follows in his own inimitable way. 'Hello, everybody,' he booms, pushing the rolled-up sleeves of his checked beige shirt further up his forearms. 'I'm Norman Woods. I have spent years campaigning to restore the cinema to its former glory so I can't tell you how pleased I am that this group is now in existence. The cinema has such an illustrious history and it's right and proper that it's saved from what could have been a devastating fate, not just for the picturehouse but for the whole of Westholme.'

We all stare at him for a moment, swept up in his passion and alarmed by the devastation none of us had realised was about to befall Westholme.

'Well, let's see if we can avert that fate,' says Daniel smoothly. 'I'm Daniel Lewis, head of Lewis & Co. and owner of an extensive property portfolio that includes the Parade. I'm no film buff, but I do love old buildings and the cinema is a beautiful example of art deco architecture. I'm with Norman in that I believe it would be a huge loss were it ever to be sold off and knocked down, and I'm glad to say that, when we succeed, it won't be.'

Navy is obviously Daniel's colour too, as he looks good in it today, with his clean white shirt providing a stunning contrast to both the dark suit and his olive skin.

He nods at me and I force myself to concentrate. 'Thank you, Daniel,' I reply. 'Emma, would you like to introduce yourself?'

'Hi, everyone,' she sings brightly, giving a quick wave to illustrate her greeting. Her long blonde hair swishes against the beige polo neck of her top as she flashes a charming smile around the room that encapsulates us all in one go.

Her forehead looks particularly wax-like today. Like someone's pulled it in all directions to make it as taut as is humanly possible then stuck Sellotape around each side. It still looks better than my lined one though.

'I'm Emma Ronson and I'm the marketing director for the Chill Out chain of hotels. I'm here to provide whatever help I can in terms of marketing. Obviously, we have a ready-made media outlet in the form of *The Good News Gazette*, but we will certainly need other types of support at different stages in the campaign, so I can advise on those too.'

Eva, seated next to her, takes up the mantel. 'I'm Eva Grant,' she says, picking out a pleat from the skirt of her brightly patterned mini-dress and running her fingers along it as if to reinforce the edges. 'I run Vintage Vibes at the Parade. Zoe asked me to join you all and I'm really looking forward to being a part of it.'

'I'd also like to introduce Candice,' adds Daniel, nodding at the red-haired woman I recognise from my two trips to his office. 'Candice will take the minutes for the meetings and send them to you all within forty-eight hours, so please make sure she has your email address before you leave here today.'

He does a quick visual sweep of the room. 'Cath from the café not joining us?' he asks. There are definite notes of trepidation in his voice and I know he's recalling the hard time she gave him over his plans for the Parade last year.

'She says she's too busy at the moment,' I reply. 'She's been run off her feet at the café since Antonio went back to Italy.'

I swear I see his shoulders relax, then, introductions made, he starts working his way through the agenda that I've hastily drafted to give the impression that I know what I'm doing.

'Zoe has put together the agenda for today's meeting,' he begins, 'which I think you should all have?'

Everyone shuffles the A4 sheet of paper set out on the table in front of them in response.

'First point of action is to agree on a name for the group. Has anyone had any ideas so far?'

I think of the name Ollie's been calling them since the idea was first mooted and giggle. Somehow I don't think the suggestion of Big Screen Queens will go down particularly well here.

'Zoe?' says Daniel, spotting me laughing. 'Was there something you wanted to suggest?'

I battle to ignore the name that's on the tip of my tongue and instead respond with, 'How about the "Back to the Future" group?'

Various noises of agreement are made as, around the table, people voice their approval.

'A very clever play on words, my dear,' Starr replies, clapping her hands enthusiastically.

But Norman's shaking his head. 'The old cinema was called The Albany,' he says. 'Our group should reflect the name of the place.'

'Actually, I think you'll find it was called The Rio,' Starr contradicts. 'Or at least, that's what it was called when *A Hard Day's Night* was shown there.'

'Yes, my dear, but it was actually called The Albany when it was launched,' responds Norman. 'That's the name I'm proposing we go back to.'

Starr rolls her eyes. 'Well, I always liked The Rio – and I'm sure that's what John would have preferred.'

'John?' checks Norman.

'You know, John…Lennon,' Starr replies, shaking her head as if to confirm the absolutely uselessness of Norman, while everyone else ignores the painful name drop and instead takes a sudden intense interest in the previously uninteresting agenda.

Daniel is observing both Starr and Norman with some fascination, a slight frown suggesting that this isn't the sort of conversation that usually takes place at the meetings he attends.

'Are we still talking about the name of the cinema?' Eva interjects. 'Because I was wondering about calling it something like "The Blue Unicorn". We could make it look really cool and urban with zebra carpets and bright-pink neon lights at the bar.'

'Ooh yes,' says Starr, who I suspect is on the verge of breaking into a round of applause. 'That would be excellent.'

Norman, whose colouring is becoming more and more purple as Eva describes the sort of twenty-first-century cinema I suspect has, until this point, only existed in his worst nightmares, looks as though he's at very real risk of spontaneous combustion.

'I really don't think—' he splutters before Daniel, who I've spotted taking a few deep breaths during the exchange, steps in.

'We seem to have veered off track a little,' he interrupts, 'but seeing as we've jumped a few points ahead of ourselves on the agenda, let's continue discussing the name of the cinema instead. Does anyone else have any proposed name changes they'd like to share?'

We all shake our heads.

'Right then,' he continues, 'let's take the name change to a vote. Those who want The Rio, put your hands up.'

Starr's hand shoots up and Lynne makes a tentative climb through the air with her own.

'Lynne, is that a yes?' Daniel says.

She nods.

'Those who prefer The Albany?'

The rest of us – minus Eva – raise our hands.

'The Blue Unicorn?'

Eva puts her hand up.

Daniel does a quick count. 'Right, The Albany it is.' Norman flashes a delighted smile at Starr, who glares at him.

Daniel glances back at the agenda and I marvel at his ability to keep things moving quickly. Our 'Friends of Westholme Parade' meetings used to take hours to get through and I often felt we hadn't achieved a great deal other than having a good chat at the end of it. This meeting is a different beast altogether.

'Next point: fundraising,' he says. 'I had one of my team out to look at what needs doing and give us a ballpark figure, and he's estimated around £50,000.'

We all gasp, except Norman, who leans back in his chair, his mouth curled into a smug smile. 'Told you so,' he says, raising his eyebrows at me.

'I'm sure this won't be a problem for such a creative and proactive team,' Daniel continues. 'Zoe has told me all about Lynne's crowdfunding abilities...' Lynne nods and smiles '...so I'm confident we have the right skillset amongst us, but I would imagine we'll need to raise some funds through other activities too. So, with that in mind, let's do a quick brainstorm and get some fundraising ideas down on paper. Candice, if you wouldn't mind jotting them down?'

Candice stands up and strides to the front of the room, her beige, wide-legged trousers billowing beautifully around her slim legs as she walks. I make a mental note to Google wide-legged trousers and see if I can find something similar, even though past experience has taught me that clothes bought on the basis that they look good on size eight models tend to look rubbish on me.

She stands, pen poised, in front of the flip chart and waits as everyone silently competes to come up with the best idea in order to win Daniel's approval.

'I could stage a performance,' offers Starr, somewhat predictably. She's still riding high on the viral success of last year's dance video but I'm not sure how, at eighty-five, she's going to top her previous five minutes of fame.

'We could hold a fundraising art competition and throw it open to schools and children in the area. Ask them to draw scenes from their favourite movies,' Emma suggests.

'How about Photoshopping images to put people's heads on famous actors' bodies and selling them for a fiver each?' asks Eva. She's met with a few murmured replies and a swift dismissal from Daniel.

I take a deep breath, then go for it. 'What would your thoughts be on a pop-up cinema?'

Margaret looks flummoxed.

'What's a pop-up cinema, dear?'

I'm thinking on my feet now and I can feel my heart pounding in my chest as I try and turn the stream of consciousness running through my head into a form of communication that makes sense.

'It's a cinema that's open for one night only. We could set up a projector somewhere – at the Parade perhaps, tell people to bring their own picnics, charge an entrance fee for it.'

'But wouldn't it be too cold?' cautions Starr. 'We're almost in October.'

'We could make a feature of the fact. Schedule it at the end of November, around the time of the Christmas lights switch-on, and make it a Christmas movie. With heaters, of course.'

'Ooh, I'm thinking mulled wine, hot chocolate, food stalls with twinkling fairy lights, holly...even a spot of mistletoe,' says Emma, running with the theme.

'That's not a bad idea,' Daniel replies. 'We could set up a marquee.'

'We'd need a bit more creativity with the Christmas lights though,' scoffs Emma. 'No offence, Daniel, but you skimped a bit on the decorations last year.'

Daniel drops his eyes to the table for a second, then rallies. 'Point taken. I'm not big on Christmas.' He looks at me. 'Maybe this year I'll enlist some help for ideas in how to make it more closely resemble a grotto.'

Emma winks at me again. My cheeks colour. Again.

Eva, who has been scrolling through her phone during the exchange, now thrusts the device at me.

'You know, this could work really well. There's loads of stuff online about places that have held similar events – look at these photos.'

I take her phone and start scrolling through the pictures. She's right – there's some amazing set-ups that we could try and recreate.

'We may not even need a marquee...' Daniel's exhaling his own stream of consciousness now. 'Just some sort of canvas cover might be enough. That would allow for more people to attend, raising more money in the process.'

I look around the room. Everyone's chatting to each other,

excited about my idea, and I can't deny that I feel pretty good about the fact.

The agenda falls apart a bit after that, but by the time we've come away from the meeting we're all agreed on two things: We're definitely going to bring the cinema back from the dead, and my idea – the Christmas Cinema night – might just be the way to do it.

And once again, I wonder how I managed to find myself in the position where the fate of a Westholme landmark rests on my shoulders.

———

Westholme Community Facebook Page:

Lisa Seddon: Well excited about filming for that big movie starting at the town hall tomorrow. Can't believe we're going to see Westholme on the big screen!

Ricky Arnside: Scratching me hed over why any of yous wud pay to go the cinma. Yous can get all the films on the dodgy box for free.

Chapter Thirteen

I might be a hardened journalist with years of experience under my belt, but even I'm moderately excited about today's assignment – heading down to the town hall to document the film crew's arrival.

Yesterday's meeting has put me in the mood for all things cinematic, and I drive out of the Parade's car park, revelling in the cinematic double whammy of having glamorous, bona fide Hollywood actors filming in Westholme at the same time as we're embarking on a project to bring the cinema back to life.

OK, I'd obviously prefer them to be filming somewhere a little more visually stunning than the Orchard Estate, but they're using the large car park at the back of the lovely old town hall as their base, so at least they'll see that there's a bit more to the area than graffiti and dog poo.

Naturally, the movie is all anyone's talking about right now, so it's vital that I upload as much footage as I can to both the *Gazette's* website and social medial platforms ASAP before others beat me to it.

Mentally, I give myself a little pat on the back. That's the sort of winning attitude I need to make the *Gazette* a success. I can do this. I can.

There's congestion on both the pavement and the road as I near the town hall, with diversion signs and temporary lights redirecting cars and buses away from the familiar route. I shuffle closer to the barrier in front of the old, imposing grey stone landmark – one of Westholme's treasures that has, thankfully, remained in place – and my heart sinks as I see a welcoming committee that looks anything *but*.

Directly opposite the building is a row of shops and it's here, perched on the wall in front of them, that a dozen or so gang members in their compulsory uniform of black tracksuits, caps and hoodies sit, smoking weed and knocking back Special Brew.

At a guess, the boys are aged between thirteen and sixteen so should probably be in school, but I suspect that truancy may be one of the less problematic aspects of their existence. As the production lorries head in through the grand gateway, a few wayward cans flung from their direction bounce off the vehicle's steel sides.

Fortunately, there are other, more sociable residents and office workers making their way over, as well as film buffs and celebrity hunters who've headed down to see what all the fuss is about. I film their arrival, trying to capture the air of excitement without emphasising the supporting role the lads are playing.

Because while we may want the world to see the presence of Hollywood on a film set in Westholme, absolutely no one needs to see stoned Orchard Estate boys here too.

Once the trailers have all filed into the town hall's car park, the whole area becomes a hive of activity. Tents are set up, Portaloos are unloaded, cables doing presumably crucial stuff are laid out across the ground and the loud hum of generators kicks in, punctuated by the occasional heckle from the increasingly off-their-head teenagers.

I film and photograph all of it from behind the barriers, aware of the growing restlessness of the crowd behind me and the sense that, for all the busyness, nothing particularly interesting is going to happen today. There's not even a whiff of the presence of the film's two main stars, Lily Lonsdale and Joshua Hartley, which means there's a good chance they've probably got their feet up in their hotel rooms rather than hanging out in their trailers, watching us.

One by one, onlookers start drifting off, satisfied that they've witnessed the best of the activity and I think I'll do the same. I'm meeting Sam for a quick coffee at Cath's in half an hour anyway, so it's probably time I headed back to the Parade.

I'm about to leave when the low chatter around me cranks up a gear or two.

'That's him,' a woman next to me hisses to her mate.

A man with pink hair wearing a tweed jacket tugs my arm and points in the direction of the trailer. 'Look! LOOK!' he squeals at me, his pupils dilating furiously.

I follow the man's finger. There, in full Technicolor glory, leaning against the door frame of his trailer in a pair of ripped blue jeans and nothing else at all, stands possibly the most beautiful actor on the planet: Joshua Hartley.

Oh. My. Goodness. He's there, literally fifty yards away from me. I can see his golden chest, his rippling abs, his chiselled cheekbones. I have to capture this on film. With trembling fingers that don't seem to move fast enough, I jab at my handset, trying to bring up the camera function.

Come on, come on, I murmur through gritted teeth, desperate not to miss the only sniff of celebrity that I've encountered in years.

The camera powers into life. The viewfinder appears on my screen and I tap at the video function and press the red button. *'Thank you, God, thank you, God,'* I whisper, overwhelmed with relief that I stayed long enough to be here for this moment, that my phone is working perfectly and that I am now committing his very presence to film.

I check the screen. It's black. I look back up at the scene I'm trying to film. Which is not. It's very much in colour. Panic squeezes my chest. *No, please don't say my battery's gone dead.* I press hard at the home button. *No, no, no, no, nooooooo.*

It is as dead as a dodo, as Lewis Carroll might say, although admittedly he probably wouldn't follow it up with the various expletives that I string on to the phrase.

I look in one direction, then another. I'm desperately trying to magic up a way to rescue this situation, but I have no idea what to do. Then I spot him. The short, bald, suited man next to me who, mid-text, seems oblivious to what's going on. Or, more specifically, his mobile.

'Please can I borrow your phone?' My words pour out in a rapidly flowing torrent.

'Urgh?' he looks up.

'Joshua Hartley,' I say pointing in the general direction of the town hall. 'Over there. I want to film him.'

He looks at me blankly. With no words available to convey my needs fast enough to be of any use, I grab his phone out of his hand and start prodding the screen like a woman possessed.

'How do I do this?' I'm still prodding. 'How do I get it to film?'

'Oi! I was in the middle of sending a text there.'

'Sorry.' The prodding's still not working. 'But I'm trying to film Joshua Hartley for my website. I need to do it NOW, before he goes back inside his trailer.'

'Who?' The man wrinkles up his big nose. I can see his pulse throbbing away in his temples. I wonder if he drives his wife up the wall.

'Joshua Hartley, the actor. THERE.' I point to the trailer where I've just missed capturing the beautiful image of him raising his arm and – biceps bulging – running his hand through his hair.

'Ohhhhh, so this is a film set.' He's grinning now. 'I wondered what was going on.'

I blink at him. 'Yes,' I say, speaking slowly in the hope that the slower I speak the faster it will sink in. 'And I need to film it. My phone's gone dead. Please, please, please will you just show me how to use yours?'

His face relaxes into complete understanding.

'Why didn't you say that earlier? Here you go, love, let me do it for you.' And with a few swift actions he powers his phone into action, holding it up just in time to capture Joshua Hartley's trailer door slowly closing, encasing him back in his metal tin, hidden once more from public view.

———

Westholme Community Facebook page:

Jimmy Hunter: A few pics of filming outside the town hall today. Thought I might have seen the *Good News* girl today, but she was a no-show. Obviously a Hollywood film crew arriving in Westholme isn't quite as good news as us getting those wheelie bins that no one even wants.

Lisa Seddon: I love my wheelie bin.

Elaine Short: Me too

The Good News Gazette: Many thanks for supporting the vital work that *The Good News Gazette* carries out in the community by photographing the filming. If at any point you'd like to further assist the small team at *The Good News Gazette* by sending said pictures or videos our way, please feel free. Many thanks, Zoe (Editor).

Chapter Fourteen

By the time I reach the Parade, I am a big, seething ball of frustration.

I walk quickly past all the shops, not even pausing to look at the latest book releases in the windows of The Lower Story, or to spot the beautiful creations I still can't afford, despite Daniel's generous wage, in Vintage Vibes. In fact, it isn't until I reach Cath's Caff that I slow my pace, determined not to present Sam with this particular version of my best self.

The café's large glass panes make it easy for passers-by to catch a glimpse of the food and drink experience they're not currently part of and, squinting, I peer in, trying to spot Sam in the sea of customers.

He's standing by the counter, throwing his head back in complete abandon as he laughs heartily at something that Cath has said – and given that she's not known for her cheery humour, it's an indication of the very special effect he seems to have on people.

Watching Sam walk into a room is like seeing the sun come out from behind the clouds. I'm not the only one who thinks so. Many a time I've spotted women looking at him, then looking at me, then looking at him again, and I *know* they're wondering how someone like me got so lucky.

I wonder that myself, sometimes. Wonder how I managed to end up in a relationship with my childhood crush. Wonder why all my bad traits haven't yet managed to put him off. Wonder why he insists on telling me he loves me even though I've not yet been able to find the words to say it back to him. I'm very, very lucky.

But sometimes I also wonder why I don't always feel it. Why I feel like there's something not quite right. Like nabbing the best dress in the shop then getting it home and finding there's a mark on it. Or buying a new book then taking it out of the bag and realising the corner's been bent during transportation. You still love it, but the flaws take the edge off the joy you should be feeling at having it.

But Sam doesn't have any flaws, so I'm not sure that that analogy works.

Maybe it's my flaws that are making me feel like this. Because I wonder, too, if he might look at me sometimes and realise he's made a huge mistake and that he should have gone back to San Francisco after his mum died. Should have waited for the day that the unhappily married love of his life built up enough courage to leave her husband and run away with him instead.

Adina moves into view. Now she's laughing too. I pull myself together and silently shout enough happy mantras to drown out the negative voices. Sam and I are together. We are a couple. The only person who could possibly ruin that is me.

I plaster a smile on my face and push open the café door.

It's as welcoming as ever – well, since Cath's nephew Antonio and Adina turned it around, anyway. Before then, back in the days when Cath was left to her own devices, it was notably more hostile.

The coffee machine is gurgling away, something that smells like cheese toasties is being made in the kitchen, and the Chatty Table that Adina introduced specifically to enable people to feel confident enough to talk to each other is full of strangers becoming friends.

A couple with laptops pass me and make their way upstairs to the hot-desking area. Downstairs, every table and booth is full of people drinking, eating and making time for each other in a way that the world outside often doesn't allow.

Sam turns around immediately, as though he's been awaiting my arrival, and on spotting me his face is lit up by his smile.

'Here she is,' he says, his outstretched arm pulling me towards him. 'Cath's just been telling me about the latest brownies Paula's been baking for her: Christmas specials with Irish cream in them. I knew you wouldn't be able to resist so I've ordered you one.'

My heart sinks. He's right, that sounds like *just* the kind of thing I can't resist. It also sounds like just the kind of thing that will result in me gaining a stone by my next weigh-in. But neither I or my willpower have the heart to say no.

'Are you having one too?'

He looks bashful. 'Er, I've just bought an apple and a banana. You know I'm not that keen on cake.'

'As you know, Zoe, I'm not a big cake eater either,' lies Cath, digging a fork into one of the brownies, double cream pooling in a dip on its surface and overflowing onto the plate. 'But these are bloody lovely.'

She swallows one, smacks her lips and sticks one thumb up to confirm the cake's excellence. Adina sets down another identical dessert in front of me before popping outside for her lunch break.

'In fact,' Cath adds, 'I'll have to take one home for Ralph.'

It's a leading question if ever I heard one, so I decide to indulge her.

'Oooh yes, Ralph. I've been meaning to ask you about him since Slim City. Tell us all the details. Where did you meet?'

She looks a little bashful, then whispers, 'Online.'

'What's wrong with that?' I reply. 'Doesn't everyone meet online these days?'

'Do you think?' she asks uncertainly.

'I'm sure of it.'

She smiles, then notices I haven't started on my brownie yet.

'Come on, eat up,' she says, shaking the plate.

I groan. 'Cath, what about our diets?'

'Oh, sod the diet.' She's already going in for another mouthful. 'You've gotta live, haven't you.'

'Suppose so.' And it's then, at exactly the moment that I pitch a fork into the brownie and pop a big chunk into my mouth, that I look up to see Slim City leader Barbara watching us through the window, face like thunder and an emotion very close to disgust in her eyes.

Five minutes later I'm still thinking about how I'm going to explain the brownie to Barbara at the next Slim City meeting.

Cath clearly couldn't care less about being spotted, her only response being to forage an extra big piece for the next bite, but having Barbara catch me in the act reminded me of the fact that the scales have been creeping up lately.

It also reminded me how I don't want to be back there again, in that awful place where you're held hostage by food, feeling like there's an invisible force inside you that's making you reach for whatever it is that's going to quell that longing, whether you actually want it or not. Which is why I end up leaving half of it on my plate.

'You look deep in thought.' Sam's watching me intently.

'Just trying to come up with a believable excuse that I can give to Barb as to why there was no other option than to eat the first half of that brownie.'

Satisfied that my thoughts are of nothing more than cake, Sam takes a bite out of his apple. 'Don't worry about it,' he says through crunches. 'You're fine. I meant to ask...' He spins the apple around to reach the previously untouched side, 'How did your cinema meeting go the other day?'

I take a sip of my coffee, swallowing it slowly to give myself time to think about how I want to respond.

'I'll admit, it was a little more challenging than I was expecting,' I eventually reply. He raises his eyebrows, an invitation for me to continue.

'You know how it is, lots of different personalities, visions of the end result that couldn't be more diametrically opposed, an ambitious fundraising target, a ticking clock...'

'Is it doable?'

'I think so. As long as people can put their differences aside and work together. We do have to raise a fair bit of money in a relatively short time though, which puts the pressure on.'

'How much do you have to raise?'

'Fifty grand.'

Sam lets out a long, slow whistle and I start to relax at the fact that he's showing an interest in the project I know he resents.

'Can you raise that much?'

I sigh. 'I don't know. I hope so. We're going to hold a pop-up Christmas cinema. That should raise a bit. And Lynne's working hard on the crowdfunding. We'll be tapping up corporate sponsors too.'

'That all sounds very hopeful.'

'Thanks, Sam,' I say gratefully. 'I know you weren't over the moon at the thought of me taking this on, but I think, eventually, it will all work out fine.'

He takes the last bite of his apple and puts the core on the plate, next to what's left of my brownie.

'Sure,' he replies, noncommittedly, looking around the room so he doesn't have to look me in the eye.

I'm feeling a bit flat when I get back to the office. It must be the run-up to the time of the month. Or maybe it's because the weather's a bit miserable. Something's off today, and I can't quite put my finger on what it is.

Adina's there, taking her lunchbreak at Ollie's desk, where they're both pointing at his computer screen, making comments like 'Look at the size of that one' and 'That's huge!'

'What are you up to?' I ask dubiously.

'Looking for apartments to rent,' replies Adina, her English still heavily punctuated by her Romanian accent. 'We're moving in together.'

'Really?' I raise an eyebrow at Ollie, who studiously ignores me in return. 'Wow, I had no idea you were planning on doing that.'

'We decided to get a new place away from the Parade,' Adina explains.

'Yeah, you know,' adds Ollie, even though he's well aware I know nothing about this new plan. 'Put a bit of distance between work and play for both of us.'

I take a sharp breath, a physical response to the very real sensation that someone's punched me in the stomach.

'Well, this is great news.' I flash them my best effort at a smile that screams 'delighted'. 'Congratulations, you two.'

'It's the right time, I think. Margaret's been amazing, but Adina can't stay there for ever. And we both need some space together. After all, it's been a year now.'

Ollie turns then and shares a look with Adina that's so intimate and filled with love that it feels as though someone has driven a stake through my heart.

'It's going to be great,' he says, squeezing her hand.

'It is.' She smiles.

And for some reason I suddenly want to cry.

'So,' I address Ollie as soon as Adina returns to work. 'Kept that quiet, didn't you?'

'For good reason,' he says huffily. 'If I'd told you what I was up to, you'd probably have tried to convince me that it would be a complete disaster and it would all end in tears.'

Stung by his comments, I look for a good comeback but find one isn't forthcoming.

'Hey,' I say instead. 'I'm not *that* pessimistic.'

Ollie snorts.

'I'm not!'

'If you say so.' He pushes his chair back and heads over to the kettle. 'Want one?'

'Yes please.' I start typing up a story about the arrival of the film crew then, unable to concentrate, look up. 'Do you really think I'm that miserable?'

'When it comes to relationships? Yes.'

'I don't understand why you'd say that though.'

He tries to run his fingers through his quiffed hair, then, remembering that the amount of hairspray keeping it in place means he won't be able to get through it, drops his hand.

'What's going on with Sam?'

I make a face.

'You know what's going on with Sam, we're going out with each other.'

He turns to the tap to fill up the kettle, but I can see he's shaking his head.

'What do you want me to say?' I plead. 'We're going out with each other, he's a lovely man, we have a great time, it's going well… I don't know what more I can tell you.'

Ollie carries on with the coffee-making process, chatting away as he scoops the granules into the mugs.

'You've been together around the same length of time as Adina and I. Surely you have some plans. You must have talked about going on holiday together, moving in together, maybe even getting engaged?'

I shrug. 'Not really, no.'

He stirs the coffee and I spot him dunk the same spoon into the sugar.

'Ollie, new spoon!'

He spins around, rolls his eyes and plonks the mug down on my desk.

'Are you like this with Sam?'

'What do you mean, am I like this with Sam? There's nothing wrong with me.'

'You probably are like this with Sam,' he muses. 'Which might be why he hasn't asked you to move in with him yet.'

'How do you know he hasn't asked me to move in with him?'

'So he *has* asked you to move in with him?'

'Yes, I mean no— Ollie, what are you doing, where are you going with this?'

'Nothing. *You're* the one who's making a big deal about it. I just asked you what was going on, that's all.'

There's a distinctly uncomfortable feeling in the room, and we both bury our heads in our computers, typing so quickly I'm surprised the monitors don't start hissing with steam.

Eventually he slows down and looks up.

'Do you love him, Zo?'

I carry on typing. 'We're not that sort of a couple.'

Ollie frowns. 'What sort of a couple? The type that love each other?'

I let my hands fall onto the keyboard.

'The type that *say* they love each other.'

Ollie's expression relaxes into complete understanding. 'Ah, so you're *the other* type of couple then. That explains it.'

Now I'm confused.

'What other type of couple are you talking about?'

He leans his elbow on the desk, rests his chin in his palm, then delivers his killer blow.

'The type that don't.'

Westholme Community Facebook page:

The Lower Story: Just a reminder to those attending our Wine for Words event next week to be courteous to those living in the flats above the Parade when they leave. There were a few complaints after last month's event. In hindsight, introducing vodka as Anna Karenina's perfect pairing in what we thought might be a fun addition to the evening was probably not the best idea. The fact that it's a spirit means it deviated from the theme, plus it resulted in a few of our lovely attendees behaving in a way we're sure they wouldn't usually. We'll be sticking strictly to wine from now on.

Chapter Fifteen

E mma, Beth and I met on day one of secondary school, when we were all hanging out on our own at break time, feeling like those misfit kids you see on American teen dramas.

We've supported each other through births, deaths, break-ups and some seriously bad hair-dos, and I would be totally lost without them. I'm seriously on board with the power of friendship.

So, when the woman on the other end of the video call tells me that the lady I'm sitting next to is her best friend in all the world, and vice versa, I completely understand the depth of the relationship they're talking about.

What I'm finding harder to understand is how these women have managed to establish such a deep bond. Because in the sixty-three years that the women have been friends, they have never, ever, met.

'We were first introduced when our school set up a pen pal programme,' says Janet, a gentle woman with light-brown, shoulder-length hair that's beautifully curled under and seems to retain its shape no matter how much she moves her head. 'The school paired me up with Elizabeth and we hit it off immediately.'

'Janet's letters were always so prim and proper – just like I'd always imagined you English would be,' says Elizabeth, her Texan drawl echoey over the internet but her plump cheeks and bright blue eyes perfectly clear on the screen. 'But she was a blast, always so funny, and her tales about English life, the boys she used to like and how much she hated school would have me in stitches.'

The women start telling me a story about one of the boys in particular that Janet had a crush on and an unfortunate mishap at a school disco and I bask in the warmth of a friendship that clearly runs deep.

In an age of text, email, WhatsApp, Facetime, Instagram, Facebook and the many other ways that people now use to keep in touch, there's something so romantic about the notion of letter writing. It's the thought of putting pen to paper and spilling out your innermost secrets to your best friend, then sealing them all up, going to the Post Office and sending them to a land far away, that has me longing for those days lost in time. When friendship was about more than dashing off a quick text or commenting on a social media post. It was about investing those precious minutes and hours in building a relationship with someone you were sure would last a lifetime.

As I watch these women chatting intimately, despite there being almost five thousand miles between them, I feel wistful for those days.

The pair are laughing now, recalling Elizabeth's letter detailing the events of her wedding night. As they chat, they unintentionally walk me through their lives, recounting events they only know about because they took the time to share the details with each other.

The early days of their friendship were clearly all about the topics that have affected teenagers for generations: boys, fall-outs with mates, the jobs that they were shoehorned into despite clearly having so much more potential.

Then they were catapulted into their twenties, a heady era for both of them by the sounds of it, with never-ending parties followed by boyfriends – a couple of which turned into husbands – and children.

'Oh, children,' says Elizabeth, rolling her eyes and letting out a sigh. 'That was tough.' She talks about the strain parenting put on her marriage, reiterating what a lifeline Janet's words of support were to her.

Janet, meanwhile, remembers letters that were written in numerous parts due to the unending interruptions of demanding babies and toddlers, and her joy at seeing Elizabeth's written responses – and the hilarious spin she put on her own motherhood failures – landing on her doormat.

'Then there were *your* dark years,' says Elizabeth ominously.

'Hmmm,' says Janet, clearly unsure how much of her life she wants to re-read in the *Gazette*.

She turns to me. 'My husband left me when I was pregnant with our third child.'

'For his *secretary*,' Elizabeth intervenes, her words no less powerful over the internet. 'Can you believe it? Could he *be* any more of a cliché?'

'And then my mum died shortly afterwards,' Janet continues. 'And I became very down.'

'Janet, it was total depression,' Elizabeth says, possibly revealing a little more than she should in the way that well-meaning good friends often do.

Janet smooths her skirt down over her thighs. 'All's well that ends well. I met a lovely chap at the factory and he took on all three of my children as his own. We were together until the day he died.'

'I'm sorry to hear that,' I say. 'When did he pass away?'

'Five years ago.' Janet sniffs and looks over at his photograph on the wall. 'We were all set to go and see Elizabeth that summer. Howard had been telling me for years how important it was that I met her in person and we'd been saving for a long time to make the trip. But then he died – heart attack, very sudden – and a big chunk of the money had to go on his funeral. I could never really afford it after that.'

'I couldn't afford it either,' says Elizabeth. 'Still can't. But we've managed to stay firm friends through the magic of pen and paper.

'Hey, Jan,' she says suddenly, 'do you remember the first time we heard each other's voices on the telephone?'

Janet beams. 'I do. It was in the eighties, wasn't it? Although we only spoke for about five minutes because of the cost. I'd spent so long imagining your voice, it was lovely to finally hear you.'

'You were exactly what I expected you to sound like,' Elizabeth continues, chuckling. 'Just like the Queen.'

Now Janet's giggling too, probably at the idea of our late Queen ever having sounded anything like as Scouse as her.

'What about our first video call?' she shoots back. 'When Kevin appeared nude in the background?'

'Crazy,' drawls Elizabeth, throwing her head back and laughing raucously. 'He's free and easy and that's how he always walks around the house. We were both pretty new to the whole video call thing and didn't realise how much Janet would be able to see.'

They're so at ease, so comfortable, that it's hard to grasp the fact that not only have they not lived in close proximity for dozens of years, popping round to each other's houses for cups of tea and coffee on a regular basis, they have never even met. Never squeezed each other's hands, wiped each other's tears, smelt each other's perfume.

'How did you feel when you saw each other over video call for the first time?' I ask. I'm intrigued by the idea of creating a long-standing friendship with someone whose face you've only seen on a grainy photograph or over a computer screen.

'We both cried,' says Janet.

'We bawled like babies,' adds Elizabeth.

'It felt like a miracle, to be able to see and speak to each other as though we were in a room together.' Janet's eyes look misty now and they both pause to reflect on what was clearly a landmark moment in their friendship.

'Not the same as a hug though, is it, Jan?' says Elizabeth after a moment or two.

'No, it's not. But we'll get there. Maybe next year.'

Elizabeth nods wistfully. 'Maybe next year.'

And as they launch into a clearly much-repeated conversation about the afternoon teas they'll enjoy, the landmarks they'll visit and the stage shows they'll see, I suddenly want to go and find Beth and Emma, throw my arms around them and tell them how glad I am that they're here in Westholme and not five thousand miles and a ten-hour flight away.

Fortunately, the fact that we all live within a three-mile radius of each other, combined with the arrangement we've already made to meet up tonight, means that I can do just that.

Having displayed a canny appetite for tapping into exactly what people want when he launched the Classics for Beginners series last year, Neil Bell, the owner of The Lower Story, is now staging another evening, Wine for Words. These eagerly anticipated events recognise the fact that most book clubs are secretly a front for mini wine-fests and combine the two in one handy format.

I wasn't sure whether Beth would fancy this event, given that she has no time to read and her current breastfeeding status means she doesn't want to drink either. Fortunately, she's so desperate to escape that she jumps at the chance to act as the designated driver while Emma and I get merrily – and literally, of course – sloshed.

Mum's out at her Zumba class so Dad's agreed to babysit and by the time the text comes to say Beth and Emma are outside, he and Charlie are so engrossed in a game of FIFA that they barely register my departure.

After planting swift kisses on the tops of both their heads, I crash out of the house and into the car, issuing more head-kisses as I climb in.

'Hello, my lovelies.' I stick my head between the two front seats in order to be closer to them. 'You are the best friends anyone could ever wish for, you know.'

Emma leans forward and turns her head so she can see my face. 'Have you started without me?'

'No!' I say indignantly. 'I haven't had a drop. I just interviewed these amazing women today who have never met each other – one lives in America and various events have stopped them getting together – but have been best mates for over sixty years. It made me think about you two and how lucky I am to have you, that's all.'

'Ahhh,' Emma says, sitting back in her seat and patting the side of my face. 'We're lucky to have you too, aren't we, Beth?'

Beth sniffs. 'Uhum.'

I peer around the seat. 'Is that even a word?' As her profile comes into view, I spot a single tear rolling down her cheek.

'Beth?'

She quickly wipes it away with her fingertips.

'Take no notice of me, I'm hormonal.'

Emma's looking at her too now.

'What's wrong?'

'Nothing,' she insists. 'I'm tired. Darcy's still struggling to sleep, which means we are too.'

'Ah, Beth, it's so difficult,' I sympathise. 'I feel so sorry for you.'

'It'll pass.' She sniffs again. 'It's just a stage, isn't it?'

'Well, yeah, but a stage that can leave you feeling as though you're losing the plot,' Emma confirms. 'Believe me, I remember it well. Have you asked your health visitor for advice?'

Beth nods. 'She's suggested a few techniques, but none of them seem to be working. If I put Darcy down before she's asleep she cries until I pick her up again. If I put her down when she *is* asleep she wakes within thirty minutes wanting to know where I am. At the moment her night-time sleeping pattern seems to be one hour asleep, then the next ninety minutes resisting our attempts to try and send her off again. And it continues like this, one hour asleep, ninety minutes awake, all through the night.'

I blow air out through my lips. 'Beth, you must be exhausted. What about that controlled crying? I know it's controversial but some people swear by it.'

'We tried it a couple of weeks ago. Tony and I were close to divorce by the time I gave in and went to her.'

Beth wipes the other eye now, checking in the rear-view mirror for wayward mascara, rather than for cars.

'Sorry, guys,' she apologises, removing a black smudge with her fingertips. 'I'm just feeling a bit low tonight. I'm sure everything will seem better in the morning.'

'You know we're always here if you need us, don't you?' I squeeze her shoulder.

She gives my hand a squeeze back.

'I know,' she mumbles. 'Love you guys.'

'We love you too,' Emma and I chorus, then giggle at our simultaneous response.

'Anyway,' Beth starts, trying to move the conversation away from herself. 'How are you both?'

'Oh, we're fine, chick,' replies Emma. 'At least, *I'm* fine. My life's currently pretty non-eventful at the moment – which is just the way I like it. Zoe, how about you? How are you enjoying your new job...' She glances back at me. 'With Daniel?'

I pull a face at her. 'He's not really that bad.'

Emma smiles. 'I didn't think he was.'

'And it's good that it's flexible,' I continue. 'I still have more time with Charlie than I would have if I'd said yes to that London job.'

The girls look across at each other, then Emma shifts around in her seat to look at me.

'What London job?'

I kick myself. I'd deliberately not told anyone about the London job, on the basis that it wasn't up for discussion, so wasn't worth discussing. Now it looks like we're about to discuss it.

'It's nothing, absolutely nothing, it's just that my old editor called a few weeks ago to ask if I'd be interested in working with her on a new magazine. But I said no, obviously.'

'Your old editor?' Emma says thoughtfully. 'What was her name? Annabel? Angela?'

'Amanda,' Beth cuts in. 'Don't you remember? We had that night out with her once for Zoe's birthday and she kept ordering us all those shots and demanding we took her to a male lap-dancing club?'

'Urghhh.' Emma buries her head in her hands. 'I *do* remember that night. I was sick for days afterwards.'

'That's the one,' I confirm. 'Anyway, it was a deputy editorship role on a new women's magazine, nothing special.' I wonder why it stings as I say it.

The atmosphere in the car changes a bit. Emma turns back around to face the road.

'That must have been a hard one to say no to,' Beth says quietly. 'You always wanted to edit a glossy mag, didn't you?'

The one downside to having old friends who know you so well is that they know you so well. They know your life's ambitions, your lost dreams, your old boyfriends. They know everything, so you can't spin past events the way you can with more recent acquaintances.

'That was a long time ago,' I scoff, as though they matter not a jot anymore. 'Everything's different now.'

'That's right.' Beth is resolute. 'You have Sam now. And Charlie's settled here. Of course you wouldn't want to leave. Would she, Em?'

Emma glances across at her, then turns her head back to the windscreen, staring straight ahead. 'No, of course not,' she repeats unconvincingly.

'Exactly, so that's that. There'll be plenty more opportunities, and in the meantime I have a good news movement to keep going. So, let's forget about all this and enjoy our night. It's ages since we've been out together. Let's have some fun.'

———

'Now, as we all know,' says John Greenwood, who, despite never having been introduced as such, is generally understood to be Neil's partner. 'Bridget Jones was about as fussy with her drinks as she was with her men. But there was one wine in particular with which she enjoyed a long-lasting relationship and that was…' He looks around the room, confident that the group of middle-aged women and a couple of men in attendance will know the answer.

'Chardonnay,' we cheer in unison. Because by now, three book pairings in, we've all shared enough drinks and laughs to believe we're in a room filled with our new best friends.

'Exactly,' he replies, a broad smile visible beneath his grey moustache. 'And with that in mind, I'll let Alfie…' he gestures to the forty-something proprietor of the Parade's newly opened wine bar, Vino '…talk you through the many attributes of a wine that has fallen in and out of fashion more times than a pair of black leggings.'

We all laugh at his joke, aware of the love/hate relationship every woman shares with leggings, a truth which only serves to strengthen our solidarity.

I glance over at Beth, expecting to see a giggle, a smile… something that shows she's with us on this, that she's enjoying the night, that she too is experiencing this feeling of female togetherness.

But while her smile says she's on board with it all, the small crease between her eyebrows reveals that, unlike the rest of us, she is not recalling Bridget Jones' many encounters with alcohol or her own encounters with the ubiquitous black leggings. In fact, I'm not sure she's recalling anything at all.

My best friend is lost, wandering aimlessly in a strange and scary land.

And I have no idea how to reach her.

———————

Westholme Community Facebook page:

Emma Ronson: Does anyone have any good tips for helping babies get to sleep on their own? Asking for a friend.

Jackie Dodds: Try a tot of whisky in their bottle. I used it on my three and it worked a treat for them. Or maybe Baileys if they don't like the taste of whisky.

Helen Carthy: As one of Westholme Surgery's health visitors, I would advise that under NO circumstances should you give your baby alcohol. This is advice backed up by the Chief Medical Officers and should be adhered to.

Johnny H: Nah, don't give the kid the alcohol – sounds like yer mate needs it more!

Chapter Sixteen

It's the end of Dad's first six weeks at Slim City and, having pretty much stuck to the diet, losing a stone in the process, he's acting as though he's got the staying power of Joe Wicks.

'How've you been finding it all so far, Terry?' says Emma, trying to involve him in a conversation that's so far centred around black leggings – an item of clothing that appears to be featuring heavily in this week's conversations – and selection boxes.

'Easy!' he booms. 'Don't know what all the fuss is about. All you have to do is stick to the instructions and you lose weight. In fact, now I've done it I'm starting to wonder what took our Zoe so long.'

'Dad,' I hiss. 'It's not that easy. People always get a good weight loss at first. Wait until you're six months rather than six weeks in before giving it the big I am, will you?'

He tuts loudly. 'No self-discipline. That's what's wrong with you all. It's not rocket science, is it? You've just got to do the diet.' He hitches his red sweatshirt up to reveal a white podgy tummy. 'Look at my tracksuit bottoms. Hanging off me, they are!'

Emma gives me a sympathetic smile. I look over at Beth, statue-like in her plastic chair, clearly scared to move, speak and possibly breathe for fear of waking Darcy, who's enjoying a blissful sleep in her arms. I try and catch her attention, but she's starring off into space again, that same faraway look in her eyes.

'Right, class,' Barbara shouts, calling us all to attention. She's clearly overjoyed at having a member who's come in with a loss, even if it is my dad, and starts the session positively beaming.

'Terry,' she says, smiling broadly. 'Would you like to tell everyone how your week went?'

Personally, I would have demanded the rest of the class explain our disastrous results first then let Dad finish the class on a high, but Barb's obviously taking the 'shame them into action' route.

'It was a breeze,' Dad declares. A deathly hush falls across the class. 'I lost another four pounds this week, which takes me to a stone in six weeks.'

'Is he kiddin'?' I hear a woman further down the line whisper to her friend.

Someone in the back row is uttering a portfolio of expletives.

Dad simply leans back, stretches his legs out in front of him and crosses his arms.

'Nope,' he says by way of reply, a self-satisfied grin bedding in on his face. 'The diet's easy. It's you lot that's making it difficult.'

My cheeks are so hot I'm sure they could power the central heating in my home, for an hour or two at least. I close my eyes and imagine that it's all just a bad dream. A very bad dream that I'll shortly wake up from.

Even Barb, usually the first to let us all know we've underperformed, looks perturbed.

'Yeah,' my dad continues. 'I just gave the missus the diet book and let her sort it all out. And then I only ate what she told me to. See? Easy!'

'Are you saying your *wife* sorts all your food out for you?' The woman on the opposite row with the short black hair is not happy.

'Course she does.'

'So you haven't had to go to the shops, prepare or cook any of this *easy* food. All you've had to do is eat it?'

Dad looks exasperated. 'The problem with you women is, you make too many excuses for yourselves. *I've had a hard week in work, I've had a row with my fella, my jeans don't fit me.* I've heard them all off our Zoe. Just get your arse into gear, eat less, and you'll lose weight. It's not rocket science, is it?'

I am mortified.

Around me I can feel looks being exchanged by dieters incredulous about the fact that this man – *who has no part in the food process other than eating it* – has the audacity to tell them what they're doing wrong.

I glance at Barbara. If I didn't know better, I'd swear there's a smile flitting across her face. But she manages to hold it in and, pre-empting a riot, attempts a change in tack.

'Have you ever tried to make any of the Slim City recipes, Terry?'

Dad frowns. 'Well, no. That's Sue's job. She does all the cooking in our house.'

I sit with my head bowed, trying to dodge the daggers being shot in our direction from most of the members of Slim City

'Lazy arse,' mutters Cath, loud enough for us all to hear.

'Oi, Cath, there's no need for that,' Dad replies, indignant. 'I'm at work all day.'

'What d'you think Sue's doing? Putting her feet up? She's at work too.'

'Yeah, but she's only on the checkouts. She's sitting down all day. I'm doing proper work. *Manual* work.'

I sink further into my seat.

'Are you having a bloody laugh?' This is from a long-haired, large-chested woman I've seen a few times in the chippy.

I cast a sideways glance at Dad. His brow is furrowed and his cheeks are even more red than usual.

'I think what we're trying to say, Terry, is that it might be beneficial to both you and your wife if you had a little go at trying to rustle up a little something yourself at home,' says Barb, taking on an unusually conciliatory role. 'It would help you to think about what you're choosing to eat, and to learn a bit more about cooking in the process. You never know, you might even enjoy it.'

Dad looks at me, grimaces, then turns back to Barb.

'I don't think that's for me.' He's shaking his head.

Barbara considers this. 'Terry, do you know *how* to cook?'

Dad looks at his knees. 'Er, not really, no.'

'How about you give it a go. Have you got an air fryer?'

I jump in to save his blushes. 'They're meant to be brilliant, those things. They do chips brilliantly – everyone says so. And they're cheaper than the oven too, apparently.'

'I stick everything in there,' adds Emma.

'Me too,' adds Cath.

Dad shifts in his seat. 'I could always give it a go, I suppose.'

Barb raps her fingers on the table. 'Yes, give it a go. You just might surprise yourself. And us.'

———

In line with our agreement, Daniel has promised to try and introduce me to as many financially secure businesses – as opposed to the ones that I seem to deal with – as possible.

That's why this afternoon he's set up a 'casual' coffee between me, him and an 'aesthetics' business, which sells a wide range of youth-enhancing services, all of which appear to involve needles, collagen and sometimes a very sharp scalpel.

Our meeting is taking place in Lawton, which, like Presthill, the very leafy, very expensive suburb where Daniel lives, is another more desirable, more affluent area than Westholme. It may not have as many multi-million-pound houses as Presthill, but it's still got a pretty cool vibe that's undeniably powered by money.

There's a chill to the air this grey morning, a reminder that summer is well and truly over and we're on the precipice of winter. In fact, we're only days away from Halloween, and the little town has been decorated to celebrate the fact, with pumpkins and orange bunting dotted about.

I'm not clear on exactly why Daniel needed to accompany me – other than the fact that he's acting as a very effective go-between – but as a rake-thin, wrinkle-free glamour-puss purrs into the swanky bar at which he's arranged for us to meet, I'm really glad he has. I have a feeling that, were it not for Daniel's presence, the woman would take one look at me, hand me an astronomical quote for urgent filler work and then run a mile on the basis that her business may be harmed by any association with someone so 'unfilled'.

Daniel stands up and kisses her on both cheeks and I marvel at how someone I know to be so socially awkward can turn on the charm so easily when required.

'Nikki, how are you?' he greets her warmly, touching my arm at the same time. 'Let me introduce you to Zoe. Zoe's the proprietor of *The Good News Gazette*, which, as I was telling you, is proving to be an extremely attractive advertising proposition.'

Nikki's plump lips remain frozen into a smile as she gives me an almost imperceptible up-down look. It's the sort of split-second evaluation that many women – whether consciously or not – give each other on first meeting; that assessment to work out who comes off best in the Top Trumps comparison of hair, make-up, clothes and – increasingly – 'aesthetics'.

I didn't used to engage in this sort of behaviour. I never liked it, let alone dreamt I'd do it. But these days I can't help it. I look. I compare. And despite the weight loss, I tend to always come off worse.

Nikki's assessment must put me somewhere in the middle of the hierarchy tree. Not low enough for her to walk off in disgust, but not high enough for her to see me as any sort of threat. Because her lips alter their shape now, forming a more genuine smile, and while there's no real change to her facial muscles, her eyes appear warmer and friendlier than they did prior to our Top Trumps contest.

'Really pleased to meet you,' Nikki greets me, ignoring my outstretched hand and going straight in for the air-kiss instead. She gives my shoulders a little squeeze as her cheek touches mine. 'Daniel's told me so much about you.'

I'm dying to know what he's said, but instead settle for asking her about herself and her business and listening politely while wondering exactly what he might have told a woman like her about a woman like me.

As we chat, Daniel sorts out the drinks order and asks for menus in case we're peckish. If the conversation veers off track, he expertly guides it back to how *The Good News Gazette* could reach potential clients and he sells the whole advertising proposition so well that even *I'm* tempted to sign on the dotted line.

For her part, Nikki appears genuinely interested by what I'm doing and tells me over and over again how important it is that something so positive exists. I wasn't expecting the meeting to be a confidence-boosting exercise, but by the end of it I feel as though I'm turning around the entire community rather than just publishing a paper filled with good news.

'I really like this and I believe it's important to support it,' she says firmly. 'I also think another contact of mine would be interested in this. He works for an NHS integrated care board and

I know that mental health is a key part of their agenda at the moment. I'll pass on your contact details in case he wants to get in touch.'

'That would be brilliant – thank you,' I reply, clueless as to what an integrated care board is but assured by the fact that it sounds important.

'As for my investment,' Nikki adds, running her long nails through the ends of her hair, 'I think *The Good News Gazette* would be the perfect way to reach potential customers, so I'd like to take out a full-page advert in the next issue and then on a month-by-month basis. Let's talk about the online advertising options too.'

I pull out a rate card and explain what each level of advertising means and she chooses one that was definitely more than I was expecting.

Eventually Nikki glances at her phone and says that she'll have to leave for her next client.

I nod politely and manage to hold it together long enough to exchange another air-kiss and a promise that I'll be in touch, but the minute I see her silver Audi purr away from the kerb outside, I allow my spirits to soar.

'Well done,' praises Daniel, his dark eyes looking warmer and softer as the light hits his face through the windows. Through this filter, he seems younger, less brooding…more real. Although the way my stomach lurches reminds me that he's like a fire, raging, dangerous. There's so much going on there that even just reaching out to touch him would almost definitely result in a first-degree burn. I wonder at the brave women who even try.

Despite all that, I'm so pleased at how the meeting has gone that I'm biting my lip to keep my beam in check. After spending the past hour talking about aesthetics, I'm more mindful than ever that I don't look great if I let my smile get too wide.

I allow myself to hold his gaze as he beams at me, like a proud mentor cheering on his protégée.

'Thank you,' I say simply. 'Thank you so much.'

'No thanks required. It was all down to you.'

He's being kind. I know it wasn't but I don't want to embarrass either of us. 'Well, thank you,' I repeat. 'You were amazing.'

For a moment I could swear I see his own cheeks colour. Then he signals for the waiter, asks for the cheque and smoothly pays the bill.

Westholme Community Facebook page:

Julie Connors: Just want to give a shout out to my friend **Craig Hartnett** who's won a place in the English Paralympic Basketball team. Really amazing guy, ex-army. Please show him your support.

Tori Hindle: That is brilliant. Congratulations and good luck.

David Larson: Fantastic mate, well done.

Sam Milner: Zoe Taylor – one for you?

Chapter Seventeen

I'm not really one for exercise. Every now and again I'll see a nice pair of trainers or someone athletic-looking on Instagram and resolve to get fit, but then I'll remember how tired I am and decide I'll start tomorrow when I've had one Last Supper and a good night's sleep.

So, the fact that I'm talking to a double amputee war veteran who's been chosen to represent Team GB in Wheelchair Basketball at the Paralympics is bringing home to me just what a sloth I really am.

His name is Craig Peller, he's twenty-eight, and he has more get up and go in his well-rounded biceps than I have in my entire body. And despite the fact that I've come to the Orchard Estate to interview *him*, we seem to be talking a lot about me.

'Is there any reason why you can't exercise, or is it more of a "can't be arsed" situation?' he asks. Not out of the blue, I might add – that would be plain rude. He's continuing a conversation I unwittingly started when I told him that the only regular exercise I did was running late.

'Hmmm, a reason I can't exercise?' I'm struggling to answer

this one. How can I tell this man, who'd give anything to have his own legs back, that I just can't be bothered to use mine? But then really, what other excuse is there?

I bite my lip and look around the lounge of the two-up, two-down in which he lives. It's sparsely decorated, with all the necessities that a man might require; humungous TV, PlayStation, stairlift at the bottom of the stairs…

'I guess it's a more "can't be arsed" situation,' I admit.

He tuts and tosses his head back, a move that creates barely a ripple in his short brown crop. 'You're missing out, you know. Forget wine, beer, chocolate – exercise gives you a natural high, makes you feel great about yourself, good about the world.'

I look at him in awe, wondering how someone has had to contend with so much can be so upbeat.

'It's all up here,' he explains, tapping his pale forehead as he reads my mind. 'What you can achieve, what you can make possible, how you think, how you feel, it's all within your control. Exercise isn't just good for your body, it gives your mind a workout too.'

Never mind a workout, Craig's enthusiasm alone is exhausting me.

'Have you always been so positive?' I ask him. 'Even before…' I trail off, unsure of how to finish the sentence.

'Before the explosion?' he finishes for me, then manoeuvres his chair towards the kitchen. 'Why don't we park this here for a moment – the conversation, not the chair.' He winks. 'I'll get us both a drink and then I'll tell you the whole sorry tale. Green tea all right for you?'

'I don't suppose you have any coffee, do you?' I ask hopefully.

He shakes his head. 'Poison, that stuff. I'll make you something better than coffee. And it won't leave you feeling like you've been at an all-night rave when you come down from it either.'

'Great.' I conjure up a show of enthusiasm to match his own. 'Green tea it is.'

I raise the mug to my lips, suspicious of its contents but prepared to exercise my mind and give it a go. I can smell mint and liquorice and something else I can't put my finger on.

I take a sip, feeling Craig's eyes on me. I swallow, trying to do that thing where you imagine you can't taste something and just knock it back, but a taste remains. I smack my lips together. It's definitely not coffee.

'So, tell me what led to your basketball career,' I start, then freeze. 'Er – other than the obvious, of course.'

He pauses for a minute, looking down at the space where his legs used to be. Then slowly, hesitantly, he begins.

'I'd always wanted to be a soldier,' he says. 'I grew up here, on this estate and I loved the idea of escaping, getting out of Westholme, seeing the world.

'Two days after my twenty-first birthday, I was serving in Afghanistan with a great group of lads, lovely girlfriend back home... I couldn't have been happier. I was in a truck with a couple of other soldiers, heading back to the barracks when everything went black. We'd been hit by a bomb.'

I'm scribbling away, trying to make sure I don't miss a word of his story. I glance up at him to let him know I'm still listening, but he's not looking at me. Instead, his brown eyes are staring into the distance as he relives his own personal hell.

'When back-up came, they thought I was dead like the others. When I came out of the coma, I wished I *was* dead. My entire existence was about being able to do stuff with my body – move quickly, rescue people, react to situations. I couldn't do that anymore.' He taps the wheelchair. 'This is great when you're trundling round supermarkets at eight o'clock at night, not so good when you're trying to escape being shot at.'

He pauses and gulps down his drink, probably the best way to consume the stuff if I'm honest. I take a gulp of my own.

'What happened next?' I ask gently.

'I came back here. Back to my mum and dad's. And I lay in bed and cried for about two years.

'People were good. Mum and Dad were amazing. The girl I was seeing was nice about it. Promised me it didn't change anything, that she still loved me. She visited every day at first. Then every couple of days, then once a week. Within a few months she was barely dropping by. Eventually I heard she'd moved to Magaluf to hand out flyers. I didn't see her again after that.'

'Wow. Sounds as though you were in a pretty bad place.'

He nods. 'I was. And then one day another injured serviceman got in touch and told me about a support group. Those guys changed my life, changed how I thought about life. I started to focus on what was possible. I made myself independent, not just practically, but mentally too. Made sure I didn't have to rely on anyone for anything. That was important, that feeling of not being a burden.

'Some of the guys knew people who were involved in the Invictus Games, others in the Paralympics. I used to love basketball as a lad and decided I was going to get into the Paralympic basketball team. I didn't for one minute question whether I'd be good enough – I just put my mind to it and did it.' He taps his head. 'It's a powerful tool, the brain,' he adds. 'You'd be amazed at what it can do for you if you focus it in the right direction.'

I think of the amount of time I've spent focusing my brain in the direction of a romance with Idris Elba and how successful that's been, but decide not to rain on Craig's parade by contradicting him. After all, he's clearly doing something right.

Craig throws back the rest of his drink. 'What about you then? What are you going to achieve?'

'Oh, you know.' I smile. 'Hit my dream weight, turn *The Good News Gazette* into a resounding success, be an amazing mum while I'm doing it, make my millions…'

'And how are you planning to do that?'

I bite the end of my pen while I consider what to say. 'The usual things – work hard, eat less, exercise more.'

He tilts his head. 'Yes, but what's your plan? Have you written it all down? Broken it into specific goals?'

'Hmmm,' I muse, rubbing my chin. 'My goals are somewhat fluid.'

Craig points towards my notepad. 'Write down your goals. Come on, do it. You're not leaving here until I've helped you come up with a plan.'

I feel the all too familiar heat start to prickle my cheeks.

'Point one.' He's still talking. 'What was it, achieve your dream dress size?' I nod. 'Write it down. Now let's work through how it can be done.'

We spend the rest of the afternoon like that, me pulling aims out of thin air, breaking them into achievable goals, and working out a plan of action for each. By the time I leave, I'm exhausted. Which, when you throw the fact that I have not had so much as a sip of coffee into the mix, is no surprise. I also feel as though I've had an appointment with my own private life coach.

'This was supposed to be about you,' I say, embarrassed at how self-indulgent I let the entire interview become.

'It was about me,' he hits back, a smile lighting up his face. 'As well as basketball, it turns out this is one of the other things I'm good at: getting people to move their arses. So, do me a favour, just give it a go?'

I clutch my notepad to me and nod, promising I'll make the necessary changes to achieve my dreams.

And then I spend the entire journey back to the office thinking about our conversation and trying to remember exactly when it was that I stopped dreaming in the first place.

'Ollie, we've got another one!'

Ollie looks up from the Rightmove website and raises an eyebrow.

'Another what?'

I read the email again to make sure I haven't imagined it. No, the words are still there. A kitchen company with a showroom in Presthill wants to drum up business in Westholme and thinks we might be the way to do it.

'Another advertiser. They're taking out a full page.'

Ollie leans back in his chair and starts fiddling with his hair. 'Was this another Daniel special?'

'No!' I shriek. 'I sorted this one out completely by myself. All Daniel did was make the introductions.'

'So it *was* a Daniel special,' he affirms, triumphant.

I ignore him.

'They want to take out a half page in the next couple of issues with a view to upgrading to a full page in the future.'

Even Ollie's smiling now.

'Do you think, oh great one, that we could actually allow ourselves to believe that we're seeing a glimmer of light at the end of a dark and extremely damp tunnel?'

I pause. 'Let's not count our chickens and all that. We're not there yet.'

'We nearly are though, aren't we, Zo?'

'I don't want to speak too soon, but yes – it looks as though we very nearly are.'

———————

Westholme Community Facebook page:

Margaret Kemp: Just wanted to post a picture of the flowers left outside my house today, on the anniversary of my husband's death. I don't know how whoever it was knew to leave them today, but they couldn't have picked a better day. It's boosted my spirits no end. Thank you so much. You are an angel xxx

Chapter Eighteen

There's more cakes at the second cinema meeting. Fudge brownies cut neatly into squares, gooey caramel tarts and carrot cake topped with thick buttercream.

Yet the sugar content of the treats on offer is doing nothing to sweeten the atmosphere that's taken a distinctly sour turn, thanks to another stand-off between Starr and Norman, who are trying their best to continue an argument in between each and every agenda point that Daniel raises.

It's all to do with the colour of the cinema. The cinema, might I add, for which we haven't yet raised enough money to even take out the lease, let alone to pay for interior decoration.

The 'disagreement' began when Eva mentioned another renovated cinema she'd come across in an internet search that had been beautifully kitted out in pastel colours – a comment that Norman had taken as nothing short of blasphemy – and it's been rumbling on ever since.

'The cinema was originally painted in a berry red, and that's the colour we should use again,' Norman argues, his face colouring with the now-familiar purple hue that lets us know his anger levels are becoming difficult to contain.

'Don't you think that's a little "predictable"?' Starr tuts, looking down her nose and through her purple tortoiseshell glasses. 'Why don't we use flamingo pink?'

'I still think zebra carpets and those neon lights would work,' adds Eva.

'Well pardon me,' replies Norman. 'I thought we were trying to recreate the beauty of the cinema in its heyday. Not turn it into some sort of monstrosity.'

Then Colin raises his hand.

'I've been thinking about seating,' he says. 'Do we want to reinstall the row seating of the period, or would we prefer to use a combination of couches and armchairs instead?'

'We should, without a doubt, replicate the original seating arrangements.' Naturally, that comes from Norman.

'Too old-fashioned,' croaks Starr. 'We need couches. Although don't make them too low. The old dears won't be able to get up from them. And they should definitely be pink – to go with the decor.'

I glance at Norman. He looks as though he's about explode. I can tell by Daniel's expression he's wondering just how much involvement he really has to have in this in order to tick the CSR box. And I can't help but think of how Sam would have charmed the pants off everyone if he was here now.

I'm so lucky to have him, I remind myself. I realise that every time women turn their heads to look at him in the street; every time I watch him coaching the boys at football; every time I remember how I used to idolise him at school.

I'm having to remind myself of this a lot lately.

Never mind, it's Bonfire Night tomorrow and Charlie and I are spending the afternoon and evening with him. A bit of time together will be good for us all.

'Zoe?' Daniel's looking at me as though he's waiting for an answer to a question I didn't hear him ask.

I blink. 'Sorry, Daniel, what did you say?' I feel weird around him today and I'm not sure why. I need to shake it off.

'We seem to be struggling to come to an agreement over the seating. I was wondering whether you might be able to look into some of the options available and report on your findings?'

I jot down the action point and plaster on a reassuring smile. 'Absolutely,' I say, as though I'm already on to it. 'I'm sure we'll be able to find an option that will be acceptable to everyone.'

'That would be grand,' Norman responds. 'Just as long as you find seating options that replicate the originals.'

'I've arranged a trip for us,' announces Norman out of the blue.

Starr rolls her eyes, while the rest of us wait expectantly for the punchline. 'Ooh, where are we off to?' I enthuse after a painful period of awkward silence, trying on an expression that I hope will convey overwhelming interest in his answer.

'The Phoenix in Calstarn.' He adopts a superior tone. 'I'd be surprised if any of you had heard of it, but it was left derelict for years, just like ours, before being brought back to life by a group of dedicated volunteers.'

We all exchange glances, not sure whether to applaud or groan. Then Daniel steps in.

'That sounds like an excellent idea,' he replies. 'I've heard of The Phoenix. I believe it's been a huge success. A trip to see it will be a good way of bringing this whole project to life for us all.'

Norman practically glows with delight, then doubt flickers across his face.

'I'm not sure whether the number 51 bus route goes that far.'

'Not a problem, Norman,' Daniel reassures him. 'We can all take cars.'

Emma twirls a chunk of her hair around her finger. 'I think I may be able to borrow our local Beavers' van. My husband's one of the leaders, so we've used it before.'

'Who would drive it though?' I wonder out loud, then kick myself as it occurs to me that Starr's usually up for giving anything a go.

'I will,' Emma jumps in, before Starr gets the chance. 'We borrow it now and again – unofficially of course – for the boys' birthday parties. I can drive it. It's all good.'

'I never knew—' I start across the table to her, my eyes wide. She flashes me a grin.

'We've all got our hidden talents. I may not be able to successfully cook, clean or keep my children in check, but driving a minibus I can *definitely* do.'

We're sixty minutes into our two-hour-long meeting now and Daniel is clinging to the structure of the agenda like a life-raft.

'Moving on to our next point,' he rushes, looking suitably rattled. 'Lynne, please can you update the group on how the crowdfunding is going?'

Lynne sits up a little straighter. 'Within the first twenty-four hours of launching we'd raised almost £3,000,' she announces proudly. 'The fund is now up to £10,000, with donations coming in from all over the world. The international donors are mainly people who've grown up here then moved away. It seems they're as keen to see the cinema rescued as the rest of us.'

Daniel allows himself a smile. 'Very good. There's obviously an appetite for what we're doing then. Zoe, I know it's been a very quick turn-around organising the open-air cinema, but you were heading up the sub-committee for that. Is there anything you need or are all the plans in place now?'

I look over at Margaret, who gives me a nod and a wink. Straight after the last meeting, she'd sidled over to me and offered her assistance in helping out with planning the cinema night. She also assured me that, just as they saved my backside last year when I somehow landed myself with organising the ill-fated community fun day, she and her lovely group of friends were more than capable of doing the same again.

I'm extremely aware that my reputation for getting things done has been created entirely by Margaret's ability to rally enough people together to actually do the things that need doing. As she rebuffs every attempt I make to share the glory, however, we seem to have developed an understanding based on the premise that she'll pretty much always make me look good and I'll always let her.

'Everything is in hand. Margaret has taken on the lion's share of the work and, along with her former Rotary Club friends, has powered into action in terms of sorting out the logistics. We were thinking *Home Alone* might be the best film for the occasion. It's family-friendly, Christmassy and enough fun to get us all in the mood.'

'Perfect.' Norman beams.

'Great idea,' praises Daniel.

'What's *Home Alone*?' asks Starr. 'Is it a musical? I haven't heard of that one. I thought you might go for something like *White Christmas* or *Meet Me in St Louis*. A Christmas classic, perhaps?'

Norman's eyes bulge and his chest puffs out. It's as though someone's just pressed the 'inflate' button.

'*Home Alone is* a Christmas classic!' he spits out. 'I have never, *ever* before in my life heard anyone suggest otherwise.'

Starr looks around, clearly trying to read the room, then peeps coquettishly from underneath her glasses.

'My dear, it can't be that much of a classic if I've never heard of it.'

There's a moment's silence as everyone waits to see what will happen next, then Margaret jumps in before anything can.

'The date we have scheduled is at the end of November, so, Daniel, you may want to combine it with some sort of Christmas lights switch-on at the Parade?'

A few appreciative 'ooh's and 'ahh's go up around the room, which makes it difficult for Daniel to do anything other than agree, and, despite his best attempts to steer us back to the agenda, it quickly descends once more into a free-for-all as we all shift into Christmas mode.

'We must make sure that, *this year*, the Parade is awash with colour and sparkle,' asserts Starr, who has now moved on from the movie and is practically jumping up and down in her seat at the thought of the festival of colour about to be created outside of her dance shop.

'It'd be good to have some cool decorations this year,' Eva agrees. 'Maybe something that reflects the association with the cinema. A single colour to give it a classy vibe.'

Starr straightens her back. 'What a wonderful idea. I'll look into that for you, Daniel.' She starts jotting something down in her floral diary while Daniel looks on helplessly. 'Decorations that tie in with the cinema,' she mutters as she writes. She looks pointedly at Norman. 'I'll research flamingo pink then.'

With Starr and Norman keen to take a swipe at each other every opportunity they get and Daniel looking bored to tears by the whole thing, by the time we remove the clingfilm from the sweet treats and savouries, I'm feeling as though, metaphorically speaking at least, I've bitten off more than I can chew.

As the others pile their plates high with sandwiches, mini pies and sweet creations, I battle to resist the call of the cakes, digging miserably instead into a bowl of salad, while trying to scoop up as many croutons as possible within each pile of lettuce. I firmly believe that croutons are practically one of your five-a-day as long as you eat them with salad.

'That looks like an extremely healthy lunch.' Daniel appears at my shoulder.

'Still trying to be good,' I virtue signal, adding a few peppers to demonstrate the huge success I'm having.

'Well, whatever you're doing, it's working,' he continues, helping himself to a large scoop of pasta. 'You look great.'

'Daniel Lewis, was that a compliment you just paid me?' I sound as though I'm joking, but my arms are prickling with goosebumps at his words.

He looks down at the food and concentrates on placing the pasta very carefully on the edge of his plate.

'Credit where credit's due,' he says briskly. 'You've put the effort in and I'm just recognising the fact. That's all.' He picks up a napkin and clears his throat. 'Right, everyone, shall we continue the meeting over lunch?'

I suppress a smile and this time have no problem turning my back on the cakes. Despite my scales suggesting I've gained a few pounds recently, I still look all right. And now that Daniel's said it, I know it must be true.

'This is your best cover yet,' I shout over to Ollie as I slice open the tape binding the newspapers together.

This month, with the exception of the one bundle they've dropped off at the office for me to inspect, the printers have finally delivered the papers direct to the distribution centre and the joy I feel at not having to haul the papers around like a carthorse anymore cannot be overstated.

I hold up a copy and my stomach churns at the combined sensations of delight at seeing our creation in a tangible form and terror that I'll spot a typo on the front page.

Ollie's done a cracking job of designing this month's splash – the revelation that we're bringing the cinema back to life. He's incorporated a perfectly punned headline into a beautifully laid out page with a stunning artist's impression of how the outside of the revamped cinema will look.

Inside, there's another artist's impression; this time of the redeveloped cinema's interior. Fortunately, I'd had it created before 'seat-gate' broke out this morning, so this, completely unbiased, image, reflects Norman's vision of refurbished red velvet seats and plush carpets. And honestly, the result is beautiful.

Ollie wanders over, nudging me out of the way so that he can pick up his own copy of the *Gazette* out of the pile. 'It *does* look good, doesn't it,' he says, his eye for detail appraising his own work.

I nod, a yawn hijacking my attempt at a verbal answer.

'Charming,' Ollie tuts.

'Sorry. I'm tired today.' I yawn again.

'I noticed. I'd ask if someone was keeping you up all night, but I'd be amazed if Sam was seeing any action at the moment.'

'Ollie!' I whack him with my copy of the newspaper.

'I'm serious, you're working here, you're still doing the freelance work, sparse as it is, your phone's going by the minutes with calls and texts about the cinema, you're looking after Charlie too…' He does a mock and exaggerated wiping of his brow. 'No wonder you're tired.'

I sigh. 'It's not for ever. Things will calm down after the cinema re-opens. And you know what it's like here at the moment...' I wave my arm around '...but we'll be OK.'

We both fall silent as we examine the paper format of our work, and I flick through my copy, taking in the tales of dogs reunited with owners, more flowers being delivered anonymously and school uniform swap shops being set up to help those struggling.

'It's important, you know, Ol. What we're doing. It *is* making a difference,' I say eventually.

'I know it is,' he responds, without a trace of his usual mockery.

'We have to find a way to keep this going. To find the advertisers. To fund this whole thing. We can do it. I know we can.'

'You will.' His voice is determined, strong. He looks from the paper to me and winks. 'And I'll be right behind you, propping you up with industrial-strength coffee, every step of way.'

Westholme Community Facebook page:

Claire Phillips: See that *Good News Gazette* girl is taking on the old cinema now. It's on the front page of this month's issue. Artist's impressions look amazing.

Pete Owen: Another money-grabbing exercise, no doubt.

Eyelash Lucy: Don't think so – it says it's going to be run as a community business. Paid jobs and everything.

Jimmy Hunter: Sounds dodgy to me.

Chapter Nineteen

As much as I love my home town, I'm the first to admit that it's at its best when you're positioned five miles away from it.

That's where I am now, way up the steep incline that leads towards Presthill, on a walk with Sam and Charlie through the farmers' fields that cover the area between the two towns, three little dots moving slowly through the landscape.

I've convinced – well, bribed – Charlie to join Sam and me by promising him an additional thirty minutes on his Xbox tomorrow in return for his presence today. It's a deal that he reluctantly agreed to on the basis that a bag of Skittles was also added into the terms and conditions. Despite the nagging feeling that this probably isn't best practice parenting, like so many other things lately, I've decided to let it go.

A sudden wind drags my hair away from my face and I shiver in response. Admittedly, it's colder than I expected, but the cloudless sky is blue and clear, providing a decidedly upbeat feel to the bright November day.

Our elevated position provides a beautiful view over

Westholme and, much further into the distance, the cranes that operate at the docks at Seaforth and the mouth of the River Mersey. In eight hours' time this spot will be packed with people watching colourful fireworks being propelled into the night sky, but for now it's a quiet haven away from the madding crowds.

I stop walking and close my eyes, enjoying the silence that's punctuated only by the odd exchange between Charlie and Sam and the bleating of the sheep in the fields beyond. It all feels so peaceful and I inhale deeply, enjoying the distinctly rural smell of cowpats.

The once-so-familiar warmth of a small, soft hand wriggles its way into mine, interrupting my mini-meditation as Charlie makes a surprising but very welcome gesture of affection. I squeeze his fingers instinctively. These days, as he moves with increasing speed into 'older boy' status, he does his very best to avoid public displays of affection with his mum. But there are the odd occasions, like now, when he'll drop his inhibitions and, for a moment at least, I get my little boy back.

He leans into me, pressing his cheek against my arm. Then he whispers the words no parent wants to hear when they're enjoying a pleasant afternoon out.

'When can we go home?'

I sigh and snap my eyes open. 'Charlie, we've come up here to get away from your Xbox. We're certainly not racing back to it. Look around you, look at the view. Isn't it pretty?'

Charlie stares off into the horizon for all of two seconds, then moans, 'No, it's boring.'

'Come on, Charlie.' Sam's jogging on the spot like a racehorse ready to compete in the Grand National. 'Let's do some sprinting. It'll be good for your fitness levels. Help you on the pitch.'

'That's boring too,' Charlie huffs.

'I thought you wanted to be a footballer,' Sam continues. 'How are you ever going to be a footballer if your fitness levels aren't high enough to see you performing at your best during a match?'

'Let's walk down this path.' I sound like an over-enthusiastic CBeebies presenter. 'Remember they used to have horses down here, Charlie? You loved those horses, didn't you?'

'Yeah,' he sneers, adding under his breath, 'when I was *five*.'

I thrust a plastic bag in his face and nudge him along the cycle path. 'I've brought carrots. We can feed them.'

'You're not supposed to feed horses carrots. There's too much sugar in them.'

'Too much sugar in carrots?' I stop dead in my tracks.

'Of course.' He rolls his eyes. '*Everyone* knows that.'

I didn't know that.

'Charlie, I really hope you're not being off with your mum because you'd rather be at home playing computer games.' Sam's frowning so much he looks almost fierce.

'He's not, are you, Charlie?' I say anxiously. I turn to Sam. 'I think he's just tired,' I whisper.

'Hmmm. *I* think maybe he's too used to getting his own way.'

I stare after him as he marches off down the path, shaking his head as he goes. He's never criticised my parenting before. Or tried to reprimand Charlie for that matter. Where on earth did that come from?'

'*Now* can we go home, Mum?' Charlie hisses, rolling his eyes. 'I'm cold.'

'No, we cannot,' I snap. 'Stop moaning and start walking. We're going to feed the horses.'

'I don't want to feed the horses.'

'Tough. We're going.'

'Well, you can feed the horses. I'm not feeding them. I'm going home.'

Charlie's feeding the horses.

Despite his many protestations, he's holding his hand out flat as instructed, giggling as a massive Shire who's obviously appointed himself chief of the field nudges the other two horses out of the way in order to gently take the carrot from Charlie's palm.

'See?' Sam says loudly. 'Isn't this better than playing on devices?'

Charlie grunts his disagreement, then chuckles involuntarily as a smaller horse sneaks in while the chief isn't looking and whips the next carrot out of his hand.

Sam drapes his arm around my shoulders. 'You OK?' he says, resting his head against mine.

'Yeah.' I reach for his hand on my shoulder and lay my own on top of it. I'm not really over the 'getting his own way' comment, but I've decided to put it in a box for now rather than let it spoil the day. After all, he was only trying to help.

'Still worried about the advertising situation? I've been having words with a few contacts I know. Trying to spread the word. I'm sure it won't be long before one of them bites.'

I hesitate before answering, never quite sure how much to reveal about any subject that involves Daniel.

'A new advertiser came on board this week, but it's still at a critical point,' I say carefully. 'It was already a struggle even before we lost Parry's, so being a full-page advert down as we are at the moment has put us in a really tough situation.' I pause. 'It's also making me wonder whether this is the right path for me, or whether I should be looking towards a new job entirely.'

Out of the corner of my eye, I see Sam angle his head so that he can see my face. 'But what would you do? There can't be many other newspaper jobs round here, surely?'

I nearly tell him about the London job offer at this point. I'm actually on the verge of it. But something stops me.

'There aren't,' I reply instead. 'Most of the other publications are like me – one or two-man bands, struggling to make ends meet.'

'You'll manage,' says Sam, squeezing my shoulder. 'And you know if you need money, you can always ask me.'

It's a kind gesture, but I shudder at the thought. It's vital that Charlie and I are self-sufficient. It's the only way I know that, come what may, we'll be all right.

After a semi-successful day – successful in that everyone managed to keep their irritation at the 'passive aggressive' stage rather than accelerating it to full-on 'fight night' levels, we devour a quick chippy tea at mine before heading out again to the annual Bonfire Night celebrations.

These nights used to be run by the council, until someone somewhere realised that Bonfire Night celebrations weren't a selling point on any party manifestos and removed the budget. Now it's up to one of the community groups to raise the money and stage the event instead.

As always, they're being held at the town's main park, Bluebell Fields, about a five-minute walk from the Parade. When Charlie was younger, we would spend hours there, doing endless laps of the swings, slide, roundabout and climbing frame, then, as he grew, we returned to kick the ball around. Now he wouldn't be seen dead kicking a ball around with me in a public place unless he'd done a thorough risk analysis to make sure no one could see him first. So, trips back to the park, in whatever capacity, are always tinged with rose-tinted nostalgia that I want to bottle and conserve for ever.

We pull up in the Parade car park and join the crowds heading to the event. It's a cold, fresh night and the scent of gunpowder fills the air as, across the town, fireworks pop a rainbow of colours into the night sky.

As we near the fields, we're enveloped in a scented cloud of fried onions and mustard combined with deep-fried donuts and candy floss puffs, confirming the presence of the junk food vans that are practically compulsory at community events.

It used to be easy keeping an eye on Charlie when a firm grasp of his hand meant I could attach him to me like an appendix. Now, his refusal to partake in any kind of physical interaction means I have to watch him like a hawk on nights like this, one eye on him, another eye on the ground in front of me to avoid stumbling in the dark.

I sigh. If only I could stick him back in the pushchair, a handy device that could carry Charlie, my coffee and a whole host of treats for me, all in one singular contraption. I miss those days.

As we reach the gates and pause to throw money into the bucket being violently shaken by a disheartened-looking volunteer, the distinctive scent of pot rises through the air. We pass a group of around twelve teenage boys in black hooded tracksuits, all with their hoods up. It's an outfit I now recognise to be the unofficial uniform of the Orchard Estate gang – and Charlie visibly shrinks as we near them.

'All right, Sam,' one of the lads mutters, nodding as we walk past, the few parts of his face actually on show jogging something in my memory.

Sam looks evenly back at him. 'All right, Jono. Keeping out of trouble?'

'Course, lad.' He smiles a toothy grin then lets out a menacing cackle as another boy arrives on a bike and he and Jono cross over the road and disappear into a side alley.

'Who are they?' I whisper once we're at a safe distance. 'I recognise the one you were talking to.'

'They're off the estate. Used to come to the academy before life took over. The one I spoke to is Tommy Johnson – the lads call him Jono. The other, taller one is Gary Spindle. Spin to his mates.'

'The first one was the ringleader that day when the gang were attacking Adina.'

Sam sighs. 'That sounds about right.'

I glance down to make sure Charlie's still there, then continue.

'They're dealing right now, aren't they?' I'm irritated by the fact that Sam looks completely unperturbed about this illegal activity going on right under his nose.

'It's all they know.'

'But aren't you going to do anything about it?' I persist. 'We're at a family *Bonfire Night* for goodness' sake.'

He stops dead in the field, oblivious to the hordes of families trying to make last-minute manoeuvres around us.

'What do you want me to do?' he hisses. 'Go and take on all twelve of them? Read them the riot act? Call the police? No, it's not ideal, but neither are their lives. You've got to pick your battles carefully – you can't hammer them over every little thing.'

'Every little thing?' I whisper back. 'Sam, they're *drug dealers*.'

Sam looks pointedly at Charlie who, thankfully, has taken advantage of the distraction to pickpocket my mobile again and check out that afternoon's football scores.

While I realise this probably isn't a conversation that should be taking place in front of him, I'm still not quite done.

'How old are they?' I start again.

'Fifteen, sixteen maybe.' Something catches Sam's attention. 'Look,' he says, pointing at a couple a few metres away. 'There's Emma and Dave. Let's go and say hi.'

———

Emma and Dave are exchanging hushed giggles with each other, looking more like teenagers with a crush than long-suffering marrieds who very nearly split up last year due to Dave's one-night stand.

I watch them for a moment, intrigued as to how they've made it work; how they've managed to find their way through such a betrayal. Then Dave, with his cropped salt and pepper hair and thick shoulders, stoops to whisper something in Emma's ear that causes her to laugh out loud and I realise that, however they've done it, I'm really glad that they have.

'Hi, guys,' I shout, as we make our way over to them. 'Good to see you, boys,' I add, greeting their twelve and-ten-year-olds, Ethan and Jacob. They grunt a reply in pre-pubescent language, first to me and then to Charlie who, being of the same species, immediately grunts back.

Within minutes, Sam and Dave are bantering over the weekend's football results, leaving me free to ask Emma about something that's been preying on my mind.

'How do you think Beth looked the other night?' I say quietly.

'Like crap.' She pushes her fingers through the length of her blonde hair and pulls it into a topknot. 'Why?'

'I'm worried about her, Em.' I bite my lip. 'I think she could be suffering…you know, in the same way that you did.'

She looks over at the boys that bring so much joy to her life but who, at the very beginning, triggered so much pain.

'I've wondered the same thing,' she agrees. 'But when she's getting so little sleep, it's hard to know whether it's post-natal depression or just sheer exhaustion.'

'Either way, I think she needs our help.'

'I think you're right. But what can we do?'

We're parted by a big family group then, grandparents swinging a little girl by the arms while her mum wheels a toddler in a pushchair, Dad walking alongside them both. To most people, they wouldn't stand out in a crowd. But as I take in the squeals of delight from the little girl and the smiles on the parents as they watch the scene, I can't take my eyes off them. I bat away a sudden stab of sadness and concentrate on Beth.

'Why don't I say I'll take Darcy for an afternoon?' I suggest. 'It would give Beth a chance to catch up on her sleep if nothing else.'

Emma frowns with her eyes. 'She's still breastfeeding her though, isn't she? That might be a problem.'

'Beth said she's taking a bottle now. All she has to do is feed her, wind her and then I'll take her for a walk in the pram. It'll be easy.'

A series of pops and crackles hijacks our conversation and we pause to watch the colours dotted across the sky – and to make sure our boys are still there, sharing extended grunts with each other.

'Are you sure?' Emma asks, as the run of fireworks disappears. 'It's been a while since you dealt with a little baby.'

'Charlie survived, didn't he? And he's survived for almost ten years since. I can't see anything going wrong.'

Emma laughs and shakes her head. 'It really has been a while, hasn't it!'

'Don't be so cynical,' I tut. 'It'll be fine. Nothing to it.'

Westholme Community Facebook page:

Tori Hindle: Did anyone read that story on *The Good News Gazette* website about those two penpals who've been best friends for years? Heartbreaking that they can't afford to see each other.

Irene Wilson: I know. I'm thinking of setting up a

GoFundMe page to try and pay for a plane fare for them –
would anyone throw in if I did?

Kim Hughes: I would

Alan Boyd: Me too

Rob Littlewood: Defo.

Chapter Twenty

I f you'd asked me to pick out of a line-up the person least likely to be able to master the art of driving a minibus, Emma would probably be at the top of my list.

My gorgeous, stylish friend is more of an Audi-driving, nails-done-in-a-salon type of gal. She's absolutely not the sort of woman who'd turn up in a battered old van with '12th Westholme Beavers' emblazoned on the side.

Yet here she is, trundling merrily towards the Parade, looking pleased as Punch that our trip to The Phoenix Cinema has finally provided her with the opportunity to put her previously hidden skill on display.

We're all standing in the Parade car park, huddled over our coffees from Cath's, as we wait to board our transport, and I'm bracing myself for this, our first cinema group trip.

Everyone's here; Margaret, Jack Germaine – Margaret's fellow Westholme Gardner (who, despite having had no previous interest in the cinema, has turned up 'just in case anyone needs me' – the 'anyone' clearly being Margaret), Norman, Emma, Colin, Lynne,

Eva, Starr and Candice. And, of course, Daniel, who's looking slightly less 'businessman' today. More 'autumn and winter Next catalogue model' in fact, even though I know his clothes wouldn't be seen anywhere near a Next store whereas mine aspire to a place there.

Boarding the bus is interesting. I'd usually sit with Emma, but she's driving, and Colin has requested a seat up front on account of his previously undisclosed travel sickness issue. He immediately winds the window down and sticks his head out of it, with Lynne sitting in between him and Emma, holding a sick bag and rubbing his back.

Jack ushers Margaret into the window seat and plonks himself next to her, wedging her in just in case she decides to do a runner. Margaret is huffing and puffing now as Jack hands around his Murray Mints, but she hasn't yet made any effort to move.

Norman sits on the single seat on the other side of the aisle to them. He's already started on the Lucozade.

Eva and Candice have teamed up to be each other's pairing for the trip, sitting behind Margaret and Jack and dumping their collective bags and coats on the seat behind Norman.

Starr, meanwhile, is curled up across the third pair of seats as though she's a 1950s movie star on a Hollywood casting couch, the faux fur blanket that she brought with her for the hour-long trip covering her black PVC-clad legs and red ankle boots. She's currently waxing lyrical about how she nearly had a one-night-stand with Sean Connery.

Which leaves Daniel, me and the four seats across the back of the bus. He goes first, heading for the window seat to the left of the row, then I squeeze through to the one on the right, leaving two spaces between us. But he's big and long, and within seconds he's shuffled along so that he's now sitting across the middle, closer to me, with his legs stretched out towards the other side.

I look down at my own legs, which seem thinner and smaller when placed next to his. I feel a wave of self-satisfaction. It's a good look for them.

Emma starts up the engine, and we all cheer as the minibus chugs towards the exit of the car park. Then Emma takes the corner a bit too sharply as she pulls into the road and I slide into Daniel, our sides pressed together like red hot pokers.

'Sorry,' I mumble, my cheeks burning as we hastily scramble back into our own spaces to the soundtrack of Colin retching in the front.

'No problem,' replies Daniel, crossing his long legs and paying an inordinate amount of attention to the sky as the minibus zigzags its way out of Westholme.

Someone's given Norman a clipboard.

Five minutes into the journey, he whipped it out and conducted a register of attendees, despite Emma hollering from the front seat that it was a bit bloody late for all that and there was no way she was going back if it turned out we'd left anyone behind.

Now he's working through a list he's compiled of particular points of interest we should all grill the cinema people on, most notably the red seating, in order to ensure that we make the most of this research trip and recall every single detail upon our return.

'He's making me feel as though I'm underperforming in my role,' Daniel mutters, as Norman proceeds to give everyone a plotted history of how The Phoenix came to rise from the ashes. Daniel's safely positioned back in the window seat now, clearly as conscious as I am that we're only one sharp bend away from another full-on body collision.

'He makes everyone feel as though they're underperforming in their role,' I reply. 'I have never seen anyone quite so dedicated to whatever task has been assigned to them as Norman.'

'He loves the cinema with a passion, doesn't he?'

'Always has done.' I nod. 'He used to make weekly visits to *The Northern News* back when I worked there, to try and get us to start a campaign to have it brought back to life. No one could ever get hold of the owner though.'

Daniel shifts in his seat. 'That would have been Peter,' he replies quietly, almost to himself.

'Peter?'

'The current owner's dad,' he confirms. 'Joanne inherited it when he died, but I think it's been a poisoned chalice. Too costly for her to renovate on her own, but she hasn't been able to raise any interest in a sale either.'

I process these facts. 'So, I guess we're doing her a favour really, aren't we? Taking on the cinema, renovating it, providing her with an income. No wonder she agreed to it.'

Daniel looks uncomfortable. 'It wasn't really about that, but yes, I suppose we are.'

The conversation suddenly feels awkward, and I'm not sure why.

'So, it's a win-win for us all then, isn't it?' I throw in to try and make it feel better.

'I guess so.' Daniel smiles at me, but it's a smile with limitations.

Then Norman's voice echoes around the van as he raises it a few hundred decibels in order to ensure no one misses the words that follow.

'Can you listen at the back please; I need to talk you through the risk assessment I've completed and I want to make sure *everyone* understands what's expected of them.'

Melanie and Jean-Paul Benoit, the couple behind the renovation of The Phoenix cinema, are just lovely. He is French, she is English, and between them they've created a thing of unique beauty.

The story goes like this: they met online on a film buffs' dating website, hit it off and have been overachieving ever since. Within three years of virtually hooking up, they had married, had a baby and recreated The Phoenix Cinema, and I get the impression this is only the start.

The Benoits are one of those kooky couples that are clearly meant for each other and each other alone. They hang on each other's every word, finish each other's sentences and obviously operate in tandem, whether that's as parents, spouses or even business partners.

'Imagine working with your fella all day, every day.' Emma shudders, then nods at Jean-Paul. 'Although maybe it wouldn't be quite so bad if your fella looked like him.'

I giggle, but secretly agree. Jean-Paul's blond hair is probably jaw-length once it's free of the confines of the band that's currently just about keeping it tied back in a stubby ponytail. An old-school Levi's T-shirt covers his narrow frame and he's wearing black skinny jeans on his slim legs. He has high cheekbones and huge blue eyes with a look that's more Scandinavian than French.

But then Melanie is equally stunning, with light-brown hair that falls in waves and no visible signs of make-up. She's tall and toned, and is rocking a pair of battered pale-blue jeans as though they were tailored just for her. Even their baby looks as though he's been created by a White Company marketing team to be used specifically as a prop for their catalogue.

While Norman's asking them for the ins and outs of their community project, I'm watching with interest how they interact with each other; the way they catch at each other's fingers as they show us the different elements of the building; how they touch each other's backs as they move around. It's different to how Sam and I are together, more tactile, more at ease.

At one point, I look up to find Daniel watching me watching them and I feel embarrassed, like he's seen something he shouldn't. So, I grab the clipboard off Norman and take up point thirty-seven on his list, which reads: 'Bathroom cleaning product suppliers', until he snatches it back off me and uses his finger to underline three times the fact that we're still only on point twenty-four.

'Isn't that your clipboard?' I whisper to Candice, who seems quite happy to have been relieved of her duties.

'I left it in Cath's when I popped to the loo before we left,' she whispers back. 'By the time I got back he'd pinched it and clipped his notes on top of mine.'

'Aren't you going to reclaim it?' I ask hopefully.

She looks at Norman, who's currently clutching it to his checked-shirted chest, then looks back at me with one eyebrow raised.

'Let him keep it. He's doing a far more thorough job than I ever could.'

I assume, by the way the Benoits gloss over the least interesting of the questions on the list, that they've met a few Normans in their time. They do a superb job of distracting him from the technicalities of how the audio system works, for example, with promises that they'll email all relevant details across to us.

Instead, they focus on the red velvet recliners in one of the cinema rooms, the black leather chairs with the small round tables in another, the menu of food and drinks they serve up during the film...it's all I can do not to ask them to stick on the first *Sex and the City* film and bring me some fries.

'How did you raise the money for all this, love?' asks Jack, who despite only having joined the trip because Margaret was on it seems genuinely interested in how it all works.

'Crowdfunding mainly,' Melanie explains, and we all nod our heads in agreement that this is indeed a good way to go. 'We were awarded some grants, which helped, but it was definitely the support of the local community that made the dream a reality.'

As they talk, a group of volunteers in smart uniforms whose ages must range between sixteen and sixty bustle past and smile at us all.

'Just some of our many volunteers,' Melanie says, greeting them with a wave. 'We have around thirty in total, each of them just as dedicated to the project as we are. We were able to bring the cinema back to life, but it's this amazing bunch that keep it going.'

'We love it,' shouts one twenty-something who's busy behind the ticket desk, and we're suddenly pelted in all directions with shouts of agreement from volunteers quietly going about their work.

There's such a feeling of 'togetherness' about it all that it's impossible to do anything but smile, and we look around at each other, our bond strengthened by seeing a real-life version of what it is we're working towards.

'People are wonderful,' Starr exclaims.

'They really are,' adds Margaret, and everyone else agrees.

Everyone except Daniel, who looks at the floor.

———

Westholme Community Facebook page

12th Westholme Beavers: Can anyone recommend a valet for a minibus? Particularly interested in hearing from those who specialise in removing the smell of sick.

Chapter Twenty-One

I t took some convincing, but eventually Beth went for the idea of me taking Darcy off her hands for an afternoon.

I mentioned it to her at Slim City and while the creases in her forehead and the chewing on the inside of her mouth indicated that she was nervous about the idea, the bags under her eyes and general exhaustion in her face meant it was unlikely she was ever going to put up much of a fight.

Fortunately, she didn't and earlier this afternoon Darcy was deposited at my house. Well, her, three holdalls and a printed list of instructions that ran to four pages and included telephone numbers for practically everyone Darcy had ever had contact with in the five months since she'd been born.

She's been here for fifteen minutes now and, after sticking around long enough to poke a slender finger into her pudgy palm and giggling as she clenched it tightly, Charlie spotted a window of opportunity and disappeared upstairs, where I suspect he's currently sneaking in unofficial time on his Xbox.

Sam's decided to join us – I think more for the entertainment value of watching me deal with a baby than anything else – and he already seems enchanted by her noises and many, many smiles.

Because while Beth might be struggling, Darcy is positively thriving. She is, hands down, the happiest baby I've ever seen. Every new face seems to generate a huge grin and an assortment of noises; every object she encounters is a thing of endless fascination. Even the slightest sound causes her big brown eyes to almost double in size as she tries to work out which of the limited objects she knows and understands it could be.

'Look, she's laughing,' says Sam as he twirls her around the room and I watch him with her, a pang of sadness at the thought of how different Charlie's early years could have been if he'd had a dad like Sam around.

'I wouldn't twirl her too much,' I warn. 'Beth fed her before she dropped her off so she might be—'

Sam stops twirling and stares at his sweatshirt.

'Sick?'

'Don't worry.' I power into action like the sort of cool, calm, composed mum I wish I'd been when Charlie was this age. 'I'll get the kitchen roll. There's wipes in the bag. Don't worry,' I repeat firmly. 'It'll be fine.'

Darcy waited until approximately four minutes after we'd cleaned her up before she vomited again. Then, while I was trying to clean Sam's top for a second time, her little head sunk into her neck and an explosion took place somewhere between her lower back and Sam's hands.

I say her lower back; that's where it started. Where it ended up was at the nape of her neck, covering every inch in between with a mustard-yellow gunge. Even the soft brown tufts of hair that overlapped the back of her babygro were drenched in the stuff. It was, even for a seasoned mum, truly gross.

Sam's holding her in the bath now, as I pour copious amounts of lukewarm water over her little body to try and remove the poo. It's tricky, trying to remove this kind of gunk without the help of soap or shower gel and I'm terrified to use any in case it's too harsh for her sensitive skin. Eventually there's nothing else for it – I have to use my fingers to rub it off.

The whole thing is such a palaver that even Charlie's deemed it interesting enough to get involved and he's trying to turn her ear-piercing screams into laughter by pulling funny faces as Sam keeps her in position and I remove the poo. I think back to when Charlie was young and wonder at what point bathing a baby turned into a three-man job.

Finally, after our combined efforts, Darcy's clean, dressed in a cute pink outfit I retrieved from one of the bags, and smiling again. I check the time, then check it again and sigh.

'Has it really only been forty-five minutes since Beth dropped her off?' groans Sam. 'What time's she picking her up again?'

'Five o'clock. We've still got another four hours and fifteen minutes to go.'

After all the excitement of the first hour, I feel quite sure that Darcy must be ready for a sleep, so I issue strict instructions to everyone to make absolutely no noise whatsoever and curl up on the couch with her.

As she cuddles into me, eyes looking curiously into mine, little fingers flexing involuntarily, I feel nostalgic for a time that's unlikely to ever come again.

Would I have wanted more children? It's not as though Charlie was planned.

The answer, unequivocally, is yes. Having been brought up as an only child (Mum says a second just never happened and they didn't pursue it), I was always clear on what my family goals were: three children, two years apart, a boy, a girl and another boy, preferably in that order.

This imagined family used to be so real to me. The mum (me), the dad (Idris Elba) and the children would live in a big house somewhere in the country. I'd spend weekends making cakes and doing crafts with the kids, Idris or his counterpart would play football with the boys in our huge garden. Mum and Dad would call and we'd have barbecues and drink wine, our tinkling laughter confirming the perfectness of it all. We'd be so overwhelmingly happy. And no one would own an Xbox.

I look down at Darcy, who, in accordance with the plan, is drifting off to sleep, her little eyelids fluttering involuntarily as the land of Nod beckons her ever closer. Sam's sitting further down the couch, watching us both with a curious smile on his face.

Then Charlie, once again cocooned in his bedroom, lets out a massive celebratory roar, presumably at the goal he's just scored playing FIFA and Darcy wakes with a start, screaming at the unwelcome intrusion into her dreams.

'Charrrrlieeeee!' I yell over the din, passing Darcy to Sam as I climb off the couch. 'Get your coat on. We're going out!'

'Muu-uuuum, I'm in the middle of a game,' he shouts back.

'I'm in no mood for discussion. NOW!'

We've been trekking around the streets of Westholme for fifty-three minutes and Darcy is gurgling happily, blinking at the sky as though it's the most impressive creation she's ever had the good fortune to come across.

Sam's quiet, deep in thought. Every now and then I hear his phone beep and see him check it.

'Everything OK?' I ask, and he shoves the device back in his pocket quickly.

'Fine,' he replies, keeping his eyes fixed on the pavement. 'Just work stuff.'

'Mum, I'm tired,' whines Charlie, who, despite being able to run around a football pitch for a good ninety minutes every week, seems challenged by the sheer exertion required to pound the pavements for an hour.

'I must admit, our walk isn't really having the desired effect,' I concede. 'What does it take to send babies off to sleep these days? When you were young, you used to go off within minutes of me taking you out for a walk. I can't understand why Darcy's resisting it.'

'Could it be something to do with every baby being different?' asks Sam unhelpfully.

'That must be it,' I mutter.

A fire engine roars past us on the street, its siren so deafening that I hold my breath as I fix my gaze on the baby. Her eyes are like saucers. And then it comes. The chin wobble. The pursing of the lips. And then, finally, the tears.

'Oh no, Darcy, oh please no, don't cry, little one,' I soothe, picking her up out of her pram and nestling her into the crook of my arm. 'It's OK, it was just a fire engine, off to save lots of people. Nothing to worry about.'

I look up, hoping to find Charlie pulling a funny face or extending his finger for Darcy to clutch or doing any one of a number of things that would surely ward off the tears, but he's kicking a stone around the pavement instead. Sam is using the brief interlude to check something – probably the football scores – on his phone.

'Guys,' I say, exasperated. 'Anyone want to help me out here?'

'She's probably hungry,' Charlie says. 'I know I am.'

I do a quick calculation as to how long it's been since she must have had her last bottle, then, keeping tight hold of a now screaming Darcy, gingerly crouch down and pull the instructions out of the bottom of the pram.

Scanning over them, I look for the part where it says to feed her, then check my watch. Yes, she's due a feed round about now. That'll be why she's not settling.

Take the bottle out of the fridge and gently warm for thirty seconds in the microwave...

I freeze. The bottle's in the fridge. At home. Which is fifty-three – no – fifty-four minutes away from where we are.

'OK, little problem. Darcy needs her bottle now and it's at home.'

'Shall we head back then?' suggests Sam, not once taking his eyes off his phone.

'We're almost an hour away,' I snap.

He looks up at me now, finally sensing the urgency as Darcy raises her cry to the next level to ensure we're all aware of the high stakes of the situation.

'No problem, I'll run back, get the car and bring it to her.'

I try and do a quick calculation as to how much time that'll save us.

'I don't think that will work, Sam.' Panic is well and truly setting in. 'I don't think I can keep her occupied for that long.'

'The only other option is to start walking back then, isn't it? Come on, let's go.'

Darcy's already alarming cry turns into screams. 'Sam,' I wail, any feeling of competence gone.

He finally pockets his phone and, reaching out his arms, gently takes her off me and places her onto his chest. 'Come on, Darcy,' he whispers soothingly into her cheek, 'let's take you home. Are you all right with the pram?' he asks over his shoulder as he starts walking, whispering and rubbing her back along the way.

And I round up Charlie and the wheeled contraption and walk

behind like a spare part as, under Sam's care, Darcy's cries eventually grind to a slow and shuddering halt.

By the time Beth arrives I have never been more in need of wine and, safe in the knowledge that Darcy's now back in the care of her mother and Charlie's happily kicking a ball around in the garden, I open a bottle before I've even offered her a cup of tea.

'Sorry, Beth,' I say as I take a gulp, 'but needs must.'

Beth grins as she hugs and kisses a delighted Darcy. 'Tell me about it,' she sympathises. 'If I wasn't breast-feeding, I'd be a raging alcoholic by now.'

I enjoy the heat the alcohol brings to the back of my throat and, as it makes its way into my chest, I feel the knot of tension start to dissolve.

'I'd forgotten how tough it was,' I admit. 'You literally don't get a minute, do you?'

She shakes her head. 'Nope. Today was the first time I've been on my own for longer than an hour since she was born.'

'No wonder you're so tired.' I take in little Darcy's expression as she gazes devotedly up at her mum, drinking in her features. 'Doesn't Tony take her out for you?'

'He does, but I think he's nervous that he'll do something wrong.' She laughs ruefully. 'As if I have all the answers.'

I look at her. 'You don't need to have all the answers, Beth. You're doing great. Darcy's a demanding baby, that's all. Anyone would be on their knees. *I* certainly am and I've only had her for a few hours.'

Sam, who is clearly intent on outperforming me today, pops his head around the door and offers Beth the cuppa that I haven't yet managed.

'I'm fine, thanks. She gives Darcy another kiss. 'Better take this little one back so we can get her in the bath.'

'She's already—' Sam goes to say, then sees the expression on my face and thinks better of it.

'It never stops, does it?' I throw my arms around her shoulders and squeeze her into me. 'But it does get easier, I promise you.'

'That's what everyone keeps saying.' She sighs. 'The only problem is, no one can tell me when.'

It's then, as I'm trying to think up a realistic answer, that I hear the sound guaranteed to put the fear of God into any parent.

An animalistic, ear-piercing, child's scream.

And it's not coming from Darcy.

Westholme Community Facebook page:

Zoe Taylor: Thanks so much to Beech Dental Practice for giving my son an emergency appointment this afternoon after he tripped over a football and snapped one of his front teeth in half. Through what seemed like a sea of blood and tears, they managed to work their magic and make the broken tooth look as good as new. Can't thank you enough. You are lifesavers!

Beech Dental Practice: You're very welcome, Mum. We're glad that Charlie is OK. And we hope you recovered quickly too. You're not the first parent to pass out and you won't be the last!

Chapter Twenty-Two

I t couldn't be a more perfect night for an open-air cinema.

The sky is a beautiful shade of inky blue, without a single cloud to block the shimmering stars dotted throughout the darkness. The moon is full and seems to have doubled in size in honour of the occasion. Even the rain has stayed away. It's as though all of the elements have conspired in our favour to make sure we have a damn good night.

Shakin' Stevens is being blasted through the loudspeakers at the Parade, singing about the snow falling all around him. And flamingo-pink lighting is being tested by decoration specialists who are probably scratching their heads at being given what appears to be a Valentine's lighting brief at Christmas.

I inhale the scent of mulled wine that cuts through the sharp mid-November air to create the sort of aroma that makes you feel all excited about the fact that Christmas isn't too far away and look around, satisfied at the scene before me. There's a stall selling gingerbread, another flogging Christmas candles, and my dad, having shown his penchant for dressing up as superheroes last year, is being held hostage in the site-office-turned-grotto by some elves in his role as Father Christmas.

Even the Parade's own permanent fairy lights are getting in on the act, playing their part in creating a pre-festive atmosphere. It's just so...Christmassy.

We arrived early in order to set everything up, which meant that Charlie was able to nab the best seats in the house for him and his friends. His mouth has recovered pretty well since last week's broken tooth incident. I'm still flummoxed by how my little boy can act like a teenager one day and trip over like a toddler the next, but if there's one thing I've learnt by now, it's to take these little occurrences in my stride. They always strike when you least expect them.

I glance over to the Parade's pedestrianised square where Margaret, ably assisted by Jack, is setting out rows and rows of fold-up chairs. Margaret spots him placing a chair – I suspect deliberately – out of line and he catches my eye and winks as she turns around to scold him.

Emma's chatting to a reporter who's just turned up from *The Northern News*, with Starr hovering closely behind, while Eva's filming everything for social media.

A whole host of other volunteers, mainly roped in by Margaret, are working together in a hive of activity, carrying out all of the tasks that I've asked Margaret to give to them, as well as many more that I haven't.

And over on the road side of the Parade, Colin and Lynne are standing at the cordoned-off 'entrance', ready to take in the money from the paying customers that are already starting to mill around.

Sam is sitting on one of the rows with Dave, Emma's husband, and their two boys, all aware of the fact that they're unlikely to get a look-in when it comes to our attention this evening. Because tonight, mine and Emma's focus is on one thing and one thing only: the biggest event to hit Westholme since last year's carnival.

A rainbow of multi-coloured lights wound around a naked Santa starts flashing across my body while tinny music blares out from my chest. I look down and sigh. We'd all agreed to wear Christmas jumpers for the event but I'd made the mistake of letting my dad get mine from one of the lads at the factory who was selling them on the side.

There's a button you're meant to be able to press in order to turn this whole sound and lights show on and off, but it doesn't work properly. This means that every now and again my jumper will break into a rendition of 'Jingle Bells' without warning, all while flashing furiously as though it should be playing a starring role in the Blackpool illuminations.

'Nice jumper,' comments Daniel, who's chosen this moment to appear right in front of me and is trying not to stare at my chest but failing dismally. I glance over at Sam, uncomfortable at the thought of him watching me with Daniel, but he's laughing at something Dave's telling him and seems too distracted to have spotted our interaction.

'Awful, isn't it.' I turn my attention back to him. 'Just blame my dad.'

'Aha.' He nods his head as if to communicate that he completely understands. I think back to last year's community festival and remember that he's one of the very few people that actually does.

I look at his own chest, and bravely reach out to part the two sides of his wool coat with my hands to better see the design.

'Daniel, is that a snowman on your top?'

He smiles ruefully and wraps his coat back around him.

I giggle. 'Don't tell me you've actually embraced the Christmas theme?'

He raises his voice in order to compete with Starr's enthusiastic attempt at manning the soundboard.

'When in Rome—'

We're interrupted by a large figure appearing at my side. A big hand squeezes my forearm.

'Zoe.' It's Norman. 'Zoe, do you have a minute?' He continues without waiting for an answer. 'I'm a little worried that the volume isn't in accordance with the council's environmental policy. Can you come and tell Starr she needs to turn it down?'

I sigh. Norman's red face and thunderous expression suggest his own attempts at doing just that have so far fallen on deaf ears.

'Sorry,' I say to Daniel. 'I'd better go and sort this out.'

'It's OK,' Daniel shouts as the volume increases again. 'Go. I'll catch up with you later.'

'Quickly, Zoe,' Norman yells, tugging my arm. 'Before someone calls Environmental Health.'

'Why have a drama when you can turn it into a crisis, hey, Norm?' I mutter under my breath. Then I turn to him and shout, 'Let's go and take her to task,' just because I know the very suggestion of it will please him immensely.

'Zoe, we're late. The film should have started four minutes ago!'

Not for the first time, I contemplate how useful it would be to have a Norman as a virtual assistant – you know, in the same way people use Siri or Alexa.

A Norman could wake you in his terribly earnest voice, urging you to get up and make the most of the day rather than give in to your desire to switch off the alarm and pull the covers back over your head. It could alert you to the fact that you were about to go over your free hour on the landline, or that you were in danger of using the posh shampoo on a working-from-home day.

A Norman could even jump in just before you opened one of the five Christmas tubs of Cadbury's Roses you'd bought in September because they were on offer, listing the calorie content and issuing a public health warning about the dangers of consuming any of them.

Yes, in day-to-day life, a Norman could be very helpful. But right now, as I'm trying to deal with numerous other issues, his constant nagging is driving me up the wall.

Having relaxed over the volume issue after Starr dutifully turned it down with a wink and a whispered promise to crank it back up once the film starts, he's now moved on to time management.

'Zoe, it is my duty to inform you that we are now five minutes late, I repeat, five minutes late in starting the film. We must press play.' He grabs my wrist between his plump fingers and stares at me, panic in his bulging eyes. 'We. Must. Press. Play!'

I shake off the urge to tell him where to go and instead say, 'Don't worry, Norman, I'm on it.' I then hotfoot it over to the projectionist to find out what the hold-up is, only to be told in no uncertain terms that the hold-up came in the form of Norman giving him a potted history of The Albany while he was conscientiously trying to go about his job.

It's only as I'm marching back to Norman that I catch sight for the first time of his own Christmas jumper. It's black, with the words 'I'll be Home Alone This Christmas' and while I applaud him for having found a sweater that ties in with the film, I feel a pang of sadness at the thought that this may actually be the case.

Before I have the chance to give him the edited version of the projectionist's response, the opening credits start up. And as the Parade becomes enveloped in the glow of Hollywood Technicolor, his tense expression gives way to one of such pure joy that I feel a wave of affection for him.

Even *I* start to relax as the audience settles down, the only noise being the rustling in their carrier bags as they retrieve their crisp and sweet packets, and the discreet but undeniably increasing volume of the film.

All of the seats are full, which means we must have reached our fundraising goal for this event. I feel a sudden sense of contentment as I observe families and friends, young and old, enjoying the festive feeling of being together as a community, all working towards the same goal. Which is, naturally, the creation of a lovely town where we can live together in harmony, appreciating Westholme for what it is: a down-to-earth, warm, friendly place that we all adore.

Or something like that.

We're halfway through *Home Alone* when the first firework is thrown.

It happens on the street next to the Parade and everyone jumps at the flash of light and unexpected bang that's nothing to do with the movie in which – until that point – they had been so engrossed.

I whip around to the source of the noise. A group of ten or twelve older teenagers, all dressed in black hoodies and tracksuit bottoms, are shouting and jeering. As one of the boys turns, a streetlight picks up some features I recognise and I realise immediately who it is: Jono from the Orchard Estate gang.

A second, then third, then fourth explosion quickly follows, as more spears of light are lobbed with abandon onto the road next to the crowd, and the distinct smell of Bonfire Night steps on the toes of our Christmas evening.

The amiable silence that had accompanied the film just moments ago disappears as event-goers turn to their companions, wondering out loud exactly how much on a scale of one to ten they need to panic.

And just as they're in the process of deciding, one of the boys launches a rocket. Right into the middle of the crowd.

Westholme Community Facebook page:

Rob Littlewood: It's all kicking off here at the Parade. Fireworks being thrown, chairs upended as people run off, it's carnage!

Lisa Sheldon: Pointless trying to do anything like this round here. It just creates problems. Should've known better than to even try.

Chapter Twenty-Three

Ear-piercing screams rip through the crowd as everyone scrambles to move out of danger, while through the noise, the unmistakable sound of a child howling in pain sends chills down my spine.

Suddenly there's a mass of bodies moving in all different directions. I look over to where Charlie's been sitting. He's not there. The child howls again. 'Charlie.' I don't even know whether that's my voice or someone else's. All I know is I can't see my child. 'Charlie!'

As everyone moves away from the chairs, I run towards them, searching desperately for the sight of that little face that will make everything all right. I call his name, over and over, but I can't see him, he's not there.

And then suddenly he is. Standing in front of me, perfectly safe, Daniel close behind him. The child screams again and I turn to see a mum tending to a young boy who's unharmed, just terrified by it all.

I wrap my arms around Charlie. 'Are you OK?' I'm turning his face from side to side, checking it for any cut or scratch, for any sign of injuries.

'Mum, I'm fine,' he reassures me.

'He really is OK, Zoe. Nothing to worry about.' Daniel raises his hand to squeeze my arm, but then spots something behind me and drops it quickly. 'I'll just go and check over there,' he says, a statement that makes no sense at all, but before I can ponder on it, Sam appears.

'Zoe, Charlie.' He pulls us both to him, either possessively or protectively – I'm not sure which. I look around with the eye that's not pressed against his shoulder, then lean away from him, searching unsuccessfully for the gang that seem to have scarpered.

'Did that rocket hit anyone?'

Sam shakes his head. 'Don't think so.'

'It was the Orchard Estate gang, wasn't it?'

Yeah, it was.'

I turn towards the road, ready to inflict some serious pain on any of the lads who might have had the nerve to hang around, but they're long gone – just like our fundraising night.

'Right,' I say, turning back to him. 'I need names. Proper names. They're definitely getting reported for this one.'

'Zoe, you know I can't do that. I'm not going to grass them up.'

I stare at him. 'Are you kidding me?'

'Zoe,' he repeats. 'I'm not a grass.'

We stand there, toe to toe, looking each other square in the eyes.

And after over a year together, it's as though we're really seeing each other for the very first time.

The event might only have lasted a couple of hours, but the rubbish that's been left behind indicates that the good folk of

Westholme managed to get through a fair amount of junk food while they were here.

There's chip wrappers, crisp wrappers, chocolate wrappers and pic 'n' mix bags all over the floor. The lovely volunteers did their best to remove it all, but I had to send them home after I spotted poor Margaret trying to peel a piece of freshly chewed gum off the pavement, which probably counted as the lowest point of the entire evening.

Once I've given my statement to the police, I set to work clearing up the mess, struck by the fact, as I crawl around trying to stuff rubbish from under the chairs into a black bin bag, that I'd do anything for one of Mrs Pople's litter pickers right now.

'What are you doing?'

It's Daniel, naturally, who spots me on my knees.

I look up, a half-empty tray of curry and chips in my hand.

'Cleaning up,' I reply, my voice flat. Sam's taken Charlie back to the house while I stay behind and try and put the square in some sort of order. The only thing that's keeping me going right now is the knowledge that there's a 'celebratory' bottle of wine in the fridge ready for me to neck the minute I get home.

'You don't need to do that,' he says, frowning down on me from his great height. I carry on anyway. '*Please*, don't do that.'

He reaches out and, cupping my elbow in his hand, helps me to my feet.

'Are you OK?'

I shrug. 'Fine.'

He tilts his head to one side. 'Are you sure?'

'I'm fine,' I repeat, then turn away, my head down, as I feel my eyes fill with tears.

Daniel puts his hand on my shoulder and gently turns me back to face him.

'Zoe?'

A sole tear trickles down my cheek as tension and disappointment rush out of my body in one deep sigh.

'It's just…we never even managed the Christmas lights switch-on.'

Daniel manages a smile. 'I'm not convinced that's a bad thing. And I'm sure your night hasn't been ruined by our failure to light the Parade up in flamingo pink.' He looks around at the square, shaking his head, then fixes his gaze back on me.

'This isn't the end of it,' he says firmly. 'They might have spoilt tonight, but that's just a small part of the bigger project. Which is still very much going ahead.'

I fold my arms. 'Are you sure about that? I mean, what's the point? What's the point in doing any of this? In trying to make Westholme nice? Those lads, that gang – they're always going to ruin it. To ruin whatever we do.'

He hesitates for a minute, two lines forming between his eyebrows as he watches me thoughtfully.

'What's going on with you?'

His dark eyes search mine so intently that I have to look away for fear he can actually read my mind through them.

'What do you mean?'

'This attitude. It's defeatist. I didn't have you down as a quitter.'

'I'm not a quitter.' I recognise my tone. It's the one Charlie uses when he's sulking. 'But does anyone really care?' I can feel the tears drowning my eyes, the flash of anger originally sparked by the fireworks triggering the frustration I feel at the way things are versus the way I want them to be. 'Who cares, really?'

'The residents care,' Daniel says, his calmness a marked contrast to my growing frustration. 'The cinema group cares. *I* care.'

'Yeah, right.'

'Zoe,' he says, taking a step closer so that we're just inches apart. 'I care.'

Finally, I'm silenced.

I look back into his dark eyes, his pupils huge as they try and soak up the low light. I heard something once about eyes being a window to the soul, and at that moment, I swear I can see every emotion he's feeling as we stand there, locked in our visual exchange.

A prickly heat starts in the tops of my shoulders, spreading across my back and up to my neck and face, freezing and heating all of my body parts simultaneously. I am rooted to the spot by this powerful, horrifying feeling.

And then a familiar voice crash-lands into our moment.

'Zoe, I wanted to check that you've been given everything you need by the police? They should have provided you with a crime reference number that Daniel will need to have to hand if he or indeed we need to make any insurance claims.'

Turns out Norman does have his uses after all.

Wrenching my eyes away from Daniel's, I turn to him. 'Thanks, Norman.' I'm on autopilot, dazed. 'Yes, they've given us a reference number. I'll be sure to check that it's kept in a safe place.'

I busy myself picking up the last bits of rubbish around me as I start to babble.

'And thank you, Daniel,' I continue, suddenly unable to look at him, the prickly sensation still coursing through my body, relentless in its quest to reach every nerve ending of each of my limbs. 'We'll pick all this up at next week's meeting, but for now I'd better get going.'

And with that, I tie up the rubbish bag, throw it in the nearest bin and all but run to the safety of my home.

Westholme Community Facebook page:

Linda Smith: What a waste of time that pop-up cinema was. They'd better be giving us all refunds.

Paul Gregory: I won't be asking for my money back. I appreciate what the group are trying to do with the cinema. It's not their fault if those Orchard Estate lads go out of their way to f*** it all up.

Tori Hindle: I don't want my money back either. I want to see the cinema re-opened.

Beryl Goodwin: Me too. Don't let a few bad 'uns ruin things for the whole community.

Eva Grant: Thanks so much, guys, for your support. We're all devastated at how the night unfolded, but reading your kind words really helps.

Linda Smith: That's nice. Still be grateful if you could reimburse me though.

Chapter Twenty-Four

While I might have experienced one of the worst evenings I've had in quite some time, when I return home it's clear the events haven't affected Sam or Charlie in anything like the same way.

I hear the din before I've even put the key in the door and I pause for a moment, feeling all topsy-turvy, upside-down, as though my tummy's going through the high spin cycle of an ultra-powerful washing machine.

Daniel said nothing, really. Nothing that you would take to be important, meaningful. But I saw something tonight. Something in his eyes. And it scared and thrilled me in equal measure.

I shake my head, as if to empty it of its thoughts, and slot the key into the lock. My strict instructions for Charlie to go straight to bed have, predictably, been completely ignored. Instead, I find Charlie and Sam engaged in a game of bedroom football that involves Charlie trying to kick the ball into the mini-net on one side of his bedroom while Sam aims to score in the footwell of his desk in the other.

'Hi, Mum,' Charlie chirps breathlessly, as he dribbles the ball around Sam and straight into the goal.

'Erm, bed?' I respond, dousing his victory dance in ice-cold water.

'Sorry,' Sam tries to placate me. 'Charlie was heading in that direction but we got a little…distracted.' He goes to ruffle Charlie's hair, but Charlie ducks quickly enough to avoid him.

Sam catches sight of my expression then, and says, 'Charlie, maybe you should go and brush your teeth.'

'Arrrrgh,' Charlie starts to protest but Sam jerks his head in the direction of the bathroom and he resignedly complies.

'You all right?' Sam puts out his arms and pulls me towards him, but his impromptu game of football has made him sweaty and I push him away.

'Not really.'

'What's up?' His face is puzzled, as though he genuinely can't work out why I don't want to cover my coat with his sweat.

'You're sweaty, that's all.'

'Am I?' He shrugs. 'That's what happens when you play football with a boy who's a quarter of your age.'

I'm still not smiling.

'Come on.' He reaches out for my hand instead. 'It was a good night. Don't let the boys make you think otherwise.'

'The police came,' I reply. 'I told them it was the boys from the Orchard Estate, but I couldn't remember their names so I didn't say it was anyone in particular.'

Sam drops his hand and turns to Charlie's bed, where he busies himself by folding up the hoodie that's been flung there. 'That's probably best.'

'I think *you* should tell the police their names instead,' I press. After all the hard work we put in to make tonight a success, I'm really struggling to let this go.

He breathes in sharply. 'Me?'

'Yes, so they can question them.'

'I can't do that.' He turns to me now. His eyes look bigger than usual, his lips tight. The dimples in his cheeks are nowhere to be seen and instead, there's a new crease between his eyebrows.

'You know I can't do that. Think of the effect it would have on the academy and the lads there.'

I look at him carefully, noting the fear in his eyes, and feel irritated by his weakness. It's been almost twenty years since he last lived on the Orchard Estate, but he's still very much part of it.

Charlie returns smelling faintly of mint and Sam says goodnight and leaves me to tuck him in.

'You OK, Mum?' Charlie snuggles down under his duvet, his not-so-little feet catching me as I perch on the side of the bed.

I sigh. 'I'm OK. Thanks, love.'

His hand sneaks out and squeezes mine.

'Those boys are horrible, aren't they?'

Usually I would stay elevated on the moral high ground, wheeling out my monologue on how some people aren't as lucky as us, don't have a nice home life, how we should always be kind, etc., etc. But tonight, I have nothing.

'They are, Charlie,' I agree.

Charlie throws the duvet back, inviting me inside. I climb into his bed and enjoy the welcome feeling of him snuggling into me.

'Don't worry, Mum,' he soothes, stroking my arm. 'I thought it was brilliant. It wasn't your fault those stupid boys ruined it.'

'Thank you, love.' I kiss the mass of dark hair topping his head, then whisper, 'I love you more than anything. You know that, don't you?'

'I love you more than the entire universe.'

'And I love you more than the entire galaxy.'

He pauses then, thinking about how he can outdo my comparisons to demonstrate his love for me, then eventually settles on one he knows I can't beat.

'I love you more than football.'

'Wow. That's it then, you win.'

He hugs me, content that he's emerged victorious from this particular battle, and I luxuriate in the one perfect moment of my day.

I squeeze him back, remind him to say his prayers, then reluctantly I leave the warmth of his bed, take a deep breath and follow Sam downstairs.

———————

Wine helps, of course. Wine always helps. I've had half a bottle now and the hard edges of the evening that were prodding and poking my insides have softened. The wonderful effect of alcohol has blurred the many thoughts I have whizzing around my head, whisking me off the floor to a little above ground level where I hover, weightlessly, in a slightly warmer world of fuzz.

I'm in the kitchen pouring another glass when Sam wanders in and starts drumming his fingers on the worktop.

'Zoe, I have something to ask you. I had planned to do it tonight, when I thought you'd be on a high, but I wasn't sure what to do when it all went a bit wrong.' He scratches the front of his head. 'I thought about it and decided that I should probably ask you anyway, so here goes…'

He thrusts his arm towards me to reveal a small ring box, clutched tightly between his fingers as though he's in possession of the world's most valuable diamond. I stare at it, wishing I could press pause on this moment so it didn't progress any further.

'We've been together for fourteen months now,' he starts. I can hear his tongue hitting the roof of his dry mouth. He starts fiddling with the clasp, ready to open the box.

'Sam, I—' I try and intervene with something, anything, that will put the conversation onto safer footing.

'Look,' he interrupts, 'I know things have been a bit off between us lately, but I think that's probably because we're not seeing enough of each other. You're always so busy, I'm busy…it can be hard making things work. But I think I know a way to change that.

'My house,' he continues, pulling me towards him with one hand, 'is too big for me. It's a family home, a home that needs a family living in it.' He pauses. 'A home that needs you and Charlie living in it.'

He flicks the box open to reveal a key. A house key.

There it is. The sucker punch that makes me take a sudden gulp for air. And all at once it's as though the walls are closing in, making my space smaller, trapping me.

'I, er, I thought we were fine as we are,' I reply, wriggling out of his grasp.

He winces. 'We *have* been fine as we are. But I had hoped we might be able to turn fine into something more…meaningful?'

I back away from him, trailing my hand along the kitchen worktop in a bid to make my retreat seem much more casual than we both know it is.

'This is meaningful,' I reassure him, pausing in my tracks as I see the hurt in his eyes. 'Sam, this *is* meaningful. This last year has been the best year in a long time. So why not carry on doing what we're doing and make the next year great too?'

He moves towards me and taking both of my hands in his, pulls me towards him again. 'Why not move in and make it even better?' He kisses me long enough to feel me melting beneath him then pulls away and cups my face in his hands.

'Zoe we're good – no, great – together. Moving in with me would be the logical next step.' He smiles encouragingly. 'Come on, let's do this. It will be great, I promise you.'

I stare up at him, into his eyes so full of love and hope. Such a good man. So kind. Great abs. I can't expect him to just date me for ever, can I?

'Or at least,' he adds hopefully, 'say you'll think about it.'

I nod then, or at least I nod as much as I can considering there's two hands still holding my face.

'OK,' I concede, my hand feeling around for the wine glass on the worktop. 'I'll think about it.'

The minute he drops his hands, I neck the glass.

Westholme Community Facebook page:

Nazia Ahuja: Many thanks to the lady who came to my dad's rescue at the supermarket today when he forgot his PIN. He usually pays in cash but didn't have enough and he was quite upset about it. Not only did this fantastic woman reassure my dad and calm him down, she also paid for his shopping too. If the woman concerned reads this, please can you DM me so I can repay the money?
Thank you.

Brenda Harris: Your lovely dad is very welcome. Absolutely no repayment required.

Chapter Twenty-Five

H ome looks different once Sam's gone.

I click the white PVC door shut behind him and feel a stab of sadness in my gut as I consider not living here anymore. It's only small, a two-up, two-down with more DIY jobs on my 'to do' list then I could ever feasibly complete, but it's mine. Well, mine and the mortgage company's.

I've worked really hard on making it a home for Charlie and me, and it's one that has been filled with love, laughter and a million happy memories. A mounting wave of regret threatens to overwhelm me and I slump back against the front door. Why, oh why, did I say I'd think about moving in with Sam? Why didn't I just tell him I was staying here?

I drag my heavy feet up the stairs, my gaze lingering on the photographs hung in a neat pattern on the off-white walls with the grubby fingermarks that I swear I'll clean every time the afternoon sun picks out their rounded edges.

Every single one of them is of Charlie and me. Charlie in my arms as a baby; Charlie and I on our first holiday; Charlie and I on our first trip to see Father Christmas; Charlie and I on his first day at nursery; Charlie and I on his first day at school; Charlie and I when he scored his first-ever goal on his 'debut appearance' with Sam's team. They're all testament to our journey through life together – a life that has been fantastic despite the infrequent appearances by his dad – and I wonder how he'll feel about this change in proceedings.

As much as he likes Sam, I'm not sure it's a change he'll particularly welcome. We've been happy here, just the two of us. It's one of the reasons I had reservations about getting together with Sam in the first place – the fear that it would interfere with Charlie and me; with what we have, with what we *are*.

I catch my breath as I realise that's exactly what's happening.

'Mu-uum.'

Charlie's hollering, probably to indicate that he's ready for the next course of his never-ending breakfast.

'Coming.' I turn around and head back down the stairs to the lounge, where he's lying on the couch in the manner of an eighteenth-century lord, arm outstretched, empty cereal bowl in his hand.

'Don't forget we're going to buy my new boots after football today,' he shouts over the noise of the TV.

I groan. Despite the very sound advice I received from Westholme's Money Man last year, the volatile nature of the *Gazette* means that I'm still constantly broke.

Even though Daniel's paying me an undeniably generous wage, with everything costing a hundred times more than it did before, Christmas just around the corner and too many presents bought during one a.m. shopping sprees accompanied by wine, my redundancy fund is dwindling fast.

But Charlie's football boots probably stopped fitting him six weeks ago and after my last disastrous attempt to stretch them with a long-handled brush ended up with a broken brush and a hole in the heel, I've finally accepted I need to cough up the cash.

'No, Charlie.' I sigh, automatically taking his cereal bowl out of his hand. 'I won't forget.'

We'll just have to eat beans on toast for a few days. Beans are one of your five-a-day, right? And the bread's wholemeal, so it's practically a nutritionist's dream. Even if it does mean a hurricane of wind and a smell that could make Norman's body odour seem like a dream in comparison.

'Sam's asked me to move in with him,' I announce to Emma and Beth the next day as we set the table for our monthly mums and sons – and, now there's Darcy, daughters too – roast.

It takes a split second for Emma and Beth to exchange a look, but it's enough time for me to spot it.

'What?'

Darcy, who, for the past five minutes, has been happily suckling away, suddenly starts screaming, giving Beth a bona fide excuse to duck out of the conversation as she stands up and tries to soothe her daughter.

'Sorry about this,' she apologises over Darcy's screams. She fixes her bra and shuffles into the lounge. 'I'll just walk her round a little bit.'

Once the screaming has subsided, I look at Emma. 'So, what was that about?'

'What do you mean, chick?' She widens her eyes as though she's entirely innocent of any wrongdoing.

'What was that look? Last time I saw it, you were telling me that *The Northern News* wasn't right for me anymore. So, what is it this time? Are you going to tell me now that Sam's not right for me either?'

Emma blinks, surprised. 'What's rattled your cage?'

Turning away from her, I peer through the glass pane into the oven, feigning great concern over how well done the roast potatoes are, then slowly turn back around.

'Sorry, Em,' I say lightly, 'that came out a bit, well—'

'Arsily?'

'Yeah,' I admit, pulling up a chair next to her. I squeeze her arm. 'Ignore me. Time of the month.'

'OK,' she replies, as though it's not really but she'll get over it. 'Congratulations. Not about it being time of the month, obviously – commiserations on that one. I mean the other thing. The moving-in thing.' She pauses. 'And are you going to?'

Beth wanders back in before I can answer, Darcy re-attached to her breast, and sits down very, very slowly.

'What did I miss?' she murmurs, looking from me to Emma.

'I was just asking Zoe if she was going to take Sam up on his offer,' Emma whispers, being careful not to meet Beth's eyes.

'Oh yes.' I'm still not one hundred per cent sure Beth remembers what we're talking about, but then I see a shift in her expression, as though her brain has caught up. 'Great news. How lovely for you. How does Charlie feel about it?'

My reply catches in my throat and I buy myself a few seconds by looking out of the window to check Charlie's still happily involved in his game of football with Emma's boys.

'I haven't told him yet. I'm still thinking about it.'

A wall of silence envelops the room and I start to babble, determined to break it down. 'I mean, Sam's house is obviously bigger than this one and he's said I can decorate it however I want. It's got some lovely nineteen-thirties character features, stained-glass windows, nice panelled doors, it's even got those vertical strips of wood running along the hall.'

'I know the type you mean.' Emma takes up the thread. 'A girl in work had those in hers, but she took them all down in the end and plastered over them. We could never work out why there were there.'

'No, me either,' I admit. 'But they're part of the original house so it feels wrong to rip them out. Besides, panelling's a thing again now, isn't it?'

We all agree it is.

Beth's watching me closely. 'Is there an engagement on the cards then? Marriage?'

I shudder. 'Good grief, no. He's asked me to move in with him, that's all.'

'Why then?' Emma asks. 'Why are you even considering it?'

'Because he asked me.' I shrug.

'Because he asked you,' Emma repeats slowly.

'What's wrong with that?' I can't understand why she's being like this. 'And because he has a lovely house,' I quip, trying to lighten the mood.

'It's not really about the house though, is it?'

'I know that, Emma.'

'But you're seriously thinking about moving in with him?'

I drop my head and sigh. 'I'm not sure. I suppose this is what people do though, isn't it? They take the next step. They progress. They move in together.'

'They don't *have* to move in together,' Beth offers.

'Not if they feel deep down that it's not right,' adds Emma in a tone that's softer than her usual one.

'But if you feel it *is* right, then that's great,' reassures Beth, one eye on Darcy, who, having drained her mum dry, is wriggling as though she's about to start protesting at the quantity of food on offer. 'I'm sure you'll be very happy together. You love him, he loves you. You're right, this is the next natural step.'

I slip up then, by saying nothing at all.

'You do love him, don't you?' asks Emma. I sigh loudly. I don't know why people keep asking me that, but it's getting on my nerves. I'm about to tell her so when Darcy starts screaming again.

'Give her here,' I snap, gently prising her off Beth, putting her over my shoulder and tapping her back. 'She's probably had enough of all the questioning.' I push my feet into my boots so that I can take her out into the garden. 'As have I.'

I venture outside, glad to escape Emma's pessimism. Despite the outward signs, she's obviously still feeling a little battered and bruised after Dave's affair last year. But to be fair to him, it was a one-off, he was desperately sorry and he worked hard to get her back. He's trying. I'm trying. We're all trying. She needs to back off. Because, in the absence of the fairy tale, isn't trying all that any of us can do?

Westholme Community Facebook page

Simon Crossley: Anyone know the name of the scumbags who beat up my nephew last night? They'll be sorry they ever messed with my family.

Rob Horton: I'll DM you.

Chapter Twenty-Six

It's an altogether more subdued bunch of volunteers that gather in the site manager's office for the next cinema meeting.

A forgotten school bag means I'm one of the last to arrive, and as I rush in, Daniel greets me at the meeting room door, demonstrating just how good a burgundy crew-neck jumper can look over a shirt and tie when it's worn by the right person.

'Hello, Zoe.' His voice is as stiff as ever.

'Hello, Daniel.' I'm trying a new look, so I'm in cigarette pants and flats today, which has the dual effect of making me feel very short and Daniel seem so tall I have to tip my head back to look up at him.

'How are you feeling after Friday night?'

I freeze, wondering exactly which part of Friday night he means. I've been unsettled all weekend – not just by the disastrous event itself, but by the exchange that followed – and I've been trying to forget any of it ever happened.

'The fireworks,' he adds helpfully.

'Oh, you know,' I say breezily. 'Onwards and upwards.'

'I was wondering whether you could join me for a quick trip to the cinema after this? There's something I'd like to show you.'

His words unleash a wave of panic inside my chest and I concentrate on my breathing to try and clear it away.

'Oh no, what's happened now?'

'Nothing at all to worry about.' He smiles. 'But we're probably due a site visit.'

I relax a little. 'No problem. I have to be back at the office for an interview this afternoon, but other than that I'm free today.'

He looks excited, like Charlie used to when he wanted to show me a drawing he was particularly proud of.

'Great. Let's walk over after that then.'

'Admittedly, Friday night didn't go entirely according to plan,' Daniel says, fiddling with the arm of his glasses as he addresses the meeting room. 'But the good news is that, even taking into account those people who demanded refunds, we still managed to raise over £2,000. Lynne, how much is the crowdfunding appeal up to now?'

Lynne looks down at her notepad. '£15,732.'

A series of appreciative noises goes up around the room.

'Candice also has some news on the fundraising front,' he adds. 'Candice, would you like to explain?'

Everyone turns to Candice, who's looking particularly stylish today with her long hair parted in the middle and tied back in a low ponytail.

'Daniel and I have been discussing the project with our contacts, and I'm pleased to say that we've managed to raise some corporate sponsorship – a lot of corporate sponsorship actually.'

She glances at Daniel and he nods at her to continue.

'The amount raised has just surpassed £25,000.'

There's one loud, collective gasp, before everyone turns to the person next to them, exclaiming that it can't possibly be true and that there's no way anyone could raise that sort of money in such a short space of time, but then conceding that when that person happens to be Daniel Lewis maybe it could be possible, which means that maybe it might be true after all.

I look from Candice to Daniel.

'Are you serious? How on earth did you manage that?'

Even Daniel, the master when it comes to controlling his emotions, is clearly delighted at the achievement. His face has crinkled into a huge grin, with laughter creases peeking through his dark stubble. It's an unusual look for him, and not an unattractive one.

'Let's just say I called in a few favours.'

I glance at Emma, who's already watching me in a way that makes me feel as though I'm being assessed. I raise my eyebrows as if to ask her what's wrong, but she shakes her head and looks away.

Then a special aroma wafts past my nose and a chunky upper-arm pushes against my shoulder as Norman leans forward in his seat to press Daniel on the specifics.

'We're short on another ten thousand or so then?'

'We are. But my team can do some of the labouring, which should save some money and I'm confident that between the ongoing fundraising activity of this group and Lewis & Co. we'll be able to make up the shortfall.'

Around the table, we all exchange looks and more murmurs. Eventually I decide to speak for us all.

'Thank you, Daniel,' I say. 'That is incredibly generous of you.'

He takes off his glasses and then puts them back on again.

'Not at all,' he protests, shuffling his agenda papers. 'Happy to help. Right, moving on. First point – staffing. I know we discussed a volunteer staffing structure up until the point where we can afford to employ a full-time general manager and I believe Margaret has managed to fill the positions within that now, haven't you, Margaret?'

Margaret wraps her brown cardigan across her large bosom and beams.

'We have a little band of merry men and women who are all very excited about the whole thing, and we're lining up dates for training. I've explained we're planning on opening just before Christmas and everyone's working within that timeframe.'

'Excellent.' Daniel consults the agenda and his cheery expression drops. 'Cinema seating.'

'All sorted,' I assert. 'I've spoken to both Starr and Norman about the seating, and between us we've agreed that rows of red velour seating with cerise trim is exactly the way to go.'

That wasn't exactly what happened, but I don't think it would benefit anyone to recount word-for-word the part of the conversation where I told both of them they'd better agree to my proposals or they'd be jointly responsible for the cinema not re-opening on time.

'So, we're all agreed that's the way to go?' Everyone holds their breath.

'Agreed,' says Starr reluctantly.

'Agreed.' Norman is slightly more enthusiastic, having had more of his way than Starr did hers.

Then there's a collective sigh of relief as Daniel draws a final and defiant line through that point on the agenda.

After drifting in and out of meeting points, I'm relieved to eventually hear that we're drawing to a close. I'm finding it difficult to concentrate today, my head pulling me in all directions over the decision I have to make regarding Sam's offer. Sitting in a meeting room pretending otherwise requires a little more acting than I'm up to right now.

'Before we finish,' Daniel almost concludes, catching my attention, 'There's something I wanted to discuss that's not on the agenda.'

We all look up, our interest sparked by this non-agenda point.

'I very much appreciate the hard work that everyone's put into this project, and Candice suggested that it might be a nice idea to have a sort of team gathering, in order to thank everyone for their efforts.

'With that in mind, I – well, Candice,' he interrupts himself, casting her an apologetic glance, 'has arranged a Christmas night out for us all.' Whispers of excitement start up around the table. 'Candice, would you like to elaborate?'

Candice smiles at the room. 'Cranthorpe Manor is staging a Hollywood-themed evening a couple of weeks before Christmas. As it's only a week before the scheduled Christmas opening, I thought it might be a good opportunity for us all to enjoy an outing together at an event that has an admittedly tenuous link to our cinema project.'

'What a splendid idea,' Starr exclaims. She looks around the room then settles on Colin. 'Colin, would you be a dear and pop round to mine after this to fetch my ballgowns out of the loft?'

Colin exchanges a glance with Lynne, then clears his throat. 'Of course, Starr.'

'You'll all need to take your ballgowns out of the loft actually,' adds Candice. 'It's a black-tie event.'

My dress! My beautiful red dress that I bought from Vintage Vibes! I finally have a place to wear it!

My heart soars. At least I won't have to go to *this* do dressed as an octopus.

Emma makes her way over to me at the end of the meeting. 'Fancy a coffee?' she asks, as we wrap up against the bitter cold that's crept in over the past few days.

'I…er… I can't today. Daniel's asked me to go and look at something at the cinema with him.'

'Ri-ight,' she responds, one eyebrow raised. 'I'll catch you later then?'

'Catch you later,' I reply casually as Daniel appears at my side. He's buttoning up his coat, a dark wool, single-breasted tailored affair that looks, and probably is, incredibly expensive. The extra layer bulks him up even more, adding extra width to his tall frame.

'Ready?' He wraps a grey scarf around his neck.

I swallow and nod.

'Let's go.'

Westholme Community Facebook page:

Jenny Holland: My eight-year-old daughter has clearly been watching too much American TV as she's informed me she wants to do a 'yard sale' this weekend to raise money for the new cinema. We live in a close with only three other houses in it, and I'm a bit worried no one will come. If anyone thinks they might be free to boost the numbers, just drop me a line and I'll DM you our address.

Beryl Goodwin: I'd love to attend.

Paul Gregory: My wife says she'll come along.

Tori Hindle: I'll pop by too. I'll even bring some Dr Pepper and a corn dog '-)

Chapter Twenty-Seven

I t might be freezing but the blue sky is free from clouds and the sun's creating shadows out of everything that dares to stand in its way. It's one of those bright, sunny winter days that bring with them a reminder that it won't always be cold and grey, and we comment on its beauty a number of times as we walk along the road to the cinema, our breath making hot clouds in the air as we chat away.

'I hope it wasn't inconvenient, me dropping this on you today,' Daniel says, once we've squeezed all the mileage we can out of the weather.

I'm having to do a little run every few seconds so that my short legs can catch up with his long ones, and the fact that I haven't been for a jog since around 2002 means I'm starting to feel breathless.

'I'll be in Palma for the next few days,' he continues, 'and after the events of the weekend, I thought it was probably best that you saw what I'm about to show you sooner rather than later.'

'Jetting off to Majorca, hey?' I manage to wheeze out, a pang of envy – or possibly the onslaught of a heart attack – hitting me somewhere in the chest. 'For work, is it?'

He shakes his head. 'No – there's a property out there I'm thinking of buying. I wanted to fly out and take a look at it. Next week I'll be in Italy looking at a potential development site. That one's for work.'

I trot the next few steps and he looks down, smiles and slows his pace.

'Wow.' I sigh, taking a few moments to inhale some extra air. 'I remember a time when trips abroad were all part of my working week.'

'Was that when you worked for the nationals?'

I glance up at his profile and notice a little cut on his clean-shaven jaw. 'How do you know about that?'

He stares off towards the road, devoting a huge amount of attention to a Vauxhall Cavalier that's making its way past and says airily, 'I can't really remember. I think someone must have mentioned it to me.'

We walk in silence for a few seconds, then Daniel picks up the topic again.

'Do you miss it? I imagine that sort of a job would be quite exciting, mingling with celebrities, chasing after stories, seeing your name on the front page of newspapers in the shops.'

He's making some assumptions here about what my life as a national journalist was like. But they're actually all correct. And the truth is, I still miss it so much it hurts. Not that I'd tell him that, of course.

'It was certainly an experience,' I reply instead. 'And I worked really, really hard to get there. But then I fell pregnant with Charlie and…things changed.'

Neither of us says anything for a moment, but this time the silence isn't an awkward one. In the half a mile or so that we've walked, a shift has taken place in the atmosphere. This feels easier;

more intimate. Which is why Daniel probably feels empowered to say what comes next.

'You never mention Charlie's dad.'

It's unfamiliar territory this, but I brazen it out. 'He's not worth mentioning. We don't speak much anymore since he failed to turn up for Charlie's first ever football match, though there has to be some contact unfortunately. I still have to accept financial help from him from time to time – for Charlie of course. But our conversations tend to be functional and Charlie hasn't mentioned him in a while.'

'You loved him once though?'

I bite my lip. Not even Sam has ventured this far down the path of questioning when it comes to Ryan. I think he prefers to pretend he doesn't exist and that Charlie was the product of an immaculate conception. I'm considering how to respond when Daniel says, 'I'm sorry. That's none of my business.'

'It's fine.' I force a smile. 'I did love him once, yes. I was head over heels, in fact. But when I fell pregnant, he made it clear that children were not in his life plan; that I had to choose between him and the baby. I made my choice. And I've never regretted it.'

'It's *him* who should be regretting it,' Daniel mutters darkly. Then he takes a deep breath, as if checking himself. 'So how *is* Westholme's resident football genius doing?'

He's referring, I know, to the time I drove him home and Charlie quizzed him on his favourite topic for the entirety of the journey.

I groan. 'Growing up way too fast. I think his hormones might be kicking in. Last night he told me he hated the world, loved everybody, wanted me to sit next to him, wanted me to leave him alone, insisted I play chess with him then told me it was for losers, all in the space of about a minute. Plus, football now seems to be making way for his Xbox, YouTube and TikTok. Whereas he used to talk non-stop about his favourite player, now it's all about someone called Logan Paul.'

'Logan who?' Daniel scrunches up his nose.

'I haven't got a clue either. But he's huge on YouTube apparently.'

Daniel chuckles, his laughter deep and throaty. 'I don't know how you keep up – that sounds exhausting.'

'It is.' I sigh. 'I also think it's a sign that my baby books are just not going to cut it anymore and that I'm pretty close to having to swap them for "what's happening to my body" books instead. I just hope I can explain it all in a way that doesn't scare him to death.'

'From what I've seen, you're an amazing mum. I'm sure you'll find a way.'

'I don't think he'd necessarily agree with that statement,' I reply, batting away the compliment. 'Not from Monday to Friday when I'm in sergeant major mode, anyway.'

'Take it from someone who knows,' Daniel says quietly, 'He would.'

I'm lost for words, so I watch our feet for a moment, now walking in tandem, a momentary pause in traffic allowing the birdsong and the sound of our footsteps on the pavement to provide a new soundtrack. We're silent, each lost in our own thoughts, until mine lead me to the question of Daniel's parents.

'Where do your mum and dad live now? Are they in Presthill, like you?'

He stuffs his hands in his coat pockets. 'My dad is. My mum lives in London. With her second husband.'

'Oh, right,' I reply awkwardly, detecting a sour note in his voice.

'Yeah, she's been there since I was about twelve,' he continues. 'She wasn't really the shirt-ironing, tea-cooking kind of mum.

Motherhood wasn't for her, but unfortunately, she didn't realise it until she'd had both my brother and me. By then it was too late.'

This is unusual for us, talking like this, but I'm not ready for it to stop.

'Is that why you don't like Christmas?'

He inhales deeply, then lets it out slowly as though he's using his own breath to buy himself some time.

'My Christmases probably weren't the same as yours.' He states it as fact, with not a hint of self-pity.

'What, you mean no one ever bought you naked flashing Santa jumpers?' I joke, then realise we've gone a little deeper than jokey.

He kicks a stone out of his way without breaking his stride.

'Christmas for my mum was like a two-week party. She spent half of it hammered, loving the festive period, my dad, my brother and me and the world, and the other half of it hungover, lashing out at everyone and everything. Possibly a bit like how Charlie is now.'

I already knew – thanks to the combination of a fascinating interview in *The North West Business News* and stuff that Sam had told me – that Daniel's brother was drawn into the Orchard Estate's drugs scene as a teenager and was now in jail. But this – the fact that his mum had issues too – is completely new to me.

'We were living on the estate back then,' he continues, 'and I used to see all our neighbours' houses decorated like a grotto and kids boasting about their new toys. We didn't even have a tree. Dad always bought a couple of presents for us, but it was a token gesture. Santa never visited our house.'

There's a bitterness to his voice as he says that last bit and I slow my footsteps, put my hand on Daniel's arm to bring him to a halt, and turn to face him. This is *not* a conversation that should be had on the move.

'Daniel, that's awful.'

He looks at his feet. 'Ironically, it got better after she left. Ran off to London with one of the regional managers from Kwik Save. Then my dad's business took off and we moved to Presthill. He did his best; presents, decorations, a tree, but I still hated it. Every year felt like a reminder of the ones that had gone before.' He raises his eyes to meet mine. 'They still do.'

I stare up at him. 'That's heartbreaking.' My hand is still on his arm and I squeeze it gently.

He shrugs. 'It's life.'

We stand there for a moment, Daniel looking down, me looking up, silent, contemplating what's gone before.

Then, his mobile goes off and he digs his hand into his pocket to retrieve the handset, letting my hand fall away from his arm.

By the time he's finished the call, businessman Daniel has returned and it's clear that our previous conversation is over.

'I'm intrigued as to what you're about to show me,' I enthuse as we start walking towards the cinema, a once great building standing proud and detached from the wasteland rotting away on either side. I'm deliberately keeping my voice light and playful and hoping he doesn't spot the shakiness in it.

'Don't get too excited,' he replies, the familiar detachment back in his voice. 'It's really nothing special.'

Westholme Community Facebook page:

Lisa Sheldon: Can anyone recommend a spark to come and fix a light fitting?

Elise Harvey: Try Luke Whiston. Haven't got a clue whether he's any good or not, but it's worth paying the call-out fee to watch him work for a couple of hours ;-)

Chapter Twenty-Eight

I t's the skip I see first. The bright-yellow skip with 'Frank's Skip Hire' emblazoned on the side. Filled with all sorts of wood, general rubbish and old plastic toilets.

'Daniel?' I say questioningly as we draw closer, trying to keep up with his ability to pull our relationship from professional to intimate then back again faster than I can say "hot and cold".

He puts his index finger to his lips. 'Don't say anything yet. Wait until you've seen inside.'

The entrance is a hive of activity, with workmen in hard hats coming and going, barking instructions at each other along the way. They're already working at speed, but as they spot Daniel, I notice everything suddenly seems to move even faster.

'All right, boss,' an older bloke with a bulging tummy and thinning hair greets him.

'Morning, John.' Daniel nods. 'How's it all looking in there?'

'Coming along nicely. We'll have it back to its best in no time.'

I freeze. 'What's going on? We haven't raised all the money yet.'

'But we're getting there. And we don't invoice until we've completed the job. No point waiting around when we could be cracking on with it. Some of the students at a college I have links with have agreed to help us out. Plus, the lads are between jobs at the moment so it made sense for them to make a start.'

He opens one of the entrance doors, pops his head around it, then beckons me inside. I hesitate, nervous of what I could be walking in to. 'Daniel Lewis, what have you been up to?'

'You won't know unless you come inside and have a look. Come on in – I think you'll like it.'

Wow. Just wow.

'Obviously, there's still a long way to go, but the lads have been working flat out over the weekend and I think you'll agree they've made a lot of headway in a short space of time.'

There's so much to take in that I can't squeeze any words out.

In the foyer, rotting skirting boards are being replaced by new ones, and two men positioned precariously up ladders are very carefully taking down the ornate chandelier that hangs in the centre. The wooden framework of the original ticket office and tuck shop is being rubbed down and cleaned, as are the beautiful ornate wrought-iron balustrades on either side of the room that lead up to the balcony above. It's as though *DIY SOS* has descended on the cinema and taken immediate action.

'Zoe, this is Jim Steiner,' he introduces, winking at the familiar, weather-beaten face of the man standing in front of me. 'Although I think the two of you may have met before.'

My cheeks colour as I remember the reconnaissance exercise I went on last year, back in the days when I was determined to prove that Daniel was nothing more than a big bad wolf. His public relations team had sent me a press release about his company winning an award for giving back to the community and I'd met Jim when I visited the building skills academy he had reportedly helped, searching for any signs of wrongdoing.

I was pretty sure at the time that Jim suspected I was trying to dig up some dirt on Daniel. So I can't help but feel a little ashamed now that it's me who's benefiting from his support.

'Hi, Jim,' I greet him sheepishly.

'Good to say you again, love,' he replies, dipping his head to reveal the bald circle that crowns his grey hair.

'I explained to Jim what we were trying to do here,' Daniel explains, 'and he generously offered us the services of his students. They've been working all weekend to help us.'

'Ah, it's nothing, Dan,' Jim says dismissively. 'It'll be good to see this place back on its feet again. Why don't you have a look in the main auditorium and see what's going on in there?'

With Daniel leading the way, we head through the double doors and into the main cinema and it's all I can do not to gasp out loud as the full picture comes into view.

The rubbish has been cleared, the wood at the front of the stage is being sanded, the ripped curtain has been taken down and an elderly gentleman is stripping the old red velvet and foam from a row of seats.

Above us, workmen are varnishing the wooden railings of the balcony, the front of which is covered in a slick of fresh off-white paint. It's a work in progress, but all this activity has already turned a stale old shell into a living, breathing thing. In fact, so much change has taken place that I'm struggling to take it all in.

'Daniel…' I'm breathless with excitement. 'How…? When?'

He clears his throat. 'After the other night, it felt as though our efforts needed an extra boost, so I reallocated some of my team and asked Jim for his assistance. That's all.'

He wanders off then to examine the work, every touch of his hand on the railings, the walls, the rows of seating a testament to the emotional investment he has in this. I feel my heart swell. Westholme, a place that only a year ago he was ready to bulldoze the heart right out of, is working its magic. This rough-around-the-edges suburban town is slowly but surely charming the life out of him. And the attention to detail he's bestowing on this grand old dame only goes to emphasise the fact.

I watch him as he questions the workmen, pointing out improvements he wants them to make, his serious expression breaking into a smile now and again as their cheery and cheeky responses tickle his sense of humour.

He is a powerhouse. A force to be reckoned with. When Daniel Lewis decides something needs doing, it gets done. It's an impressive quality.

He looks up and catches me watching him and, embarrassed, I pretend to examine the old paper on the wall. Moments later, when I think it's safe, I glance back at him, but he's still looking and this time when he catches my eye, neither of us look away.

Daniel smiles first, a gentle, tentative smile as though, despite his ability to make everyone stand to attention just by entering the room, he's slightly unsure of himself. Slowly, I allow myself to smile too, an acknowledgement of what, together, we're starting to achieve.

I'm suddenly aware of the rhythm of my heart pounding in my chest and a wave of heat permeating my nerve endings, from my temples to my toes.

Then Jim calls him over to check on something. The moment he breaks eye contact, it's as though an invisible force has released me, leaving me reeling from its intoxicating power – and feeling as though I'm on the edge of a precipice that I really shouldn't be anywhere near.

Westholme Community Facebook page:

Frank's Skip Hire: Please can I ask again that people stop dumping their crap in our skips outside the old cinema. They're for our paying customers to use, not for every Tom, Dick and Harry to fly-tip in. Much obliged.

Chapter Twenty-Nine

After an unproductive morning that's been largely spent wandering in between Vintage Vibes, The Lower Story, Cath's Caff and the office, I'm driving to Charlie's school, where I've arranged to speak to a six-year-old on his lunch hour for a piece I'm writing for *The Good News Gazette*.

The headteacher, Mrs Pople, has been in touch to tell me that this one boy has single-handedly started a movement to ensure that the entire world receives a Christmas card this Christmas, and while I haven't yet verified the accuracy of this statement, it'll be a damn good story if it's true.

I pull up at the school. In the distance, at the far side of the field, a group of boys and girls that I recognise from Charlie's class are running around kicking a ball, some with a greater degree of success than others. I crane my head to try and spot Charlie. I see him all the time at home, obviously, but there's something about watching him in a different setting that makes my heart ache and soar, all at the same time.

Mrs Pople has arranged an indoor sleepover for Charlie's year in the school hall to help raise money for the cinema renovations this weekend, and it's preying on my mind. I'm excited for him, but my heart does a little somersault every time I think of him sleeping anywhere but in a warm bed, under the supervision of a few teachers who may or may not be knocking back shots on the side.

I shudder. I'm giving this way too much thought. I need to think about something else. Where's my phone? That always distracts me. I grab it out of my bag and check the screen.

Ooh, there's a new email from Nikki Long, the aesthetics woman Daniel put me in touch with who had been so impressed with the *Gazette* that she had all but signed on the dotted line to advertise with us.

Opening it up, I expect to see confirmation that she's put her signature to the form I sent her setting out our advertising agreement.

But instead, there's a kindly worded message explaining that she's reconsidering her advertising spend and advising us to put the paperwork on hold for the time being.

And by "the time being", I'm pretty sure she means "for good".

William Bradshaw is picking his nose, examining whatever he's retrieved on his finger, and then, according to his findings, either eating them or wiping them on his trousers. It's pretty gross, but the Head's busy with an older boy and I'm not about to rain on William's parade, so I simply watch him, possibly as fascinated as he is about what's inside.

In the background I can hear Mrs Pople trying to bring to an end the conversation with the other pupil, issuing assurances through the door that's slowly but forcibly closing behind him.

Eventually it clicks shut and I see her shoulders rise and fall as she takes a deep breath and turns to me.

'Sorry about that, Mrs Taylor.' She brushes her hand across her forehead. 'Lucas is… How can I put it… A very *diligent* head boy. Very concerned with keeping me informed of the activities of some of his *less diligent* classmates.' She smiles again, but I'm sure I spot her roll her eyes first and I wonder how she keeps her cool dealing with a bunch of tell-tales, troublemakers and nose-pickers.

'Ahem, it's Ms,' I say, in a tone designed to match her own, 'but yes, I understand *entirely*.' I decide to move on. 'Thank you for letting me come here to interview William today. I know his mum was finding it difficult to pin down a good time to chat at their home so she said it might be a good idea to meet here in her lunch hour.'

'Ah yes, poor Mrs Bradshaw. She works so hard, your mum, doesn't she, William?' William carries on picking his nose in a manner that conveys he neither knows nor cares about how hard his mum works. Then, suddenly conscious he's being watched, he buries his finger and goodness knows what at the end of it between his thigh and the dark fabric of the chair.

'Mrs Bradshaw's a care assistant in a care home, you see,' Mrs Pople continues. 'She's just called to say she'll be ten minutes late, but that it's fine for us to make a start without her.'

She turns to William. 'In fact, it was her job that inspired William to start his Christmas card campaign, wasn't it, William?'

William nods, his eyelashes blinking against his silky blonde fringe.

'Would you like to tell Mrs Taylor about your mum's job?'

I choose not to correct her this time and let William talk instead.

Except he doesn't. He just nods again.

There's an awkward silence while we wait for him to speak and then I lean towards him and say, 'William, do you know

Charlie Taylor? He's a few years older than you but you might have seen him on the playground.'

He thinks for a few agonising seconds and then nods.

'Well, I'm his mum, and my job is to write news stories for my newspaper.'

He stares at me blankly but I continue undeterred.

'So, my job is to meet people like you and ask them all about the interesting things they're doing. Your mum has a job too – can you remember what she does?'

He's still nodding.

'What does she do then?'

He starts to poke his finger up his nose again, then, thinking better of it, lets it drop to his lap and says, 'She looks after old people.'

'There you go,' I say with a measure of relief. 'And Mrs Pople says it's your mum's job that made you think about getting people to write Christmas cards to the people she looks after. How did you come up with the idea?'

He looks at Mrs Pople for reassurance then turns his startled blue eyes back to me. 'Because Mummy says that a lot of people she looks after don't get any cards at all. Off anyone,' he clarifies.

I make a sad face to convey my empathy. 'That's a shame, isn't it?'

He nods and I try again.

'So, what did you decide to do?'

'I wrote Christmas cards for all of them in my very best handwriting,' he declares proudly. 'Then Mummy said there were lots of other old people in Westholme, but I didn't know their names or where they lived so I couldn't write them cards.'

'And what did your mummy say you should do?' Mrs Pople prompts.

'I wondered whether anyone else could help us, and Mummy

said we should ask our friends if they would write Christmas cards too. Then our friends asked their friends and now EVERYONE in the world is writing Christmas cards.'

Now it's my turn to nod as I carry on taking notes, because who am I to say that six-year-old William Bradshaw hasn't created a worldwide campaign to make sure no one's lonely this Christmas.

A knock on the door interrupts our stilted conversation and the school secretary shows Mrs Bradshaw, who visually is simply an older version of William, into the room.

She manages to take two steps into the room before William shouts, 'Mummyyyyyy!!!' and she crouches down to greet him as he flings himself into her arms. As they squeeze each other tight, clearly over the moon to be reunited despite having only been apart for a few hours, I feel a sudden pang at the thought that the time when Charlie might have done that has long since passed. These days, he won't even be seen holding my hand. It's a natural progression, I know, but it's a painful one.

'Sorry I'm late,' she says, raking a hand through the top part of her ponytail. 'One of the residents kicked off when she found out it was soup and a sandwich for lunch.'

I make a sympathetic smile. 'Soup and a sandwich not her favourite then?'

She rolls her eyes. 'It was yesterday. Today the lady says she never touches the stuff.' She shrugs then. 'Can't win 'em all.'

I jot down some notes as she gives me more details about where she works and it turns out it's a place I've visited before: the dementia care home which offers a 'Memory Lane' for their residents; a fantastic place with a replica Post Office, pub, café and corner shop, just like in the old days.

'Christmas can be such a difficult time for older people,' she explains. 'Some of our residents don't have children, and their husband or wife has died, so they're completely on their own. Imagine being so disconnected to the world that you're on absolutely no one's Christmas card list.' We all fall silent as we consider how lonely that would feel.

'William, stop that.' We're brought rudely back to the present by Mrs Bradshaw issuing a stern reminder to her son to stop picking his nose and he reluctantly retracts his finger from his nostril.

'Sorry,' she apologises, shaking her head. 'He never has his finger out of his nose lately.'

I smile. 'There's worse places to put it, I suppose.'

She grimaces. 'He puts it in those places too.'

'Shall we continue?' Mrs Pople says briskly, clearly keen to move on from the 'finger in inappropriate places' chat.

I stifle a giggle and instead cough out, 'Absolutely.'

'So, Mrs Bradshaw, William tells us he wrote Christmas cards for all the residents *in his very best handwriting*,' I offer, 'and you said on your email that that small act of kindness inspired other people to start writing cards for people that they knew of who were on their own, or other care home residents. How did that come about?'

She looks at William with warmth and pride in her eyes. 'William was worried about all the other people who wouldn't receive Christmas cards, and my sister was there at the time and said that she and her two children would write cards too. Then our neighbours heard about it and said they'd join us. Slowly but surely, more and more people heard about what we were doing and said they wanted to join in.

'We now have about forty people who are actively writing Christmas cards for those on their own, which translates into hundreds of people receiving cards who might have otherwise been forgotten about this Christmas.'

I jot down her words in shorthand, a skill I learnt as a trainee that fortunately I've never lost, and I'm struck by how simple yet how effective the campaign is.

'Once we'd sent cards to everyone we could think of in Westholme, we moved on to Presthill and Lawton,' continues. 'It's so sad how many people are forgotten about – in some cases even by their own family – at Christmas. But this year everyone's getting cards. Some people are even writing back to the people that have sent them cards to thank them. Friendships are being formed that never would have happened.' She smiles then. 'It's so lovely when a plan comes together.'

'Is there still a need for people to be involved? I'm sure many of our readers would want to take part – they seem to be a good-hearted bunch.'

'The more the merrier,' Mrs Bradshaw agrees. 'There's a whole world of lonely people out there. Let's see how many new friendships can be forged by Christmas.'

Westholme Community Facebook page:

Caroline Freeman: I run Westholme's foodbank and a lot of our customers have been telling us how worried they are about the school party and Christmas jumper days that are coming up and the fact that they can't afford to buy outfits for them. If anyone has old Christmas jumpers or occasion wear that their children have grown out of, please can you drop them off at the foodbank? We'll be sure to find a home for them so they can enjoy a second life.

Terry Taylor: There's a lad in the factory I work in that can get Christmas jumpers on the cheap. They might be a bit rude, and some of the batteries are a bit faulty, but if your kids want something edgy then these would be great. DM me for more details.

Chapter Thirty

There's just two weeks to go before the grand cinema opening, and while our group meetings are helpful, sometimes we have to sit through a fair bit of Norman- and Starr-related waffle before it feels that anything much is achieved.

As a result, we're now running a teensy bit behind schedule, which is why Daniel's suggested that I "pop over" so that we can complete some of the outstanding tasks on our never-ending to-do list.

It's not the first time I've been to Daniel's, of course. I inadvertently ended up at his house when I gave him a lift home last year and Charlie decided he had an urgent need to empty his bladder the minute we pulled up outside.

But there's no Charlie with me this afternoon, as he's at the dreaded school hall sleepover. It would have been a good opportunity to spend some time with Sam, but when I mentioned it, he said he needed to catch up on some work and, confusingly, I felt relieved.

So, I'm driving to Daniel's in the twilight, providing backing vocals to Slade's 'I Wish It Could be Christmas Every Day' and nosy-ing at the various different displays people have created with their Christmas lights, when the music pauses as a call comes through. I glance at the dashboard screen. It's Amanda. Strange.

'Hey, sweetie, how are you?' Her voice fills the car's speakers and I marvel at how strong and confident she always manages to sound.

'Good, thanks, Amanda, how's things with you?'

'Great. Little problem. The editor I had to appoint didn't work out. He was crap. So we're looking for someone else. I don't want to go through the whole search thing again when you're the perfect person for the job. Please will you reconsider?'

A jolt of excitement washes over me, a bit like that feeling of anticipation you get on Christmas Eve, before it fades when I remember that this is an offer I can't possibly accept.

'Amanda, you know I'd love to, but I just can't.'

'Hmm, you said that. But is it can't or won't? I mean, really, sweetie, what's actually stopping you? We have schools in London, you know. We have childcare too. And happy children. And they don't *all* turn out to be serial killers. Plus, you'd make a packet.'

It's that last bit that stops me in my tracks. Imagine being able to go to the supermarket without having made a meal plan first. Or being able to turn the heating on impromptu without wondering if that one unscheduled click would be the difference between financial solvency or bankruptcy.

'Honestly, Amanda, I just don't know. I want to stay here, but I would *love* that job. Is there any way I could do it from here?' I ask hopefully. 'Maybe I could juggle it with the *Gazette*.'

She snorts. 'Sweetie, this is *not* the sort of job you could juggle with anything. Except Charlie, of course,' she adds quickly. 'I mean,' she continues, 'there's people down here who could do the job with their eyes closed, but they're a bit...argumentative, forceful. I want *you*.'

I say nothing. But I do it forcefully.

'Listen, think about it. We've got a couple of weeks' grace on this. But don't take too long to tell me that the answer's yes.'

'OK,' I agree, even though I know the chances of me saying yes are practically nil. I've done the London thing. Those days are over. I think.

I pull up outside the gates of Daniel's house, roll down the window and tap on the button beneath the slate plaque that confirms I'm at Harper Lodge, bracing myself against the rain that's started up and is now spattering my face.

'Come on in,' a familiar voice filters through the intercom, and the gates slowly shift aside, allowing me temporary access into this beautiful world.

Off-white gravel crunches beneath the tyres as I drive slowly towards the house, and through the swishing of my windscreen wipers, fractured images come into view.

The whole setting is even more beautiful than I remember it to be. The unmanicured grounds that surrounded the property when I was here last year have been replaced by lush green gardens either side of the approach. Where once there were weeds, there are now dozens of hydrangea bushes, flowerheads forming somewhere within the branches, waiting for the seasons to change so they can once more reveal their beauty.

But it's the house that's the real show-stopper, and the fact that this is the second time I've seen it detracts in no way from its 'wow' factor.

The red brick contrasts sharply with the green of the grass that surrounds it, and the two rows of windows that stretch across the width of the building. There are more rooms in the attic space above, with small windows jutting out from the grey-tiled roof.

Daniel's already at the door, leaning against one of the two Tuscan columns that flank the entrance, just far enough back to avoid the sheet of rain that's now hammering against the roof of the car. His hands are in the pockets of his jeans, a black half-zip, funnel-neck jumper revealing a hint of the black T-shirt that lies beneath. Something lurches in the pit of my stomach and I try and ignore the sensation as I pull up in front of the house, my new-to-me but old-to-everyone-else Nissan Note incongruous with the perfection of it all.

I grab my bag from the passenger seat, the cold, wet air biting my face as I fling open my car door and dash towards the house and out of the rain.

Daniel laughs as I reach him, my hair, trainers and sports leggings dampened by the large drops that pelted me as I made the three-second journey from car to porch.

'Sorry, my umbrella's at the office, or I would have come out and rescued you,' he greets me as I shake the water off my hair and run my fingers underneath each eye to catch any smudged mascara.

'Good thing I came dressed for a run,' I joke, shrugging off my padded coat.

He turns to walk ahead of me into the house, then looks back when I don't immediately follow him.

'What are you doing?'

I look up.

'Taking my trainers off.'

He wrinkles his nose. 'Why?'

I pull the second trainer off my foot. 'So I don't mess up your floor.'

The look he gives me takes me by surprise. It's filled with an affection I didn't know Daniel even possessed. He chuckles. 'You're good. Leave them on.'

I leave them off. There's no way I'm being held responsible for sullying this Farrow & Ball interior by bringing the outdoors in.

The place is even more stunning than I remember. Huge sash windows sit either side of the door, with a grey velvet chaise longue stretching luxuriously beneath the one to the right.

The parquet floor feels smooth and warm beneath my feet and I pad across the huge square hallway, my heart weeping with longing for the gorgeous oak banister that runs from the far end of the hallway all the way up the staircase then continues around the U-shaped galleried landing beyond. A gigantic crystal light installation hangs from the ornate double-height ceiling while modern art pops from the pale grey wall. There is, of course, no Christmas tree.

Pervading the entire scene is a musky, spicy scent with hints of orange, and I'm surprised when I immediately recognise it as being his. I hadn't realised before that he had his own aroma, yet this house definitely smells like Daniel. I dread to think what my house must smell like. Boy, definitely boy. And catfood.

The kitchen lies on the other side of the hallway, and I follow Daniel into it.

Running a good way across the back of the house, latticed windows and French doors framing the trees, lawn and views across the valley down to the Mersey beyond, it looks even more beautiful on second viewing.

'Coffee?' Daniel offers, and I notice the full cafetière on the white marble island and nod. He pours it into two tall glass cups and after a few minutes of small talk moves us over to the black dining table with the grey velvet seats where we spend the next couple of hours hammering out the finer details of the plans.

It's the first time I've worked on my own with Daniel, and, by the end of it, I can see why he's so successful. He spots everything – improvements that could be made, potential pitfalls – and he has a lawyer-like grasp of the relevant legalities.

He's thorough, but in a supportive way, so I feel like he's trying to make everything better rather than looking to find fault. I see now why everyone spoke so highly of him when I went to visit the college he won a community award for last year. He seems like a brilliant employer. One that you actually want to work for, rather than moan about.

I lean back in my seat, both exhilarated and exhausted, and stifle a yawn.

'Sorry,' I say hastily, 'I don't know where that came from!'

He smiles. 'Too much partying?'

'Not likely.' I laugh, shaking my head. 'Just too many late nights and early mornings lately. My boss is a real taskmaster.'

Daniel's brow furrows. 'You know, we can redistribute the work if it's too much for you?'

'No, no,' I reply quickly. 'Honestly, I'm fine. In fact, I'm really enjoying it. I don't need to pass any on.'

'If you're sure.' He takes his glasses off and starts polishing them on the bottom of his jumper. He carries on talking, something about how I should tell him if it all gets a bit too much, how he's aware of the numerous pressures I must be dealing with, but I'm not really listening now. Because looking at Daniel without his glasses on is like looking at a different face entirely, and I've never had the chance to examine it in such detail before.

The smooth olive skin is still there, as is the hint of stubble that he had five minutes ago, but without his glasses he looks less business-like, more casual. I can see more clearly the crinkles around his eyes, the scar on his cheek that I now know came from the ill-fated night when he was beaten up and left for dead, the horizontal line on the bridge of his nose that the frame of his glasses usually slots into. Those full, pink lips.

His short black/brown hair sticks up a bit where he's gelled it, but tiny wisps still feather his hairline along his forehead.

Then he stands up and I tune back into his words.

'Come on,' he says, rubbing the lower part of his back, 'these chairs are only comfortable for so long. I'll make us another drink and we can carry on chatting in the lounge.'

'OK,' I reply. There's no excuse to be made, nowhere else I need to get to for a while. I love being in this house, and if staying here for ever meant drinking 1,000 cups of coffee, right now I think I would happily comply.

Daniel's funnier than I expected when he's out of the office. His isn't a ta-dah, punchline, laugh-a-minute type of humour; it's more of a dry, understated wit, with wry observations on everyday life. But he's made me laugh, really laugh, a few times since we moved into the living room. Despite the lack of alcohol in my cuppa, any nervousness I felt at being in his house is starting to melt away into the thick cushions of his champagne-coloured velour couch in one of his many reception rooms.

One thing I have noticed is this: with every joke, with every laugh, it's as though yet another layer is peeled back and discarded as we gain the confidence to reveal a little bit more of ourselves to each other. It's starting to feel, dare I say it, suspiciously like a friendship.

'I've been thinking about what you said about missing your life on the nationals,' Daniel says, his head tilted to one side as though he's giving the matter some very serious thought.

'And?' I reply, stroking my fingers along the arm of the extra-long sofa on which we're seated at either end.

'I was thinking what a shame it was that you had to give it all up.'

Something catches in my throat as I process this unexpected empathy.

'I was also thinking how frustrated that must make you feel, and wondering whether there was a chance you might end up moving back down to London again one day?'

Honestly, it's as though this man has telepathic powers. I've feared before that he could read my mind. Now I'm almost certain it must be true.

'Actually,' I say slowly, wondering whether I should tell him what I know I'm about to anyway, partly to impress him and partly to get it off my chest. 'I've been offered a job at a new magazine that's opening up down there. It's a glossy one,' I add quickly. 'Apparently they have a year's worth of advertising lined up before it's even launched.'

His eyebrows lift a little.

'That sounds impressive. Are you going to take it?'

I sigh. 'No, I don't think so. I mean, it *was* the dream once, but that was a long time ago. Things change, don't they? And I might not feel like I'm living the exact life of my dreams, but it's not all about your career, is it? Or the money? I'm happy here. And it would be nice to work for an amazing international publishing company with sick pay and a pension and a printer that always works, but I have Charlie to think about. And I know we'd be able to afford a nice place in a decent area, but we live in a lovely community here. And the wage might be amazing, and I suppose it would be good not to worry about money, but money's not everything, is it? Although it is important. And it would be nice not to stress about how I'm going to pay the bills each month. And it would be so good to be "successful"...' I do that quotes thing with my fingers to emphasise that part '...like you. Well, maybe not quite like you – you're on another level. But successful all the same. Not constantly pedalling forwards and feeling like I'm going backwards. But it might end up meaning less time with Charlie. And he's growing up so fast anyway. Which means he probably won't need me as much over the next few years. But he'll still need me. And he loves his grandparents. And his friends. And his school. So no, I'm not taking the job. Definitely not.'

When I pause for breath, I realise that Daniel's smiling.

'That was quite an answer,' he replies, nodding sagely.

I sigh. 'Sorry. That was a lot.'

'Do you feel better?'

'What do you mean?'

He stretches his legs out. 'Releasing all those thoughts from your head? They must have been taking up a lot of space in there.'

I give a gentle laugh. 'I suppose they were. More than I'd realised.'

'You have a lot going on, don't you? It must be hard for you at times.' His features look soft, his expression concerned, and I suddenly feel as though I've returned to the edge of that precipice, not sure whether to jump off or step back.

Panic floods my thoughts. I've revealed too much. I've let him see an unguarded part of me. The messy, anxious, unfulfilled, ugly part. And it feels all wrong.

'What time is it?' I suddenly throw out there. I make a great show of checking my phone and then smack my head with my palm. 'I'm so sorry, I totally forgot I have a delivery coming. I'd better get back home.'

I stand up and head towards the hall, aware of him following behind me.

'A delivery? What are you having delivered at eight-thirty at night?'

I say the first thing that comes into my mind.

'An epilator.'

'Of course,' he replies, although I'm sure I catch him smirking when I glance back at him.

'Sorry to have stayed so long,' I say, flustered, as I retrieve the trainers I've left neatly by the front door and crouch down to pull them back on.

'Don't apologise. It was…pleasant.'

He reaches for my hand to help me back up and the intimacy of the unexpected touch takes us both by surprise. We stand completely still as he continues to hold on, his touch setting my fingers, my arm and my heart on fire.

The effect is a rush of adrenalin that flies through my body like a run of dominoes in full flow. And he's looking at me in a way that's so hungry, so filled with desire, that I *know* he wants to kiss me.

So, I do what I always do when something scares me. I grab my coat, make my excuses and leave.

———

Westholme Community Facebook page:

Gina Norris: I don't usually post stuff on here, but I'm struggling tonight. I lost my mum six months ago, and I can't seem to get over it. It's been even worse over the past couple of weeks, probably because Christmas is getting so near and I'm dreading it. I just feel so lonely. Don't expect anyone to respond, just needed to offload.

Paula's Bakehouse: You are not alone. DM me your address and I'll drop you off a little something to cheer you up.

Tori Hindle: You are not alone honey. I'm sending loads of positive vibes your way and hoping you'll feel much better soon.

Leah Moreton: You're not alone babe. If you want to drop me a line with your telephone number, I can give you a call.

Cath's: Our Chatty Table is always very popular with those who'd like to meet new people. Please feel free to call in anytime.

Beth Hurst: You're not alone. I'm here too.

Chapter Thirty-One

I've been trying everything to get on to the set of the new film, but no one's playing ball. I'm desperate to speak to Lily Lonsdale and Joshua Hartley, the two A-list celebrities starring in the movie, but I also want to interview the director, Tony Hanlon.

From what I managed to pull together when I wrote a story last year about the fact that he was bringing a film crew to Westholme, Tony Hanlon is originally from the area but won a scholarship to the private school in Presthill, which is where he met Daniel. From there, he went to university, then straight to film sets in London, then on to Los Angeles, which is where he appears to have set up home for the last ten years.

Although he's long since left Westholme, there's clearly a local link, plus when it comes to good news stories, his is right up there with the best of them, so I'd love to feature him in *The Good News Gazette*. If only I could get hold of his email address or convince *someone* at his company to reply to me.

Despite it being Daniel who told me about the film being shot here in the first place, I've tried to avoid asking him for help. He's done enough for me lately, plus I want him to think I'm capable of at least doing *some* things for myself.

But after making no headway with either the council's film officer or the film company, I decide there's no other option; I'm going to have to speak to him.

Fortunately, after appointing himself as my unofficial advertising pimp, Daniel's set up another lunch meeting between myself and one of his high-school buddies who now runs a wildly successful window-fitting company. So, while we're waiting for his friend to arrive at the swanky Presthill restaurant Daniel's chosen, I have the perfect opportunity to drop it into the conversation.

'Daniel, there's something I wanted to talk to you about,' I say once he's ordered the drinks, the pounding of the rain on the full-length windows only serving to make the modern dining room feel colder than it actually is.

'Oh yes?' He raises an eyebrow.

I take a deep breath. 'I hesitate to ask this, seeing as you've helped me so much already...'

'Go on.'

'Do you remember telling me about that friend of yours who's directing that movie they've just started filming for?'

'The story that saved the first edition of *The Good News Gazette* last year, just hours before it went to print?' he recalls, a smug smile dancing across his lips.

I grimace. 'Yes, that one. I've tried every way I can think of to arrange an interview with Tony Hanlon but I've found it impossible to make contact with him. I wonder whether you'd mind... I wonder whether you'd mind putting me in touch with him?'

He laughs, a simple gesture that causes the skin around his eyes to crease under his glasses, making him look more approachable and even better looking all in one go.

'Is that all? You looked so apprehensive I was expecting a request for a million-pound loan.'

I feel my bum-cheeks unclench. 'Is that how people tend to look when they approach you for million-pound loans?' I tease.

'Sometimes,' he replies and I realise he's not joking. 'But with regards to the interview, I assumed you'd want to speak to Tony so I've already mentioned it to him. He's told me to pass on his details and you can take it from there.' He starts scrolling through his phone. 'I'll send you his number now.'

Within seconds the contact details have arrived and I stare at them, unable to believe that after so many weeks I finally have Tony Hanlon's mobile number right here in my hands.

'Thank you,' I say, more grateful than I want him to know. A sense of unease settles in the pit of my stomach as the thought that I'm coming to rely on him too much flits through my head like a butterfly that won't quite settle. It pauses just long enough to make its presence felt before being shooed away by an unfamiliar face coming into view.

The woman is tall, with dark, wavy hair like mine and olive skin like Daniel's. Her blue-sky-on-a-sunny-day eyes stand out against her St Tropez colouring and I find myself staring as she sashays up to our table, approaching Daniel from behind, and places her hands over his glasses.

'Guess who,' she purrs, as Daniel shuffles around in his seat to see who's gate-crashed our business meeting in such an unbusiness-like manner.

He squints for a minute as he refocuses his eyes, then his frown changes to an expression of surprise.

'Hello,' he says, standing up and turning around to greet her. He bends down to kiss her cheek, but she turns her head and what I had expected to be a quick peck turns into a lingering kiss on the lips.

My face erupts into a festival of heat and I'm torn between

conducting a forensic examination in order to assess exactly what type of a kiss this is and looking at any – in fact every – other inanimate object in the room to distract me from the animated scene unfolding just feet away from my face.

He pulls away first, relatively quickly, and turns awkwardly to me.

'Joanne, this is Zoe, the woman I told you about who's leading the cinema's revival. Zoe, this is Joanne – the owner of the cinema.'

For a moment I fear my heart may have stopped. Breathing no longer feels natural and when I try and speak the words won't come out. *I've had dealings with her.* That's what Daniel had said about Joanne. 'I've had dealings with her.' Not 'I have dealings with her on a regular basis – and they're not the type you'd read about in the business pages.'

This time it's me doing that up-down look. And a split second is all it takes to tell me everything I need to know about Joanne. Her spotless cream wool coat and matching trousers contrast beautifully with the blue silk shirt that seems to have been colour-matched with her eyes. Her long, glossy hair has that 'just stepped out of a salon' bounce to it and her 'aesthetics' look genuinely real.

Where I'm doing the compare/contrast thing, she's simply looking at me with interest rather than any jealousy or concern at what I might be doing in a restaurant with her boyfriend.

She grasps my shoulders and pulls me to her, and as she air-kisses me on both sides, a whiff of deliciously expensive perfume surrounds my Tesco blazer. She looks down at me, her dainty white teeth like pearls in a cushioned shell as she smiles and tells me how glad she is to finally meet me.

Our meeting passes quickly and, for my part, in something of a daze. She touches Daniel a lot as we exchange pleasantries, her hand landing on his arm, his wrists and then, as she prepares to say goodbye, snaking around his back as she kisses him again. It's a series of actions, each simple, each innocent, but joined together they leave me reeling.

As Joanne leaves, James the window-fitting man arrives and for the next hour, Daniel and I studiously avoid each other's glances, each of us talking through James who has unwittingly become a safe medium for our conversation.

Images of what I've just seen fill my head and it takes every ounce of effort I possess to try and block out both those and the even more alarming thoughts of unseen images and concentrate instead on the golden opportunity that Daniel's placed in my lap.

Somehow I get through the next forty-five minutes. I say everything I'm supposed to say. I even manage to convince him to take out an advert.

But this time, when the meeting ends, there's no overwhelming thrill. There's no prospect of a good mood. Instead, all I feel is flat and inexplicably duped. I have no idea why. Daniel doesn't owe me anything. We're business contacts – that's all – yet I feel as though I've been horribly let down. I'm also mortified for feeling that way.

The minute James leaves, I stand up and start putting on my coat.

'Do you fancy staying for one more?' Daniel says, not quite meeting my eyes.

'Oh, I can't, I'm afraid,' I say with forced cheerfulness, not meeting his, either. 'Very busy, lots to do. Anyway, once again, thanks for that, Daniel, really helpful. Brilliant. Thanks a lot.'

And with that, I move quickly towards the door, inhaling deeply as I step out into the rain. 'Nothing's different,' I say to myself. 'Nothing's changed.' Yet as I hurry along the street, I know I'm lying to myself. Everything is different. Everything has changed.

Westholme Community Facebook page:

Tori Hindle: I met Joshua Hartley in El Corazon today! He was sitting there with some of the people from the film set and I went over and asked for his autograph and got loads of pictures of me with him! I even sat on his knee!

El Corazón: You'll all be aware that we have some celebrities in town at the moment, but we would be very grateful if all of our customers were to bear in mind our non-harassment policy. We did receive some complaints after a particularly over-enthusiastic member of the public started molesting one of our guests. We trust that that won't happen again. *Gracias*.

Chapter Thirty-Two

There's Christmas music playing on the radio station as I drive to the office the next morning. Everyone's in a jovial, upbeat mood – Charlie who's on a festive-induced high, his teachers with their Christmas decoration earrings and Santa hats, the radio presenters who are chatting about what's on their Christmas list – but all I feel is miserable. Miserable and let down. And ashamed and angry that I feel that way.

I can't believe I've let us all be so horribly, horrendously duped by Daniel Lewis. And it's not even as though it's the first time he's done it. He fooled me last year when he let me think that I had a chance of changing his mind over the Parade, a fact that, now that I come to think about it, I never really did get to the bottom of. Now he's done it again, by convincing us all to get involved with Joanne's cinema, persuading us it's for the good of the community, when it's obviously all about financing her property.

He's a con artist. A trickster. None of this has been about making things better for Westholme. It's all about impressing his tall, pretty businesswoman girlfriend by getting a band of unwitting locals to not only raise the funds to have her white elephant cinema renovated, but also to pay rent on top. He's scheming, conniving and duplicitous. And I am so, so stupid to have been taken in by him.

On the passenger seat next to me, my mobile phone lights up and Sam's name flashes across the screen. I didn't speak to him last night, preferring instead to converse by text, a medium through which I could more easily hide my mood. I'm not quite ready to deal with the 'told you so's I suspect might be on the cards when I reveal what Daniel's done, so I ignore the call. I'll speak to him later.

'Are you going to tell me what's going on then?'

'Er, I would, but I have no idea what you're talking about.' I've met Emma for a quick coffee at Cath's, expecting conversation rather than confrontation. I look around, noting the fairy lights draped around the window, the backs of the booths and along the wall. In the corner of the room stands a Christmas tree, saturated with decorations of all colours, shapes and sizes. Adina's done Cath's proud. This place looks like a staffroom for Santa's elves.

'This thing with Sam. This other thing with Daniel. It's like some weird love triangle that you haven't even noticed exists.'

My stomach does a few flip-flops and I focus for a moment on Ella Fitzgerald, whose voice sounds far more chilled than I feel as she provides the perfect juxtaposition to the conversation with her joyous take on Christmas classics.

'I really don't know what you mean.'

Emma takes a deep breath, then puts her hand on mine. 'You know I love you, don't you?'

'Hmm-mmm,' I say uncertainly.

'And I would never, ever say what I'm about to if I didn't think it was for your own good.'

'Hit me with it.'

'I don't think you should be moving in with Sam.'

I reach for the words of protestation I know should come. The ones that would explain why moving in with Sam is *exactly* what I should be doing; that explain how he's the love of my life; that make it clear, once and for all, that Sam is the man for me.

But they're not there.

Instead, all I can do is stare miserably into my coffee as Emma draws back her hand and waits for me to respond.

Eventually I look up and as I meet her eyes I instantly know she understands everything I haven't been able to say.

'Oh, Zo,' she says, her hand back on mine again, squeezing it tight. She leans in close. 'What are you going to do?'

A solitary tear makes the leap from my eye onto my cheek and I brush it away quickly. Then I shake my head and shrug at the same time, a catch-all that I hope will convey the sheer hopelessness of the situation.

'Is it just…not there?' Emma says gently.

Another tear spills out of my other eye, sending a two-fingered salute to my attempts to remain in control of my emotions.

'It's not that it's not there. It just sometimes feels that there's not *enough* of it there.'

We fall silent, each taking in the ramifications of these finally spoken words.

'But he's such an amazing man,' I blurt out. '*Why* don't I want to take it further? He's pretty much perfect. So, what's wrong with *me*?'

Emma sighs. 'Perfection is boring. Far better to keep the magic alive with a husband who's cheated on you.'

I look up sharply.

'Does that still play on your mind?'

Emma picks up a section of her hair and starts looking for non-existent split ends. 'We're in a much better place now. I don't think it's going to happen again. But I'd be lying if I said I never found myself lying awake at three a.m. thinking about it.'

Now I squeeze *her* hand. 'I'm sorry, Em.'

She shrugs. 'Do you remember when we were in school, all the plans we had for our lives? We were going to meet our dream man, find our dream job, make loads of money and basically do everything perfectly?'

I nod.

'It was as though our lives were laid out before us like a silk sheet, flawless, spotless, perfect. But now I'm in my thirties, I realise this: life isn't a silk sheet. It's a patchwork quilt, made up of the times we got things right, the times we got things wrong, the happy times, the sad times…and that's just the way things are. What's the point dwelling on the flawed squares on the quilt when there are so many others to focus on?'

'I like that analogy,' I sniff.

'Deep, isn't it?'

'For you, yes.'

'Look, Sam's brilliant,' she continues. 'One of the best. But a lifetime with the same person is long. It can also be hard. At times, it's only that sense of longing for the other person that pulls you through. And if it's not there at this point in your relationship, maybe it never will be.'

In the background, I hear the opening bars of Mariah Carey's Christmas song. It's usually all I need to put me right into the Christmas spirit. But today I feel as though Mariah's mocking me, boasting about the fact that she's found the man she wants while the realisation is slowly dawning on me that it's quite possible I haven't.

'What about Daniel?' Emma says.

My breath catches in my chest and a sudden rush of anger takes me by surprise as I remember what he's done. 'Forget Daniel Lewis,' I shoot back. 'He's made fools of us all.'

Emma sits back and listens as I tell her about the meeting, Joanne, their kiss and the way in which he's managed to convince us this is all for the community when it's clearly just a way for the two of them to build their empire together.

'Isn't that awful?' I say, expecting her to agree wholeheartedly. 'Isn't he the worst person ever?'

'It does seem weird,' she admits. 'But it doesn't sound like the bloke I've seen so far. I can't help but think there might be more to this than meets the eye.'

'There isn't.' I'm emphatic. 'It is what it is. Let's just get this cinema opening out of the way and then try and find a way to never have to deal with him again.'

'And Sam?'

I drop my voice. 'Can you leave that with me for now? That one's a little harder to answer.'

That afternoon, I finally get the email I've been waiting for. The one from the director Tony Hanlon. He's invited me to visit him on set at the Orchard Estate where I can chat to the actors, then interview him over lunch.

'Yeeeess,' I shriek, jumping up in my seat, a reaction that knocks my coffee over onto Ollie's phone.

'Oi!' he yells, moving quickly to wrap the device in sheets of kitchen roll. We spend the next couple of minutes manically trying to rescue various papers, phone leads and biscuits from the dangers of liquid infiltration, before Ollie says, 'What were you "yessing" about, anyway?'

'Tony Hanlon's agreed to an interview.'

His expression is blank.

'Tony Hanlon, the director of the movie.'

'The one you've been after for ages?'

'The very same.'

'When is it?'

I re-check the email. 'Tomorrow morning. Eleven-thirty. Then lunch at El Corazón straight afterwards.'

He sighs. 'We really need more restaurant choices in Westholme, don't we?' Then, seeing my expression drop, he adds, 'El Corazón is lovely and everything, but it would be nice to have another option that wasn't there or Cath's when we want to meet up with people for lunch.'

'S'pose.' A thought strikes me. 'Sorry, Ol, I haven't even asked you how the house search is going?'

He types something into his keyboard, then smiles.

'We've found somewhere – look.'

I scoot round our desks to see the agent's pictures on his screen and recognise the area instantly. It's at the cheaper end of town, not too far from where I live. It's a two-up, two-down like mine but unlike my house it's already been rendered white, with ivy growing up the side of the door. The front garden has neat borders filled with winter flowers that lie either side of the gated path that splits the front lawn in two, while the interior is all white and clean-looking.

'What a gorgeous house,' I exclaim, making a mental note of all the ideas I could pinch to make my own look a bit better. A lick of paint on the hall walls would be a start.

'Lovely, isn't it? And Adina loves it – that's the most important thing.'

A wave of sadness that's almost overwhelming crushes my heart as it hits me just how much Ollie adores her. All his little quirks – the cynicism, the sarcasm, the witticisms – disappear when her name is mentioned and in their place is a soft expression, kind words and a full heart.

And I realise at that moment that that's exactly what's missing between Sam and me. It's that look that Ollie has in his eyes when he talks about Adina. The look of love.

———————

Westholme Community Facebook page:

Elise Harvey: Some pics of the film crew parking up at our estate. Must mean Joshua Hartley and Lily Lonsdale will be around tomorrow.

Eyelash Lucy: Make sure ur wearing ur best PJs then.

Elise Harvey: Best PJs? I've just been The ASDA and bought a brand-new dressing gown!

Chapter Thirty-Three

I've made an extra special effort with my appearance today and am wearing some slim-fitting navy trousers, a white bodysuit (I know!) and a matching navy blazer that just about fits under the thick blue coat that's trying but failing to keep the cold out. I've even experimented with using my straighteners as curling tongs, and apart from an odd piece of hair that just wouldn't curl, the loose waves that emerged means the experiment could almost be deemed a success.

It's not that I actually care what any of the Hollywood actors think, of course. It's more the fact that they've come all the way over from Los Angeles. I consider it my civic duty to look nice for them.

I look around. It's a shame the housing association responsible for many of the houses on the Orchard Estate isn't operating on the same premise.

Despite the best efforts of the majority of residents, the estate itself is as run down as it ever was, with abandoned homes still punctuating the streets of well-kept ones.

No one quite understands why they're still boarded up –

surely there are enough people in need of houses to justify smartening them up again? But deprived of the opportunity to be someone's forever home, at least one of the houses is doing a sterling job acting as a narcotics mini-mart for the kids who've found their own ways in to the 'secure' property, so I assume the housing association think it's all good.

I pull up alongside an immaculate grass verge – the closest spot I can see to the street where the crew are scheduled to film today.

Dozens of people are lining the barriers that separate mere mortals from the elusive actors and actresses cocooned in the trailers set up further down the road. And while the day may be cold and grey, the various multi-coloured Christmas lights in the windows and huge bows adorning the front doors are adding a distinctly festive atmosphere to proceedings.

Making my way towards the set, I can sense a buzz freewheeling its way through what tends to be a notorious part of Westholme.

Those residents not in work are out on the street, either at the barriers or hanging around on their paths, watching as the most exciting event in town for decades unfolds before them.

I apologise as I almost walk into a middle-aged woman in slippers, smart jeans and a big pastel pink jumper carrying trays of hot drinks for the crew. Another lady in a cream tracksuit is shivering as she hands over a Victoria Sponge cake to someone wearing a headset.

Across the road, an older gent in a pair of trousers and a golfing jacket is passing a set of ladders through the barriers to a thirty-something male wearing an Iron Maiden sweatshirt and a pair of scruffy jeans.

I smile. The estate may not be awash with cash, but it's saturated with goodwill. The crew won't go short of anything here – whether they like it or not.

'Zoe Taylor, I have an appointment with Tony Hanlon,' I introduce myself to a tall, thin security guard who's being stalked by an ultra-glamorous blonde in extremely high-heeled black boots, black jeans, a very low-cut top and a fake-leather jacket.

The man nods, then takes a few steps towards a woman with a clipboard where he mumbles something and points in my direction. The woman consults the list in front of her, then beckons me over and moves the barrier a few inches to allow me to pass through.

I trail behind the security guard along the street that's so familiar but today, touched as it is by the star of Hollywood, feels completely different. I'm so busy watching all of the activity – including the cameras set up around one of the ugliest, most dilapidated homes – that I don't notice the man with the thinning brown hair until I'm right in front of him.

He's peering over a monitor, pointing something out to a petite brunette in a trendy grey jumpsuit and is completely oblivious to my presence.

'Scuse me, Tony,' says the Cockney security guard, 'it's the girl from *The Good News Gazette*.'

Tony Hanlon smiles at me, all capped white teeth and sparkly eyes. Balding head aside, he literally couldn't look more Hollywood if a flash of light had sparked out of his front tooth.

'Zoe Taylor,' he drawls in a posh English/American hybrid accent. He stands up and extends his hand for me to shake. 'It's so good to meet you. Daniel's told me all about you.'

I frown and reach out my own hand. 'Has he?'

He grins. 'Maybe not *all* about you. But enough to know you're a good friend. Which immediately makes you a good friend of mine.' He utters something to the woman next to him then checks his watch. 'We're about due for a break now,' he says. 'Let me introduce you to the guys.'

I follow Tony down the road, stepping over and around all

sorts of filming paraphernalia, until we reach a huge white trailer. I make my way up the steps behind him, my heart beating extraordinarily quickly, unsure of exactly what awaits me inside. And then I'm in. Not just in the trailer, but in a parallel universe to the one I've just stepped out of. Everything about it is gleaming, from the smooth marbled vinyl that eventually gives way to a thick beige carpet, to the spotless kitchen cabinets and worktops.

The entrance area leads into the kitchen with its booth-style dining, then onto a lounge with a cream settee and a couple of armchairs. At the far end of the trailer I spot a couple of steps into what looks like a bedroom.

Bricks and mortar are so over-rated. I'd happily give up my house if it meant I could live in this aluminium-clad construction for the rest of my days.

'You've got the paper,' I exclaim, as I spot a copy of *The Good News Gazette* casually lying on the table.

He nods. 'Daniel sent it to me. And a great read it is too.'

I look at it again. It *does* look good. Fortunately, Ollie puts as much care into the look he creates for the paper as he does into his own appearance and it's definitely paid off.

Tony heads to the coffee machine to make us drinks and I jot down some information about where he grew up (Westholme), how he came to go to private school (a combination of a scholarship and a wealthy grandad) and his thoughts on Daniel ('Love him – brilliant bloke').

He brings the coffee over and gestures for me to sit down on one side of the booth as he takes the other.

'I know Westholme is a bit rough around the edges,' he continues, 'but I always loved it as a kid. The people were warm and friendly and it was important to me, when I found myself in a position to do so, to put something back. I always swore I'd bring a crew here one day. It's great to see it finally happening.'

Voices approach the trailer then, followed by a rapid tap on the door.

'Come on in, guys!' Tony yells. And then there they are. Joshua Hartley and Lily Lonsdale. As I live and breathe. Standing no more than ten feet away from me.

One of the perks of being a journalist is having access to the most remarkable people from all walks of life. I take most of it in my stride. But they're here! Right in front of me! Looking so perfect it's as though they've stepped inside the most flattering filter on Instagram!

They're mid-conversation as they walk in, laughing about something that happened earlier on-set and I gawp at them, a fixed grin on my face, as I wait for them to notice my existence.

'Joshua, Lily, meet Zoe,' Tony introduces us once their chatter has subsided. 'Zoe's the editor of an upbeat newspaper.'

'One that only publishes *positive* news,' I add as a form of introduction.

'Hey,' says Joshua, stepping forward to shake my hand. 'Pleased to meet you, ma'am.'

I gulp.

'Are you free for a half-hour to have a drink and a conversation with her?' Tony asks.

'Of course,' replies Lily, who is as enchanting as her colleague, her numerous smiles providing her with the opportunity to flash her beautiful white teeth over and over again.

In fact, every moment only serves to showcase another perfect part of her: her swishy blonde hair, her long slim limbs, her precisely positioned features.

They're both absolutely charming, showing an embarrassing amount of interest in *The Good News Gazette* and providing me with lots of great quotes, spoken with an endearing mixture of humour and self-deprecation.

In fact, they're so friendly that I forget we're not actual friends and embarrass myself a little bit by asking for their numbers so we can keep in touch. Fortunately Tony realises my error before I do and changes the subject before they're forced to refuse.

I do manage to engineer a few selfies, but all too quickly we're faking cheek kisses (except me – mine are real) before we move on to the one part of the day I've been dreading – lunch with Daniel.

I'm still trying to work out how I'm going to 'be' with Daniel.

Should I be cold and uninterested, play it cool so that he knows just how unbothered I am by this knowledge that I now have in my possession; the knowledge that he's together in every sense of the word with Joanne? Or do I let him know that I'm on to him and that I'm not going to stand for it; that I'm not prepared to be part of the Big Screen Queens anymore?

The whole thing is complicated by the fact that Tony will be there, having organised what he thinks is a friendly lunch. Acting otherwise could make the next hour or so extremely awkward, not just for Daniel and me, but for Tony as well.

But then, before I have the chance to decide, Daniel's there in front of me, amidst much back-slapping with his old private-school chum. It's extremely difficult to do anything other than go along with this general air of frivolity, so I do so reluctantly; saying all the right things, making all the right faces, but keeping eye contact with Daniel to an absolute minimum.

The amount of small-talk going on between them makes it relatively easy for me to paper over the cracks with Daniel. Even if there are the odd couple of occasions when I spot him studying me while Tony's speaking and the attention should really be on him, I successfully manage to avoid any meaningful interaction with him and keep a lid on my growing levels of anger. It's a strategy that's working well. Until, that is, Rafa comes to take away our mains and asks us how the cinema's restoration project is progressing.

'Ah yes, Daniel told me you're saving the local cinema together,' Tony says. 'It's incredibly impressive, the community coming together to preserve such a great part of Westholme's history.'

'I don't know whether you're aware,' I reply, 'but this isn't the first time the community have come together to save a precious part of it.'

'Is that so?' Tony asks.

'It is.' I nod. 'Daniel, maybe you'd like to tell Tony about what happened last year.'

Daniel shifts uncomfortably in his seat.

'You know, when you tried to knock this place down and turn it into a supermarket?'

Tony's looking between us, unsure of the direction that the conversation is taking. Daniel is staring at me, a slight frown finding the familiar lines in his forehead. I can tell he's confused and I feel a rush of satisfaction at being the one who's in charge of the situation for once.

He smiles, but I can see I've thrown him off his stride. 'Fortunately, you came along and set me back on course.'

'On course for what? Shafting the locals a second time?'

There's a collectively sharp intake of breath as we all consider what I've just said and I realise too late that this isn't really the time or the place to reignite my feud with Daniel. So, I laugh as though I've just made a corker of a joke and make enough eye contact to convince them both to laugh along with me.

I leave before either Daniel or Tony in the hope that I'll escape any questioning over my odd behaviour, but Daniel catches up with me as I'm cursing the Range Rover driver who's blocked me into my parking space.

I'm hanging around both cars, probably looking as though I'm about to break into the vastly more expensive one, when from the corner of my eye I see his tall frame approaching.

He stops at my car, stony-faced.

'What was that all about?'

I shrug. 'What?'

'That little "shafting the locals" comment, for one.'

'It was a joke,' I scoff. 'I didn't *mean* anything by it.'

'You sure about that?'

'Of course. Whatever arrangement you and Joanne have to renovate the cinema is totally between you. I just don't like seeing good people being taken advantage of, that's all.'

He screws up his face as he tries to pick through what I've just said.

'Who's taking advantage of them? I hope you're not suggesting that I'm not acting in their best interests?'

The Range Rover driver turns up then, a twenty-something, skinny tracksuit-wearing lad who narrows his eyes at me in the same way that I've just narrowed mine at him. We try and out-narrow each other for a few seconds before it dawns on him that the fact that he's driving a Range Rover makes him the ultimate winner and he laughs as he speeds off out of the car park.

I turn my attention back to Daniel and sigh. 'Let's just get this done and move on. We're nearly at the end of it now, thank goodness.'

He raises his eyebrows, eyes wide in surprise, and it actually stings to see the hurt in them.

'Right, well. Good to know how you feel.' He does something with his keys that makes his own car flash a 'hello' and turns to walk towards it. Then he stops and glances round at me and my heart stops for a second as I think he might come back.

But he doesn't. He just looks at the floor, shakes his head and walks away.

———————————

That night, after putting Charlie to bed, I head straight to the fridge to pour myself a large glass of wine.

It's been a strange day – the high of hanging out on a Hollywood film set dulled massively by the low of having to be nice to Daniel. Then having to be nicer still after slipping up with my 'shafting the locals' comment.

And then, as it turns out, not being very nice at all.

At least I said what I needed to say; let him know he's not getting away with it. But still, I feel unsettled and agitated. Not quite right. As though I discovered a fairly unimpressive aspect of my character today, dusted it down and put it on show for all to see.

I'm too wound up to catch up on the work I should really be doing, so, in the absence of any better distractions, I find a series two episode of *Bridgerton*, which, for the record, is my favourite so far. *So* romantic.

I'm more than ready to lose myself in Kate Sharma and Anthony Bridgerton's dramas instead of my own when my mobile goes. My stomach lurches when I see the name on the screen. It's Sam.

'Hey, how's your day been?' I can hear a forced brightness in my voice that I hope he's not picking up on.

'Good thanks, how about you?' His cheerfulness sounds forced too.

I tell Sam about my trip to the film set and, as always, he's interested, asking the right questions and making all the right noises in response.

But when I try and move onto him, he replies to my questions with one-word answers, his voice tense. There's clearly something on his mind. Then he comes out with it. 'Have you thought any more about moving in?'

There's a momentary pause while I try and come up with a suitable answer.

'Erm, I haven't really had a chance. Why?'

'I… I don't know. If I'm being honest, I get the feeling this isn't something you're exactly jumping with joy about.'

My face feels hot, then cold, then hot again. 'Honestly, Sam, it's not that at all, it's just, well, there's been a lot going on, hasn't there?'

He tries again. 'Look, all I'm saying is that if you're not ready… If this isn't what you want…'

I think about Charlie, about how he would feel about it all. Then I think about Sam and wonder why he's even asking. *Surely* he can feel the same weirdness that I can. Then I think about me. What do I want, really? I have no idea.

I'm aware that right here is the point at which I should tell him. Where I should 'fess up and explain that he means an awful lot to me but that Charlie won't want to leave our home, that *I* don't want to leave our home. That I really, really like him, but that there's something extra I'm still waiting to feel; something I hope will kick in.

OK, so it hasn't yet, but there's time. After all, we've got all the time in the world, haven't we? Why do we need to rush anything?

'Have you even spoken to Charlie about it?' He's sounding mildly irritated now.

'Not yet,' I admit. 'I've just been so, you know—'

'Busy,' he cuts in. 'You said.'

I suddenly want this conversation to end.

'Look, it's no problem,' Sam says quickly. 'Let me know when you're ready. It doesn't have to be immediately.'

I feel as though a weight has been lifted off my shoulders. 'Really, Sam? Are you sure?'

'Yeah, of course. Tell me at the weekend if you like. There's no rush, is there?'

The weekend. And with that, the weight of the world is placed firmly back on my shoulders.

Westholme Community Facebook page:

Billy Reed: Got some autographs from Joshua Hartley and Lily Lonsdale today. Will sell for a tenner.

Tommy Jenkins: Stick 'em on ebay mate – I got £14.73 for Lily's signature and it was only on the back of a petrol receipt!

Chapter Thirty-Four

I 'm missing my mum and dad at the moment.

It may sound strange; after all, I can talk to them whenever I want and they only live around the corner, but I often feel guilty about the fact that the only times I see them are when they look after Charlie for me. In all honesty, I'm bringing little else to the family table.

So, this morning, I decide to pop in on my way to work and have a cuppa and a catch up with them, a move which I'm hoping will have the dual effect of keeping them happy and easing my guilt.

My mum's expression when she opens the door is one of such pure delight, I resolve to make a point of visiting more often and I give her a massive squeeze as I hurry in out of the cold.

'This is a nice surprise,' she says over her shoulder, as she bustles ahead of me into the kitchen. 'But shouldn't you be in work?'

'I'm on my way.' I head straight for my dad who's standing by the cooker fiddling with some new contraption. 'I just thought I'd pop in and see how you're doing first. I feel like it's been ages since we had a good chat.'

Wrapping my arms around his waist, I rest my head on his shoulder. It feels nice, comforting, as though I've suddenly been transported back a good twenty-five years in time and I'm nine years old again.

Dad returns my hug. 'Well, I'm glad you did. It's good to see you, love.' He jabs at some buttons on the machine in front of him. 'And maybe you can help me to work this, too.'

I pull away, examining the black machine in front of him. 'You bought an air fryer? Sam's got one of these, they're brilliant.'

'I did!' he exclaims, triumphant. 'I've spent the past couple of weeks on the John Lewis website waiting for them to be restocked. They finally came in, so I jumped on it and got one of the last ones.' He scratches his head. 'But I think it's broken. I've been trying to fry this bacon for forty-five minutes now and look...' He lifts a frying pan, complete with raw bacon, off the top of the machine and pats the surface 'It's not even heating up.'

I put all of my efforts into keeping my face straight.

'Dad, explain to me how you think it should work.'

He presses a button labelled '1', then presses another button, then another, then presses start.

'See? I've set it just like it says on the instructions, but it's not heating up on the top.'

'Why would it need to heat up on the top?'

He looks at me like I'm stupid.

'So I can airfry my bacon in the frying pan.'

I reach over and pull out one of the drawers. Inside, he's stored the half-empty pack of bacon and a can of lager.

'You're meant to cook the bacon in the drawer, not on top of the machine.'

Dad turns to me, and the look of utter confusion on his face causes my shoulders to shake, as laughter I didn't know I had in me starts to build up speed.

'How is it going to fry bacon in there? There's no frying pan!'

'I don't know,' I manage, between snorts. 'It just does.'

'But I thought that part was a mini-fridge.' He looks so disappointed that this new contraption isn't both a hob and fridge in one that I almost feel sorry for him, and I pat his arm in consolation.

'Look,' I say. 'I'll show you how it works. It's easy when you know how.'

I use a fork to pick the bacon out of the pan and move it to the drawer, spray it with some cooking oil, then close it and do my best at reprogramming the fryer.

'There you go. Done. It should be ready in five minutes or so. You just need to keep checking on it to make sure it doesn't burn.'

Dad scratches his head and picks up the frying pan. 'I don't need this, then?'

I take it off him. 'No, you definitely don't need that.'

He looks embarrassed and I feel bad. 'Bloody idiot, aren't I?'

I squeeze him again. 'No, you're not. In fact, I'd give you top marks for trying.' I glance at Mum and wink. 'But maybe we won't share this particular attempt at doing the cooking at the next Slim City group, OK?'

'If you don't mind,' he says, nodding. 'Maybe this one's best kept between us.'

I've just received an email from the head lice advertiser, who is very sorry to inform me that she can no longer afford our rock-bottom advertising rates due to her own business pressures.

Instead, she's decided to accept a 'too good to be true' deal from *The Northern News* and advertise with them instead.

Ollie, who is merrily singing along to a Little Mix song on the radio, catches my expression and stops.

'Oh no, what's wrong?'

I look up. 'What?'

'Has your cat died?'

I shake my head. The last time Lola made her way home to feast on Whiskas' finest and use her luxury toilet tray, she was very much alive.

'Don't tell me *this* car's started dying too?'

'No, but I think the *Gazette* is.'

He laughs. 'It might be seriously ill, but it's not dead yet. Come on, think positive. I'm sure things'll pick up soon.'

'We've just lost head lice woman.'

His ever-ready smile fades.

'Oh.'

'I know.'

'I can't understand why this isn't working,' I say, gulping to swallow away the lump in my throat. 'What is it that's putting people off? We were going great guns last year... But over the last couple of weeks it's as though everyone's suddenly got cold feet.'

He shakes his head. 'I don't know, Zoe. I really don't. Do you think it's your new look? Personally I like it, but maybe you're making other people feel threatened.'

I pull a face. 'What? It's only a bit of weight loss – it's not like I've had plastic surgery.'

He tilts his head to one side and examines me. 'Zoe, you've changed your hair, updated your clothes... Even your *skin* colour has changed.'

I look down at my orangey-brown arm. It's not exactly the Mediterranean look I always dreamt of, but this shade is better than my previous grey – interspersed with broken veins – coloured limbs.

'It makes me look better,' I argue.

'Oh, I'm the first to agree you look much better now than you did twelve months ago,' he says. 'But one man's treasure and all that.'

I sigh. 'I have no idea what you mean.'

'You know, one man's treasure is another man's junk.' He thinks for a minute. 'Or maybe that should be the other way around. Anyway, you know what I'm saying.'

I don't, but decide to let it go for the sake of my sanity.

'My point, Ollie, is that we now only have enough advertising to cover the cost of production. Once this advertising contract comes to an end, I can no longer pay you – or myself for that matter – and much as we love the *Gazette*, I think we've both had enough of working voluntarily.'

He looks crestfallen. 'I don't mind doing a bit of work for free,' he says. 'Obviously, I'd probably struggle to design the whole paper without getting paid but—'

'Thanks,' I interrupt. 'I appreciate that, but I wouldn't expect you to.' I stand up. 'I need to clear my head. I'm going to go to Cath's and pick up a coffee. Can I get you anything?'

'Don't worry, thanks. I'm meeting Adina there for lunch in an hour.'

'OK,' I reply, heading towards the door.

'Zoe, WAIT!'

I spin around. 'What's up?'

'Just a reminder. Stay away from the cakes. I've got enough on my plate at the moment without having to deal with the fall-out of you putting on half a stone out of sheer misery too.'

I tut and shake my head, outraged that he'd suggest I might be seeking solace in a chocolate mint cupcake, and ignore the fact that it had actually been the sole reason for my trip.

I'm queuing up for a coffee – minus the cake – when I hear a gentle 'Hi, Zoe' from the queue behind me.

I turn around to see Neil and John from The Lower Story.

'Hi, guys. Sorry, I was miles away.'

'We noticed,' John replies, his red jumper and navy hipster cords bringing a spot of sun to an otherwise grey day. 'We weren't even sure whether to bring you back from wherever you were, in case it was much hotter and sunnier than our current location.'

I grin as though my daydream had taken me to the Maldives rather than back to choosing my outfit for the dole queue.

'If only. How's business at the moment?'

'Been better, been worse.' Neil rubs his sparse grey beard. 'We're still battling to make our voices heard and, as you know, it's not always easy.'

'But the themed events and book signings have been helping,' John adds, his flat cap casting a shadow over the top part of his face.

'Well, I, for one, love Wine for Words,' I enthuse. 'Such a great way of taking us all out of our comfort zone and getting us to try new reads – and new wine.'

'Thanks, Zoe,' Neil replies. You've always been so supportive of us and the business. I'm sorry to hear the *Gazette's* going through some difficulties at the moment.'

There's a sudden thump in my chest, as though I've been hit really hard by one of Charlie's footballs.

'Where did you hear that the *Gazette* was going through some difficulties?'

Neil and John exchange a look.

'Oh…' Neil purses his lips and starts pulling nervously at a loose thread hanging off the bottom of his green striped shirt. 'Nowhere. Actually, I think I heard that about *another* business, not the *Gazette*.'

John interrupts. 'Always getting so mixed up, aren't you? Too much going on in that little head of yours.' He taps Neil's head gently and Neil flashes him a grateful grin.

'I'm sure I'd be eating breakfast for tea if it wasn't for you,' he agrees.

Our conversation's brought to an end then by Cath asking what we want and I ignore what Ollie said and add a cupcake to the order anyway. Sugar cravings don't stop when you get thin. You just get better at managing them – most days anyway

Today is definitely not one of those days.

I'm walking past Vintage Vibes on my way in to the office when I see Eva dressing a mannequin in the window in a dress that is so spectacularly jaw-droppingly stunning that it literally brings me to a standstill.

Spotting me, she beckons me in and as I walk in through the door she turns to me, her eyes sparkling with excitement.

'Look at this beauty,' she says, holding up the skirt of the garment she's arranging. It is a pale-blue, sequinned ball gown, with a full skirt, a strapless top and a matching pale-blue bolero, all in satin. If ever there was a Cinderella dress, it's this one. She arranges the small train of the skirt in a pool on the floor then stands up, delighted at her skilled arrangement of this work of art.

'It's gorgeous. Where did you get it from?'

'That vintage fayre in Paris I went to last week. Everyone wanted this dress, but I saw it first.'

We stand in awe, both silent for a moment as we admire the pretty colour, the flawless fabric and the crystals embellishing the bodice.

'I don't think I'll ever in my lifetime have a place to go that would be good enough for this dress,' I say eventually.

'I'm a bit concerned no one will buy it for that very reason,'

Eva admits. 'It's not exactly the sort of thing you'd wear for weekend drinks at the Stag and Unicorn, is it?'

I shake my head. 'I'm thinking more Kate Middleton at a state banquet.'

Eva's eyes widen. 'Do you think Kate Middleton might buy it?'

'I think if Kate Middleton ever came to Westholme, stopped off at the Parade and saw this dress in your window, she'd definitely buy it.'

A few more seconds passes, then Eva says, 'Probably not all that likely though, is it?'

I pause to consider the chances. 'Probably not.' Through the window, a pair of large purple glass frames floats past below a puff of red hair. 'But I'm pretty sure Starr would bite your hand off for it.'

Eva watches me for a minute, then says, 'Is everything all right?'

I sigh. 'Yeah.'

'You sure?'

Across the room, a teal halter-neck jumpsuit hanging on a railing catches my eye.

'Oh my goodness, will you look at that,' I say in awe, relieved at finding a way to avoid answering. 'Talk about head-turning. How much is it?'

'Gorgeous, isn't it? I've just priced it up this morning.' Suitably distracted, she turns the price tag round to show me the figure on the back.

'It's amazing. I just wish I could afford it. But with Christmas a few weeks away, I'd better not.'

'Ah, I know – I heard you were struggling,' she sympathises.

I look up sharply. 'You heard what?'

She bites a fingernail. 'What do you mean?'

'What did you hear about me struggling?'

She wrinkles her nose. 'Not that you were struggling as such, more that advertising was slow – you know, in the same way that business is slow for all of us at the moment.'

I'm suddenly feeling very paranoid. First Neil, now Eva. What on earth have they heard? And more importantly, where have they heard it from?

'Anyway, about this jumpsuit,' says Eva and I hesitate, wondering whether I could get away with interrogating her any further.

Then I do what anyone in my situation would do.

I put the jumpsuit on my credit card.

As soon as I get back to the office, Ollie leaves to meet Adina and I'm left alone with my thoughts. My head is spinning with the events of today: the lost advertiser, the whispers about the *Gazette's* struggles, the fact that it's true and my concern that just as success breeds success, there is a direct link between the perception and the reality of failure.

What I can't understand is where the rumour has come from in the first place. The only people I've discussed it with are my trusted group of friends and family, and I know none of them would ever repeat that sort of information – not even my dad. But it can't just be a coincidence that both Neil *and* Eva have mentioned it at the same time that advertisers are pulling out, so what's going on?

My phone beeps and I cast it a cursory, then a second glance, then grab my bag, lock the office and race to my car.

Even at the best of times, a CODE RED message – the one phrase that Emma, Beth and I use to let each other know we need immediate support – would see me dropping everything and racing to their side.

But even more frightening is the fact that this CODE RED didn't come from either of the girls.

It came from Beth's husband.

It came from Tony.

Westholme Community Facebook page:

Dot Baker: Went into that Vintage Vibes shop today. Can't for the life of me understand why anyone would pay so much for second-hand clothes. The hospice charity shop is just a few doors down and they sell dresses for a fraction of the price.

Joanie Reed: Ooh no, I don't bother with that one anymore – their prices are way too high. Try Barnardos instead. Much better deals in there.

Chapter Thirty-Five

I pull up at Beth's at the same time as Emma, and we move in tandem towards Beth's detached 1960s home.

We're only a few steps up the path when Tony wrenches open the door. He looks dreadful. His eyes are bloodshot, his face grey, shadows filling the hollows around his eyes and highlighting the lines on his forehead. Darcy is in his arms, her cries loud and shrill, and he's patting and shushing her simultaneously.

'What's the matter? Where's Beth?' I fire rapidly at him. The 'panic' part of my brain is on high alert.

'She's in here. I don't know what to do.'

He ushers us into the hall, apologising for the cluttered assortment of baby paraphernalia strewn around it and the folded washing in piles at the bottom of the stairs, then hangs back and nods us through to the lounge.

There, sitting on the grey carpet with her back to the wall, is Beth.

'What the...' says Emma at the same time as I gasp out loud.

Our beautiful, capable friend looks anything but. She's huddled against the wall in the corner of the room, all folded up with her arms wrapped around her knees and her head buried into them in such a way that all I can see of it is the caramel-brown bob, once so smooth and chic, that's currently sticking out at all angles. Her whole body is shaking with the sobs that are ravaging her body from the inside out.

Emma and I both cover the length of the living room in quick long strides, dropping down to the floor and wrapping our arms around her skinny frame.

'What's happening?' I whisper gently into her hair. But she doesn't look up, simply shakes her head underneath my lips and sobs even harder.

I look at Emma over the top of Beth's head. Her expression is filled with alarm, and she shrugs her shoulders slightly to confirm my own fears: that neither of us have a clue what to do.

'Beth, please,' I try again. 'Talk to us.'

Tony appears at the door, Darcy now draped over his shoulder, chirruping cheerfully. 'I don't know what's going on. I came home early from work. Beth was sitting like that on the floor and Darcy was upstairs in her cot, crying. I can't get a word out of Beth and I didn't know who else to text but you two.'

'Don't worry, Tony, I'm sure it's nothing serious,' I lie. 'Why don't you take Darcy for a walk and we'll have a little chat to Beth.'

Tony nods gratefully and disappears in a flash. Within roughly ten seconds he's banged the pram out of the front door, taking what sounds like half of the door frame with him, and is halfway down the road.

'Right,' Emma says to Beth's hair. 'It's just us now. We need you to talk. What the hell's going on?'

After evicting a couple more sobs, Beth slowly raises her head.

Her beautiful brown eyes are bloodshot, swollen and encircled by big, dark hollows. Tears make her eyelashes glisten. Beneath them, burst blood vessels spread across her wet cheeks. Her lips are dry and cracked. She looks like a drug addict going through cold turkey. Not a new mum whose daughter has made all her dreams come true.

Beth takes a deep breath. It's clearly almost too much of an effort for her to speak, but eventually the words come out.

'I. Can't. Do. This. Any. More,' she sobs.

'Do what?' I probe, sure that I already know the answer.

'Be. A. Mum,' she forces out through shudders, body and mind ravaged by the little girl whom she and Tony fought so hard to create.

I hug her even harder.

'I know it's been very difficult for you, chick, but what's different about today? What's pushed you over the edge?' asks Emma.

'Nothing,' Beth spits out, then thinks again. 'Everything. The baby's crying all the time and we can't work out why. We haven't had more than a couple of hours' sleep in one go since she was born. It's hell.'

The sobs scupper any further attempt at talking for a few minutes, and we sit with all four of our arms around her, waiting for them to pass.

'Have you been in the house on your own all day?' I ask once her body stops shaking.

She nods. 'I thought I'd made a mum friend. Someone I met at baby sensory last week. She told me about a playgroup that was happening at the United Reformed Church today and I wanted to take Darcy and meet her there.'

'What happened?' I nudge gently.

Beth takes a deep breath. 'I was struggling to get us both ready in time to go, so we were late anyway. Then just as I was about to put her in the car, she pooed. It went all over her. I had to strip her off and clean it all off her. She screamed the whole time. And by the time I'd got her ready again, it was too late. We were too late.'

Beth's voice becomes higher pitched as the tears gather speed. 'I let the other mum down. She was waiting for me there and I didn't turn up. Look at me. I can't even manage to get us to a playgroup in time.' She drags the back of her hand across her eyes, a move which seems to produce even more tears. 'I can't do this anymore. I'm a MESS.'

I lean back on my heels and watch as she buries her face back into her knees. I have never, ever, seen Beth like this. Out of the three of us, Beth's the calm, quiet, rational one. She's not the one who has a breakdown in the middle of the day and talks about giving up.

It's Emma who eventually speaks first. 'Not to kick you when you're down, but you're right about one thing. You *are* a bit of a mess.'

'Emma,' I give her a sharp warning. Sometimes I wonder if she is actually my dad's secret lovechild, the number of traits she shares with him.

'Well, she is a bit,' she says sulkily. Then she takes Beth's hands in her own and squeezes them.

'You remember what happened to me when I had the boys, don't you?'

Beth nods without taking her head out of the valley of peace that lies between her knees.

'You remember I had to go and see the doctor and go on some tablets for a while, don't you?'

Beth lifts her head out of her knees. 'I don't want to do that. I'm not seeing the doctor. They'll think I can't cope. They'll take Darcy off me.'

'They won't, Beth, they'll try and help you.'

She shakes her head. 'They won't, they'll take her. That's what they do. I saw it on *EastEnders*.'

Emma looks at me. 'Right, so we won't call the doctor. But you need to talk to someone. What about your health visitor?'

Beth shakes her head again. 'I can't tell her how I'm feeling. She'll *definitely* report me.'

Emma snorts. 'Who's she going to report you to? The sleep police?'

Beth looks up at me helplessly and another tear rolls down her cheek. 'You don't understand. None of you understand.'

I scoop my hair into one hand at the back of my neck and pull it around and over my shoulder, buying myself some time before I have to respond.

Then, just as I'm about to announce that I'm all out of ideas, the solution falls right into my lap.

'I can't believe I let it get this far without intervening,' I exclaim. 'Especially when the answer's right on our doorstep.'

'What do you mean?' Beth sniffles.

'Margaret Kemp. She used to be a health visitor, she runs the Meals for Mums service...she totally gets it. She'll know how to help you. I can't believe we didn't think of her before now. Emma, her number's in my phone – can you pass it to me?'

Emma picks up the bag I'd slung down next to her, takes out my phone and types in my passcode. I don't even ask how she knows it.

'Where will I find her?' She's scrolling through the names and numbers in my contacts. 'She's not under M.'

'No,' I smile. 'She's filed under A.'

'A?' Emma repeats, confused. 'Why's she filed under A?'

'For Angel,' I explain. 'Angel of Westholme.'

As expected, Margaret knew exactly what to do. And it began, as all British rescue plans should, with a nice cup of tea.

She arrived within minutes of our call, bustled into the living room with smiles and reassurances and managed to convince Beth

284

that the couch would be a far more comfortable place to have a 'little chat' than the carpeted floor, even if the carpet *was* one of the more expensive ones that cost £19.95 per square metre.

Now Beth is on the sofa, flanked by Emma and me, and Margaret's in the adjacent couch, having the chat that really does sound like a chat rather than the first stage of a social services investigation.

As they talk, I'm kicking myself for not having thought to ask for Margaret's help sooner. I know she runs the Meals for Mums scheme – in fact, I accompanied her on one of her trips last year – but it never occurred to me that Beth would need her services. I'd left my day trip with Margaret under the impression that the service was for people who didn't have anyone. Beth has people. Yet even we, those people that love her, hadn't realised how completely isolated she was feeling.

I watch as Margaret slowly teases it all out of her: how much she hates being in the house by herself all the time, how lonely she feels when Tony's at work, how much she loves Darcy but is desperate to have some of herself back again, and how absolutely shattered she feels every second of the day.

'I'm supposed to go back to work in three months, but the way I'm feeling now I don't think I'll ever be able to work again,' she mumbles, sniffing.

Margaret listens to every word, patiently waiting when the tears engulf her, encouraging her to go on when she's ready to talk again, taking it all in, working it all out.

I feel the cogs turning as she computes the information Beth's giving her, putting the pieces of the jigsaw together in order to see the overall picture.

Key facts filter through; Darcy cries a lot. She's often sick. Every poo is like a mini-explosion that requires a change in clothes for Darcy and often Beth too. Beth has become terrified to go out, so messy have these occurrences become. And even when she tries, like today, the monumental effort required to leave the house is overwhelming.

'It sounds as though something may be irritating Darcy's stomach,' Margaret says eventually. 'Are you still breastfeeding her?'

Beth nods. 'I've just started introducing her to solids, but it hasn't made much of a difference.'

'And do you drink cow's milk?'

'It's in the cold tea I drink all day long.'

A series of bangs in the hall, followed by the baby wail that appears to have become the soundtrack to Beth's life, indicates that Tony's home. He pops his head gingerly around the door, a whimpering Darcy perched on his hip, then offers a nervous smile once he sees that Beth's stopped crying and is off the floor.

'Are you OK?'

'Better than I was.' Beth issues a small smile and extends her arms to take Darcy.

'Can I take her for a moment?' Margaret intervenes, then quickly introduces herself to Tony. 'I just want to try and work out what it might be that's upsetting her.'

Tony hands Darcy over, relieved, I suspect, to temporarily suspend parenting duties for a couple of minutes, and we watch in awe as Margaret deposits her on the couch and turns her this way and that, examining her to assess what could be wrong.

She lays Darcy out flat across her knee and gently rubs and kneads her little back until eventually Darcy lets out the biggest trump, then slowly stops crying, wriggles around and beams at us all.

'Hmmm,' says Margaret thoughtfully. 'I think it would be worth getting her checked out for some sort of intolerance or allergy.'

'We have been to the doctors a couple of times,' Tony responds, 'but they just told us it was colic and that it was completely normal. We've tried all the remedies, though, and nothing's worked. We had a feeling there was more to it than that, but assumed we were just being over-dramatic.'

'Never think that,' replies Margaret. 'Parents know. If you're worried, keep pushing for answers. And, in the meantime, let people help you. You're having it extremely tough at the moment, but there are things we can put in place to make life easier for you.'

By the time Margaret leaves, she's arranged Meals for Mums deliveries for the next month, established a schedule involving us all, which ensures Beth can have regular breaks, and made some calls to the GP's surgery to ensure Darcy's doctor is under no illusion as to what needs to happen next.

'Thank you so much, Margaret,' I whisper as I see her to the door.

She smiles, and then surprises me by saying, 'Not at all, my dear. It was nice to feel useful for a while.'

And as I watch her trundle off to her car, I feel mildly reassured to know that we all need a bit of help sometimes – even angels of Westholme like Margaret.

I'm back at the office, finishing up for the day, when the phone goes. Daniel. I frown. We haven't spoken since the other day and I can't shake the feeling that we've all been totally screwed by him.

'Hello?' I answer warily, as though I'm expecting it to be a cold call.

'Zoe?' His voice is as brisk and business-like as usual.

'Daniel?' I've adopted the coldest tone I own.

'I've heard some concerning news today and I wanted to make contact to see if you needed some help.'

He is literally the last person on earth I'd accept help from right now.

'I have absolutely no idea what you're talking about.'

'The *Gazette*. I heard that it's on the verge of closure.'

I take a sharp intake of breath and feel the hairs on the back of my neck stand on end.

'Where did you hear that?' I ask, less bullish now.

'I was talking to Bob the greengrocer. He told me you were in a very precarious situation.'

I'm confused. I haven't spoken to Bob about the *Gazette*'s situation at all.

'Is he right?'

I scramble about for the right words. 'No, no, well, as you know it's been a bit quiet on the advertising front...and we did lose a key advertiser today, but... Oh look, I don't know what's happening. The situation was already concerning and then over the last week three advertisers have pulled out.

'I have no idea what's going on and why there's suddenly been this mass exodus. I also can't understand why everyone thinks the *Gazette* is on the verge of closure. I mean, it might be but still... neither Ollie nor I have told any of the advertisers that so I'm not sure where it's come from.'

There's a moment of awkwardness as neither of us speaks, then a thought occurs to me. 'Daniel,' I say slowly. 'I don't suppose Bob told you where he'd heard that from, did he?'

'It's really not for me to say.'

'Daniel, I'd appreciate it if you would. This rumour seems to be picking up speed and I really need to shut it down ASAP or I'm going to have absolutely no business left by Monday.'

I can almost hear his brain ticking over as he considers whether to tell me what he knows.

'Daniel, please,' I'm practically begging now. 'I need to know where this is coming from.'

'OK, I'll tell you. But you're not going to like it.'
I freeze in anticipation of what he's about to say.
'Who is it? Who's spreading these rumours?'
He misses a few beats, then clears his throat.
'It's Sam.'

Westholme Community Facebook page:

Jimmy Hunter: Heard that *Good News Gazette*'s on its way out. No surprise there then – knew it wouldn't last.

Beryl Goodwin: Oh I do hope not – I love that paper.

Zoe Taylor: I'd like to reassure all of our readers that *The Good News Gazette* is still very much in operation – regardless of what you might have heard.

Jimmy Hunter: Council must be propping it up.

Chapter Thirty-Six

To say I'm incandescent with rage is to do a complete injustice to the word incandescent. Because what I feel right now is way, way stronger than incandescent but without actually going through the thesaurus, I'm at a loss as to what other word would trump it.

Sam, my *boyfriend*, the man who wants me to *live* with him, is simultaneously telling what feels like the whole of Westholme that the *Gazette* is on its knees and, in doing so, nudging advertisers to leave quicker than you can say 'failing business'.

I turn the phone over and over in my hands, my face hot with anger and my body as pumped as though it's just been given five espressos on an intravenous drip.

I'm trying to think calmly, sensibly, to not jump to conclusions but come on... What the hell is he doing to me?

Sam, can you meet me at mine immediately? I text. *It's urgent.*

My phone lights up so quickly with a *hell yes* that I suspect he thinks it's an early booty call, a fact that only serves to irritate me even more. I scribble a note to Ollie telling him I've gone for the day, then race home and spend the next ten minutes pacing up and down the living room as I wait for Sam to arrive.

By the time the doorbell goes, I'm so wound up that his chances of survival are slim. As I power open the door and see him standing there, there's a split second when sadness catapults its way through my rage as I look at his beaming face, flush with anticipation, and realise that something's about to change irrevocably.

He's about to reach for me when he spots my expression. His smile disappears and I spot a fleeting frown pass across his features before I spin around and storm back into the lounge.

The front door clicks shut, then the soft tap of his trainers on the floorboards confirms he's followed me inside.

'What's up?' I hear his voice, tentative, from behind me.

I swing around to face him. 'Have you been telling people that *The Good News Gazette* is struggling?'

For a moment, he simply stares at me, then says, 'What do you mean?'

A sudden injection of anger races through my veins and I try and stay calm as I repeat my question. 'Have you been telling people that *The Good News Gazette* is struggling? Have you, Sam?'

He steps forward and tries to take my hands but I push his own away.

'It isn't like that.'

'Oh really? Well, what is it like then?'

He's frowning now, annoyed by my tone. 'I can tell you're angry, but will you wait to hear what I have to say before you go off on one?'

I say nothing, but raise my eyebrows as high as they'll go.

'I know how hard you've been struggling with the advertising situation and I also know how much support you have from people round here who want you to succeed. So, I confided in a few of our *trusted friends* that things weren't going so well and told them that if they could think of anyone who might be interested in advertising with you then it would be very much appreciated.'

'So, you told people *The Good News Gazette* was at risk of closure?' I say, my temper threatening to boil over.

He hangs his head. 'I thought I was helping. You were trying to handle everything, but the situation was getting too difficult for you to manage on your own.'

'I wasn't on my own,' I snap. 'I had Daniel.'

Sam recoils as though he's been slapped and I instantly regret my words.

'I'm sorry,' I say. 'I didn't mean it like that.'

He hangs his head. 'I think you did.'

'I didn't, but we're getting off the point. Sam, do you know that because of what you've done, advertisers have actually pulled out? In fact, I've just lost my biggest one, meaning that *The Good News Gazette* is more at risk of closure than ever before?'

Sam sinks into the couch, his green eyes cast to the floor, suddenly seeming less like the hunk of a man he usually does and more like a naughty schoolboy in the headteacher's office.

'I was trying to fix things for you – to make it right.'

'Why can't you understand that I don't need you to fix things for me? I'm more than capable of fixing things for myself.'

'But you weren't doing, were you? You were just killing yourself trying to juggle more and more freelance work with the *Gazette*. I've barely seen you in weeks.'

I feel a new injection of anger pump through my veins. 'Barely seen me? Even when you do see me, you're always distracted, answering calls or texting. Who are you even sending messages to anyway? Surely not that many parents can be texting you?' In the heat of the moment, I'm suddenly suspicious. 'Is there someone else?'

'Of course not,' he snaps, but something in his expression changes enough for me to notice.

'Sam,' I say through gritted teeth. 'Who exactly have you been messaging?'

'It's not what you think.' He looks guilty as hell

'Tell me, *right now*, who you've been messaging.'

Sam swallows. 'She just wanted to let me know her circumstances had changed and I've been helping her through it. But I've told her that there's no way anything can start up again; that I'm with you now.'

I feel sick. 'Who are you talking about?' I ask, sure that I already know the answer.

He sighs. 'It's my ex-girlfriend, Nazia. The woman from San Francisco. She's finally left her husband.'

'But you're not free to be with her,' I mutter.

'I don't *want* to be free. Zoe, can't you see how committed I've been to us? *Am* to us? I've been trying so many different ways to make life easier for you; asking you to move in with me to help ease your money worries and give you a bit more time to spend with Charlie, trying to rally people to advertise to keep the paper – that *they love*, by the way – afloat. You've got nothing to worry about with Nazia. But you've got to work with me. I can't help you unless you help yourself.'

I stare at him. 'You asked me to move in with you to *ease my money worries*?'

He leans backwards into the seat, then forwards, then runs his fingers through his hair. 'That came out wrong.'

He stands up and walks towards me, reaching out for me, but I shuffle over to the other side of the room. I don't want him to touch me right now.

'Zoe, I asked you and Charlie to move in with me because I *love* you. Yes, I see you struggling and I want to help you but even that is because I love you. Why is that such a bad thing?'

I freeze.

'Unless…you don't feel the same way?'

Sam frowns, hurt and confusion dancing around his face in tandem.

'That's it, isn't it?' he says eventually. 'You don't feel the same way, do you?' He pauses, waiting for me to fill in the gaps, to say the things that will make it all better, that will make it all right, but they're not coming. In fact, the only thing that's coming is tears, streaming unexpectedly down my face.

I go to speak, but the words are stuck in my throat, choked by anger, emotion and uncertainty.

He shakes his head sadly. 'I really got this wrong, didn't I? I thought asking you to move in with me was the start of something; not the end.'

'Sam, I…' I start, but I really don't know where to go with it, don't know which words need to be arranged in which order to express the jumble of emotions that I can't even explain to myself.

And before I get the chance to work out the puzzle, he's picked up his coat, walked out of the room and shut the front door firmly behind him.

Westholme Community Facebook page:

Caroline Freeman: Thanks so much for all the donations of Christmas clothes to the food bank. We now have party outfits for girls and boys of all ages, as well as a plethora of Christmas jumpers. You are all very kind. Westholme Food Bank continues to be open every Wednesday and Friday from 9:30am-12:30pm. Always here for those in need.

Chapter Thirty-Seven

T he next few days are spent plodding heavily on the familiar treadmill of life.

I get up, fetch Charlie's breakfast, drop Charlie off, pick him up, make the tea, do some cinema work...but I do it all carrying the hefty burdens of sadness, guilt and fear of the future on my back. And try as I might, I can't shake them off.

The minute I close the door behind Charlie and me each night, all I want to do is put my PJs and dressing gown on, make up the hot water bottles – which we're hammering now that the fire seems to have become a treat saved for special occasions – and snuggle down in front of the TV under the blankets with him.

So, it's with an extremely heavy heart that I'm sitting at my dressing table, curling my hair, glamming myself up for that Oscars-themed cinema group night out.

It's hard to imagine that Sam, who has been by my side for over a year now, is no longer my Sam. That there'll be no more meals at his house, talk about the future, or 'family time' with Charlie.

But there's a big part of me that feels relieved by this new turn of events.

Relieved that Charlie and I will get to stay in our home, relieved that I no longer have to keep trying to fan a flame that had been dying for some time, relieved that I'm back on the familiar footing of it just being Charlie and me again.

Our break-up was a long time coming, even if it wasn't necessarily planned.

Have I made the right decision?

Only time will tell.

I've been working my way through a mini-bottle of prosecco while I've been getting ready, so by the time I put on the killer red dress I finally brought home from Vintage Vibes today, I've rallied.

My phone pings to let me know that Emma's arrived in the taxi. Charlie's staying over at Mum's tonight, so there's only Lola to wave goodbye to and even she looks at me with complete and utter contempt as I do so.

My shoes are already giving me blisters, but as they were the best match for the dress I'm determined to persevere with them, and I wobble down the drive, thankful to reach the taxi at the end of it.

I tug open the door and climb inside.

'Hi,' I sing, determined to enter into all the fun of a Christmas night out.

Emma gasps. 'Wow, you look stunning.'

I give her a half-smile.

'Thanks.'

Emma tells the taxi driver to drive on to Vino, where we're all meeting before taking more cabs to the hotel, then fixes her fringe of false eyelashes in my direction.

Saving the Good News Gazette

'What's happened?'

I give her a shortened version of the story, explaining how, despite my best efforts, Sam has single-handedly managed to kill off most of my advertisers in the space of a few weeks, and our relationship in the process.

'Oh no,' she says sadly when I pause for breath. 'I'm sorry. It sucks going through a break-up.'

'It really does. Especially when the person concerned, someone that you trusted, has destroyed everything you've worked so hard to create.'

Emma sighs. 'The only thing I can say in his defence is that I'm sure he really was trying to help. He's a decent guy, even if he might be slightly misguided.'

My heart aches. 'I know.'

'And what about the *Gazette*? Will you be able to keep it going?'

The driver takes a bend a bit too quick, so when my heart lurches I'm not sure if it's the journey or her question that's caused it.

'Honestly? I have no idea.' My eyes threaten tears and I shake my head to clear them. 'I have no idea about anything right now.'

The taxi slows as we pull up outside Vino.

'Listen,' Emma says quickly as she helps me out of the car. 'Let's just forget everything tonight, drink far more than we should and dance. It'll be fine – I'm sure of it.'

'You're right.' I sigh. 'In the words of Kenny Rogers, we've got tonight. So, let's sod tomorrow and get absolutely smashed instead.'

It's the first time I've been inside Vino during the evening, and while the fact that there's bouncers on the door doesn't usually signal that a great time is about to be had by all, I can't help but be impressed.

It's beautifully decorated for Christmas, with pine branches coupled with holly and ivy hanging in abundance around the bar and from various points on the ceiling. Warm white fairy lights sparkle on top of the greenery, and white berries and pine cones add the finishing touches.

Couples and friends dressed for Christmas are perched at the pale wooden bar tables, huddled in grey velvet booths or waiting at the white marble bar, trying to decide which of the beautifully lit spirits, beers or wines in fridges and on shelves they're going to choose tonight.

Perfume and aftershave mix together in a precursor of what may happen later on in the evening. Combined, they make for a potent and seductive scent to accompany the jazz versions of the traditional Christmas classics that are playing in the background.

'Wow,' I say out loud, 'how have we missed this?'

'I know,' Emma replies. 'Gorgeous, isn't it? I've heard great things about it but I had no idea it would be this pretty.'

We're taking it all in when the door flings open and Starr arrives, escorted by Margaret and Jack, and Lynne and Colin. And, as promised, she is indeed wearing a ballgown.

It is huge, so huge in fact that I wonder how her little frame has managed to haul it here. It has a wide, full skirt, clearly given its volume by a hoop underskirt, while the top part is modest and beautifully fitted, with a scoop neck and darts underneath the bust. But it's the fabric that's the real showstopper; emerald green satin that looks like it would be unforgiving of spilt drinks. A matching satin stole is wrapped around her shoulders, setting off her red hair beautifully. She looks incredible; and just one look at her face makes it clear she knows it.

'Starr,' I exclaim, greeting her in the only way acceptable for someone of her standing – with a double kiss. 'You look stunning!'

She grins like the cat who has not only got the cream, but has eaten it and gone back for seconds.

'I do, don't I,' she purrs, then adds graciously, 'Thank you, darling, but I think you've stolen that particular crown for the evening'.

I smile gratefully, then hug Margaret, who's wearing a very lovely navy lace mid-length affair, and Lynne, whose long purple and black sequinned dress hangs beautifully off her narrow shoulders.

'Where's mine?' cries Jack, who scrubs up very well in his smart dark suit and tie, then envelops me in his big arms before I have the chance to respond.

'You look lovely,' I reply once he's released me from his clutches. 'Nice outfit.'

'Thanks, love,' he says, winking. 'It's my funeral suit.'

Colin's greeting is a little more reserved, with a polite and quick kiss on the cheek, and we all head to the bar to order our drinks.

While we're waiting, Candice and Eva join us, each looking beautiful in their own Christmas best, with Eva wearing a fabulous mustard silk maxi-dress that would look horrendous on ninety-nine per cent of people on earth but is absolutely stunning on her slim figure.

Someone taps me on the shoulder, and I spin round, half-expecting it to be Norman.

'Well, who do we have here, Adina?' Ollie smiles conspiratorially at his girlfriend. 'I used to know someone who looked a bit like this fine lady. But it can't be her. This woman must be ten years younger. And she's got lipstick on. No, it definitely can't be Zoe Taylor.'

Adina shushes him and smiles at me. 'I love your dress,' she says, twirling me around so she can see the back. 'You look wonderful!'

I return the compliment, marvelling at how, in a pair of plain black pants, a nice top and next to no make-up, Adina still manages to outshine us all.

'Are you coming with us on our cinema night out?' I ask Ollie as Adina excuses herself to go to the ladies.

'No, but I knew *you* were, and I wanted to pop in to make sure you'd actually gone.'

I wrinkle my nose in confusion. 'What do you mean?'

Ollie looks around, then leans in towards me and whispers conspiratorially, 'I was talking to Sam today. Sorry to hear it's all gone belly-up.'

My shoulders sag, and observing this, Ollie adds, 'Why didn't you tell me?'

'I don't know,' I say. 'It was all just a bit too painful to talk about.'

His forehead wrinkles a little bit. 'I really hope it wasn't to do with anything I said. I know I've been winding you up over Sam for a few weeks now, but it was all in good fun. I really didn't mean to cause any trouble.'

A warm glow fills my heart. Who would have thought that Ollie would actually worry about hurting someone's feelings.

I toy with the idea of telling him it was entirely his fault and that Sam and I would still be together now if it wasn't for his constant mickey-taking, but then realise that's too cruel and squeeze his arm instead.

'I'm very touched that you care enough to worry about me, but I promise, it's absolutely nothing to do with you – we just weren't right for each other, that's all.'

Ollie does a mock and exaggerated wiping of his forehead.

'Phew. I can now live out the rest of my life knowing that I was not the man responsible for ruining the romance of the century.'

I let out a glum chuckle. 'No, it definitely wasn't down to you.'

He looks over his shoulder, winks, then says, 'Must have had something to do with this guy then,' just as Daniel Lewis comes into view.

I catch only a glimpse of him before Norman pops his head around the door and gesticulates to let us know that the taxis are here, then Daniel's away and guiding Margaret, Jack and Starr into his own car before you can say 'get me out of here'.

Emma leads me, Eva and Candice into one of the taxis, while Colin, Lynne and Norman head towards the other. Then, once Norman's satisfied that we're all present and correct, he gives a thumbs-up and both taxis pull away in tandem.

'Take us to Hollywood,' Emma instructs our driver, and spends the next twenty minutes grilling him on whether he's been busy tonight, what time he finishes, and how much Colin might have to pay the other taxi-driver if he's sick in his car.

I've never tasted an espresso martini before. Which, when you take into account how much I love coffee and my penchant for alcohol, adds up to a complete oversight on my part.

I'm on my third now, and it's making me feel incredibly relaxed and happy – neither emotion being ones that I've experienced in quite some time. It's a fantastic feeling. I take another sip. Almost as fantastic as this dangerously moreish drink.

Emma and Eva have gone off to the toilets to reapply their make-up, but I've hung back, not only because I've come to the conclusion that we're way past the age when it's acceptable to visit the toilet in threes, but also because I'm enjoying the people-watching that my vantage position at the bar allows.

The event has all of the key features you'd expect from a

Hollywood-themed night. On arrival, we were met by two gold Oscar statues flanking the entrance of the pretty old manor house with its ivy-covered open porchway. Then there was the prerequisite red carpet, on which Starr spent an unacceptable amount of time posing, turning left and right, twisting her body this way and that for the mock paparazzi who were kindly humouring her efforts.

Once inside, the coats came off, revealing an array of outfits – some beautiful, some awful – worn by partygoers excited to swap their lives for something a little more Instagrammable. And I'm thoroughly enjoying assessing each and every one of them now, as I sit at the bar alone.

I'm using the mirror behind the optics to spy on a glamorous couple having a passive aggressive argument when I see the outline of someone instantly recognisable approach. My stomach plummets. In his black tuxedo, white shirt and bow tie, Daniel is turning the head of every single person he passes, but his eyes are firmly fixed in one direction.

He's looking at the back of my head rather than the mirror, so although he can't see my face, I can see the expression on his own as he takes in my head, the dark curls that I've pulled to the side of my neck and the exposed skin of my back.

He pauses for a minute, still watching, then I see his chest expand as he takes a deep breath and approaches the bar.

'Hello, Zoe,' he greets me, his usual formal manner in no way relaxed by the occasion.

'Hello, Daniel.' I slowly spin around on the bar stool and greet him with a cool smile, crossing my legs to allow the split of the dress to expose the side of my false-tanned thigh. I'd usually rather wear a ski suit than get my legs out, but whether it's the espresso martinis or the devastating feeling of having very little left to lose, I feel different tonight; more reckless, harder, sexier.

Daniel's eyes betray him for a second as he glances at the flesh on show, then he clears his throat and moves his gaze back to my face, his Adam's apple bobbing in his neck as he swallows furiously.

'Are you having a good night?'

Nodding, I reach out and place my hand on the top of his wrist, my fingertips light on his skin. I'm acting strangely, I know; after all, I'm still furious over the whole Joanne thing, and this is *Daniel* – Mr Untouchable, not to mention my boss. But after that night at his when I thought he was going to kiss me, I feel as though I have some power. And tonight, I've had enough booze to use it.

'And are *you* having a good night?' I nod at the glass of water in his hand. 'Or could you be tempted to let loose just a little and have a real drink instead?'

He smiles now, clearly used to drunken women trying to persuade him to join them.

'I'm driving.' He gives a little shrug of his shoulders that's meant to imply that he's doing so reluctantly, when I've noticed before that he never drinks. 'I have to be on a flight to Dubai first thing in the morning.'

'Leave your car here. Take a cab.' I look right at him, as if I know what I'm doing, when the truth is I have no idea.

His eyes narrow for a moment and he observes me, trying, I know, to work out why I'm acting differently tonight – not at all like the straight, mumsy, slightly boring Zoe he's come to know.

I'm enjoying the feeling of knowing he's taking it all in; my dark eyes made even darker by copious amounts of eyeshadow, eyeliner and mascara; my cheeks, highlighted and blushed to within an inch of their lives, and my lips, smooth and soft, painted pink with a slick of gloss helping to create a pout.

Then he frowns and shakes his head quickly. 'It's probably best that I don't.' The air rushes out of my lungs.

'Probably best,' I repeat, and I spin back round to the bar, enjoying the confusion in his eyes that I can see in the mirror as he takes one last, longing look at the back of my head then turns to the barman and orders a water.

These espresso martinis are going down well. Too well in fact. I've just finished my third and I'm on the dancefloor, swaying to Beyoncé, feeling more than a little fuzzy. There's a man in front of me that I seem to have been dancing with for quite some time, and although I'm not quite sure who he is or how I came to be dancing with him, he's singing and grinning at me, so he's definitely a new friend.

I look to the left of me where Emma and Eva are dancing with each other, equally lost in our lovely world of music and alcohol, and somewhere in the back of my mind it hits me that this is the first time in a long time that I've felt completely carefree.

There's no Sam making me feel guilty, no one killing my joyful vibe and even my parental duties have been momentarily put on hold. I feel as though I'm eighteen again, dancing in a field of cows while coloured lights float above me in the sky. I squint. Or maybe they're coming from the ceiling. I'm not actually sure anymore.

I smile my happy smile at the grinning man, and he leans in and whispers something in my ear that's completely lost in the volume of the music. I beam back at him and nod, although I'm not sure what it is I'm agreeing with. He moves forward and then he's dancing even closer to me. I smile again as I look up at him. We're all in the happy club and it feels sooooo good.

A moment later his lips are on mine, rough, sloppy. Eurgh. I jolt my head away and take a step back, but he steps closer and does it again. I press my fists against his chest, trying to push him away, but his big hands are on my back and they're pulling me closer to him. Then they're moving down onto my bum, and he pulls it towards his crotch, gyrating and grinning and with the coloured lights shining across his face and hair, he's like some freaky multi-coloured alien monster.

Wriggling, I try and wrestle out of his grip, but he's too strong and I can't move him. Out of the corner of my eye I see Emma and Eva, still lost in the music, unable to hear my protests above the pulsating beat.

'Get off me,' I yell. 'Get off!' But one hand is snaking around to my front now, pressing upwards towards my chest while my own hands, usually so effective, appear to have no strength left in them to push him away.

Suddenly, something wrenches him off me with an incredible force that almost knocks me off my feet. I'm caught by Eva and Emma, all too aware now that something's not quite right.

I look around, trying to get my bearings. On one side of me, the alien monster's heaving himself off the floor, his grinning face now contorted with anger. On the other side is Daniel, who appears to have grown another foot in height. He's squaring up to the guy now, his shoulders broad, fists clenched, and he shakes his head, a warning not to push him any further.

Alien monster sways for a minute as he looks up at him, weighing up his options, then slinks off, his fingers making shapes to convey to Daniel exactly what he thinks about his intervention.

As soon as he's satisfied he's gone, Daniel turns to me, grabs my wrist and pulls me roughly off the dancefloor and through the throngs of partygoers to the side of the room.

'What's going on?' he shouts, his expression angry, puzzled, possibly even concerned.

'What's going on with you?' I yell back, like an insolent teenager.

'What are you talking about?' He looks even more confused than before.

'Joanne? The cinema? Using me – using all of us – to make money off her property.'

His head jolts back, as though I've hit him with my hand rather than my words. 'You're wrong.'

'Yeah, right,' I sneer. 'Because you'd never dream of using anyone to get what you wanted, would you?'

'Zoe, you're not making any sense. Who am I using?'

I start to formulate an answer, then blink slowly. As the flashing lights start to rotate around my head, it dawns on me that I might be a tiny bit drunk.

'You're using me,' I slur. 'You're making me feel all these things that I...' I look around in despair. The room spins again and I take a step back. 'I feel sick.'

He takes a deep breath, then wraps his palm around my wrist and pulls me, more gently this time, through the double doors and along the hall, pausing only when he sees the torrential rain splashing into puddles outside.

Daniel looks at the weather, then back at me, then swears a bit before steering me, my beautiful dress and my lovely curls out of the doors and through what feels like a ten-minute shower compressed into a five-second dash to the car. He wrenches open the passenger door of his BMW and places his hand on the top of my head as he pushes me firmly inside.

'Hey!' I shout at him through the window as he strides around to his side of the car, 'Where are we going?'

He gets into the driver's seat. 'I'm taking you home,' he says, shaking the water off his hair. 'No arguments.'

And surprisingly, even for me, there are none.

Saving the Good News Gazette

Westholme Community Facebook page:

Nora Baker: Be careful at the usual flooding hotspots tonight. Just driven down the main road by the Orchard Estate and the mini-lake there seems worse than usual.

Alan Boyd: It's bad by ours too – my garden's already like a bog.

Rob Horton: The council really needs to sort this out. It happens every time there's heavy rain.

Stephanie Porter: Must admit, I did think they'd do something after the river burst its banks that time when I was a kid, but not much seems to have changed.

Billy Twistle: They've given us our wheelie bins. What more do you want? Blood?

Chapter Thirty-Eight

I t's only when we're halfway back to my house that I realise I
don't have my bag, my phone or my key.

I start patting the places where pockets would usually be, as
though I'm expecting a magic opening to suddenly appear. Daniel
looks at me out of the corner of his eye.

'What's wrong?' he asks, his voice cool rather than concerned.
I've definitely gone too far this time.

'My bag. It's on the dancefloor with Emma and Eva.'

He stares straight ahead at the road. 'Can't you just get it off
them tomorrow?'

'My house key is in my bag,' I say in a small voice.

Daniel indicates and pulls over to the side of the road,
tapping the steering wheel as he works through our limited
options.

'Maybe we could go back to the hotel and get it off them?' I
make what, in my opinion, is a helpful suggestion.

He checks the clock. 'There's no point.' His voice is weary. 'By
the time we get back there they'll probably have left. It'll be like
trying to find a needle in a haystack.'

'It's fine,' I say cheerfully, 'my mum and dad have a spare key – we can just knock there.'

'At one-thirty a.m.?'

He's so negative.

Daniel starts up the engine. 'Right,' he says, pulling out onto the road. 'You'll have to stay at mine. There's no other option.'

Under any other circumstance, I'd be horrified at the very idea of it, but the buzz from the alcohol is wearing off and I'm starting to feel tired, so instead I snuggle down into the heated seats, issue a defiant, 'Fine' and promptly fall asleep.

I wake up as we turn into the drive and the gravel crunches under the tyres as we approach the house. It looks even more impressive by night, with spotlights illuminating the facade of the building, emphasising each of the many features that all add up to create a grand and imposing home. But there's still no Christmas lights, no decorations, nothing to indicate that the Big Day is less than a fortnight away.

As I shift in my seat, an extra layer moves with me and I glance down to see Daniel's jacket draped over my dress, the cause of a comforting layer of warmth that has built up around me and the heated seats that I'm reluctant to move from.

Daniel gets out of the car and I pull down the passenger mirror to check on my appearance, wiping spots of wayward mascara away from underneath my eyes and snapping it closed just in time for him to open my door.

'You OK?' he asks roughly as I wriggle out from under his jacket, relieved to see that the heavy rain has turned to light drizzle.

I nod and swing my legs out from the footwell, holding onto the car door as I step gingerly onto the gravel and wondering just how wrecked my shoes will be on a scale of one to ten by the time I reach the entrance.

Daniel walks ahead, letting me struggle on for a few seconds. Then, muttering something under his breath, he turns back and scoops me up into his arms, leaving me trying but failing to cover up as my strategically cut split falls very unstrategically to reveal an entire thigh just inches away from his face.

With nowhere else for my head to go, I rest it against his shoulder for a moment, breathing in the deliciously sexy scent of musk, pine and something almost as spicy – but not quite – as my thoughts.

I nuzzle my head closer into his white shirt with no concern whatsoever for what my make-up might do to it, and I feel hard muscle flex through the soft tissue of his chest. My tummy starts to flutter furiously and I look up at his neck, wondering why I've never noticed the strong line of his jaw before and marvelling at the strength he must possess to be able to carry me with such ease.

He opens the front door and carries me over the threshold, a thought that makes me laugh out loud.

'What's so funny?' he says, his voice low and ragged and displaying a mood that's anything but.

'Nothing,' I giggle, as he carries me up the sweeping staircase, along the galleried landing and into one of the bedrooms where he casts me onto the huge bed.

I hear his breathing quicken as he stares down at me, his dark eyes almost black as they roam up my leg, across my tummy and onto my chest, where the corset has created a cleavage that no amount of plastic surgery could achieve.

He loosens his bow tie, jerking his head from side to side as he works at the knot, then undoes the top few buttons of his shirt. Now it's my turn to stare at his chest, at the smooth golden flesh that's just crying out to be touched.

I catch my breath and we stare at each other for a few seconds before, emboldened by the espresso martinis, the setting of the house and pure, unadulterated lust, I make the drunken decision to dive in.

Shuffling to the edge of the bed, I kick my heels off, place my feet on the deep plush carpet and take the few steps that I need to reach him. Pressing my chest against his ribs, I snake my arms up his body and rest them on the back of his neck, looking up at him with pleading eyes while trying to ignore the pained expression on his face.

'What are you doing?' he murmurs, his voice catching in his throat, lower and huskier now. I don't have the answer, so instead I pull his head down towards mine, stand on my tiptoes, lean forward and tease him with my lips.

The first few seconds of the kiss are gentle, tender. But it quickly moves from nought to sixty, fervent, hungry, desperate. My fingers are in his hair, his hands are pressing all over my back, I'm pushing my body into his, he's pushing back. I'm so ready for this, for him, I can feel myself starting to let go… And then, as quickly as it began, Daniel rips himself away, stepping backwards to force a distance between us that I'm convinced neither of us wants.

We stare at each other, chests heaving, the sound of heavy breathing echoing around the room.

'What's wrong?' I pant, my eyes wide.

He keeps his eyes firmly fixed on my face, the intensity of his stare not fading for a second. 'You're drunk,' he says, his voice gruff.

'But you want this.' My earlier confidence is replaced now by uncertainty in my voice. 'I know you do.'

We stand there like that for a few seconds, a big, jumbled ball of confusion, red hot electricity and something else that I can't put my finger on between us.

Then he shakes his head. 'Not like this.'

I suddenly feel very sober, very stupid and very exposed.

'Get some sleep,' he growls, already heading out of the room.

He takes one last look at me as he reaches the door and I know he can see the rapid rise and fall of my chest as my breaths come in short, ragged bursts. Then, just as he's about to leave, he turns back around and shoots me an injured look.

'You accused me of using you tonight. Can you honestly say you're not trying to use me right now to get back at Sam?'

But before I can answer, he is gone.

Westholme Community Facebook page:

Eric Hanson: Something's going on at the cinema. Does anyone know how to reach that girl who's running it all?

Rita Hollingworth: Try *The Good News Gazette* FB page and message her through that. Although if it's not good news she may not be interested;-)

Chapter Thirty-Nine

O f course, by the time the morning comes, the very last person in the world I want to see is Daniel.

I lie there, all alone in his gigantic bed with the thick smooth white sheets, and as I stare at his off-white walls and dark wood furniture, I'm struck by the thought that this must be what it's like to stay in a really posh hotel. Except that guests in a posh hotel probably don't wake up with a vivid memory of trying to sleep with the manager. Well, unless the manager is a bit more downmarket than the hotel.

My digression buys me a few more seconds before The Fear that always strikes when I've had a drink kicks in, wringing my insides out as it tells me I've really outdone myself this time. I have officially humiliated myself more than anyone has ever humiliated themselves in the history of humiliations.

Burying my head in Daniel's puffy pillows releases a fresh burst of his scent and a wave of longing hits me with unexpected force.

I should have seen this coming. I should have listened to what my body was trying to tell me every time he came within five feet of me; what my heart was trying to tell me every time I felt the warm glow that came with spending time with him. I should have known. Then I could have kept my distance.

I groan out loud.

And now I'm stranded in this beautiful mansion with its electric gates, miles away from home and no idea how I'm going to get out of here in a cocktail dress without him, or indeed anyone, spotting me.

The thought of having to face him makes me feel even more nauseous than I already do, so I creep into the en suite, wash my hands and face and brush my teeth as best I can with my finger, a move that does nothing to remove the morning-after taste in my mouth.

I pour myself back into my beautiful red dress, retrieve my heels and, placing my hand on the satin nickel door handle, press down on it as slowly and carefully as my trembling fingers will allow. The door opens easily and I tiptoe along the landing to the staircase, peering down it to the entrance hall like it's the promised land.

Standing at the top of the stairs, I try – and fail – to hatch a cunning plan to escape the castle, like a twenty-first century Beauty trying to escape the clutches of the Beast – only in reverse.

It's at the exact moment that I realise I have no way of getting home without him, that I see a cordless phone on the console table that sits on the expansive landing, a note stuck on the handset.

Gone to Dubai. Help yourself to breakfast. Presthill Cars will take you wherever you want to go. Just tell them to put it on my account and use the PIN to open the gate. Number below. Daniel.

As apprehensive as I was at the thought of facing him, not seeing him at all is even worse. I have no idea of what he's thinking, what he's feeling, whether he's cross with me or able to laugh it all off, if he really does believe I was using him to get back at Sam.

I glance at the note again. His writing is like him; tall, strong, beautiful. I catch sight of myself in the mirror above the table and shake my head in disgust.

Then I pull the note off the phone, pick up the handset and dial the number that will get me the hell out of here.

Fortunately, my phone and keys are located at the first house I try. Unfortunately, that house is Emma's, which, with two boys whose energy levels never appear to dip below that of three cans of Red Bull, couldn't be less of an antidote to a hangover. She opens the door, takes one look at me and bundles me quickly inside.

In direct contrast to Daniel's house, Emma's is a festival of Christmas colour, with fairy lights, decorations and at least three trees visible from the hall alone. I head into the kitchen, away from the worst of the noise, ready for a coffee and a sympathetic ear. But Emma closes the door behind us, thrusts my phone in my hands and whispers, 'Quick, check it.'

I frown at her, unable to decipher the hidden meaning within her instruction.

'The cinema's been vandalised,' she hisses. 'Norman and Colin are there already assessing the damage but obviously I had your phone so couldn't reach you and I don't have Daniel's number. We didn't want to call the police until we'd spoken to Daniel and the owner. What's her name – Joanne?'

An icy chill spreads down my back. 'Daniel's in Dubai. And I have no idea how to contact Joanne. Do you know how much damage has been done?'

Emma shakes her head. One of her eyelashes is hanging off

and it's all I can do not to reach out and pull the other half from her eyelid.

I'm thinking on my feet now. My blistered, red raw, hungover feet. 'Do me a favour, Em,' I say, 'stick the kettle on and make me a coffee. I'll phone Mum and Dad and ask them to look after Charlie for a bit longer while I go home and get changed.'

'Then what will you do?' she asks, the grey tint to her otherwise orange skin indicating that I'm not the only one who over-indulged last night.

I sigh. 'Then I'll phone Daniel.'

Daniel's not answering. I've tried his mobile at least twenty times, but I can't even hear that funny ringing tone that lets you know the person on the other end of the phone is abroad. Instead, it's just refusing to connect, demonstrating perfectly just how difficult it is for Daniel and me to communicate with one another in any kind of meaningful way.

I bury my head in my hands and think. My mobile is pinging incessantly with messages from all and sundry making sure I'm fully up to speed with the events of the evening and I flick it to mute.

In the absence of all other options, I realise there's only one thing for it: I'm going to have to call Joanne. But when, thirty minutes of internet searches later, I still haven't tracked down any out-of-hours contact details for her, I take a punt and call Candice instead.

She answers immediately and I explain what's happened.

'I've just heard,' she says. 'I was about to give you a call and ask what was going on.'

'I don't know. I can't get hold of Daniel. I guess the first thing I need to do is to head to the cinema and see how much damage they've caused.'

'Good idea,' she replies. 'Give me ten minutes and I'll see you down there. Let's see how much of this we can sort out ourselves before Daniel finds out.'

Westholme Community Facebook page:

Rita Hollingworth: You were right about the cinema

Eric Hanson. I've just walked past it this morning. It's so sad. Did the *Good News Gazette* girl get back to you.

Eric Hanson: No. Feel sorry for her and all those people that have been working on it though. Did you see what they'd graffitied on the building too?

Rita Hollingworth: I dread to think.

Eric Hanson: Don't kick me off the group for the use of foul language, **Harold Kiddle**, but it's horrible. They've spray-painted *F*** Good News* on the side of the wall.

Chapter Forty

The scene at the cinema is heart-breaking.

I stand in front of it, looking at the graffiti and paint daubed across the building's brick exterior. Sharp, jagged edges are all that remain of the fan glass door panes while jagged shards and half-shells of lightbulbs are strewn across the ground beneath the new backlit sign. What only days ago was a thing of beauty is now a defiled, injured example of how quickly a labour of love can be turned into a vehicle for hate. A searing pain pierces my heart. It is devastating.

Moving almost mechanically, I push open the entrance door, bracing myself for the spectacle of ruin I already know lies behind.

It's Candice I see first. She's there, notebook in one hand, mobile in the other, photographing every last bit of damage and making copious notes. She looks as overwhelmed as I feel.

A broken mirror lies by her feet. From there, a trail of destruction snakes around the room; white paint splashed across the brand new red patterned carpets; the stunning chandelier, smashed to the ground; pipes ripped from the walls, causing water to pool in intermittent soggy patches.

As I see the balustrades, something catches in my throat. Those beautiful wrought-iron spindles that I admired such a short time ago have been bashed out of place, sticking out at haphazard angles from the panel below. There's paint on the box office counter too, with obscenities spelt both correctly and incorrectly daubed along its smooth marble surface.

'Is there anything they haven't destroyed?' I say evenly. It's not even a question, really. Because it's clear that whoever it is has been thorough in their annihilation.

Candice shakes her head. 'It's weird, the shutters still seem to be working perfectly, but they must have broken them in order to get in through the front door.'

'That's strange,' I muse. 'Because I was the last one in here and I definitely closed the…' I trail off. I closed the shutters, didn't I? I always close the shutters.

And then I remember.

I'm not convinced that I did close the shutters. I think it might have been me who left the cinema exposed. And now it's ruined, probably for a long time. Possibly for good.

'Candice,' I start, terrified to admit my mistake but aware that I have to do it all the same. 'I think it was me who—'

'Do you know, I've been thinking about those shutters,' she interrupts, 'and I'm sure there's something wrong with the electrics. There was definitely a day last week when I was sure I'd closed them, but when I came back to double-check, they'd rolled back up again. I'm certain that's what's happened.'

'But—' I persist, determined to confess.

'Listen,' she interrupts, looking me right in the eye, 'I'm absolutely *certain* that's what's happened.'

I bat away a wave of sickness. I'm way too hungover to contemplate the part that I played in all this. That can come later. For now, I need to get to grips with the situation in hand. And honestly? I don't know what I should do. Call the police? Call the insurance company? Call someone to find out who the insurance company even is? I feel useless, helpless. What was it that leadership book said? *In crisis situations, be the ship that guides your team to shore.* This is my team. I am the ship.

'Right,' I command as though I have any authority left. 'Let's make a to-do list. Are you happy to write it down?'

'No problem,' Candice replies. 'Although top of the to-do list should probably be sorting Norman out.' She nods towards the auditorium. 'He's in there.'

———

Norman is sitting on one of the few rows of seats left standing, staring at the slashed curtain and the vinyl screen behind it as though there's something to look at other than two giant rips.

I approach him from the side, able to see the downwards turn of his lips and the trembling of his chin. His spine is hunched over and his hands hang limply over his knees. He looks every inch the broken man.

He senses someone watching him, and his eyes flicker in my direction, then back again when he realises it's me.

'Are you OK, Norman?' I ask, even though it's clear he isn't.

He waits for a few moments before responding, then says, 'I don't think I am, no.'

I sit down next to him and look around.

The rows of beautifully reupholstered red tip-up seats have been kicked over with the sort of force I'm convinced only the Incredible Hulk could possess, with some of the parts ripped off and discarded on the floor. But that's just the start. More white paint has been thrown around the room with globules licking the walls, a huge hole has inexplicably appeared in the ceiling, and the LED lights that sit beneath each of the steps into the auditorium have been ripped out.

Beer cans and empty crisp packets scattered haphazardly across the room along with cigarette ends stumped out on the once-lovely floor only add to the feeling that the group of partygoers have spent a hedonistic few hours undoing all the good work that's been done here over the past few months.

'Don't worry,' I say, my voice weary with the effort of it all. 'We'll raise some more money, we can make it beautiful again. It just might take a bit longer to do than we thought, that's all.'

Norman turns his head to look at me with sad, puppy dog eyes and shakes his head. 'I don't think so. This...' He throws out his arm as he takes in the room again. 'Seeing it like this...it's just too hard.'

He's right. It is too hard. We're fighting a losing battle. Whatever we do, we're always going to lose to the gang. They'll always be there, waiting to slash tyres, set fire to stuff, throw rockets. Maybe we should just admit defeat. Throw in the towel. Call it a day.

I rub the palms of my hands across my face, aware of the dull thumping of a headache joining the nausea. The thought of what Daniel's going to say when I tell him we gave up makes me feel sicker still. Then I remember the way I threw myself at him last night and for a moment there's a very real risk that I may throw up on the already ruined red carpet.

The auditorium's double doors squeak and Candice rushes through them with what appears to be unnecessary speed considering that the damage is already done.

'There's something you need to see.'

Slowly, I raise my head.

'What is it?' Nothing could make this situation any worse. But then, nothing could make it any better either.

Candice pushes her lips together and gives me a half smile.

'We've got them. They're on CCTV.'

With all thoughts of throwing in the towel temporarily suspended, Norman and I hurry behind Candice as she leads us to the little office upstairs. We crowd into the tiny room and behind the small desk, where a number of images showing the various interior and exterior aspects of the building are set out on a grid on the computer screen. Norman has to squash the side of his body against my own in order to get a good view of the monitor and I hold my breath to avoid inhaling his unique scent.

'There's five of them,' Candice points out, as she clicks on the first of a number of videos we're about to see. 'Watch.'

Over the next fifteen minutes we do just that, unable to take our eyes off the screen as five boys who can't be more than sixteen years old casually destroy this beautiful building.

Thanks to the myriad of CCTV cameras erected by Daniel's team, we are privy to every aspect of the assault on the cinema, from the way they smash through the front doors to gain access, to the vicious way they repeatedly kick and stamp on the seats until the screws that held them to the ground are loose enough to be ripped out of the ground.

Next to me, I can sense Norman's distress. At times it's almost impossible for him to watch and his body recoils at the most harrowing parts. Because this grand old dame's revival has always been *his* dream, *his* baby. The rest of us were just facilitators. And to see these thugs treat something he's loved for so long with such contempt…well, it's almost too much for him to bear.

By the time the lads have sauntered out through the broken panels in the front doors, mission of destruction complete, we've all seen enough.

Me in particular.

Because despite the grainy footage, I can tell who some of

those boys are. It's the lads that spoke to Sam at the fireworks display. It's Jono and Gary Spindle – Spin. And a few more besides.

As I process this fact, the feeling of defeat gives way to anger. I'm disgusted. Fuming. And determined that, this time, the Orchard Estate gang are not getting away with it. They've abused Adina, graffitied the lovely white walls of the Parade, ruined our open-air movie night and now destroyed our cinema too.

Everything we've tried to do, every positive move our tight-knit community has tried so hard to make, they've tried equally hard to ruin.

But no more. This time they're not getting away with it.

Releasing a breath and then quickly inhaling a new one, I walk around the other side of the desk just in time to see Norman wiping away a tear.

'This isn't over,' I say firmly. 'Not by a long shot.'

Fishing into his pocket, he pulls out a blue-checked handkerchief and presses it firmly over his nose. The impact of my statement is lessened somewhat by the noises Norman makes as he gives it a good blow, so once I'm certain he's finished, I start again.

'Norman,' I say, more sharply than I mean to. He looks up with puppy dog eyes. 'We're not giving up.'

He sniffs again and looks at me, his expression full of uncertainty. 'Why, what are you going to do?'

I take a deep breath, then push my shoulders back. 'What someone should have done a long time ago. I'm going to speak to them. I'm going in.'

We're almost at the car when Starr pulls up next to us in her orange Renault Twingo. We wait as she fiddles around with the window switches, opening then closing the passenger window then grinning and mouthing 'oops' before successfully putting down her own.

'I've heard the news, my dears,' she almost sings, her giant gold hoops banging against her neck. 'What a dreadful turn of events. What can I do?'

Norman tuts. 'You'll be glad to hear they've wrecked the red velvet chairs.'

'What nonsense. As though something that awful would make me happy.' She takes her glasses off and polishes them on the belly of her cerise velour tracksuit. 'Have you thought about a new colour scheme?'

'Not yet,' I quickly intervene. 'That's a conversation for later on, I think.'

'Of course, of course. So where are you going now?'

'We're off to the Orchard Estate to tackle the perpetrators,' says Norman, who I'm starting to suspect is quite excited by the plan. His puppy dog eyes have disappeared, his tears are all gone and there's clearly a fire in his belly. In fact, I haven't seen him this determined since he went up against Starr over the cinema name. 'We've got them on CCTV.'

'Oooh,' she replies, clapping her hands together. 'That sounds thrilling. Jump in and I'll drive you there.'

I gulp. When I announced my 'reclaim the streets' mission, I pictured myself as the sole participant in it. Maybe Candice at a push. But now Norman and Starr are chattering excitedly about it and I'm starting to realise my attempt to scare the boys into submission may invoke laughter rather than terror.

'Do you know what,' I say, thinking on my feet. 'I totally forgot I have to pick Charlie up from my parents. Maybe we should leave it today. Go another day instead.'

'Don't worry, Zoe, we've got your back.' Norman's looking around at the others. 'We'll go, won't we?'

'Yes, let's do it! Let's do it now.' Oh, good grief. Starr's as up for this as Norman is.

'It probably would be better to wait,' agrees Candice, who's clearly not up for it at all.

'Rubbish,' scoffs Norman. 'If we go now, we'll be back by lunchtime and I'll still catch the horse-racing.' He opens the passenger door and jumps inside. 'Come on, Starr, let's go.'

'Wait!' I shriek and make a grab for the back door handle. 'Never mind Charlie, I'll collect him later.'

We all eye Candice now. 'Are you coming, my dear?' asks Starr. Candice looks from Starr to me then back again.

'Daniel's going to kill me,' she mutters, then climbs in anyway.

'To the Orchard Estate!' cheers Norman, and we chug off at approximately twenty-five miles per hour to do battle with Westholme's most wanted.

Westholme Community Facebook page

Lucy Lashes: Feel so sorry for those poor people who put so much hard work into renovating the cinema. Looks like the little scrotes have absolutely wrecked the building.

Steve Crossley: The people who have done this are absolute scumbags. It really is a battle between good and evil.

Paul Gregory: If anyone fancies fighting back, I have a plan... DM me

Chapter Forty-One

I t isn't until we turn into the estate, nausea picking at the back of my throat thanks to the combination of Norman's body odour and Starr's juddery relationship with the gear stick, that it dawns on me I don't actually know how to find the lads. They might be hard-faced but I'm pretty sure they're not just hanging about waiting for someone – albeit that someone is more likely to be the police than four community campaigners – to turn up and nick them.

We head towards the part of the estate where the movie people are completing the last few days of filming, but a quick drive-by reveals they're not there and I have no idea where to try next.

I rack my brains, trying to come up with a plan that won't result in me having to admit I've dragged everyone here on a wild goose chase. But other than simply driving around the estate hoping we'll find them knocking back some Special Brew on a garden wall, I don't have any firm ideas. After all, I only even know who a couple of them are because of Sam.

Sam.

We haven't spoken since the night it all ended and given the fact that he wouldn't tell me who threw the fireworks, I'm pretty sure he's not about to deliver the boys to my door.

Then again, he knows how hard we've all worked to get the cinema to this point and, if the lads agree to what I'm about to put to them, there may not be any 'grassing' involved.

'Guys,' I call out from the back seat. 'I might just need to make a little stop first.'

'Absolutely, dear,' chirps Starr. 'Where would you like to go to?'

'The football academy. I need to have a quick word with Sam.'

'Ah,' Starr swoons. 'Lovely Sam. He's ever so handsome, your man, isn't he?'

'Umm, er…' I'm not feeling equipped to answer this sort of question anymore, given that he's no longer my man. 'We've broken up,' I finally answer.

Starr brakes sharply to bring the Twingo to a shuddering halt, nudging me forward against the passenger seat in the process.

She turns around and looks at me through the side of her glasses, an angle which, against the magnified lens, makes the eye closest to me look unnaturally large and grotesque.

'I'm sorry, luvvie,' she clarifies, 'I thought then you said you'd broken up.'

'We have,' I confirm, buckling under the weight of two pairs of eyes – plus one extra-large one – on me.

Starr looks shell-shocked. 'But he's a hottie.'

'He is. But it just wasn't working. I mean, it didn't work out.'

'Oh dear,' Starr muses. 'I bet he'd take you back. A nice man like him, I'm sure if you just told him it was a mistake…'

'The thing is, I'm not sure that it was a mistake,' I reply, squeezing one hand with the other. 'I'm not sure at all, actually.'

I steal a quick look at Candice, whose eyebrows are raised. Ahead of me, Norman looks impatient at this interruption to proceedings.

'Very sad, very sad,' he says, checking his watch. 'But we'd better be getting on.'

Starr glares at him, goes to say something, then, thinking better of it, turns back round to the steering wheel, puts the car into first gear, then gear-change-jolts us all the way down the road.

———

Sam's typing something into his computer when I arrive at the academy. I watch him for a second through the glass door pane and my heart does a little jump as I catch sight of his face, screwed into an expression of intense concentration.

I knock on the door to let him know I'm there and his eyes widen in surprise as he sees it's me. He beckons me inside and I step tentatively into his office.

'Hi,' I say quietly.

'Hi,' he replies. I shift awkwardly.

'This is…unexpected,' he says finally.

'I know. I'm sorry to bother you, but the cinema's been vandalised – destroyed actually – and we've got the lads who did it on CCTV.' I pause. 'Sam, it's Jono and Spin, plus a few others.

'By rights, we should go straight to the police, but then where does it end? We'll always be battling against them, watching them ruin every effort we make to improve the town. They'll get arrested, given some kind of crap punishment, then it all begins again. But if you can take me to them, I can put another idea to them; one that just might offer them a way out.'

Sam bites his lip. 'What's the idea?'

'Will you show me where they live?'

He shakes his head. 'No. They might look like kids but they're dangerous. You really don't want to make them angry.'

I puff my chest out and raise my chin. 'Sam, that gang of lads have just ruined months of hard work by myself, the team and the entire community. Believe me when I say that it's not *their* anger you need to worry about.'

He sighs then, a gesture of defeat, and I feel so bad I decide to meet him halfway. 'Tell you what,' I say, 'why don't you come with us. You don't have to lead me to their exact doorways. Maybe just somewhere in the vicinity'.

I unhook his coat from the back of the door and take the few steps across the room I need to hand it to him.

As I pass it over the desk, he reaches out, but instead of taking the coat from me, grasps my hand instead.

'I'd do anything for you. You know that, don't you?'

Something squeezes my heart and wrings it out like a sponge and I can't tell whether it's guilt or regret.

'Almost anything,' I reply gently, not quite able to meet his eyes.

Neither of us speaks for a moment, lost in a wave of 'might-have-been's and 'still-could-be's.

'You and I have different ideas on how to solve the same problem, that's all,' he says eventually. 'I use football to try and change lives rather than the justice system. It doesn't mean I don't care; just that I think, in some cases, there's a better way.'

I purse my lips. 'Then you might like the plan I've come up with.'

His expression is hopeful now, expectant.

'We'd better go,' I assert. 'The others are waiting outside.'

'Others?'

'I'll explain on the way. Let's go before either of us loses our nerve.'

Of all the properties on the Orchard Estate, Jono's is probably the least attractive. There's a mattress, broken flags and an old children's slide littered across the small jungle of a front garden, with the one thing of beauty in the otherwise ugly piece of land being a single rose bush growing near to the front wall.

It's sad to think that someone must have loved this house once, of the time and effort they probably put in to making it look pretty, planting the rose bush, blissfully unaware that their efforts would be trampled on so carelessly in years to come.

We stand down the road from the house, Starr, Norman, Sam, Candice and I, examining it from afar while working up the nerve to knock on the door.

'What an ugly house.' Starr wrinkles her nose in disgust.

'I've seen worse,' says Candice ominously.

Norman glances at his watch. 'Shall we knock?'

I take a deep breath. 'Let's do this. So, Sam, you're going to wait in the car?'

He nods. 'But call me if you're in the slightest bit worried about anything, agreed?'

'Agreed.'

'And, Zoe?' I meet his eyes. 'Please be careful.'

———————

Norman, Candice, Starr and I walk towards the house like a group of prisoners heading towards a firing squad.

From the moment we reach the front path, the stench is all-pervading It stinks of rotting rubbish, dirt, sweat, and has clearly escaped the cleaning frenzy that has swept up the nation in recent years.

'This smell is foul,' utters Norman and I try not to look surprised by the observation. It's fascinating how someone with such little regard for his own personal hygiene can be so offended by the neglect of others.

I lead our gang past the broken front gate and up the path

before coming to a stop at the front door, where peeling black paint reveals a sage green shade underneath. There's no bell and the only sign of any kind of door knocker is a metal base plate which probably once held one in place.

I gingerly lift my hand up to the door and knock on it loudly, a move which catches the attention of a dog that responds by repeatedly throwing itself against the door, barking with the ferocity of a blood hound on a hunt as it does so.

We all jump back as the dog continues to howl at our presence, unsure whether we've bitten off more than we can chew. But before we can even consider the option of leaving, a woman's voice hollers, 'Jono! Get that, will you?' and the door is wrenched by the very boy I've been looking for, holding the Staffordshire Bull Terrier back by his flimsy-looking collar.

So, this is him. Jono. The same Jono who launched the assault on Adina at the Parade, the same Jono who was responsible for ruining our pop-up film night and the same Jono who led the others into the attack on the cinema.

He's tall and gangly, but I already knew that. His skin is an unhealthy shade of grey and he has clearly been blighted by the kind of acne that can make some teenagers' lives hell. His beady eyes narrow and his nose and mouth wrinkle into a sneer as he tries to work out who we are and why we're on his front doorstep.

With Starr in her cerise tracksuit, Candice in her gym gear and Norman in his cords and checked top I suspect he's already ruled out any suggestion we might be the police, but still a look of contempt forms on his face as he glares at each of us in turn.

'Are you from social services?'

I step forward. 'No, we're not from social services, Jono. We're from the cinema you've just destroyed. And I'd strongly advise you to listen carefully to what I'm about to say.'

The dog growls and pushes forward and I try to stay brave as Jono makes only a half-hearted effort at keeping hold of him.

'Oh yeah? Can't wait to hear this,' he snarls.

'I know what you did last night. I know where you were and who you were with.'

I'd love to say that at this point Jono looks panicked, scared, anything that indicates he is in any way fearful of the repercussions that his actions might bring. But his expression holds firm and I almost suggest that he might want to consider poker as a form of income rather than whatever it is he's doing right now to earn his keep.

'Thanks to the wonders of CCTV, I have a detailed recording of exactly how you and your friends tore apart the inside of the cinema last night,' I say in my most threatening tone, the one I use when Charlie back-answers me. 'And I'm going to hand it in to the police, along with the names and addresses of each and every one of you.' Obviously, I'm bluffing this part, but given that I've already managed to track down Jono himself, I'm confident he'll buy it.

'So what like?' he replies, but this time he does flinch a little.

'However,' I continue, 'there is a way you and your friends can avoid all that.'

He crosses his arms as he waits to hear what I have to say.

'Be on our cinema board.'

The face he pulls in response is so exaggerated that it immediately rubs me up the wrong way, but I somehow manage to keep calm and carry on.

'Join our board as advisers and volunteers. Help us to shape the cinema. Tell us what films you'd like to see there. Get involved with running it.'

'No chance,' Jono snorts. I shudder. I really don't want anything to do with him, but unless we get them on board, the Orchard gang are going to put the blocks on literally every positive move we try and make.

'Then I'll have to take this CCTV to the police.'

There's a rustling at the door and a woman appears next to him. She's probably only thirty-something, but the lines that surround her mouth and the fag hanging out of it make her look much older.

'Who's this?' she says to Jono without at any point removing the cigarette.

'Some cow from the cinema,' he replies.

Norman steps forward so he's standing next to me. 'Excuse me, but I think you'll find this is the very esteemed editor of *The Good News Gazette*, and she's worked extremely hard to try and make improvements within our community. Now, he can either listen to what she has to say, or we may be forced to make a citizen's arrest.'

I'm both grateful for and embarrassed by his indignation and try and harden my expression to give the impression that – pompousness and cerise tracksuits aside – we're not a group to be messed with. I have no idea how to actually make a citizen's arrest and don't fancy my chances of any attempt being much of a success, even if it would be a case of four-on-one.

'I was explaining to your son,' I address the woman with the cigarette, 'that I have CCTV footage of him and his mates wrecking the cinema last night and that, unless they agree to work with us on putting it right, I'll be going straight to the police with the recording.'

The woman glares at me for a minute then mumbles something to Jono.

He chunners something back, then she says, 'Wait here' and slams the door.

'Ooh, this is ever so exciting, isn't it?' whispers Starr, hopping from trainered foot to trainered foot.

'That's one word for it,' I mutter.

'The other being "risky",' adds Candice.

The door is wrenched open again and Jono and his mum stand beside each other, seemingly ready to confront us head-on.

'He'll do it,' she declares, reaching across her vest top to scratch her plump arm.

'And his mates too?'

Jono scowls. The woman pokes him in the ribs.

'All right,' he spits.

'Good. Then I'll expect to see you all down at the cinema by two p.m. this afternoon. Any later and I'll go straight to the police.'

The woman takes a drag. Jono curls his lip. And then the door is shut firmly in our faces.

Westholme Community Facebook page:

Paul Gregory: Everyone ready?

Steve Crossley: I am.

Tori Hindle: Me too.

Beryl Goodwin: As I'll ever be.

Alan Boyd: Present!

Rob Littlewood: Looking forward to it.

Eileen Wilson: Can't wait.

Chapter Forty-Two

I t's only two p.m. but I feel as though I've already lived a lifetime today. After dropping the others back off at the cinema, I collected Charlie from Mum and Dad's, went home and rustled up both lunch and painkillers and then headed straight back to join them.

Charlie is delighted at having been deemed old and important enough to join me on such a mission. He's currently walking around the building like someone off *CSI: Crime Scene Investigation*, pointing to various damaged parts and using my phone to photograph them and document the evidence.

My heart sinks as I look around the auditorium. How the gang managed to cause so much damage in such a short space of time is beyond me, but it's going to take more than a few hours to put it right. A few months is more realistic. But the cinema's meant to open a week today. My stomach does a weird flippy thing that makes me fear for the contents of my lunch. There's no way we're going to be able to do it in time.

Candice pops her head around the door. 'Zoe?' she calls, then spotting me, says 'Ah, you're here. Guess who's just crawled through the broken panes of the entrance doors?' And she pushes the door open wider to reveal Jono, Spin and the rest of their lowlife mates, reluctantly awaiting their instructions.

I know there's two ways I can play this. I can sink to their level, have them work like dogs and generally make their lives hell; or I can take the upper hand, offer them a drink and hope that this is the wake-up call they need to turn their lives around. I toss the two options around in my head for a second, every instinct telling me that they fully deserve the former.

And then Jono sneezes and one of his mates says, 'Bless you.' It's a phrase that's so sweet and so unexpected that it takes me by surprise.

'Good to see you, lads,' I say. 'Now who wants a cuppa before we start?'

I thought *I* was a hardened coffee drinker. But next to Jono I am little more than an amateur. He's knocked back three cups in the last forty-five minutes, but I don't want to quell his appetite for caffeine for fear it might slow him down. And, as we've already established, there is *a lot* of work to be done.

The first and most immediate task was to call out a plumber to try and put right whatever they'd done to the pipes. Because while half of the carpet was perfectly dry and usable, the other half of it was completely saturated. But it being Saturday and good plumbers – like every other reputable tradesperson – already in pretty short supply around Westholme, getting hold of one was proving impossible.

'Oi, lads,' I shout to where they're crouched with cloths and buckets trying to soak up the mini-flood they've created. 'I don't expect you've ever done any sort of plumbing work, have you?'

I'm not hopeful, but then I didn't anticipate the 'Bless you', either.

They all grunt various forms of 'no' and I sigh. Our cinema repair team is currently made up of Sam (he insisted), Candice, Norman – who returned once he'd finished watching the horse-racing – Starr, Detective Charlie, me and five criminals. And none of us have a clue what we're doing.

I head to the office for a moment's respite and put my head down on the desk. Out of nowhere, a tear I didn't see coming trickles across my nose and down the other cheek. Then another one rolls out of the other eye, falling onto the tops of my hands where I'm resting my head.

I'm a fraud, getting everyone to work like this. Even if we stayed here twenty-four hours a day for the next seven days, our little gang could never put the cinema back together in time. We're going to have to cancel the opening. Put it back for a couple of months, explain that we just couldn't do it.

The tears pick up speed.

I stay like that for a few minutes, tears pooling under the side of my head, feeling utterly sorry for myself and forcing myself to replay every bad decision I've ever made, in particular the ones involving leaving the shutters unlocked and launching myself at Daniel Lewis.

Suddenly, a little arm lands across the back of my neck, a head I've come to know just as well as I do my own presses against my cheek and I feel myself being squeezed more tightly than is comfortable.

'Don't cry, Mummy,' whispers Charlie, and just that word alone is enough to send me into freefall. It's been so long since he called me 'Mummy' and just as long since he hugged me like that. I move my hand to grip his arm and squeeze it equally tightly.

'We'll fix it, Mum,' he says, my little boy now trying to reassure me. 'I've photographed all the evidence so we can show it to the police and the new people said they'll have the cinema open on time if it's the last thing they do.'

I raise my head as I register his words. 'What new people?'

He kisses my forehead. 'The people who've just arrived. There's lots of them.'

I sit upright, instinctively wiping away the smudged make-up that I already know will be there.

'What do you mean?'

He huffs, the Charlie I've come to know and love making a swift return.

'*I* don't know. Why don't you come and see?'

I sniff and stand up. 'I'm coming now.'

'Come *on* then, before they go. And, Mum?'

'Yes, Charlie?'

'Love you.'

'I love you too. More than you could ever know.'

And just like that, my little/big boy makes everything seem infinitely better than it did before.

There are more than forty people milling about in the foyer, armed with tools, materials, bin bags and lots and lots of goodwill.

Margaret is leading the charge, standing at the front of them all like the world's most unlikely sergeant major, directing everyone into groups and allocating roles to each of them.

I recognise Colin and Lynne, Emma and Eva and a few others, but most of the people here I've never set eyes on before.

'Ah, here she is,' shouts Margaret. 'Here's our leader.'

'Margaret,' I hiss. 'What's going on?'

'Nothing to do with me.' She beams, her eyes positively shining with delight. 'It's the Westholme Community Facebook page. These people heard about what happened to the cinema and wanted to help.'

'And help we will,' says a voice I recognise from somewhere, and I look over to find Jim Steiner, the bloke who runs the course at the local community college, standing there with a tool belt slung around his hips and a dozen or so teenage boys and girls gathered around him. 'The cavalry has arrived.'

'With cakes and sandwiches,' a female voice rings out, and Paula pokes her head out from behind a pile of cake boxes.

'And hot drinks,' yells Cath, who's setting up a couple of urns.

My eyes prickle with those pesky tears again and I will myself not to start sobbing.

Even the Orchard Estate boys look taken aback by this much community spirit all in one place.

I gulp and clear my throat. 'Thank you so much, everyone,' I shout to the assembled crowd. 'It's so good of you to come. I know we won't be able to stick to our pre-Christmas opening date, but with all your help, maybe we can set a new date for some time in the new year.'

'Nonsense,' a voice hollers from the crowd.

'The cinema's opening next week, just like you planned,' yells another.

Jim steps forward and I scuttle over to him.

'They're wrong, aren't they, Jim? There's not a chance we can have this place ready for next week – is there?'

Jim looks around, quickly assessing exactly what needs doing.

'Can't see why not,' he surmises. 'As long as you're up for it, that is.'

I look at all these people, willing to give up their time to put the cinema back together again, and I'm filled with a rush of love for my home town.

Candice stands poised for action, holding the clipboard she

must have pinched back off Norman, and she nods to let me know she can help organise.

I head back to the front of the room. 'Right then!' I shout. 'Let's do this! Please make yourselves known to Candice, Jim and Margaret, who will assign jobs to each of you. Help yourselves to tea and coffee, let me know if you need anything, and between us I'm sure we'll be able to get this cinema back on its feet in no time.'

A huge cheer goes up around the room.

'Are there any jobs left for us?'

The crowd parts like the Red Sea, and as I crane my neck to see who else is throwing their hat into the ring, I hear a series of gasps spread round the foyer.

Tony Hanlon, Joshua Hartley, Lily Lonsdale and what looks like the entire cast and crew of Westholme's very own movie are standing right before us in their jeans and sweats.

'Mum,' murmurs Charlie, tugging at my arm, 'it's...it's...'

Before he manages to say it out loud, Joshua Hartley steps forward, puts out his hand and says, 'Pleased to meet you, little guy, Joshua Hartley at your service.'

And it's all I can do not to faint on the spot.

Westholme Community Facebook page:

Eyelash Lucy: Joshua Hartley is at the old/new cinema right now! Tried to go down and help, but they've got so many people queuing up to volunteer, the film crew have put their own security on the door.

Leah Moreton: Not surprised – I wouldn't mind volunteering my services to Joshua Hartley.

Hollie Cross: You might as well. You've volunteered them to everyone else in Westholme ;-)

Westholme Gardeners : If anyone's looking for volunteering opportunities, please feel free to DM us. We're always on the lookout for new members.

Hollie Cross: So's **Leah Moreton** ;-)

Chapter Forty-Three

My nightmare day has turned into something of a dream.
Within thirty minutes of the cavalry's arrival, Margaret and Candice had assigned jobs to each and every one of them and the cinema has since become a hive of activity, with people brandishing paintbrushes, dragging in dehumidifiers, fixing pipes and renovating broken chairs in record time.

Admittedly, the celebrities aren't getting much of a chance to really put their back into it, given that every time they move, someone else finds an excuse to talk to them, but as morale boosts go, they're right up there with the coffee and cake.

I catch Sam looking admiringly at Lily and realise I don't mind as much as I would have expected. As much as I would if it had been Daniel.

I check my phone again. He hasn't returned any of my calls. I bet he's returning Joanne's calls. I look around at everyone working so hard, trying to fix this mess for the good of the community, and feel a wave of shame that they're here under false pretences.

Because it's not about the community really. It's about Daniel coming to the rescue of his girlfriend's derelict property, finding a way to have it renovated, up and running and bringing in cash for her – all under the guise of a 'community business'.

A surge of anger fires me up again. I was right the first time – and every time since – when I thought he was trouble. He's duplicitous and scheming and I can't believe that, despite knowing all that, I threw myself at him.

I sigh. As soon as this project's finished, I'll never have to see him again. The London job offer pops into my mind, and I wonder for the first time whether it might actually be a viable proposition, as a form of escape if nothing else.

I'm pondering on this when Ollie struts into the auditorium. He's wearing skinny light blue jeans and a white jumper, a look that makes me think, once again, he's not here to indulge in any sort of manual labour.

'Come on in and join the fun,' I greet him, managing to summon up a grin. 'I was wondering what was taking you so long.'

I realise then that he's not smiling back.

'Ollie, what's wrong?'

He fixes me with his big blue eyes.

'It's the cinema. Zoe, Joanne's put it up for sale.'

I stare, open-mouthed, at Ollie.

'What?'

'It's true. I had a coffee this afternoon with a friend of mine, a commercial property agent. He's been off this week, so he couldn't give me the latest update, but he said his company was dealing with it and as far as he knew, it was going on the market a few days ago.'

'But I don't understand. Joanne had an agreement with us. Or with Daniel, at least. I have no idea what's happened.'

Candice wanders past. 'Just making coffee,' she says. 'Do you want one?'

I beckon her over. 'Do you know anything about the cinema being put up for sale?'

She frowns. 'What are you talking about?'

'Ollie's heard that the cinema is going on the market and I wondered whether you knew anything about it?'

Candice shakes her head. 'I can promise you, there's no way that can be right. The cinema's not up for sale, it's—'

She stops herself then, looks apologetically at Ollie and then back at me.

'Zoe, can I speak to you alone for a minute?'

———

Satisfied that the cinema's every need is being attended to, I take Candice upstairs to the office and shut the door, fighting back the headache and nausea that have returned with full force.

'So,' I demand. 'Spill.'

Candice flops into an armchair in the corner, then says carefully, 'Joanne doesn't own the cinema anymore.'

'Of course she does; we're renting it off her.'

'Er, you're not. Not anymore. The cinema's not up for sale. It's already been sold. It's changed hands in the past few days.'

I inhale deeply as I try and process what she's telling me. Nothing is making any sense at all.

'But if she doesn't own it, who does?'

Candice shifts in the chair. 'I'm sorry, I'm really not meant to say.'

This is bizarre. 'Candice. We have half of Westholme, five

criminals and the cast of a Hollywood film in here fixing the place up. Whoever owns it really needs to know what's going on.'

She sighs. 'All right, but it never came from me.' She takes a deep breath, then speaks quietly and slowly. 'As of three days ago, the new owner of the cinema is Daniel.'

'What? I don't understand, how can it be Daniel?'

She hesitates, then says, 'What I'm about to say is strictly between us, agreed?'

I nod. 'Agreed.'

'You know Joanne and Daniel had "a thing"?'

'Yes.' I gulp.

'A few weeks ago, Daniel ended it. I don't know any more details – you know Daniel would never talk about that kind of stuff – but it seems as though she got nasty. Told him he couldn't use the cinema anymore, that she would put it up for sale after all. She obviously knew how much it meant to him, and she stuck to her word, instructing agents, putting word around that it was going to be sold.'

Candice leans forward in her chair. 'But she's money-driven, isn't she? So, he made her an offer she couldn't refuse. She put him through the mill, pushing and pushing for more, but eventually accepted whatever it was he offered her. So, you see, Joanne doesn't own the cinema anymore. Daniel does.'

I think about what she's telling me. 'What does this mean for the business then?'

'From what I understand, Daniel intends for it to continue exactly as it has been doing, but instead of having the buy-back agreement with Joanne, the group will have it with Daniel – or with Lewis & Co. – instead.'

'And what about the two of them? Is it really over?' I say, not managing to meet Candice's eyes.

A smile plays across her lips.

'It's over. If it ever even begun. The question is, what are you going to do about it?'

I consider the question a lot.

I consider it when I'm making the forty-fifth round of drinks that afternoon; when I'm fielding questions from Starr about the colour of the replacement seating and when I'm telling my dad that we don't need the bloke he knows at the factory to supply us with any weapons in case Jono and Spin suddenly turn on us again.

Yes, the question is well and truly considered.

And this is my answer: Nothing. Nothing at all. It's all feeling too messy. Too ugly. Too much.

I've made an absolute idiot of myself in front of Daniel once again by jumping to the wrong conclusions, acting like a total arse at lunch with Tony, then on top of it all throwing myself at him last night.

All that respect that I've worked so hard for, that I strongly believe is inherent in a leader, thrown out of the window as I succumbed to every possible negative stereotype of women in business.

So, I won't be doing anything with this piece of information Candice has given me. I'll just let it float off into the breeze, try and learn, once again, from my mistakes, and concentrate on finishing the job I set out to do: bringing the cinema back to life for the good people of Westholme.

I am *so* glad to get home tonight.

My head is whirling, spinning. I am *so* hungover. And tired.

And totally done.

Charlie, on the other hand, is full of beans and keen to dissect the events of the day in microscopic detail.

'Mum, do you know that Joshua Hartley asked me my name TWICE today?' he babbles, while we're devouring pizza on the couch, our faces periodically illuminated by the flashing LEDs on the Christmas tree I somehow made sure went up.

'And Lily Lonsdale said, "No thank you" when I offered her one of my Monster Munch. I can't WAIT to tell the boys at school.'

'I must admit, Hollywood celebs fixing up Westholme is not the sort of thing that happens every day, is it?' I put on a great show of enthusiasm, determined to be as excited for Charlie as he is for himself. 'Or even any day, come to think of it. It's going to make a great front cover for the *Gazette*.'

Damn. I'd forgotten about that. I'm going to have to type out a story and upload it to the website ASAP once Charlie's gone to bed. The one downside of news being 24/7 now is that everything has to be transmitted immediately. It's exhausting. I take a bite of my pizza. Another reason why I love magazines.

An old episode of *Knight Rider* comes on the TV and Charlie is immediately engrossed. I wish I had a KITT car to fix everything for me. Because right now I'm in a bit of a quandary. There's a few things on my mind:

1. **Daniel:** He's bought the cinema. What does this mean? Is our community business still a community business, or is it now Daniel's business, which we have inadvertently funded? And why would he buy it in the first place? Does he actually care about it? About our little group and all the hard work we've put in?
2. **Sam:** Is it really over? I think yes.
3. **The Gazette:** Can we keep it going with only one advertiser who pays ten pounds a month for a postage-

sized advert? I think no.

4. **David Hasselhoff:** Was he the best-looking man on earth during his Knight Rider years? And has anyone actually come close since?

5. **The London job:** Too many thoughts to list.

After KIIT has dealt with the bad boys in a satisfactory manner, I make the mistake of asking Charlie how he'd feel about a move to London, sweetening the deal with the suggestion that we'd have more money to spend on football stickers and FIFA points.

'Would we live with Dad?' he asks suddenly. 'Dad lives in London, doesn't he?'

I freeze. There's a reason I hadn't mentioned that factor.

'He does,' I confirm. 'But no, we wouldn't live with Dad.'

Charlie falls silent for a moment.

'I like it here.'

My heart feels like it's being ripped in two and I almost end the conversation there. But something in me makes me try one last time.

'Do you think it's possible that you could like somewhere else a bit more? There's lots to see. The Royal Family live in London – at least I think they do. Or maybe that's Norfolk. Or Windsor. I'm not actually sure, but both Buckingham Palace and Kensington Palace are in London anyway and that's where everyone thinks they live.'

Charlie rubs his hand back and forth over the crown of his dark hair.

'Wembley Stadium's in London.'

'Well, there you go then,' I reply, silently thanking whoever it was that chose to build Wembley Stadium in Wembley. 'So is the Tower of London.'

'So's Harry Kane,' adds Charlie, warming to the theme.

'Who's Harry Kane?' I'm scratching my head.

'Mu-um, only a super-famous footballer!' Charlie rolls his eyes.

'Oh, OK.'

'Maybe we'd even be neighbours,' he says hopefully.

'Er, I don't think so,' I reply.

'No, he probably lives next door to Jermain Defoe,' Charlie concedes.

'Probably.'

Charlie shifts on the couch and throws his legs over mine.

'Maybe we could live next door to Dad then.'

I choose my answer carefully.

'I think he already has neighbours. Anyway, we don't really see him so much anymore, do we?'

Charlie strokes my hair back from my face. 'You think he doesn't love us, don't you?'

'No, Charlie, that's not it at all,' I reply firmly. Urgh. Why did I even start this conversation on a hangover?

'But I think it's just *you* he doesn't love,' he clarifies. 'I'm sure he still loves me.'

I sigh. 'I'm sure too, little man.'

'And maybe he'd want to see me a bit more if we lived closer to him.'

'Erm…maybe.'

'So yeah,' he concludes. 'It might not be so bad after all.'

He shifts again, nuzzling my shoulder, then his head pops up back into my line of sight.

'Wait, would we still see Nan and Granddad?'

Ah, now that one hurts.

'Not as much as we do now. But we'd come back and visit regularly.'

'And who would look after Lola?'

'We would,' I say. 'She'd have to come with us.'

He settles down again. 'I think I'm all right with that.'

I rest my head back and stifle a smile at the fact that Harry Kane is out there somewhere tonight, completely oblivious to the fact that the choices he's made in his career could have such a bearing on my own.

———

After Charlie's gone to sleep and I've uploaded the 'A-list celebs save Westholme's silver screen' story, I try again to watch series two of *Bridgerton*. I'm approximately two minutes in, when a text flashes up on my mobile from a number I don't recognise.

Lost my phone at the airport, sorry you've had to deal with all the cinema business on your own. Are you OK?

My heart skips a beat as I realise it's from Daniel.

No worries. Everything's fine. All's well that ends well. How's Dubai?

He texts back immediately.

Fine. We should talk when I get back.

My heart leaps with joy, quickly followed by a wave of almost overwhelming sadness. Carefully, I place the phone on the couch, face down. Then, slowly and deliberately, I pick up the remote control, point it at Kate Sharma and press play on her life, with the sole intention of pausing my own.

———

Westholme Community Facebook page:

Pete Owen: The river's at dangerously high levels again tonight. Must be all this rain we're having. Thought it was meant to be snow at Christmas, not rain.

Billy Twistle: That only happens in the movies. What do you think Westholme is? A film set?;-)

Chapter Forty-Four

Having done the rounds on all of the national media and finding there to be a distinct shortage of publications willing to run a story on her daughter playing a munchkin – paid or otherwise – Chelsea Turner's mum has emailed me to say she's had a re-think and has decided to let me interview her for free.

I'm making Charlie's breakfast when the email comes through. I say 'making' – all it actually involves is pouring cereal into a bowl and making sure Charlie sprinkles one teaspoon of sugar rather than ten on top – so I can't reply to her straight away. But by the time I drop Charlie off at school and get to the office, she's already called and spoken to Ollie three times.

'Good grief, what is with this woman,' I comment, as I read the sticky note on my desk. 'She seems obsessed with making her poor daughter a star.'

'It's not just her daughter,' Ollie says. 'She tried to tell me about at least another four children while she was on the phone. Apparently, she runs some kind of theatre company and thinks we should be writing about all the kids.'

I roll my eyes. Listening to a mother wax lyrical about her all-singing, all-dancing daughter is the last thing I need today. But I've been so tied up with the cinema business, I haven't had time to pursue many new stories over the past few days, so a little feel-good tale about a local child performer in a Liverpool play might be worth doing.

'I'll email her now. It'll make a nice picture story in the next issue, if nothing else. Coffee?'

'Love one.' Ollie holds out his coffee cup for me to collect and then, after about ten seconds of me pretending I haven't noticed, he gets up and brings it over.

'Gutted I missed all the cinema action,' he says. 'Everything sorted now?'

'Hmmm, I noticed your usual absence from any situation which requires a bit of graft. Anyway, yes, we're getting there. And having the actors join in with the rescue mission has given everyone a bit of a boost.'

I unscrew the coffee jar and start spooning coffee into our cups.

'Ollie,' I say after a moment, 'I need to talk to you about something.'

'Uh-oh.' His eyes sparkle with mischief. 'What have you done now?'

Usually, his comments would be met with mock indignation and a swatting of the arm. This time, though, there's no reaction; only a silence as I work up the nerve to get out what I have to say.

'I've been offered a job in London.'

'Oooh!' He laughs. 'I hope you told them you couldn't possibly accept, as you were far too busy sorting out the boyz in the hood and saving local landmarks from demolition.'

He nudges me with his shoulder. 'How did they take it? Did they offer you double the wage to swap Westholme for West London?'

'I haven't decided whether or not to accept it yet.'

I stare at the mugs, waiting for him to say something funny, make us laugh, make it all feel fine. But he doesn't make a sound. He just stands rooted to the spot, staring at me.

Eventually I can't bear it any longer. 'Ollie, for goodness sake, say something.' I stir milk into the coffee then hand him his mug.

'What would happen to the *Gazette*?' he asks, finally.

'Well, obviously I wouldn't be here to keep it going.'

'What about me?'

'I never – I mean – I didn't think this was something you'd want to continue on your own.'

'No,' he says sharply, 'I mean, what about me? I thought we were a team.'

All the hair on my body seems to stand on end, like a million little pin pricks all in one go.

'We *are* a team, Ollie, of course we are. But you know how difficult it's been to keep everything going over these last few months. Trying to juggle freelance work with finding stories, not to mention advertisers. The endless pressure of trying to bring new advertisers on board while keeping the very few we do – did – have. And with the wage Daniel's paying me due to come to an end soon… I'm not sure I can do it anymore. It's impossible.'

He looks at me carefully, then shakes his head. 'Just weeks after Adina and I have committed to renting this house.' He laughs bitterly.

'Ollie…' I say, reaching out to touch his forearm. 'I haven't decided whether to go or not yet.'

'Forget it,' he says, dumping his mug and grabbing his jacket from the back of his chair. 'Do what you want. I'm done.'

I waited all day for Ollie to return, but he didn't come back.

In fact, the only person who did come back to me today was Chelsea Turner's mum. She responded instantly to my email, advising that it would be best *for me* if I went along to her theatre company tonight. That way, apparently, I could both interview Chelsea as soon as was humanly possible and also see if there was anything else going on there that I might be interested in writing about.

I'm pretty sure there won't be, but there's no after-school clubs for Charlie tonight and he could really do with a break from his Xbox, so I replied telling her we'd both head along to her class at the town hall straight after school.

'Mu-um, do we have to?' he moans when I pick him up and set out the plan for the next hour or so.

'Yes, we do,' I reply. 'I only need to do have a quick chat, video her and take a photo. It won't take five minutes.'

'I'll set the timer on my watch,' he warns.

'Set it for ten then,' I respond. 'These things can't be rushed now, can they?'

Chelsea Turner is as precocious as I remember. She's spent the last fifteen minutes telling me how much stronger a performer she is than virtually everyone else in the production of *The Wizard of Oz*, and despite Charlie making numerous faces at me to ensure I know exactly how much over the allocated time I've gone, I can't seem to escape this verbal assault.

I've filmed, photographed and interviewed her and her mother to such an extent that I know exactly how dilated Mrs Turner's cervix was when she turned up at the labour ward (six centimetres) and I still haven't found anything remotely interesting in her story.

Eventually, I get my own back on Charlie by telling Mrs Turner that we'll have to go on account of his funny tummy and it's only then, as we're being shown out of the door, that I ask Mrs Turner about her theatre class.

'Oh yeah, I mentioned the class to that bloke you work with, but he said he wasn't interested,' she replies, giving me an insight into exactly how Ollie deals with potential story phone calls when I'm not there.

'It's a shame, cos I didn't get round to telling him the whole story.'

'What's the whole story?' I ask, more out of obligation than interest.

'All these kids have special needs,' she replies. 'That's the area of teaching I trained in, so I got some drama teachers in who are qualified in this area and now we run this theatre school.'

'I didn't realise you were a teacher.' Now *this* sounds like a good story.

'In the special needs school over at Lawton. Great group of kids. These are too. I keep telling them, give it a few years and you'll be as successful as our Chelsea.'

I bite my tongue so that I don't come out with anything mean, and say instead, 'How long have you been running the drama school for?'

'Only six months or so. I started it up for my son. He has special needs too. He's what inspired me in the first place. After all, look at these kids. Each and every one of them is amazing,' she says. 'Why shouldn't they be on the stage? Why shouldn't they be on our TVs?'

'No reason at all,' I agree.

'That's what I keep telling our Bailey, my son.'

'Can I speak to him?' I ask, ignoring the very pointed look that Charlie's giving me. 'It would be great to get some quotes about how the classes have helped him.'

'Well, you could do, but he's only thirteen months so he's not actually talking yet. But we have been doing a bit of roleplay with him.'

'Thirteen months?' I repeat.

'Yeah. You can't start them too early, can you? It's so competitive out there.'

Parents are gathering around the door now so I say my goodbyes and arrange to return and video him later on in the week. When I've worked up a bit more enthusiasm.

Westholme Community Facebook page:

Sharon Knox: Has anyone else received one of these lovely Christmas cards from the little boy at Westholme Primary School? My mum lives on her own and only really has me to visit. This card put a smile on her face that I haven't seen in a long time. Thank you!

Jenny Ledman: My dad got one yesterday. He was over the moon that someone had thought of him. I think the little boy who started it wanted to make sure no one was lonely this Christmas.

Jimmy Hunter: I also received a card. Very touched. Thank you.

Chapter Forty-Five

I t's become clear that the film company's involvement with the cinema rescue may not be entirely altruistic.

While I'm sure Tony Hanlon's motives are genuine – and to be fair, he's grafting with the best of them – I'm fairly certain Joshua Hartley and Lily Lonsdale's involvement is being directed by the PR woman. She turns up at regular intervals with photographers from different publications and arranges the pair into various 'working hard' poses before whisking them back to the film set faster than you can say 'media opportunity'.

The upside of all that is that the cinema's getting way more publicity than I could ever have dreamed possible. The international coverage, combined with the social media content Josh and Lily are constantly posting about how they're saving our 'small-town cinema', means that fundraising for the project has gone through the roof, with donations being sent from all over the world to help pay for the work.

Of course, we've gone to great lengths to make sure that Jono, Spin and their friends' real identities have been kept hidden. Because while we're still seething over the damage they caused, none of us are about to throw them under the bus and reveal who caused such destruction.

There's another reason why I want to protect them as much as possible. Because in the few days since Jim Steiner took them under his wing and started teaching them new skills while putting them to work, I've noticed a change in all of them. They're turning up on time, chatting to the other volunteers, and now and again they even chance a chuckle, although they quickly stop if they suspect anyone can see them.

I can't believe I'm saying this, but I think they're enjoying being a part of it all. In fact, I actually think they're having fun.

I've missed a few Slim City meetings.

There's been so much going on in my head that there's been no room to think about weight loss too, and a few (dozen) items of food that I would normally avoid may have crept into my mouth without me noticing.

But after eating a full box of the Christmas chocolates I'd bought for Charlie's teacher while I was watching *Bridgerton* the other night, I realised I was starting to slip back into my old ways so decided to recommit by turning up to class.

I'm standing in the queue now, which seems to have paused thanks to Cath taking an inordinate amount of time at the scales, chatting to Beth and Emma about Darcy's recent doctor's appointment. I can tell from the bags under her eyes that Beth hasn't quite reclaimed her sleep, but she seems happier and more relaxed now that she has additional support. She's even found a top that goes with her black leggings.

'So, they're going to refer Darcy to the hospital to work out what's going on, but the doctor said she may be allergic to something or it might be Irritable Bowel Syndrome,' she explains.

'Obviously, neither of these are great, but at least once we know what's happening, we can treat it for her. In the meantime, he's given her some probiotic drops, and they already seem to be calming things down a bit.'

'I'm so pleased for you,' says Emma. 'Finally, you seem to be getting somewhere with it all.'

'It was Margaret,' Beth replies. 'She sorted everything out. Arranged the doctor's appointment and explained in advance what the problem seemed to be. She's been a godsend.'

'Hopefully you can see some light at the end of the tunnel now,' I remark.

'I can. And it's a weight off Tony's mind too.'

We're interrupted then by the sound of Cath cackling at the scales.

'Oh no,' Beth gasps.

'Tell me she's not doing what I think she is,' Emma says, just as my dad walks in, takes one look at Cath, and walks straight back out again.

She is.

Cath is standing on the scales in her underwear. In her faded pink bra, her white/grey knickers, and absolutely nothing else.

'Yes!!!!' she hollers, oblivious to everything but the numbers on the scales. 'I did it, ladies! I got my stone award.'

A rousing cheer goes up around the room.

'Although you did resort to slightly unconventional measures to achieve it,' responds Barb. 'But well done, a stone is a stone, and it all counts on the regional figures,' she adds. 'That's the most important thing.'

The queue moves a lot more quickly once Cath's out of it, and within minutes it's my turn on the scales.

'Hello, dear,' Wendy, Cath's assistant and chief weight monitor, greets me. 'We haven't seen you for a while.'

'I know. I've been really busy and I just haven't been able to concentrate on my weight.'

'How do you feel it's going?' she asks kindly. Not well, is the honest answer. I've been squeezing myself into my work trousers to the point where they've actually started to hurt my waist when I put them on, and I now have at least one shirt that can only be made decent by the addition of two safety pins around the bust.

'Oh, you know,' I say instead. 'Up and down.'

I take a deep breath and step on.

'Unfortunately it's more up than down,' Wendy confirms.

My heart sinks. 'How much have I put on?' I'm already dreading the answer.

'Eight pounds.'

Ouch.

'Are you sure?' I appeal.

'Quite sure,' she confirms.

'Great,' I mutter. 'Barb's going to have a field day.'

'Don't worry, dear, you're not the only one. There's been lots of gains tonight.' Wendy leans towards me and whispers conspiratorially. 'It would have been worse, but I've made a slight alteration to the scales.'

I gasp. 'But Barb will kill you!'

Wendy taps the side of her nose. 'What she doesn't know won't hurt her. And believe me, my dear, judging by what I've seen on the scales so far, I've saved her from a world of pain tonight.'

Barbara is not happy.

She's just called out my name, then, expecting me to have

maintained my previous weight loss, cast a cursory glance at her little screen.

The face she is pulling in response tells a thousand words.

'Zoe,' she calls out. 'Please tell me that Wendy's input the wrong figure.'

I shake my head miserably.

'Eight pounds, Zoe? In four weeks?' Oh, the shame as I hear a collective gasp from the other members. 'Have you been on an all-inclusive holiday that you forgot to mention?'

'No, Barb,' I reply, attempting a laugh while simultaneously sinking down into the chair and wondering why my dad had to choose this exact moment to sneak back in.

'Suddenly developed a thyroid problem?' she asks hopefully.

'No.'

'Well, what on earth's happened then?'

I sink even further into my seat, and am about to apologise, when I'm hit by a sudden realisation.

I shouldn't need to apologise for my weight gain.

It's OK to put on eight pounds.

It's also OK to eat the brownies.

I sit up straight.

'I've had an extremely stressful few weeks,' I inform Barb, batting away the feeling of guilt at knowing that, due to her husband living with Motor Neurone Disease, she's not exactly on Easy Street herself.

'Haven't we all,' she mutters, then addresses me. 'Zoe, there are always difficulties to be faced in life, but that's when it is more important than ever to stick to the diet. Otherwise we'll go off the rails, as you've seen this week.'

I take a deep breath. 'I disagree,' I respond. The room falls silent. Barb pushes her shoulders back, as if ready for a fight.

'Pardon?'

'I said, I disagree.'

'Go on,' she says, but in a way that suggests I really shouldn't.

'Life can be hard. Break-ups, job losses, work stresses, any life event…it's tough. And do you know what brings me immense pleasure during those times of abject misery? It's knowing that I can return home, put *Bridgerton* on and pig out in front of the TV with some chocolates or a nice glass of wine, or a big bag of those lovely pink and white squashy sweets. Or maybe all of them.

'Anyway, my point is that while I know that, when life is a bit crap, the best thing for my body is to take a yoga class and drink camomile tea, the best thing for my head, at that moment in time, is to eat like a seven-year-old at a kids' party.'

'And have there been a lot of those moments lately?' Barb interjects.

'There have,' I confirm. 'And while I'm not overjoyed at having put on eight pounds…' I look at Wendy '…or maybe more, I also accept that sometimes, these little blips are going to happen. Because that's just life. And maybe, once I've stopped beating myself up about my complicated love life, my thwarted attempts to keep my good news operation going and the fact that all these distractions are using up mum time that I should be having with my son, I'll pass the bargain sweets shelf in the mini-market without so much as looking in their direction and buy some fruit instead. But right now, that's not on my horizon.'

I stand up and pick up my coat.

'Barbara, I really do appreciate your attempts to keep me on the straight and narrow, and I promise I will return when I've lost a few pounds, but for now I'd be lying if I sat here and promised I'd rein it in over the next week.'

I look around the room. 'Ladies, it's been a pleasure.'

'Where are you going?' asks Dad

'I…' I pause for dramatic effect '…am off to Greggs.'

And, holding my head up high, I stalk out of the room, pausing only to whisper, 'Sorry, Barb', on the way out.

Westholme Community Facebook page:

Kim Hughes: Anyone seen the old cinema? They've turned the outside lights on. Think it must be the opening night.

Jimmy Hunter: It is. Well done to the team who've renovated it. I'll admit, they've done a good job and it seems to have turned out well. For now.

Chapter Forty-Six

Τ he cinema looks beautiful.

It's ten minutes before the guests are supposed to start arriving for the launch party and I'm standing in front of it checking for any last-minute hitches.

Above the doors, lettering on the huge white light box states: 'Westholme Cinema Opening Night Tonight'. On the canopy below the wording, hundreds of warm white twinkling fairy lights provide an inviting glow to moviegoers, while Christmas garlands hanging off it give the whole place a wonderfully festive feel.

The columns of the cinema's red-brick frontage have been illuminated and three lines of blue strip lights make the top of the building glow.

Through the double doors at the entrance, the brightly lit foyer can be seen with uniformed volunteers standing behind the box office and the refreshments counter, waiting to make their first sale.

From what I've seen of Norman's old photos, even in its heyday the cinema never looked like this. My heart swells with pride as I think back to what the building was like a week – never mind a year – ago.

Norman, the man who for so long has made it his mission to bring his beloved cinema back to life, is inside organising the people who have come forward to help over the past couple of months. He's agreed to take on the cinema manager role on the condition that it's only until we manage to find someone more suitable, although I strongly suspect that we'll struggle to find anyone else with half as much passion as he has for this place.

I place my hand on the polished brass handle and push open the glass-panelled door. Ahead of me, standing in the corner next to the huge, brightly lit Christmas tree, Norman is issuing instructions to the volunteer ushers and counter assistants who are working this evening.

'Now remember,' he's saying sternly. 'Health and safety is paramount, so it's absolutely vital that you remember the protocols at all times.' He holds up a safety booklet and raps his fingers against it. 'You should all know this guide inside out by now, but if you need clarification on any of the points in there then please alert me as soon as possible.'

He sees me and nods, clearly pleased as Punch with his new role, and I head past him and into the auditorium to check it's ready for the customers.

My breath catches in my chest as I'm hit by the beauty of it all. The thick rich-red curtains, the plush red-and-pink-patterned carpet and the rows of beautiful red velvet chairs with the cerise trim all look magnificent.

Crystals hanging from the chandeliers catch the light to cast pretty patterns on the clean, white walls. I step forward and walk down the sloping floor, then look back up at the balcony with its fresh coat of paint and carved embellishment in the centre. Whatever Jono and his mates did, there's no longer any evidence of it here. Thanks to our wonderful community – plus a couple of

A-list celebrities and a Hollywood film crew – the whole place looks as good as new. Even better, in fact.

The door bursts open and Candice rushes in, coat hanging over one arm, phone nestled in the other hand. Her long red hair has been loosely curled and she's wearing a long black one-shouldered dress. She looks fabulous.

She greets me with a hug and a kiss, then pulls back to look at this 'done up' version of me, in my beautiful teal jumpsuit that I gave in and bought from Vintage Vibes. 'Wow, you look gorgeous.'

'Thank you. So do you.' We beam at each other, savouring the moment of victory.

'Come on then,' I say. 'The guests will be here soon. Let's get ready to greet them.'

It's nearly time to start officially welcoming our visitors so I head to the office to do a last-minute make-up check.

I'm about to push open the door when it's wrenched away from me and I walk straight into Norman's chest.

'Norman!' I exclaim. 'I'm sorry, I had no idea you were in here.'

He mumbles his apologies and is manoeuvring his way around me when I spot something on my desk. I take a step closer so I can work out what it is. A small but beautiful bunch of flowers.

I spin around and call to his fast-retreating body. 'Norman?' He tries to hurry on, but I shout to him again and he comes to a standstill. 'Norman, have you got a minute?'

Slowly, reluctantly, he turns around and walks back towards me, pausing at the chair to the side of the door. 'Well, all right,' he says, 'but just one minute. There's lots to do, you know.'

'Did you leave me these flowers?' I say, pointing towards the desk.

He shakes his head emphatically, but keeps his eyes firmly fixed on the floor.

'It's you, isn't it? It's you who's been placing the flowers around Westholme.' He shakes his head again. 'Why have you been keeping it secret?'

'I really don't know what you're talking about,' he protests, and I try again.

'Norman, I promise you that what we're about to discuss will be kept very firmly between you and me, but please will you put me out of my misery and admit that you're the flower-giver?'

He sinks down into the chair and puts his head in his hands. 'I didn't want anyone to know.'

'No one does know. It's just me.' I crouch down to speak to him and squeeze his arm. 'What you've been doing is absolutely lovely. I'm just intrigued as to what's behind it.'

'My wife,' he says, his expression one of wearied disappointment.

'Your wife? I didn't even know you were married.'

He nods. 'I am. Was. She died last year. It was a habit, you see, buying the flowers. I did it every week. And then when she died there was no one to buy flowers for anymore, but I kept doing it anyway.'

He sighs. 'One day, a neighbour of mine lost her mother, so I left them outside her door and watched as she found them. Seeing her face light up when she saw the flowers was the first thing that had made me happy since Audrey died.

'A week later, I heard about a nurse who was retiring after fifty years in the job, so I left a bunch of flowers outside of her door too. There were also others who were having a hard time and needed a little bit of cheering up so I made sure they received flowers.

'And then, of course, I started reading *The Good News Gazette*, which provided an endless source of people who deserved to have their kind deeds acknowledged.'

'But what have *I* done?' I ask, confused. 'Why do I deserve a bunch of flowers?'

'You did this,' he replies, spreading his hands out. 'You rescued the cinema that I've tried so hard for so long to preserve. My wife always used to say, "Keep going, Norman, you'll convince them all one day." Now, thanks to you, that's exactly what's happened.'

Guilt pricks my conscience as I remember all the times Norman, with his pompous ways and his insistence on procedure, got on my nerves. If only I'd known that behind the mask he was grieving his late wife and looking for people whose day would be made brighter by a beautiful bunch of flowers.

'Norman, that's beautiful,' I say, feeling unexpectedly emotional by this unexpected discovery. 'What a lovely gesture.'

'She was all about that, my wife. Romantic gestures. That was her thing. I did it because she liked it. And then I couldn't stop.'

'Well I, for one, am glad you didn't.' I give him a hug and delight in the aftershave that hits my senses rather than his usual smell. 'This is so kind. Your wife would have been very proud of what you've done.'

His eyes start to look glassy so I change the subject.

'It's nearly time to open the doors. Would you like a minute to yourself before we do?'

He nods. 'Thank you, that's very kind.'

I straighten myself up, stretching out my legs and wondering when it was that I reached the age where I had to groan as I moved out of the crouch position.

'You're a very special person. You know that, Norman, don't you?'

He smiles gratefully.

'As are you, Zoe, as are you.'

Westholme Community Facebook page:

Lisa Seddon: Celebrity alert – I'm hearing that Lily Lonsdale and Joshua Hartley are going to be at the opening tonight.

Eyelash Lucy: There's a bunch of us already here – I'll be livestreaming the whole thing!

Chapter Forty-Seven

M argaret arrives before the doors are officially open, with Jack following closely behind. 'Just in case you need any extra help,' she says. 'All hands to the deck and all that.'

I smile warmly. 'Thanks to you, we seem to be right on track.' A volunteer walks past with a tray filled with glasses of fizz and I grab two and hand them to Margaret and Jack.

'Your only job this evening is to relax with a few glasses of these and enjoy the reckless feeling of not having anything to do except enjoy yourself for a few hours.'

'Like a proper night out, eh, Margaret,' Jack adds, knocking back the first glass and helping himself to a second. 'Maybe we could hit the clubs after we're finished here.'

'Jack, will you behave yourself,' Margaret scolds, shaking her head in disgust. 'We're here to celebrate the opening of a community cinema, not to get drunk like two teenagers.'

'Well, maybe we should,' Jack replies. 'After all, we're a long time dead, aren't we, Marge?'

'It's Margaret, and I'm nowhere near dead, thank you,' she

snaps back, but as she turns away I'm sure I detect her mouth twitch beneath layers of disapproval.

Out of the corner of my eye I see a smartly dressed couple file through the doors. I turn to greet them I do a double-take. It's Mum and Dad.

'Good grief, Dad, what's happened to you?' I say, eyeing his suit and tie combo.

He grins, clearly delighted at the recognition.

'Had to get a new suit, didn't I, love,' he says proudly. 'There was no way I was going to let you down on your big night by looking like a scruffbag.'

'He looks great, doesn't he?' says Mum, giving him an affectionate squeeze. 'Like a real gent.'

'Oi!' Dad responds. 'I *am* a real gent.'

'We know, Dad, we know,' I say, patting his arm. 'But even gents can drink fizz now and again, so go and help yourself before Jack pinches them all.'

The rest of the gang have been here for a while, fussing around like me, but not really doing anything useful as, thanks to Margaret's organisational skills and the work ethic of the many locals who descended on here over the last week to fix everything in time, it's all been done.

The only person who hasn't yet arrived is Daniel. He ended up having to stay in Dubai longer than planned, and although we've spoken about the cinema through emails and texts, we haven't had a proper conversation since that night. He was flying back today and is due to arrive any minute and my stomach is doing somersault after somersault at the thought of seeing him again.

Our other friends are starting to wander in now, too. Neil and John are greeting everyone arm-in-arm; Cath's here with her new man Ralph, who is shorter and rounder than her and gazes at her as though he can't quite believe his luck. Paula, meanwhile, has arrived with Sean, who's immediately teamed up with Charlie and Emma's two boys to huddle in a corner and watch Mr Beast on the mobile phones they've smuggled in.

In black suits with white shirts, Jono, Spin and the rest of their gang have turned up looking like something out of *Reservoir Dogs*. The director Tony Hanlon kindly brought some old suits that the costume department had apparently discarded, and the transformation into these washed, smartened-up versions of themselves makes my heart swell.

Beth and Tony wave at me from the other side of the room, where they're chatting to Sam, who must have snuck in without me looking. After that painful afternoon when we found Beth on the floor, they seemed to accept they needed to ask for more help. Tony's mum has since turned out to be a godsend at knowing how to calm Darcy when she's unsettled, providing Beth and Tony with a brief respite while they wait to receive Darcy's hospital appointment so that they can better understand how to help her.

A blond man and brunette girl arrive, their combined beauty turning even more heads than usual. It's Ollie and Adina, and I head over to them, unsure as to the reception I'll get.

'Hi, guys,' I greet them, issuing a cautious smile.

'This is all amazing,' Adina gushes as she throws her arms around me.

'Looks great, Zo,' says Ollie and then, as Adina turns to chat to Margaret and Jack, he moves me nearer to the wall.

'About the job...' he begins.

'Oh, Ols, you don't need to worry about that. I've only got until tomorrow to make my final decision, then they'll move on to someone else anyway.'

His usual jovial face is serious. 'I hope you're going to say yes.'

'I—'

'Wait,' he cuts in. 'Before you decide, I need you to know that I've been giving it a lot of thought, and you have to do what is right for you. If giving up *The Good News Gazette* and moving to London is your dream, then you have to do it.'

'But what about you?'

He breaks his gaze for a second. 'I'm not going to pretend that this fits in with my own life plans. But there's a bit of shift work I can do on one of the Manchester papers, and there are other things I can do to make ends meet. We'll be OK.'

I give him an impromptu hug. 'Thank you, Ollie. For everything.'

He squeezes me back. 'Love you. In a totally platonic, non-sexual, old enough to be my mother kind of way, of course.'

My eyes fill up with tears as I hold the hug longer than is strictly necessary.

'I know,' I reply. 'Love you too.'

I've just let go of Ollie when a rumble of excitement trembles through the foyer. The volume of the chatter, which, until that point, had been relatively low and contained, goes up a few notches. Then someone next to me murmurs, 'Will you look at who's just turned up,' loud enough for me to hear, and I spin around to see lights flashing through the glass panes at the front of the building.

I rush to the front of the foyer, concerned that the next generation of the Orchard Estate gang may have turned up to reclaim their predecessors, and haul open the doors.

Suddenly, I'm standing right in the middle of an impromptu photoshoot, starring Lily Lonsdale, Joshua Hartley, Tony Hanlon, some other actors and actresses who have been overshadowed throughout by their more famous counterparts, and now, me.

'Zoe,' shouts Tony. 'Get in the photo with us.'

'Wait,' I yell. 'There's a few more people that need to be in the shot.'

I duck back inside. Where's Norman when you need him?

Then suddenly, I'm within shouting distance of him.

'Norman!' I yell. 'We're all needed outside immediately for a photograph with the cast of the film.'

'I'm on it,' he shouts back, nodding authoritatively.

He disappears for a few seconds, then suddenly he's halfway up one of the staircases with a Tannoy raised to his mouth.

'Where the hell did he get that?' Candice asks.

'Is it not yours?'

She shoots me a look in response.

'Ladies and gentlemen,' Norman begins. 'Can I have the original members of the Big Screen Queens to the front of the building IMMEDIATELY please. I repeat, the Big Screen Queens are needed outside the front of the building for a group photograph.'

I giggle, incredulous at the fact that that name was ever actually adopted by our little group, and join the others as we make our way through the double doors and into the middle of the celebrity line-up.

Starr, dressed in a beautiful purple cocktail dress made up of lots and lots of feathers, and sporting matching long gloves, is already there, smiling graciously in the line-up and happy, for once, to share the limelight.

'Guys!' Tony shouts to the photographers, paparazzi and everyone else who's turned up to film, photograph and record every minute of this spectacle. 'Let's have a cheer for the woman who made all this happen – Zoe Taylor and her team!'

I take my bow to the cheers of the crowd, my joy tempered by the weight of the one pair of eyes I feel on me that are way heavier than anyone else's.

And before I even see him, I know that Daniel's back.

Westholme Community Facebook page:

Eric Hanson: Flood alert tonight – the police are going up and down various roads in the town knocking on doors and telling people to evacuate.

Joan Byers: A flood alert? But it's not even raining!

Eric Hanson: It's forecast to start in the next hour and after all the rain we've had recently, the river can't take much more apparently. Levels are expected to rise even further tonight and a number of flood alerts have been issued in the town. *The Northern News* are posting regular updates.

Chapter Forty-Eight

I 'm definitely in fight-or-flight mode.

My heart is beating way faster than it's meant to, and the rest of my body feels like it's following suit. Daniel's presence has put me in full panic mode, and now my mouth's dry, my stomach's lurching as though it's leapt on a roller coaster and my legs are jelly weak.

Fortunately, before we have the chance to speak, Norman uses his Tannoy to announce that we all need to move to the auditorium immediately so that the introductory film can begin.

I'm filing back into the foyer along with the celebrities, who, after spending a fair amount of time with the locals over the past week, don't seem particularly concerned about keeping their distance and are happily chatting away to anyone who approaches them, when I feel a light touch on my arm.

I spin around, half expecting it to be Daniel, and instead come face to face with the beaming faces of two older ladies, one with light-brown hair that dusts her shoulders, the other with bright-blue eyes and a silver bob.

The first lady I recognise instantly; it's Janet Dawson, the UK half of the pen pal duo I reported on for the *Gazette*. It takes me a little longer to place the second woman.

'Zoe!' Janet exclaims, nudging the other lady towards me. 'Meet Elizabeth.'

Now I remember. The women who had been writing to each other since they were schoolgirls but had never met. And now they're here, standing together, arm-in-arm, as though they're worried that if they let go they may not find each other again.

'After reading your story on *The Good News Gazette*, lots of lovely readers donated money to pay for a flight to bring Elizabeth over here,' explains Janet.

'There sure are good folk right here in Westholme,' drawls Elizabeth. 'What a great place to live.'

'Ladies, this is amazing,' I reply, whipping out my phone to photograph them so I can post a follow-up story on the site. 'I'm so pleased to see you together in person.'

'Elizabeth only arrived here yesterday, but we have a lot planned,' says Janet. 'People donated so much money that the fund organiser gave us what was left over after the flight so that we could do some of the things we'd always talked about.'

'It's so cool,' adds Elizabeth. 'We're going to see all the Liverpool sights – I'm a big fan of The Beatles – and then we're going to go to London and see a show, have afternoon tea at a posh hotel…it's going to be a blast.'

Norman appears at my side then, cutting short the conversation in order to remind me that I need to go to the auditorium NOW as it's approximately eight minutes until the short film we're showing, documenting our journey to the opening night, begins.

After extracting promises from Janet and Elizabeth that they'll send me photos of their various exploits, I join the crowd of people making their way to the auditorium.

We've all filmed our progress at various points along the way, and Norman has been working with a video-editing whizz kid he knows to stitch our footage together and serve up what he promises will be a fitting tribute to the cinema's journey to greatness.

The idea had been that we'd actually all be shown this pièce de résistance before tonight, but the Orchard boys' involvement had derailed everything, and we just didn't manage to fit it all in. So, it got to the point where I had to just cross my fingers, trust Norman's sometimes questionable judgement and hope for the best.

Norman's cordoned off the front two rows of chairs for everyone involved in the project and I beckon Charlie over as we file in, determined that the most important person in my life will have a prime spot in proceedings.

We all squeeze in next to each other, chattering in excited anticipation of what we're about to see. Around me, I can hear people commenting on how lovely the cinema looks and what a beautiful job we've done, and the feeling it gives me makes everything that's happened to this point worthwhile.

Once everyone's seated, the auditorium is plunged into complete darkness as atmospheric music surrounds us courtesy of the cinema's new surround sound system and we all gasp and giggle in feigned fear.

The red velvet curtains swish slowly back, revealing a picture on the huge screen of the cinema back in its heyday, when Westholme residents would visit in their droves.

Other images follow, creating a nostalgic throwback to a time when cars were a luxury almost no one had and TVs were yet to be installed in our living rooms.

A voice that I recognise to be Norman's accompanies the images, providing historic background to the grainy sepia pictures and imparting all sorts of information about them that I'm sure most of us will never have heard before.

The sepia eventually gives way to colour, as the cinema enters the seventies, and we all try and spot people we might know from the cinemagoers that appear on the screens.

We hurtle through the eighties and the nineties, then, as the timeline takes us up to the millennium, a photo of the cinema all boarded up with a 'for sale' sign in the front of it leads us into the next two decades of dereliction.

That's how those of us that are my age and younger remember it: abandoned, graffitied, cut off from the busy community who no longer had time for its once-loved picture house.

I'm transfixed, watching the images of how the cinema was during that time; the weeds that sprang up around the outside of it, the smashed windows that no one ever bothered to replace, the rows and rows of abandoned seats, the rubbish left on the floor, just as it was that day when Daniel and I saw it.

And then, the music changes. It becomes cheerier, faster-paced, more upbeat as both our narrator and the photos and videos he's talking about are hauled into the 2020s. We all cheer as photographs of each of us doing various jobs are shown on the screen, interspersed with videos of us talking about what we were doing. I'd forgotten I'd even been filmed talking about my role in it all, so frantic have the last few months been, yet there I am, providing a piece to camera on why the renovation of the cinema is so important to the people of Westholme.

I smile back at the image of me on the screen. The shadows on my face suggest I'm completely exhausted, but my eyes are shining and I look happy. After I've finished talking, Daniel approaches me and says something that makes me giggle. My heart squeezes with sadness, but it's what happens next that really hurts.

The camera is still on us, but while I turn away and carry on with whatever I was doing before, Daniel continues watching me, smiling at whatever it is I shout over my shoulder at him by way of response.

It's a look that carries with it so many unspoken words that I feel goosebumps spread along my arms and legs. Its message is so unmistakable that even Charlie shifts his eyes to me and my face goes hot in response.

Because I know that look. It's the look that Ollie gives Adina every time I see them together; the look I always knew that Sam and I were missing. The look of love.

———

We'd already agreed that Daniel should make the opening speech, so once the video's ended with a modern-day photograph of how the cinema looks right now, all lit up and beautiful once more, he makes his way up to the stage, taps the mic that Norman's set up for him, and begins to speak.

Even just watching him sparks something in my chest, so I look at Charlie instead and take comfort in the encouraging smile he gives me as I squeeze his hand.

'Good evening, all,' Daniel starts. 'I'm delighted to welcome everyone here tonight to celebrate the re-opening of Westholme's new and improved Albany Cinema.'

The audience starts clapping and whooping with, ironically, the Orchard Estate boys leading the cheers.

'As with any great project, there have been bumps in the road, some big, some small. But throughout the good times and the bad, the great people of Westholme – and the odd few from Hollywood...' he winks at Tony '...have been here cheering us on, supporting us in our efforts and coming to our rescue in our hour of need.

'We have been so lucky to have had many people who have shared our vision and committed to it from day one. But there's one woman who has really driven the whole project. It's the same woman who convinced me last year that the Parade would be better kept as a shopping centre than a supermarket, the same woman who has been responsible for feeding us with a constant flow of good news, and the same woman who has opened my eyes to the meaning of community. Ladies and gentlemen, will you please put your hands together for... Zoe Taylor!'

My stomach flips as all around me, people start pushing me up towards the stage.

'Are you sure?' I manage to whisper to Charlie as I'm pushed along the line.

'Do it.' He nods.

I walk down the aisle towards the stage, accepting the hand that Daniel holds out to help me up, and feel a pang of sadness as I remember him making the same gesture at the ill-fated networking event. It was only a few months ago, but in that time our relationship has become something that neither of us could have imagined.

He catches my eye as I let go of his hand, but I quickly avert my gaze for fear I'll lose my nerve if I look at him for too long.

And then I'm in the middle of the stage, my eyes blinded by the spotlights shining down on me, trying to position the mic so I can speak into it, but failing due to it being set up for Daniel, which means it's about a foot too high for me.

After a couple of doomed attempts at standing on my tiptoes, I reach for the mic and pull it off the stand instead.

'Hello, all,' I say, jumping a little at the loud volume of my own words. 'It's been an absolute privilege to play my part in bringing this cinema back to life. I remember it being open briefly until I was about fourteen, and during that time it provided the backdrop to so many memorable events in my life.

'It was here that I saw my very first film, celebrated birthdays, had my first date and even my first kiss. Sorry, Charlie,' I add quickly because I know he'll probably want to kill me for that.

'My friends and I used to whisper together during the trailers, and we'd plan our escape from Westholme into the big brave world beyond that we only really knew existed because of what we'd seen on the silver screen.

'It's perhaps telling that, while we lived elsewhere for a while, my friends and I chose to come back home to raise our children. We wanted to bring them up in a close-knit community where they would learn the value of family and friendship. We felt that there are valuable life lessons to be learnt here. Still do, as a matter of fact.

'However, one of those lessons that we learnt here, watching those very special movies, was that sometimes opportunities present themselves that take you away from the place you call home.

'That is what is happening to Charlie and me right now, actually.' I swallow hard. 'We've been offered the opportunity to return to another place I lived for a while – London. A place which is known for being inhospitable, but where community can be found, if you look hard enough.

'So, while tonight heralds the start of even more great things for Westholme, it signals the end of an era for me. It's the end of a rediscovery of my home town, one which has both surprised and delighted me since I moved back ten years ago to raise my son. And, sadly, it's also the end of *The Good News Gazette*, which Ollie Jenkins and I have adored working on together.'

Tears are prickling my eyes now, and although the lights are so bright that I can't see the audience, I still hear the gasp, followed by the deathly silence that follows.

'I hope this doesn't put a downer on your night, but we'll be leaving in a few days, so it's probably the only time I'll have to speak to you all together, and it was so important to me to say thank you. Thank you for taking me back in, for wrapping me up and keeping me safe, for being my friends, for being my colleagues, for keeping me supplied with news stories and with cakes that have far too many calories in.' I can hear a few sniffs in the crowd, but I'm determined to see this through.

'You are all so, so special and I will miss each and every one of you.' I'm sniffing myself now. 'And while our bodies will be in London, our hearts will definitely remain with you all in Westholme; our birthplace, our home.'

Westholme Community Facebook page:

Lucy Lashes: Anyone see that gorgeous blue dress Lily Lonsdale was wearing tonight?

Leah Moreton: I did! Any idea where it's from? It looked so different from the kind of stuff you usually see around here.

Tori Hindle: I heard it was from Vintage Vibes in the Parade.

Lucy Lashes: You're kidding – it's just old tat in there, isn't it?

Tori Hindle: Well, if it is, it's old tat I wouldn't mind having in my wardrobe! Going in tomorrow to see what else they've got.

Paul Gregory: Are we really talking about dresses when Zoe Taylor's just stood on stage and resigned?

Leah Moreton: Where from – *The Good News Gazette*?

Paul Gregory: From Westholme! She's going to London. Leaving next week.

Jimmy Hunter: Thought she was meant to bring us good news?

Chapter Forty-Nine

I n hindsight, maybe the launch night of the new cinema wasn't the best moment to share my news.

It killed the after-party, for one. It's hard to maintain that party spirit when all around you people are looking glum and reaching for their tissues.

From the moment I stepped off the stage, I spent the rest of the evening batting off pleas to stay and dealing with incredulous faces wondering why on earth I'd swap what I have here for London.

I've maintained the party line, talking about the opportunities, opportunities, opportunities it offers, when the answer is that it's *because* of what's here that I have to leave.

I'm just no good in relationships. Not ones where there's a risk I could fall head over heels, anyway. I did once, with Charlie's dad, Ryan, and the way that that ended hurt so much that sometimes I wondered how a human brain could endure such pain. On the plus side, it helped me to develop a highly sensitive beacon that lights up when it spots the danger signs. And where Daniel's concerned, there's been plenty.

Charlie seems fine, thank goodness. If anything, he appears to have adopted some of the celebrity aura exuded by his new film star mates and is currently lapping up the onslaught of questions he's receiving. I make a mental note to tell him to revisit some of the answers he's been giving; case in point, we still *won't* be living next door to Harry Kane. But other than that, he seems exhilarated by the whole thing.

I'm ignoring the nagging feeling I have that a big part of the reason he's facing this move with such optimism is to do with the dad we tend not to talk too much about anymore, and keeping everything crossed that he's simply up for what will be a new and exciting challenge.

My old boss, Amanda, will be delighted with the news, and she's already assured me there should be a place for Charlie in at least one of the schools there. If not, I'll just home-school him. Amanda said I'd be able to do a fair bit of work from home anyway and, honestly, how hard can home-schooling really be?

I did think Daniel might want to speak to me – or even Sam for that matter. But I haven't seen either of them since I made my announcement so they can't have been that bothered by my news.

Emma and Beth made sure they were the first to reach me post-speech though, embracing me the moment I left the stage, covering me in hugs and kisses and reassurances that it would all be fine, that this was my chance to reclaim what I'd lost the moment I found out I was pregnant with Charlie.

Then it was Mum and Dad – who already had an inkling of what was on my mind after I confided in them, the day of the air fryer debacle – telling me how proud they are of me and how they always *knew* I'd get back to London one day. After they'd reassured me, they moved on to Charlie, squeezing him tight and promising, as they headed off with him while I cleaned up after the party, that they'd be regular visitors to our new place.

Yes, I'm definitely doing the right thing, even if I feel wretched at the thought of leaving Westholme, my parents, and everyone I love.

As long as Charlie and I are together, we don't need anyone else. We'll be fine as we are. Just us two, taking on the world and beating it hands down.

It's around midnight by the time the shutters go down on the cinema doors and I prepare to brave the heavy rain I'll have to race through in order to reach my car.

I leave by one of the emergency exits, the one that will bring me out at the nearest point to it. The car park may be well lit, but I'm never entirely comfortable being there on my own.

Locking the back doors, I scrunch up my face against the splodges of water pelting my cheeks and forehead and head into the car park. But I've only taken a couple of steps when I spot something that makes me stop dead in my tracks; the outline of a man resting against a car next to mine.

I freeze. But as I take a second look, the figure starts to look slightly familiar. And as my eyes adjust to the light, I recognise a stance that is distinctly Daniel's.

Taking a deep breath, I walk slowly towards him, the unrelenting rain soaking my face and hair, penetrating both my coat and my lovely teal jumpsuit beneath.

Ahead of me, Daniel is still perched against the bonnet of his BMW. Water is running off his dark hair and down his face onto his beautiful, dry-clean only suit, the shape destroyed, the rain reducing it to little more than rags. Underneath his open jacket, his white shirt clings to his abs, and I feel a clutch at my chest that is so violent it hurts.

I come to a halt about two feet away from where he stands, my own clothes already almost as drenched as his.

'Where did you get to?' I ask, so calmly it's barely even a question, my words almost lost in the pounding of the rain against the car.

He looks pained, anguished. His stance, usually so alpha male, appears reduced as he rests against his car, knees slightly bent to accommodate the length of his legs.

'Why are you leaving?' His voice is quiet and low.

I look away, ignoring the water that's dripping off my eyelashes.

'It's a good opportunity.'

'But you don't want to go,' he states, his telepathic eyes working overtime, forcing me to look back at him.

A huge drop of water hits the nape of my neck and I shiver.

'Yes I do.'

'You don't.'

I look away, willing the tears prickling my eyes to stay away until I'm in my car, driving home. 'It's the right thing to do.'

'So, you're just going to walk away? From your friends? Your family? The *Gazette*? The cinema?'

A rush of anger hits me. 'I have done everything I can for this community and all the people in it. EVERYTHING. I couldn't have put more into the paper, or the cinema. And my friends and family know I'd never walk away from them. But I need to do this. I need to do this for me.'

I push past him towards the driver's side of my own car, but he catches my hand as I pass, then pulls me back until I'm standing in front of him, right between his legs, my body just inches away from his.

'Don't go,' he says quietly, finding my other hand and holding them both firmly in his own. A ball of heat forms in my veins and races around my body, powered by the rapid beating of my heart.

Something stabs at my chest, but I hold firm.

'It's the right decision for Charlie and me.'

'But the wrong decision for you and me.'

Despite my best efforts, the tears rush into my eyes, spilling over on to my cheeks. This hurts so much. It's as though someone's given me the winning lottery ticket then taken it back and told me I should never have had it in the first place.

'I can't do this, Daniel.'

'Do what? Fall in love? Take a chance?' The confusion etched on his face is killing me.

'This! You... Sam... I couldn't hurt him like that. Watching the paper I love die a slow death. I am *broke*, Daniel. Or I soon will be. I need a job. A career. Some semblance of the sort of life that everyone else has.'

He stares at me, his jaw clenched, the water making his lower eyelashes so dark it's as though he's doused them in ultra-black mascara.

'You're running,' he says eventually.

I shake my head and look down at his extended thighs, grateful for the heavy rain that's masking the tears now pouring down my cheeks.

He lifts my chin with his fingertips, forcing me to look back into his eyes.

'Yes, you are.'

I'm aware, even as I stand there, that I'm at THAT crossroads. That moment that defines how the rest of your life will turn out.

Everything in me tells me to stay. But I'm stronger now than I was before. I know what Charlie and I need – and what we don't need. I make my own decisions.

So I allow myself one last, heart-breaking look at him, pull my hands away, get in my car and leave.

Epilogue

None of us expected the flood.

Yes, there may have been local weather warnings, Met Office flood alerts and police knocking at our doors telling us to evacuate, but I was at the launch night when the police knocked and, honestly, does anyone even look at those weather warning alerts unless they're telling us we're about to have either an unseasonal heatwave or snow?

I suppose I was a bit distracted. So, when I got back home, ready to climb into my pyjamas and under the covers for approximately the next twenty years, the last thing I expected was to be prevented from getting into my close by the police. They were sorry to tell me that ours was one of the houses expected to be affected and I needed to leave. They also added that under no circumstances was I to return to my home tonight.

'But my cat's in there,' I repeatedly complained, pretty sure she wouldn't be but glad of the excuse. They eventually agreed to let me go and in get her on the basis that I took no longer than five minutes, after which time they would have to risk life and limb –

despite the fact that the only evidence of rain was still a few puddles on my driveway – by going in after me.

I let myself into the house, and am now in the process of retrieving my phone from my bag, which reveals I have numerous missed texts and calls, mainly from Mum and Dad, but from Beth, Emma and Sam too. I check my ringer, wondering why it hasn't made a sound throughout all of this activity, only to realise that I'd turned it off when we went into the auditorium and haven't turned it on since.

Flood evacuation, I text Mum and Dad.
Can I come to you?

Dad phones immediately. 'If you like, love. Bloody ridiculous. We saw what had happened, so we brought Charlie back here. He's in the spare room. But you don't need to worry, love,' he continues. 'There won't be a flood here. It'll just be puddles in the usual places, that's all. Bloody snowflakes, panicking over a bit of rain.'

'Thanks, Dad. I'll grab my stuff and come over then.'

'You do that, love,' he replies. 'We haven't got any beds left, mind – there's only the single one Charlie's in, cos your Mum's got all the Christmas presents on the floor in the back bedroom, but it'll be fine. There's always the couch. If you lie in a certain way, you can avoid all the broken springs.'

After a quick peek out of the window confirms that the police are more interested in chatting among themselves than in making sure I evacuate, I decide I'll just take my chances and stay home tonight. After all, how likely is it that a flood will actually hit Westholme, destroying houses, shops and livelihoods in just a few short hours?

That would never happen...would it?

To be continued...

Acknowledgments

I'm now two books into my writing career, and if there's one thing that I've learnt above all others since I started tapping away on the first draft of *The Good News Gazette*, it is this: while it may be the author's name that appears on the cover, a book is never, ever the product of just the writer. It's a collaboration between that one person and so many others, from those in publishing to the loyal readers who share its existence on social media. And it literally could not be done without them.

To my editor, the fantastic, endlessly supportive Charlotte Ledger. Thank you for everything. To Nicky Lovick, who provides such brilliant copyedits, Tony Russell, whose proof-reading is razor-sharp and insightful, Lucy Bennett, who has art-directed both of the beautiful book covers so far, the talented Dawn Cooper who has brought Lucy's visions to life with her illustrations, and the rest of the One More Chapter team whose input always makes the books better, thank you – you are, indeed a dream team!

Away from One More Chapter and Harper Collins, a whole host of other people powered into action to help ensure *The Good News Gazette* reached as many readers as possible.

To Rachel Gilby from Rachel's Random Resources, blog tour organiser extraordinaire; thanks for working up a book tour storm, and for all the additional pointers and guidance you've provided along the way.

A massive thank you, too, to the many book reviewers and bloggers who were kind enough to take the time to read and review *The Good News Gazette*, and in particular to Linda Hill from

Linda's Book Bag, Emily from The Breakfast Book Club, and Anne Williams from beinganne.com, who were particularly supportive and encouraging. With so many brilliant books out there and so little time to read them, the fact that you gave this first-time novelist a chance is a kindness for which I'll be eternally grateful.

Thanks as well, to the newspapers, websites and radio stations that supported my new venture – it really does make such a difference.

To Bob Stone, owner of independent bookshop The Write Blend in Waterloo, who was kind enough to offer me my very first book signing and continues to champion authors at whatever stage in their careers, you are the lifeblood of the publishing industry. Thank you to you, and to all the other independent bookshops for being there for the writers who so desperately need you.

To Caroline Corcoran, a fellow author and more importantly, a good friend, thank you so much for being such a great cheerleader. I'm thoroughly enjoying our London jaunts.

To Debbie Johnson and Catherine Isaac, thanks for always being there – whether that's clinking wine/beer glasses or at the other end of an email – for advice, friendship and laughs.

As well as my long-standing writing friends, I've also been lucky enough to meet some new author pals over the past couple of years, who really are the most supportive bunch of people. A special thanks must go to Elizabeth Bailey, who was extremely generous with her time and knowledge in teaching me everything anyone could ever need to know about starting a newsletter (it's coming, I promise!).

I must also flag up, once again, the Romantic Novelists' Association, a must-join group for anyone interested in writing romantic fiction, whose members continue to provide support.

To those lovely family, friends and strangers who have rooted for me from the word go, in particular Jennie Hughes-Breen,

Sheila Maude, Ann and Julia Kerr and Elizabeth Roen, I can't tell you how much your support has meant to me. Thank you.

Thanks also to my beautiful friends Kate Walker, Karen Day, Laura Buoey, Zoe Kennedy, Sandra Flynn, Gill Harris, Sandra Bryan, Rebecca Smullen, Caroline Andrew, Aimi Clayton, Sally Edgar, Claire Grey, Laura Benjamin, Kristina Swift and Vicki Ridland for your friendship. Love you all.

Team Oakley – Laura B, Hannah Reti, and Paul and Diane Hudson – thank you for your love and support. Paul, I will never forget I owe it all to you ;-)

To my Aunty Olive, thank you for always believing in me. You'll always be a powerhouse to me.

To Glen and Viny, who are always there for us all. Thank you.

Mum, Dad, Jenny and Rob, thank you for providing so much practical and emotional support and unwavering enthusiasm – and for buying at least half of the copies of *The Good News Gazette* currently in circulation!

To Mike, Nathan and Natalie, my biggest achievements by far. Mike, thank you for the comedic contributions you've made to some of the books' most humorous scenes. I love the way you look at life through a lens that makes everything funnier and less serious that it appeared before.

Nathan and Natalie, thank you for sharing your mum with the laptop, and for championing even my smallest writing achievements. You are the kindest, funniest, loveliest little humans and I'm so proud of you both. Love you all the world and more.

And finally, to all the wonderful readers who have bought my books, thank you, thank you, thank you. I hope you enjoy reading the stories as much as I enjoy writing them.

Read on for an extract from *The Good News Gazette*

Nine years ago, Zoe Taylor returned from London to the quiet hamlet of Westholme with her tail between her legs and a bun in the oven. Where once her job as a journalist saw her tearing off to Paris at a moment's notice after a lead, now the single mum covers the local news desk. At least, she did...until she's unceremoniously let go.

When Zoe invites her friends over to commiserate, wine and whining soon turns into something more... and before the night is out she's plotted her next step: *The Good News Gazette.*

Available in eBook, audio and paperback now

The Good News Gazette: Chapter 1

'You've been robbed again, haven't you?' Ollie smirks, using the camera app on his phone to check his reflection as he fiddles with his blonde quiff.

'What?' I sling my Primark bag down onto my desk, catapulting it against yesterday's cup of coffee, a cardboard take-out container which meets the challenge with all the resistance of a plastic skittle.

'Robbed,' repeats Ollie, who is dutifully adhering to his ethos never to do any actual work during the first hour of the working day. 'It's Friday. That's always your excuse for being late on Fridays. Mondays tend to be road traffic accidents, Tuesdays are the days you leave your straighteners on, Wednesdays are always the fault of the Head not opening the school on time, Thursdays your car tends to break down and Fridays – 'he dips his head slightly to examine his razor-sharp cheekbones – 'Fridays are the days the burglars call.'

I tune out, distracted by the coffee currently flooding my workspace with complete abandon, drowning piles of council meeting agendas, old newspapers and sticky notes that keep falling off my monitor in thick, brown liquid.

Thrown by the fact that I haven't immediately hurled an insult back at him, Ollie shifts his blue-eyed gaze from the phone to me, enjoying every second of watching me try and fail to mop up half a cup of coffee with three multi-coloured Post-It notes.

'Look out,' he mutters, as something behind me catches his eye. 'Stevie boy approaching from the rear. You have approximately three seconds to come up with a new excuse for being late that he might actually believe. Three … two … one…'

I chuck the soaking Post-It notes in the bin, cover the pool of coffee with the newspapers and turn to face my greasy-haired, scruffy twenty-something news editor as I wait for the onslaught to begin.

'Good morning, Zoe,' he says loudly, enjoying the attention his booming voice commands as some of the more junior reporters slump even deeper into their seats in a bid to avoid whatever's about to come my way. 'Let me guess, you were caught in a terrifying hostage situation and despite your most ardent pleas, the kidnappers simply wouldn't accept that you had to be at work by 9am.'

I smile sweetly, a move that's meant to charm but that I suspect looks more like I'm planning ways to assassinate him. I pause for a moment and wonder whether I could get away with it, then rule it out on the basis that I keep myself to myself, which seems to be a prerequisite for a murderer.

'Good morning Stephen.' My tone is authoritative; an attempt to suggest I'm in control of the situation despite all evidence pointing to the contrary being true.

'I'm so sorry I didn't make it in earlier.' I try to adjust my smile into something a little less serial killer and more office angel. 'But I did call the newsdesk to say I was running a bit late. We were burgled last night and I've been dealing with the police.'

Over my right shoulder I hear Ollie attempt to stifle a snigger. Stephen flicks his dark, beady eyes in his direction then eyes me suspiciously.

'You were burgled last week, weren't you?' he remarks, a frown creeping across the shiny forehead and resting in two vertical lines between his eyebrows.

'I was,' I nod gravely. 'There's been a lot of burglaries recently.'

'And the week before?'

I carry on nodding, which is starting to feel like a safer course of action than speaking.

He nods in tandem with me. 'Hmmm. I suppose there *have* been a lot of break-ins lately. But in the nicer areas like Presthill. Nowhere near where *you* live.' He says this with such relish I want to pick up the soggy mass of sticky notes and newspapers and dump it on his head.

'You are also clearly unaware that we ran a story yesterday about how the police have nailed a group for the burglaries, which you'd know if you *read* the paper now and again.'

I bite my lip.

'So, I trust you won't be experiencing any more burglaries from now on?'

Ollie snorts. I shake my head.

'Good. Now we've got that out of the way maybe you can make a start on some work.' He spins on his heel and slithers off towards the newsdesk. 'Oh, and Zoe?' he shouts over his shoulder. 'Maybe you could call when you're going to be on time in the future. That seems to be the exception rather than the rule these days.'

In the time it has taken to clean up my desk, Ollie's done a round of the female trainees, set up a date on Tinder and completed a round trip to the canteen. He hands me a fresh cup of coffee, blue eyes twinkling in amusement.

'So your house *has* been burgled eh?' he chuckles. 'And on a *Friday* too. What are the chances of that happening? Do you have a crime reference number? Have you called the insurance company? Anything of particular value been taken? Oh, please say they've nicked that flowery top that looked as though it had been pinched from the Chelsea Flower Show.'

'Shut up, Ollie', I snap. 'It was Charlie's homework. We were on our way to school when I remembered—'

'Don't even attempt to blame your tardiness on your son,' Ollie cuts in. 'Anyway...' He checks who's around, then leans towards me, dropping his chest down to his desk like a spy evading the secret service. 'Have you heard the news?'

I shake my head.

'Stephen's about to be promoted to head of digital, which means that the news editor job will soon be up for grabs. Why don't you apply for it?'

A rush of air fills my lungs as I inhale sharply. 'Is it official?'

'Too right. And this opportunity has got your name written all over it. Seriously, Zoe, it's been what, nearly nine years since you trundled back from the nationals with your tail, not to mention a massive baby bump, between your legs? Surely you don't want to write about drug raids and Westholme's desperate need for wheelie bins forever?'

'But I'm rubbish. You heard Stephen. I don't even *read* the paper.'

He bites a huge chunk off his burnt sausage then leans back in his chair, making grotesque facial movements as he grinds it up into small pieces.

'No-one reads the paper,' he says between chews. 'It's crap.'

'I don't know...' I start. 'I mean...' I trail off, not exactly sure what I mean.

'Come on Zoe,' Ollie cuts in. 'You might as well go for it. After all, you're no spring chicken. You're nearly forty—'

'I'm thirty-three,' I interrupt, indignance creeping through my tone.

'Exactly. You're not getting any younger. You need to crack on, do a bit of ladder climbing if you don't want to get left behind while the likes of my good self steam on ahead of you and dominate you from above.'

He looks at me now as though appraising a prize cow. 'You're a good-looking girl, nice hair, good teeth, great legs. Make a bit more of an effort and dress a bit more,' he glances at my paisley midi-dress, 'well, a bit less like *that*, and you'd have the bosses fawning all over you. Even *I'd* take you out if you weren't old enough to be my mother.'

'I'm eight years older than you!' I exclaim.

'If you say so,' he says, winking before turning back to his computer to update his social media status. I glare at him, envious of his ability to be twenty-five with no responsibilities, then, at a loss as to how to respond to that statement with words, I tut and focus my attention on checking my emails instead. The subject headings do nothing to lift my spirits. From *Rat infestation in Moorland Road* to *Why the council are screwing us all* – which, on closer inspection, is far less erotic than it sounds – none of them imply a story full of cheer.

'Wait a minute, what's this?' I click on one promising heading: *Letter from my grandad arrives fifty years after it was sent.*

I scan through the contents. 'Listen, Ol,' I say. 'A woman's grandad sent a letter from America half a century ago, and it finally arrived this week. Isn't that incredible?'

Ollie pulls a face. 'Sounds like a nice story, but you know Stevie-boy won't go for it.'

'Why not?' I ask, though I already know the answer.

'Because all he wants is vandalism, drug deals in the park, low OFSTED ratings. He thinks the good stuff is just fluff.'

'But people need the good stuff. They need to be reminded that great things are happening as well as bad. Light and shade, isn't that what they taught us at journalism college?'

Ollie shrugs. 'Don't shoot the messenger. You know as well as I do it won't get past him.'

Looking over my shoulder to check Stephen's whereabouts, I spot him through the floor-to-ceiling windows of the editor's office, his head tilted to one side as Ray, editor of *The Northern News* and our not-very-esteemed boss, speaks.

'What's going on in there?' I say.

Ollie glances past me and frowns. 'I don't know, but I don't like the look of it.'

We watch as Stephen nods, stands up and leaves the office, closing the door behind him. He pauses, rubs his forehead then looks directly at Ollie and me. It's not a look that screams instant promotion.

Within seconds, he's behind me again.

'Ollie, the ed wants a word.'

Phew. At least it's Ollie who's about to get a rollicking rather than me.

I raise my eyebrows, wondering what antics Ollie's been up to that might have landed him in trouble with our pint-swilling editor Ray. Maybe it's to do with Becky from Advertising and that store cupboard business last week. Then again, Ray would probably steer clear of any involvement in the romantic entanglements of his employees. From what I hear, he has enough of his own to deal with.

Ollie follows him into the office and, satisfied the three of them will be tied up for a little while, I pick up my purse and head to the canteen for a very naughty but very needed breakfast. The weight of my heaving backside as I walk is a reminder that I should really opt for fruit, but sod it. I don't care.

In fact, given that not only is it Friday, it's also payday, I might even have a hash brown and some fried bread too.

———

I've just swallowed the last bite of my full English when Ollie returns to his seat, his face ashen.

'What's going on?' I ask.

Ollie looks at Stephen, who has resumed his place at my shoulder.

'Zoe,' he says, his hushed voice a marked contrast to his earlier ear-wincing tones. 'The editor will see you now.'

My heart does somersaults all the way down to my stomach. *Everything will be fine*, I tell myself. *Everything will be fine*. Except what if it's not?

———

'Zoe.' Ray issues a tight smile as he gestures for me to sit on the green fabric couch facing his. 'How are we today?'

Ray always addresses his employees as 'we', his attempt to convey the message that everyone is in 'it' together. Whatever 'it' is.

I clear my throat, smiling nervously at him and wondering if he seriously only has that one blue tie with the red slashes all the way down it. And whether it's ever seen the inside of a dry cleaner's.

'Um, good thanks, Ray. How are you?'

'I'm fine, fine,' he says cheerily, examining a spot on the floor for a moment before looking up at me, broken spider veins popping out across his bulbous red nose.

'Actually, Zoe, I'm not fine. I'm devastated.'

I try to feign concern. 'Oh no, Ray, what's wrong?'

'Zoe, it's awful. Possibly one of the worst moments of my career if truth be told.'

Good grief, what on earth's happened? I stay silent and adopt my most sympathetic look. Perhaps one of his numerous affairs has been revealed. Maybe he's been fiddling his expenses. Whatever it is, it must be bad if he wants to confide in me about it.

Ray shuffles forward in his seat and looks directly at me.

'You know we've been struggling with a decline in advertising for a long time now.'

I nod and feel a pang of sympathy. Poor Ray. The big bosses must finally have given him his marching orders.

'And you'll remember we had to let Alf go last year.'

'Yes,' I say slowly, remembering the kind-hearted arts correspondent who was unceremoniously dumped from the paper in a cost-cutting exercise.

'Unfortunately, Zoe, the powers-that-be have been at work again.' He raises his eyes to the ceiling in reference to the Finance team that reside on the floor above.

'They've crunched the numbers and they've told me I'm going to have to lose two people. One, sadly, is Ollie. The other,' he pauses for dramatic effect, 'is you.'

My brain freezes, unable to grasp the enormity of what Ray is telling me. His voice rolls into one long, meaningless noise as the room begins to spin. I hear a few random words. Restructure, garden leave, lump sums…

Ray is still talking. 'I impressed upon them how valuable you are to us. I even explained you were a single mum.' He shakes his head. 'None of it did any good.'

He's wearing a patronising expression that makes me want to punch him. 'There's a lot of hungry new entrants willing to work for next to nothing. And they've got more social media followers than you.' He coughs. 'Not that that makes a difference of course. We couldn't actually *replace* you. That wouldn't be allowed.' He shakes his head as if to emphasise his total commitment to employment law.

I gulp. 'I'm pretty sure *this* isn't allowed, Ray. Aren't we supposed to have some sort of consultation exercise or something?'

Ray looks uncomfortable. 'We did have a consultation exercise, Zoe. Last year, when Alf was made redundant. We mentioned we might have to make more redundancies then.'

'Yes, but—'

'Anyway.' He leans back and crosses his short, stumpy legs. 'Let's not worry about the semantics. We are where we are, after all.'

A wave of horror passes over me. 'Ray, is this about the staff Christmas party?' I can't even look at him as I say it.

'Gosh, no,' he roars, throwing his head back in laughter. 'I think most of us would sleep with the managing director, given half the chance.'

'But I didn't *sleep* with him. I didn't even speak to him. I just—'

'Told his wife you would,' he says, the tone of his voice far too upbeat. 'And who can blame you, as I say, even I—'

'I thought she worked in Payroll,' I cut in, the familiar heat rising in my cheeks. 'I didn't realise it was his wife. And I had had a few when I said it.'

'Anyway.' Ray waves a hand as if to dismiss the entire incident. 'I can assure you it's nothing to do with that. Honestly.' He shakes his head and chuckles, then checks himself. 'Now, Tracey from HR will be down to speak to you shortly, but in the meantime … is there anything else you'd like to ask me?'

'Not at the moment,' I say quietly, a jumble of thoughts whirling around my head.

He slaps his thighs as if to indicate that the meeting's over and I stand up to leave.

'So...'

He's smiling, relieved I haven't cried and clearly congratulating himself on his sensitive handling of the situation.

'Leaving do for you and Ollie? The Pig and Whistle?'

'I'll think about it,' I say, my voice trembling ever so slightly. I make my way out of the door, a lot less confident in the strength of my own legs than I was five minutes ago.

'Okay!' Ray shouts cheerfully behind me. 'But don't leave it too long to decide. We'll have to give them plenty of notice if we want a decent buffet, or we'll all end up eating crisp butties like we did at Alf's do...'

I leave him, still going on about the inferior quality of the last redundancy spread and head straight to the ladies' loos, where I lock myself inside the cleanest cubicle I can find, drop my head in my hands, and let the tears fall.

As if what I've done to my son isn't bad enough already, I can't believe I've failed him once again. Except this time it's worse. Because this time there is no back-up plan.

ONE MORE CHAPTER

YOUR NUMBER ONE STOP

FOR PAGETURNING BOOKS

The author and One More Chapter would like to thank everyone who contributed to the publication of this story...

Analytics
Emma Harvey
Maria Osa

Audio
Fionnuala Barrett
Ciara Briggs

Contracts
Georgina Hoffman
Florence Shepherd

Design
Lucy Bennett
Fiona Greenway
Holly Macdonald
Liane Payne
Dean Russell

Digital Sales
Laura Daley
Michael Davies
Georgina Ugen

Editorial
Arsalan Isa
Charlotte Ledger
Nicky Lovick
Jennie Rothwell
Tony Russell
Kimberley Young

International Sales
Bethan Moore

Marketing & Publicity
Chloe Cummings
Emma Petfield

Operations
Melissa Okusanya
Hannah Stamp

Production
Emily Chan
Denis Manson
Francesca Tuzzeo

Rights
Lana Beckwith
Rachel McCarron
Agnes Rigou
Hany Sheikh
Mohamed
Zoe Shine
Aisling Smyth

The HarperCollins Distribution Team

The HarperCollins Finance & Royalties Team

The HarperCollins Legal Team

The HarperCollins Technology Team

Trade Marketing
Ben Hurd

UK Sales
Yazmeen Akhtar
Laura Carpenter
Isabel Coburn
Jay Cochrane
Alice Gomer
Gemma Rayner
Erin White
Harriet Williams
Leah Woods

And every other essential link in the chain from delivery drivers to booksellers to librarians and beyond!